M000043187

EX
LIBRIS

Dear Reader,

It's hard to believe, but it's the tenth anniversary of **Silhouette Desire**! And what better way to celebrate this past decade than by reliving some of the memories, and rereading some of the books?

Between the covers of this handsome collection you'll find three stories written by some of the authors you've come to know—and love—in **Silhouette Desire**: Diana Palmer, Jennifer Greene and Lass Small.

With their stories, *September Morning, Body and Soul,* and *To Meet Again,* these talented authors have set the high standards for passionate romance and deep emotion you've come to expect from **Silhouette Desire**.

Each and every month since June 1982, we have worked to bring you the very best in short, sensuous romance. You, the reader, have been with us all the way, and we know you're looking forward to the next ten years as much as we are!

Sincerely,

The Editors at Silhouette Books

SILHOUETTE

Desire

10 TH

Anniversary

COLLECTION

DIANA PALMER
JENNIFER GREENE
LASS SMALL

Silhouette Books®

Published by Silhouette Books New York

America's Publisher of Contemporary Romance

SILHOUETTE BOOKS
300 E. 42nd St., New York, N.Y. 10017

ISBN 0-373-15222-1

Silhouette Desire
Tenth Anniversary Collection
Copyright © 1992 by Silhouette Books

The publisher acknowledges the copyright holders of
the individual work as follows:

September Morning
© 1982 by Diana Palmer
Originally published as Silhouette Desire #26

Body and Soul
© 1986 by Jennifer Greene
Originally published as Silhouette Desire #263

To Meet Again
© 1986 by Lass Small
Originally published as Silhouette Desire #322

CONTENTS

SEPTEMBER MORNING

Diana Palmer

To Ann, Anne, "George,"
"Eddard," Dannis and Dad

DIANA PALMER

is a prolific romance writer who got her start as a newspaper reporter. Accustomed to the daily deadlines of a journalist, she has no problem with writer's block. In fact, she averages a book every two months. Mother of a young son, Diana met and married her husband within one week. "It was just like something from one of my books."

Her upcoming Silhouette Books include the next two books in her *Most Wanted* series, which began in March 1992 with *The Case of the Mesmerizing Boss* (Desire #702). The series continues in June 1992 with *The Case of the Confirmed Bachelor* (Desire #715, a Silhouette Desire *June Groom*), and in September 1992, with *The Case of the Missing Secretary*. And don't miss the *Diana Palmer Collection*—the reissue volume of *Rawhide and Lace* (Silhouette Desire #306) and *Unlikely Lover* (Silhouette Romance #472)—available during the summer of 1992.

Diana Palmer says, "It is my great pleasure to participate in the tenth anniversary of Silhouette Desire. *September Morning* is one of my favorite books and I hope readers will enjoy it. Happy birthday, Sihouette Desire, and thanks to Lucia Macro for all her hard work as senior editor of Silhouette Desire!"

Books by Diana Palmer

Silhouette Desire

The Cowboy and the Lady #12
September Morning #26
Friends and Lovers #50
Fire and Ice #80
Snow Kisses #102
Diamond Girl #110
The Rawhide Man #157
Lady Love #175
Cattleman's Choice #193
The Tender Stranger #230
Love by Proxy #252
Eye of the Tiger #271
Loveplay #289
Rawhide and Lace #306
Rage of Passsion #325
Fit for a King #349
Betrayed by Love #391
Enamored #420
Reluctant Father #469
Hoodwinked #492
His Girl Friday #528
Hunter #606
Nelson's Brand #618
The Best Is Yet To Come #643
†*The Case of the Mesmerizing Boss* #702
†*The Case of the Confirmed Bachelor* #715

Silhouette Romance

Darling Enemy #254
Roomful of Roses #301
Hear of Ice #314
Passion Flower #328
Soldier of Fortune #340
After the Music #406
Champagne Girl #436
Unlikely Lover #472
Woman Hater #532
*Calhoun #580
*Justin #592
*Tyler #604
**Sutton's Way* #670
*Ethan #694
*Connal #741
*Harden #783
*Evan #819
*Donavan #843

Silhouette Special Edition

Heather's Song #33
The Australian #239

Silhouette Books

Silhouette Christmas Stories 1987
"The Humbug Man"
Silhouette Summer Sizzlers 1990
"Miss Greenhorn"

Diana Palmer Duets Books I-VI

*Long, Tall Texans
†Most Wanted Series

One

The meadow was dew-misted, and the morning had the nip of a September breeze to give it life. Kathryn Mary Kilpatrick tossed her long black hair and laughed with the sheer joy of being alive. The sound startled the chestnut gelding she was riding, making it dance nervously over the damp ground.

"Easy, boy," she said soothingly, her gloved hand reaching out to touch his mane gently.

He calmed, reacting to the familiar caress. Sundance had been hers since he was a colt, a present from Blake on her sixteenth birthday. Sundance was a mature five-year-old now, but some of his coltish uncertainties lingered. He was easily startled and high-strung. Like Kathryn Mary.

Her dark green eyes shimmered with excitement as she studied the long horizon under the pink and amber swirls of the dawn sky. It was so good to be home again. The exclusive girls' school had polished her manners and given her the poise of a model, but it had done nothing to cool her ardor for life or to dampen the passion she felt for Greyoaks. Despite the fact that the Hamiltons' South Carolina farm was her home by adoption, not by birth, she loved every green, rolling hill and pine forest of it, just as though she were a Hamilton herself.

A flash of color caught her attention, and she wheeled Sundance as Phillip Hamilton came tearing across the meadow toward her on a thoroughbred Arabian with a coat like polished black leather. She smiled, watching him. If Blake ever caught him riding one of his prize breeding stallions like that, it would mean disaster. What luck for Phillip that Blake was in Europe on business. Maude might indulge her youngest, but Blake indulged no one.

"Hi!" Phillip called breathlessly. He reined in just in front of her and caught his wind, tossing back his unruly brown hair with a restless hand. His brown eyes twinkled with mischief as they swept over her slender figure in the chic riding habit. But the mischief went out of them when he noticed her bare head.

"No helmet?" he chided.

She pouted at him with her full, soft lips. "Don't scold," she accused. "It was just a little ride, and I hate wearing a hard hat all the time."

"One fall and you'd be done for," he observed.

"You sound just like Blake!"

He smiled at her mutinous look. "Too bad he missed your homecoming. Oh, well, he'll be back at the end of the week—just in time for the Barringtons' party."

"Blake hates parties," she reminded him. Her eyes lowered to the rich leather of her Western saddle. "And he hates me too, most of the time."

"He doesn't," Phillip returned. "It's just that you set fire to his temper, you rebellious little witch. I can remember a time when you all but worshipped my big brother."

She grimaced, turning her eyes to the long horizon where thoroughbred Arabians grazed on lush pasture grass, their black coats shimmering like oil in the sunlight. "Did I?" She laughed shortly. "He was kind to me once, when my mother died."

"He cares about you. We all do," he said gently.

She smiled at him warmly and reached out an impulsive hand to touch his sleeve. "I'm ungrateful, and I don't mean to be. You and your mother have been wonderful to me. Taking me in, putting me through school—how could I be ungrateful?"

"Blake had a little to do with it," he reminded her wryly.

She tossed her hair back impatiently. "I suppose," she admitted grudgingly.

"Finishing school was his idea."

"And I hated it!" she flashed. "I wanted to go to the university and take political science courses."

"Blake likes to entertain buyers," he reminded her. "Political science courses don't teach you how to be a hostess."

She shrugged. "Well, I'm not going to be here forever, despite the fact that you and Blake are my cousins," she said. "I'll get married someday. I know I owe your family a lot, but I'm not going to spend my whole life playing hostess for Blake! He can get married and let his wife do it. If he can find anyone brave enough," she added waspishly.

"You've got to be kidding, Cuz," he chuckled. "They follow him around like ants on a sugar trail. Blake could have his pick when it comes to women, and you know it."

"It must be his money, then," she said tightly, "because it sure isn't his cheerful personality that draws them!"

"You're just sore because he wouldn't let you go away with Jack Harris for the weekend," he teased.

She flushed right up to her hairline. "I didn't know Jack had planned for us to be alone at the cottage," she protested. "I thought his parents were going to be there, too."

"But you didn't think to check. Blake did." He laughed at her expression. "I'll never forget how he looked when Jack came to get you. Or how Jack looked when he left, alone."

She shivered at the memory. "I'd like to forget."

"I'll bet you would. You've been staring daggers at Blake ever since, but it just bounces right off. You don't dent him, do you?"

"Nothing dents Blake," she murmured. "He just stands there and lets me rant and rave until he's had enough, then he turns that cold voice on me and walks away. He'll be glad when I'm gone," she said in a quiet voice.

"You're not going anywhere yet, are you?" he asked suddenly.

She darted a mischievous glance at him. "I *had* thought about joining the French Foreign Legion," she admitted. "Do you think I could get my application accepted before the weekend?"

He laughed. "In time to escape Blake? You know you've missed him."

"I have?" she asked with mock innocence.

"Six months is a long time. He's calmed down."

"Blake never forgets," she sighed miserably. She stared past Phillip to the towering gray stone house in the distance with its graceful arches and the cluster of huge live oaks dripping Spanish moss that stood like sentries around it.

"Don't work yourself into a nervous breakdown," Phillip said comfortingly. "Come on, race me back to the house and we'll have breakfast."

She sighed wearily. "All right."

Maude's dark eyes lit up when the two of them walked into the elegant dining room and seated themselves at the polished oak table.

She had the same olive skin and sharp, dark eyes as her eldest son, the same forthright manner and quick temper. Maude was nothing like Phillip. She lacked his gentleness and easy manner, as well as his pale coloring. Those traits came from his late father, not from his maverick mother, who thought nothing of getting a congressman out of bed at two in the morning if she wanted a piece of pending legislation explained to her.

"It's good to have you home, baby," Maude told Kathryn, reaching out a slender, graceful hand to touch the younger woman's arm. "I'm simply surrounded by men these days."

"That's the truth," Phillip said wryly as he helped himself to scrambled eggs from the bone china platter. "Matt Davis and Jack Nelson nearly came to blows over her at a cocktail party last week."

Maude glared at him. "That isn't so," she protested.

"Oh?" Kathryn asked with an impish smile as she sipped her black coffee.

Maude shifted uncomfortably. "Anyway, I wish Blake were home. It was bad timing, that crisis at the London office. I had a special evening planned for Friday night. A homecoming party for you. It would have been perfect..."

"I don't need Blake to make a party perfect," Kathryn burst out without thinking.

Maude's pencil-thin gray brows went up. "Are you going to hold it against him forever?" she chided.

Kathryn's fingers tightened around her coffee cup. "He didn't have to be so rough on me!" she protested.

"He was right, Kathryn Mary, and you know it," Maude said levelly. She leaned forward, resting her forearms on the table. "Darling, you have to remember that you're just barely twenty. Blake's thirty-four now, and he knows a great deal more about life than you've had time to learn. We've all sheltered you," she added, frowning. "Sometimes I wonder if it was quite fair."

"Ask Blake," she returned bitterly. "He's kept me under glass for years."

"His protective instinct," Phillip said with an amused grin. "A misplaced mother hen complex."

"I wouldn't let him hear that, if I were you," Maude commented drily.

"I'm not afraid of big brother," he replied. "Just because he can outfight me is no reason . . . on second thought, you may have a point."

Maude laughed. "You're a delight. I wish Blake had a little of your ability to take things lightly. He's so intense."

"I can think of a better word," Kathryn said under her breath.

"Isn't it amazing," Phillip asked his mother, "how brave she is when Blake isn't here?"

"Amazing," Maude nodded. She smiled at Kathryn. "Cheer up, sweetheart. Let me tell you what Eve Barrington has planned for your homecoming party Saturday night . . . the one I was going to give you if Blake hadn't been called away . . ."

The arrangements for the party were faultless, Kathryn discovered. The florist had delivered urns of dried flowers in blazing fall colors, and tasteful arrangements of daisies and mums and baby's breath to decorate the buffet tables. The intimate little gathering at the nearby estate swelled to over fifty people, not all of them contemporaries of Kathryn's. Quite a number, she noticed with amusement, were politicians. Maude was lobbying fiercely for legislation to protect a nearby stretch of South Carolina's unspoiled river land from being zoned for business. No doubt she'd pleaded with Eve to add those politicians to the guest list, Kathryn thought wickedly.

Nan Barrington, Eve's daughter, and one of Kathryn's oldest friends, pulled her aside while the musicians launched into a frantic rock number.

"Mother hates hard rock," she confided as the band blared out. "I can't imagine why she hired that particular band, when it's all they play."

"The name," Kathryn guessed. "It's the Glen Miller ensemble, and Glen spells his name with just one 'n.' Your mother probably thought they played the same kind of music as the late Glenn Miller."

"That's mother," Nan agreed with a laugh. She ran a finger over the rim of her glass, filled with sparkling rum punch. Her blond hair sparkled with the same amber color as she looked around the room. "I thought Blake was going to come by when he got home. It's after ten now."

Kathryn smiled at her indulgently. Nan had had a crush on Blake since their early teens. Blake pretended not to notice, treating both girls like the adolescents he thought them.

"You know Blake hates parties," she reminded the shorter girl.

"It can't be for lack of partners to take to them," Nan sighed.

Kathryn frowned at her. She cupped her own glass in her hands and wondered why that statement nagged her. She knew Blake dated, but it had been a long time since she'd spent more than a few days at Greyoaks. Not for years. There was too much to do. Relatives she could visit in faraway places like France and Greece and even Australia. Cruises with friends like Nan. School events and girl friends to visit and parties to go to. There hadn't been much reason to stay at Greyoaks. Especially since that last bout with Blake over Jack Harris. She sighed, remembering how harsh he'd been about it. Jack Harris had turned every color in the rainbow before Blake got through telling him what he thought in that cold, precise voice that always accompanied his temper. When he'd turned it on Kathryn, it had been all she could manage not to run. She was honestly afraid of Blake. Not that he'd beat her or anything. It was a different kind of fear, strange and ever-present, growing as she matured.

"Why the frown?" Nan asked suddenly.

"Was I frowning?" She laughed. She shrugged, sipping her punch. Her eyes ran over her shorter friend's pale blue evening gown, held up by tiny spaghetti straps. "I love your dress."

"It isn't a patch on yours," Nan sighed, wistfully eyeing the Grecian off-the-shoulder style of Kathryn's delicate white gown. The wisps of chiffon foamed and floated with every movement. "It's a dream."

"I have a friend in Atlanta who's a budding designer," she explained with a smile. "This is from her first collection. She had a showing at that new department store on Peachtree Street."

"Everything looks good on you," Nan said genuinely. "You're so tall and willowy."

"Skinny, Blake says." She laughed and then suddenly froze as she looked across the room straight into a pair of narrow, dark eyes in a face as hard as granite.

He was as tall and big as she remembered, all hard-muscled grace and blatant masculinity. His head was bare, his dark hair gleaming in the light from the crystal chandelier overhead. His deeply tanned face had its own inborn arrogance, a legacy from his grandfather, who had forged a small empire from the ashes of the old confederacy. His eyes were cold, even at a distance, his mouth chiseled and firm and just a little cruel. Kathryn shivered involuntarily as his eyes trailed up and down the revealing dress she was wearing, clearly disapproving.

Nan followed her gaze, and her small face lit up. "It's Blake!" she exclaimed. "Kathryn, aren't you going to say hello to him?"

She swallowed. "Oh, yes, of course," she said, aware of Maude going forward to greet her eldest and Phillip waving to him carelessly from across the room.

"You don't look terribly enthusiastic about it," Nan remarked, studying the flush in her friend's cheeks and the slight tremor in the slender hands that held the crystal glass.

"He'll be furious because I haven't got a bow in my hair and a teddy bear under my arm," she said with a mirthless laugh.

"You're not a little girl anymore," Nan said, coming to her friend's defense despite her attraction to Blake.

"Tell Blake," she sighed. "See?" she murmured as he lifted his arrogant head and motioned for her to join him. "I'm being summoned."

"Could you manage to look a little less like Marie Antoinette on her way to the guillotine?" Nan whispered.

"I can't help it. My neck's tingling. See you," she muttered, moving toward Blake with a faint smile.

She moved forward, through the throng of guests, her heart throbbing as heavily as the rock rhythm that shook the walls around her. Six months hadn't erased the bitterness of their last quarrel, and judging by the look on Blake's rugged face, it was still fresh in his mind, too.

He drew deeply on his cigarette, looking down his straight nose at her, and she couldn't help noticing how dangerously attractive he was in his dark evening clothes. The white silk of his shirt was a perfect foil for his olive complexion, his arrogant good looks. The tang of his Oriental cologne drifted down into her nostrils, a fragrance that echoed his vibrant masculinity.

"Hello, Blake," she said nervously, glad Maude had vanished into the throng of politicians so she didn't have to pretend more enthusiasm.

His eyes sketched her slender figure, lingering at the plunging neckline that revealed tantalizing glimpses of the swell of her small, high breasts.

"Advertising, Kate," he asked harshly. "I thought you'd learned your lesson with Harris."

"Don't call me Kate," she fired back. "And it's no more revealing than what everyone else is wearing."

"You haven't changed," he sighed indulgently. "All fire and lace and wobbly legs. I hoped that finishing school might give you a little maturity."

Her emerald eyes burned. "I'm twenty, Blake!"

One dark eyebrow went up. "What do you want me to do about it?"

She started to reply that she didn't want him to do a thing but the anger faded away suddenly. "Oh,

Blake,'' she moaned, ''why do you have to spoil my party? It's been such fun...''

''For whom?'' he asked, his eyes finding several of the politicians present. ''You or Maude?''

''She's trying to save the wildlife along the Edisto River,'' she said absently. ''They want to develop part of the riverfront.''

''Yes, let's save the water moccasins and sandflies, at all costs!'' he agreed lightly, although Kathryn knew he was as avid a conservationist as Maude.

She peeked up at him. ''I seem to remember that you went on television to support that wilderness proposal on the national forest.''

He raised his cigarette to his firm lips. ''Guilty,'' he admitted with a faint, rare smile. He glanced toward the band and the smile faded. ''Are they all playing the same song?'' he asked irritably.

''I'm not sure. I thought you liked music,'' she teased.

He glowered down at her. ''I do. But that,'' he added with a speaking glance in the band's direction, ''isn't.''

''My generation thinks it is,'' she replied with a challenge in her bright eyes. ''And if you don't like contemporary music, then why did you bother to come to the party, you old stick in the mud?''

He reached down and tapped her on the cheek with a long, stinging finger. ''Don't be smart,'' he told her. ''I came because I hadn't seen you for six months, if you want the truth.''

''Why? So you could drive me home and bawl me out in privacy on the way?'' she asked.

His heavy dark brows came together. "How much of that punch have you had?" he asked curtly.

"Not quite enough," she replied with an impudent grin and tossed off the rest of the punch in her glass.

"Feeling reckless, little girl?" he asked quietly.

"It's more like self-preservation, Blake," she admitted softly, peeking up at him over the empty glass as she held its coolness to her pink lips. "I was getting my nerves numb so that it wouldn't bother me when you started giving me hell."

He took a draw from his cigarette. "It was six months ago," he said tightly. "I've forgotten it."

"No you haven't," she sighed, reading the cold anger very near the surface in his taut face. "I really didn't know what Jack had in mind. I probably should have, but I'm not very worldly."

He sighed heavily. "No, that's for sure. I used to think it was a good thing. But the older you get, the more I wonder."

"That's just what Maude was saying," she murmured, wondering if he could read other people's minds.

"And she could be right." His eyes narrowed to a glittering darkness as he studied her in the revealing little dress. "That dress is years too old for you."

"Does that mean it's all right with you if I grow up?" she asked sweetly.

One dark eyebrow rose laconically. "I wasn't aware that you needed my permission."

"I seem to, though," she persisted. "If I try to do anything about it, you'll be on my neck like a duck after a June bug."

"That depends on what growing-up process you have in mind," he replied, reaching over to crush the cigarette into an ashtray. "Promiscuity is definitely out."

"Not in your case, it isn't!"

His head jerked up, his eyes blazing. "What the hell has my private life got to do with you?" he asked in a voice that cut her like sheer ice.

She felt like backing away. "I . . . I was just teasing, Blake," she defended in a shaken whisper.

"I'm not laughing," he said curtly.

"You never do with me," she said in a voice like china breaking.

"Stop acting like a silly adolescent."

She bit her lower lip, trying to stem the welling tears in her soft, hurt eyes. "If you'll excuse me," she said unsteadily, "I'll go back and play with my dolls. Thank you for your warm welcome," she added in a tiny voice before she pushed her way through the crowd away from him. For the first time, she wished she'd never come to live with Blake's family.

Two

For the rest of the evening she avoided Blake, sticking to Nan and Phillip like a shadow while she nursed her emotional wounds. Not that Blake seemed to notice. He was standing with Maude and one of the younger congressmen in the group, deep in discussion.

"I wonder what they're talking about now?" Phillip asked as he danced Kathryn around the room to one of the band's few slow tunes.

"Saving water moccasins," she muttered, her full lips pouting, her eyes as dark as jade with hurt.

Phillip sighed heavily. "What's he done now?"

"What?" she asked, lifting her flushed face to Phillip's patiently amused eyes.

"Blake. He hasn't been in the same room with you for ten minutes, and the two of you are already avoiding one another. Talk about repeat acts!"

Her rounded jaw clenched. "He hates me, I told you he did."

"What's he done?" he repeated.

She glared at his top shirt button. "He said . . . he said I couldn't be promiscuous."

"Good for Blake," Phillip said with annoying enthusiasm.

"You don't understand. That was just what started it," she explained. "And I was teasing him about not being a monk and he jumped all over me about digging into his private life." She felt herself tense as she remembered the blazing heat of Blake's anger. "I didn't mean anything."

"You didn't know about Della?" he asked softly.

She gaped up at him. "Della who?"

"Della Ness. He just broke it off with her," he explained.

A pang of something shivered through her slender body, and she wondered why the thought of Blake with another woman should cause a sensation like that. "Were they engaged?"

He laughed softly. "No."

She blushed. "Oh."

"She's been bothering him ever since, calling up and crying and sending him letters . . . you know how that would affect him." He whirled her around in time to the music and brought her back against him loosely. "It hasn't helped his temper any. I think he was glad for the European trip. She hasn't called in over a week."

"Maybe he's missing her," she said.

"Blake? Miss a woman? Honey, you know better than that. Blake is the original self-sufficient male. He never gets emotionally involved with his women."

She toyed with the lapel of his evening jacket. "He doesn't have to take his irritation out on me," she protested sullenly. "And at my homecoming party, too."

"Jet lag," Phillip told her. He stopped as the music did and grimaced when the hard rock blared out again. "Let's sit this one out," he yelled above it. "My legs get tangled trying to dance to that."

He drew her off the floor and back to the open veranda, leading her onto the plant-studded balcony with a friendly hand clasping hers.

"Don't let Blake spoil this for you," he said gently as they stood leaning on the stone balustrade, looking out over the city lights of King's Fort that twinkled jewel-bright on the dark horizon. "He's had a hard week. That strike at the London mill wasn't easily settled."

She nodded, remembering that one of the corporation's biggest textile mills was located there, and that this was nowhere near the first strike that had halted production.

"It's been nothing but trouble," Phillip added with a hard sigh. "I don't see why Blake doesn't close it down. We've enough mills in New York and Alabama to more than take up the slack."

Her fingers toyed with the cool leaves of an elephant-ear plant near the balcony's edge as she listened to Phillip's pleasant voice. He was telling her how much more solvent the corporation would be if they bought two more yarn mills to add to the conglomerate, and how many spindles each one would need to operate, and how new equipment could increase production...and all she was hearing was Blake's deep, angry voice.

It wasn't her fault that his discarded mistresses couldn't take "no" for an answer, and it was hardly prying into his private life to state that he had women. Her face reddened, just thinking of Blake with a woman in his big arms, his massive torso bare and bronzed, a woman's soft body crushed against the hair-covered chest where muscles rippled and surged....

The blush got worse. She was shocked by her own thoughts. She'd only seen Blake stripped to the waist once or twice, but the sight had stayed with her. He was all muscle, and that wedge of black, curling hair that laced down to his belt buckle somehow emphasized his blatant maleness. It wasn't hard to understand the effect he had on women. Kathryn tried not to think about it. She'd always been able to separate Blake who was like family from the arrogant, attractive Blake who drew women like flies everywhere he went. She'd kept her eyes on his dark face and reminded herself that he had watched her grow from adolescence to womanhood and he knew too much about her to find her attractive in any adult way. He knew she threw things when she lost her temper, that she never refilled the water trays when she emptied the ice out of them. He knew that she took off her shoes in church, and climbed trees to hide from the minister when he came visiting on Sunday afternoon. He even knew that she sometimes threw her worn blouses behind the door instead of in the clothes hamper. She sighed heavily. He knew too much, all right.

"...Kathryn!"

She jumped. "Sorry, Phil," she said quickly, "I was drinking in the night. What did you say?"

He shook his head, laughing. "Never mind, darling. It wasn't important. Feeling better now?"

"I wasn't drunk," she said accusingly.

"Just a little tipsy, though," he grinned. "Three glasses of punch, wasn't it? And mother emptied the liquor cabinet into it with our hostess's smiling approval."

"I didn't realize how strong it was," Kathryn admitted.

"It has a cumulative effect. Want to go back in?"

"Must we?" she asked. "Couldn't we slip out the side door and go see that new sci-fi movie downtown?"

"Run out on your own party? Shame on you!"

"I'm ashamed," she agreed. "Can we?"

"Can we *what?*"

"Go see the movie. Oh, come on, Phil," she pleaded, "save me from him. I'll lie for you. I'll tell Maude I kidnapped you at gunpoint..."

"Will you, now?" Maude laughed, coming up behind them. "Why do you want to kidnap Phillip?"

"There's a new science fiction movie in town, and..." Kathryn began.

"...and it would keep you out of Blake's way until morning, is that how this song goes?" Phillip's mother guessed keenly.

Kathryn sighed, clasping her hands in front of her. "That's the chorus," she admitted.

"Never mind, he's gone."

She looked up quickly. "Blake?"

"Blake." Maude laughed softly. "Cursing the band, the punch, the politicians, jet lag, labor unions, smog and women with a noticeable lack of tact until Eve almost wept with relief when he announced that he was going home to bed."

"I hope the slats fall out under him," Kathryn said pleasantly.

"They're box springs," Maude commented absently. "I bought it for him last year for his birthday, remember, when he complained that he couldn't get any rest..."

"I hope the box springs collapse, then," Kathryn corrected.

"Malicious little thing, aren't you?" Phillip asked teasingly.

Maude slumped wearily. "Not again. Really, Kathryn Mary, this never-ending war between you and my eldest is going to give me ulcers! What's he done this time?"

"He told her she couldn't be promiscuous," Phillip obliged, "and got mad at her when she pointed out that he believed in the double standard."

"Kathryn! You didn't say that to Blake!"

Kathryn looked vaguely embarrassed. "I was just teasing."

"Oh, my darling, you're so lucky you weren't near any bodies of water that he could have pitched you into," Maude said. "He's been absolutely black-tempered ever since that Della toy of his started getting possessive and he sent her packing. You remember, Phil, it was about the time Kathryn wrote that she was going to Crete on that cruise with Missy Donavan and her brother Lawrence."

"Speaking of Lawrence," Phillip said, drawling out the name dramatically, "what happened?"

"He's coming to see me when he flies down for that writers' convention on the coast," she said with a smile. "He just sold another mystery novel and he's wild with enthusiasm."

"Is he planning to spend a few days?" Maude asked. "Blake has been suspicious of writers, you know, ever since that reporter did a story about his affair with the beauty contest girl...who was she again, Phil?"

"Larry isn't a reporter," Kathryn argued, "he only writes fiction...."

"That's exactly what that story about Blake and the beauty was," Phillip grinned. "Fiction."

"Will you listen?" Maude grumbled. "You simply can't invite Lawrence into the house while Blake's home. I've got the distinct impression he's already prejudiced against the man."

"Larry isn't a pushover," Kathryn replied, remembering her friend's hot temper and red hair.

Maude frowned, thinking. "Phillip, maybe you could call that Della person and give her Blake's unlisted number just before Kathryn Mary's friend comes, and I'll remind him of how lovely St. Martin is in the summer...."

"It will only be for two or three days," Kathryn protested. Her soft young features tightened. "I thought Greyoaks was my home, too...."

Maude's thin face cleared instantly and she drew Kathryn into her arms. "Oh, darling, of course it is, and you know it is! It's just that it's Blake's home as well, and that's the problem."

"Just because Larry's a writer..."

"That isn't the only reason," Maude sighed, patting her back. "Blake's very possessive of you, Kathryn. He doesn't like you dating older men, especially men like Jack Harris."

"He has to let go someday," Kathryn said stubbornly, drawing away from Maude. "I'm a woman now, not the adolescent he used to buy bubble gum for. I have a right to my own friends."

"You're asking for trouble if you start a rebellion with Blake in his present mood," Maude cautioned.

Kathryn lifted a hand to touch her dark hair as the breeze blew a tiny wisp of it into the corner of her mouth. "Just don't tell him Larry's coming," she said, raising her face defiantly.

Phillip stared at Maude. "Is her insurance paid up?" he asked conversationally.

"Blake controls the checkbook for all of us," Maude reminded her. "You could find yourself without an allowance at all; even without your car."

"No revolution succeeds without sacrifice," Kathryn said proudly.

"Oh, good grief," Phillip said, turning away.

"Come back here," Kathryn called after him. "I'm not through!"

Maude burst out laughing. "I think he's going to light a candle for you. If you're planning to take Blake on, you may need a prayer or two."

"Or Blake may," Kathryn shot back.

Maude only laughed.

The house was quiet when they got home, and Maude let out a sigh of pure relief.

"So far, so good," she said smiling at Kathryn and Phillip. "Now, if we can just sneak up the stairs..."

"Why are you sneaking around at all?" came a deep, irritated voice from the general direction of the study.

Kathryn felt all her new resolutions deserting her as she whirled and found herself staring straight into Blake's dark angry eyes.

She dropped her gaze, and her heart thumped wildly in her chest as she dimly heard Maude explaining why the three of them were being so quiet.

"We knew you'd be tired, dear," Maude told him gently.

"Tired, my foot," he returned, lifting a glass of amber liquid in a shot glass to his hard, chiseled mouth. He glared at Kathryn over its rim. "You knew I'd had it out with Kate."

"She's been gorging herself on the rum punch, Blake," Phillip said with a grin. "Announcing her independence and preparing for holy revolution."

"Oh, please, shut up," Kathryn managed in a tortured whisper.

"But, darling, you were so brave at the Barringtons," Phillip chided. "Don't you want to martyr yourself to the cause of freedom?"

"No, I want to be sick," she corrected, swallowing hard. She glanced up at Blake's hard-set face. The harsh words all came back, and she wished fervently that she'd accepted Nan's invitation to spend the night.

Blake swirled the amber liquid in his glass absently. "Good night, Mother, Phil."

Maude threw Kathryn an apologetic glance as she headed for the staircase with Phillip right behind.

"You wouldn't rather discuss the merger with the Banes Corporation?" Phillip grinned at Blake. "It would be a lot quieter."

"Oh, don't desert me," Kathryn called after them.

"You declared war, darling," Phillip called back, "and I believe in a strict policy of non-interference."

She locked her hands behind her, shivering in her warm sable coat despite the warmth of the house and the hot darkness of Blake's eyes.

"Well, go ahead," she muttered, dropping her gaze to the open neck of his white silk shirt. "You've already taken one bite out of me, you might as well have an arm or two."

He chuckled softly and, surprised, she jerked her face up to find amusement in his eyes.

"Come in here and talk to me," he said, turning to lead the way back into his walnut-paneled study. His big Irish Setter, Hunter, rose and wagged his tail, and Blake ruffled his fur affectionately as he settled down in the wing armchair in front of the fireplace.

Kathryn took the chair across from his, absently darting a glance at the wood decoratively piled up in the hearth. "Daddy used to burn it," she remarked, using the affectionate name she gave Blake's father, even though he was barely a distant cousin. He was like the father she'd lost.

"So do I, when I need to take the chill off. But it isn't cool enough tonight," he replied.

She studied his big, husky body and wondered if he ever felt the cold. Warmth seemed to radiate from him at close range, as if fires burned under that darkly tanned skin.

He tossed off the rest of his drink and linked his hands behind his head. His dark eyes pinned Kathryn to her chair. "Why don't you get out of that coat and stop trying to look as if you're ten minutes late for an appointment somewhere?"

"I'm cold, Blake," she stammered.

"Turn up the thermostat, then."

"I won't be here that long, will I?" she asked hopefully.

His dark, quiet eyes traveled over the soft, pink skin revealed by her white dress, making her feel very young and uncomfortable.

"Must you stare at me like that?" she asked uneasily. She toyed with a wisp of chiffon.

He pulled his cigarette case from his pocket and took his time about lighting up. "What's this about a revolution?" he asked conversationally.

She blinked at him. "Oh, what Phil said?" she asked, belatedly comprehending. She swallowed hard. "Uh, I just..."

He laughed shortly. "Kathryn, I can't remember a conversation with you that didn't end in stammers."

Her full lips pouted. "I wouldn't stammer if you wouldn't jump on me every time you get the chance."

One heavy dark eyebrow went up. He looked completely relaxed, imperturbable. That composure rattled her, and she couldn't help wondering if anything ever made him lose it.

"Do I?" he asked.

"You know very well you do." She studied the hard lines of his face, noting the faint tautness of fatigue that only a stranger would miss. "You're very tired, aren't you?" she asked suddenly, warming to him.

He took a draw from the cigarette. "Dead," he admitted.

"Then why aren't you in bed?" she wanted to know.

He studied her quietly. "I didn't mean to ruin the party for you."

The old, familiar tenderness in his voice brought an annoying mist to her eyes and she averted them. "It's all right."

"No, it isn't." He flicked ashes into the receptacle beside his chair, and a huge sigh lifted his chest. "Kate, I just broke off an affair. The silly woman's pestering me to death, and when you said what you did, I overreacted." He shrugged. "My temper's a little on edge lately, or I'd have laughed it off."

She smiled at him faintly. "Did you . . . love her?" she asked gently.

He burst out laughing. "What a child you are," he chuckled. "Do I have to love a woman to take her into my bed?"

The flush went all the way down her throat. "I don't know," she admitted.

"No," he said, the smile fading, "I don't suppose you do. I believed in love, at your age."

"Cynic," she accused.

He crushed out the cigarette in his ashtray. "Guilty. I've learned that sex is better without emotional blinders."

She dropped her eyes in mortification, trying not to see the unholy amusement in his dark face.

"Embarrassed, Kate?" he chided. "I thought that experience with Harris had matured you."

Her green eyes flashed fire as they lifted to meet his. "Do we have to go through this again?" she asked.

"Not if you've learned something from it." His gaze dropped pointedly to her dress. "Although I have my doubts. Are you wearing anything under that damned nightgown?"

"Blake!" she burst out. "It's not a nightgown!"

"It looks like one."

"It's the style!"

He stared her down. "In Paris, I hear, the style is a vest with nothing under it, worn open."

She tossed her hair angrily. "And if I lived in Paris, I'd wear one," she threw back.

He only smiled. "Would you?" His eyes dropped again to her bodice, and the boldness of his gaze made her feel strange sensations. "I wonder."

She clasped her hands in her lap, feeling outwitted and outmatched. "What did you want to talk to me about, Blake?" she asked.

"I've invited some people over for a visit."

She remembered her own invitation to Lawrence Donavan and she held her breath. "Uh, who?" she asked politely.

"Dick Leeds and his daughter, Vivian," he told her. "They're going to be here for a week or so while Dick and I iron out that labor mess. He's the head of the local union that's giving us so much trouble."

"And his daughter?" she asked, hating herself for her own curiosity.

"Blond and sexy," he mused.

She glared at him. "Just your style," she shot at him. "With the emphasis on sexy."

He watched her with silent amusement. Blake, the adult, indulging his ward. She wanted to throw something at him.

"Well, I hope you don't expect me to help Maude keep them entertained," she said. "Because I'm expecting some company of my own!"

The danger signals were flashing out of his deep brown eyes. "What company?" he asked curtly.

She lifted her chin bravely. "Lawrence Donavan."

Something took fire and exploded under his jutting brow.

"Not in my house," he said in a tone that might have cut diamond.

"But, Blake, I've already invited him!" she wailed.

"You heard me. If you didn't want to be embarrassed, you should have consulted with me before inviting him," he added roughly. "What were you going to do, Kathryn, meet him at the airport and then tell me about it? A *fait accompli?*"

She couldn't meet his eyes. "Something like that."

"Cable him. Tell him something came up."

She lifted her eyes and glared at him, sitting there like a conqueror, ordering her life. If she buckled under one more time, she'd never be able to stand up to him. Never. She couldn't let him win this time.

Her jaw set stubbornly. "No."

He got to his feet slowly, gracefully for such a big man, and the set of his broad shoulders was intimidating even without the sudden, fierce narrowing of his eyes.

"What did you say?" he asked in a deceptively soft tone.

She laced her fingers together in front of her and clenched them. "I said no," she managed in a rasping voice. Her dark green eyes appealed to him. "Blake, it's my home, too. At least, you said it was the day you asked me to come live here," she reminded him.

"I didn't say you could use it as a rendezvous for romantic trysts!"

"You bring women here," she tossed back, remembering with a surge of anguish the night when she had accidentally come home too early from a date and found him with Jessica King on the very chairs where they were now sitting. Jessica had been stripped to the waist, and so had Blake. Kathryn had barely even noticed the blonde, her eyes were so staggered by the sight of Blake with his broad, muscled chest bared by the woman's exploring hands. She'd never been able to get the picture of him out of her mind, his mouth sensuous, his eyes almost black with desire....

"I used to," he corrected gently, reading he memory with disturbing accuracy. "How old were you then? Fifteen?"

She nodded, looking away from him. "Just."

"And I yelled at you, didn't I?" he recalled gently. "I hadn't expected you home. I was hungry and impatient, and frustrated. When I took Jessica home, she was in tears."

"I...I should have knocked," she admitted. "But we'd been to that fair, and I'd won a prize, and I couldn't wait to tell you about it...."

He smiled quietly. "You used to bring all your triumphs straight to me, like a puppy with its toys. Until that night." He studied her averted profile. "You've kept a wall between us ever since. The minute I start to come close, you find something else to put up in front of you. Last time it was Jack Harris. Now, it's that writer."

"I'm not trying to build any walls," she said defensively. Her dark eyes accused him. "You're the mason, Blake. You won't let me be independent."

"What do you want?" he asked.

She studied the delicate scrollwork of the fireplace with its beige and white color scheme. "I don't know," she murmured. "But I'll never find out if you keep smothering me. I want to be free, Blake."

"None of us are that," he said philosophically. His eyes were wistful, his tone bitter. He stared at her intently. "What is it that attracts you to Donavan?" he asked suddenly.

She shrugged and a wistful light came into her own eyes, echoing his expression the minute before. "He's fun to be with. He makes me laugh."

"That's all you need from a man—laughter?"

The way he said it made shivers run down her stiff spine, and when she looked at him, the expression on his hard face was puzzling. "What else is there?" she asked without thinking.

A slow, sensuous smile turned up the corners of his mouth. "The fires a man and woman can create when they make love."

She shifted restlessly in her chair. "They're overrated," she said with pretended sophistication.

He threw back his head and roared.

"Hush!" she said. "You'll wake the whole house!"

His white, even teeth were visible, whiter than ever against his swarthy complexion. "You're red as a summer beet," he observed. "What do you know about love, little girl? You'd pass out in a dead faint if a man started making love to you."

She stared at him with a sense of outrage. "How do you know? Maybe Lawrence..."

"...maybe not," he interrupted, his eyes confident, wise. "You're still very much a virgin, little Kate. If I'd had any fears on that account, I'd have jerked you off Crete so fast your head would have spun."

She grimaced. "Virginity isn't such a prize these days," she sighed, remembering Missy Donavan's faintly insulting remarks about it.

His silent appraisal lasted so long that her attention was caught by the faint ticking of the big grandfather clock in the hall. "Don't get any ideas about throwing yours away," he warned softly.

"Oh, Blake, don't be so old fashioned," she grumbled. "Anyway," she added with a faint, mischievous smile, "where would you be today if all the women in the world were pure?"

"Rather frustrated," he conceded. "But you're not one of my women, and I don't want you offering yourself to men like a nymphomaniac."

She sighed. "There's hardly any danger of that," she said dully. "I don't know how."

"That dress is a damned good start," he observed.

She glanced down at it. "But it covers me up," she protested. "It's a lot more modest than what Nan was wearing."

"I noticed," he said with a musing smile.

She peeked through her lashes. "Nan thinks you're the sexiest man alive," she said lightly. "She knew you'd be at the party."

His face hardened. "Nan's a child," he growled, turning away with one hand rammed in his pocket. "And I'm too old to encourage hero worship."

Nan was Kathryn's age, exactly. Her heart seemed to plummet, and she wanted to hit out at him. He always made her feel so gauche and ignorant.

She studied his broad back. He was so good to look at. So big and vibrant, and full of life. A quiet man, a caring man. And a tyrant!

"If you won't let me invite Larry here," she murmured," I suppose I could fly down to the coast and go to that writers' convention with him."

He turned, staring at her, hard and intimidating even at a distance. "Threatening me, Kate?" he asked.

"I wouldn't dare!" she replied fervently.

His dark face was as unreadable as a stone sculpture. "We'll talk about it again."

She scowled at him. "Tyrant," she grumbled.

"Is that your best shot?" he asked politely.

"Male chauvinist!" she said, trying again. "You do irritate me, Blake."

He moved toward her lazily. "What do you think you do to me, little Kathryn?" he asked, his voice a low growl.

She looked up into his arrogant face as he came within striking distance. "I probably irritate you just as much," she admitted, sighing. "Pax?"

He smiled down at her indulgently. "Pax. Come here."

He tilted her chin up and bent his head down. She closed her eyes, expecting the familiar brief, rough touch of his mouth. But it didn't come.

Puzzled, she opened her eyes and looked straight into his at an unnerving distance. She was so close that she could see the flecks of gold in his dark brown irises, the tiny crinkled lines at the corner of his eyelids.

His fingers touched the side of her throat, warm and strangely caressing.

"Blake?" she whispered uncertainly.

His jaw tautened. She could see a muscle jerk beside his sensuous mouth.

"Welcome home, Kate," he said roughly, and started to move away.

"Aren't you going to kiss me?" she asked without thinking.

All the expression drained out of his face to leave his eyes smoldering and they looked down into hers. "It's late," he said abruptly, turning away, "and I'm tired. Good night, Kate."

He walked out the door and left her standing there, staring at the empty doorway.

Three

Blake was strangely reserved for the next few days, and Kathryn found herself watching him for no reason at all. He was Blake, she kept telling herself. Just her guardian, as familiar as the towering old house and its ring of live oaks. But something was different. Something . . . and she couldn't quite grasp what.

"Blake, are you angry with me?" she asked him one evening as he started upstairs to dress for a date.

He scowled down at her. "What makes you think that, Kathryn?" he asked.

She shrugged, and forced a smile for him. "You seem . . . remote."

"I've got a lot on my mind, kitten," he said quietly.

"The strike?" she guessed.

"That, and a few other assorted headaches," he agreed. "If you're through asking inane questions, I am on my way out."

"Sorry," she said flippantly, "Heaven forbid that I should keep you from the wheat fields."

"Wheat fields?"

"Where you sow your wild oats, of course," she said with what felt like devastating sophistication as she turned to go back in the living room where Phillip and Maude were talking.

He chuckled softly. "Your slip's showing."

She whirled, grasping her midi-length velveteen skirt and staring down at her shapely calf. "Where?"

He went on up the stairs with a low chuckle and she glared after him.

Later, she watched him come back downstairs, dressed in a pair of dark slacks with a white silk shirt open at the neck and a tweed jacket that gave him a rakish look. What woman was he taking out, she wondered, and would she know how to appreciate all that dark, vibrant masculinity? Just the sight of him was enough to make Kathryn's pulse race, and involuntarily she thought back to the night of her homecoming party and the strange look in Blake's eyes when he started to kiss her and didn't. That hesitation had puzzled her ever since, although she tried not to think about it too much. Blake would be frighteningly dangerous in any respect other than that of a cherished adopted brother.

Nan Barrington came over early the next morning to go riding with Kathryn. Petite and fragile-looking in her jodhpurs, she was wearing a blue sweater, very tight, that was the exact shade of her eyes.

She brushed by Kathryn with a tiny sigh, her eyes immediately on everything in sight as she searched the area for Blake.

"He's gone out," Kathryn said with an amused smile.

Nan looked wildly disappointed. "Oh," she said, her face falling. "I just thought he might be going with us."

Kathryn didn't bother to mention that Blake was doing everything short of joining a monastery to avoid her. That would have led to questions she didn't want to face, much less answer.

"Well, there she is, the golden girl," Phillip said from the staircase, gazing with exaggerated interest at the petite blonde. "You luscious creature, you."

Nan laughed delightedly. "Oh, Phil, you're such a tease," she said. "Come riding with us and let me prove that I can still beat the socks off you."

He made a mock pose. "No girl exposes my naked ankles," he scoffed. "You're on!"

Kathryn led them out the door, tugging her green velveteen blouse down over her trim hips as she went, delighting in its warmth in the chill morning air. "It's nippy out here," she murmured. Her slender hand went up to test the strength of the pins that held the coiled rope of hair in place on top of her head. The wind was brisk, invigorating.

"Nice and cool," Phillip agreed. "Strange how Blake's run out of time to ride," he mentioned with a curious glance at Kathryn. "He's literally worked every minute he's been home. And with the Leedses arriving Saturday, he's going to be lucky if he can manage time to pick them up at the airport."

"Fighting again?" Nan probed, shooting a glance at Kathryn.

Kathryn lifted her head and watched the path in front of her as they took the old shortcut to the big barn, with its white-fenced paddocks. The path led through a maze of high, clipped hedges, in the center of which was a white gazebo, carefully concealed, and ringed all the way around with comfortable cushions. Kathryn had always thought it a wildly romantic setting, and her imagination ran riot every time she saw it.

"Blake and I are getting along just fine," she said, denying her friend's teasing accusation.

"Nothing easier," Phillip agreed with a grin. "They never see each other."

"We do," Kathryn disagreed. "Remember the other night when Blake was going out on that date?"

Nan glanced at Phillip. "Who's he after now?" She laughed.

Phillip shrugged fatalistically. "Who knows? I think it's the little blonde he's got in the office. His new secretary, if office gossip can be believed. But I hear she can't spell cat."

"Blake likes blondes, all right." Kathryn laughed with an amusement that she was far from feeling.

"Here's one he sure avoids," Nan groaned. "What's wrong with me?"

Phillip threw an avuncular arm across her shoulders. "Your age, my dear," he informed her. "Blake likes his women mature, sophisticated and thoroughly immoral. That leaves you out of the running."

Nan sighed miserably. "I always have been."

"Blake used to pick us up after cheerleading practice, remember," Kathryn said, eyeing the gazebo longingly as they passed it. "He still thinks of us chewing bubble gum and giggling."

"I hate bubble gum," Nan pouted.

"So do I," Phillip agreed. "It leaves a bad...well, hello," he broke off, grinning at Blake.

The older man stopped in their path, dressed in a sophisticated gray business suit, with a spotless white silk shirt and a patterned tie. He looked every inch the magnate, polished and dignified.

"Good morning," Blake said coolly. He smiled at Nan. "How's your mother?"

"Just fine, Blake," Nan sighed, going close to catch his arm in her slender fingers. "Don't you have time to go riding with us?"

"I wish I did, little one," he told her. "But I'm already late for a conference."

Kathryn turned away and started for the barn. "I'm going ahead," she called over her shoulder. "Last one in the saddle's a greenhorn!"

She almost ran the rest of the way to the barn, shocked at her own behavior. She felt strange. Sick. Hurt. Empty. The sight of Nan clinging to Blake's arm had set off a rage within her. She'd wanted to slap her friend of many years, just for touching him. She didn't understand herself at all.

Absently, she went into the tackroom and started getting together bits and bridles and a saddle. She barely noticed when the lithe chestnut gelding was saddled and ready to mount. He pranced nervously, as if he sensed her uneasy mood and was reacting to it.

Nan joined her as she was leading Sundance out into the bright morning.

"Where's Phil?" Kathryn asked, trying to keep the edge out of her voice.

Nan shrugged curiously. "Blake dragged him off to the office for some kind of council of war. At least, that's what it sounded like." She sighed. "Blake seemed very angry with him." Her face brightened. "Almost as if he didn't like the idea of Phillip going riding with me. Kate, do you suppose he's jealous?" she asked excitedly.

"It wouldn't surprise me a bit," Kathryn lied, remembering Blake's remarks about her friend. But, frowning, she couldn't help wondering if he meant it. Why in the world didn't he want Phillip to ride with the girls?

Kathryn knew that Blake felt Phillip's attitude toward the multi-company enterprise was a little slack sometimes. But why drag him off at this hour of the morning unless . . . She didn't want to think about it. If Nan was right, she didn't want to know.

"Get saddled and let's go!" Kathryn called. "I'm itching for a gallop!"

"Why did you run off back there?" Nan asked before she went into the stable to saddle her mount.

"Do hurry," Kathryn said, ignoring the question. "Maude wants me to help her plan some menus for the Leedses' visit."

Nan hurriedly saddled her mount, a little mare with the unlikely name of Whirlwind, and the disposition of a sunny summer day.

The two girls rode in a companionable silence, and Kathryn gazed lovingly at the rolling green hills in their autumn colors, trees in the distance just beginning to don the soft golds that later would become brilliant oranges and reds and burgundy. The air was clean and fresh, and fields beyond the meadows were already being turned over to wait for spring planting.

"Isn't it delicious?" Kathryn breathed. "South Carolina must be the most beautiful state in the country."

"You only say that because you're a native," Nan teased.

"It's true, though." She reined in and leaned forward, crossing her forearms on the pommel to stare at the silver ribbon of the Edisto River beyond.

"Do you know how many rice plantations there were in Charleston just before the Civil War?" she murmured, remembering books she'd read about those great plantations with their neat square fields and floodgates.

"I'm afraid I don't share your passion for history, Kate," Nan said apologetically. "Sometimes I even forget what year they fought the War of 1812."

Kathryn smiled at her friend, and all the resentment drained out of her. After all, Nan couldn't help the way she felt about Blake. It wasn't her fault he was so wickedly attractive. . . .

"Let's ride down through the woods," she said abruptly, wheeling Sundance. "I love to smell the river, don't you?"

"Oh, yes," Nan agreed. "I'm with you."

* * *

Blake was home for dinner that night, an occurrence rare enough to cause comment.

"Run out of girls?" Phillip teased as they sat around the table nibbling at Mrs. Johnson's chicken casserole.

"Phillip!" Maude chided, her dark eyes disapproving as she paused in the act of lifting a forkful of chicken to her mouth.

Blake raised an eyebrow at his brother. His blue-checked sports shirt was open at the neck, and he looked vibrant and rested and dangerously attractive to Kathryn, who was doing her best to keep her eyes away from him.

"You had more than your share this morning," Blake remarked dryly.

"Was that why you dragged me off to the office before I could enjoy being surrounded by them?" Phillip laughed.

"I needed your support, little brother."

"Sure. The way Sampson needed a herd of horses to help him tug the pillars down."

"I would like to point out," Maude said gently, "that Mrs. Johnson spent an hour preparing this excellent chicken dish, which is turning to bile in my stomach."

Kathryn darted an amused glance at the older woman. "You should have had daughters," she suggested.

Maude stared at Blake, then at Phillip. "I'm not sure. It's very hard to picture Blake in spiked heels and a petticoat."

Kathryn choked on her mashed potatoes, and Phillip had to lean over and thump her on the back.

"I'm glad Kathryn finds something amusing," Blake said in that cold, curt tone that she hated so much. "She wasn't in the best of humors this morning."

Kathryn swallowed a sip of coffee, and her dark green eyes glared at Blake across the table. "I don't remember saying anything to you at all, Blake," she murmured.

"No," he agreed. "You were too busy flouncing off to offer a civil greeting."

How could he be so blind? she wondered, but she only glared at him. "Excuse me," she said haughtily, "but I never flounce."

He lifted his coffee cup to his chiseled lips, but his eyes never left Kathryn's face. Something dark and hard in them unnerved her. "Push a little harder, honey," he challenged quietly.

Her small frame stiffened. "I'm not afraid of you," she said with a forced smile.

His eyes narrowed, and a corner of his mouth went up. "I could teach you to be," he said.

"Now, children," Maude began, her eyes plainly indicating which of the two she was referring to as they glared at Kathryn. "This is the meal hour, remember? Indigestion is bad for the soul."

Phillip sighed as he tasted his lemon mousse. "It's never stopped them before," he muttered.

Kathryn crumpled her napkin and laid it beside her plate before she got to her feet. "I think I'll play the piano for a while, if no one minds."

"Not for too long, dear, you'll keep Blake awake," Maude cautioned. "Remember, he had to get up at five in the morning to drive down to Charleston to pick up the Leedses at the airport."

Kathryn threw a gracious smile in Blake's direction. "Of course," she said with honey in her voice. "Our elders must have their beauty rest."

"By heaven, you're asking for it," Blake said in a voice that sent chills down her spine.

"Go, girl!" Phillip said, pushing her in the direction of the living room. He closed the door behind them with an exaggerated sigh and leaned against it. "Whew!" he breathed, and his dark eyes laughed at her when he opened them again. "Don't push your luck, sweet. He's been impossible to get along with for days now, and this morning he made a barracuda look tame."

"Doesn't he always?" she grumbled.

"Yes," he conceded. "But if you had his secretary, it might give you ulcers as well."

She glanced at him as she went to the piano and sat down flexing her fingers. "If he wants secretaries who decorate instead of type, that's his business. Just hush, Phil, will you? I'm sick of hearing about Blake!"

She banged away at Rachmaninoff's Second Piano Concerto, while Phillip stared at her profile thoughtfully for a long time.

Four

Maude had the housekeeper, buxom Mrs. Johnson, and the two little daily maids running in circles by late afternoon. It was almost comical, and Kathryn had to force herself not to giggle.

"Don't put the urn of dried flowers *there,*" Maude wailed when one of the maids placed it in the entrance to the living room.

Kathryn decided she had better go outside and keep out of the way.

Phillip was just getting out of his small sports car as she emerged from the house. He hesitated for an instant when he saw Kathryn coming, then got the rest of the way out and closed the door.

"What's the matter with you?" he asked cheerfully.

"It's the dried flowers," she explained enigmatically.

Phillip blinked. "Have you been into Blake's whiskey, Kathryn?"

She shook her head. "You had to be there to understand," she told him. "Honestly, you'd think the head of state was coming. She's rearranged the furniture twice, and now she's going crazy over flowers. And just think, Phil," she added in a conspiratorial whisper, "Leeds can't even save the river!"

He chuckled. "Probably not. Blake should be back soon," he said, after a glance at his watch.

Kathryn looked out over the sculptured garden, with its cobblestone path leading through the hedges to the concealed white gazebo. "I wonder what Miss Leeds looks like?" she murmured thoughtfully.

"Vivian?" he asked, smiling. "The cover of a fashion magazine. She's an actress, you know, quite well-known already, too."

She felt ill. "Old?" she asked.

"Twenty-five isn't old, sweet." He laughed. "Blake can't be without a woman for long. He really can pick them."

She wanted to hit him. To scream. To do anything but stand there with a calm smile plastered to her face and pretend it didn't matter. Suddenly, terribly, it mattered. Blake was her... She stopped, frowning. Her *what?*

"Kathryn, you aren't listening," Phillip said patiently. "I said, would you like to go into King's Fort with me and buy a new dress or two?"

She looked up at him. "Whatever for?" she asked indignantly. "I don't dress in rags!"

"Of course not," he said, placating her. "But Maude suggested that you might like some new clothes since we're having guests."

She drew a deep, angry breath. "Put on my best feathers, you mean?" She thought about it, imagining an outfit daring enough to make even Blake take notice. A tiny smile touched her pink mouth. "All right. Take me someplace expensive. Saks, I think."

"Uh, Kathryn..." Phillip said.

"Blake won't get the bill until next month," she reminded him. "By then, I can be on St. Martin, or Tahiti, or Paris...."

He chuckled. "All right, incorrigible girl, come on. We've got to hurry or we won't be here when Blake's guests arrive."

Kathryn didn't tell him, but that was just what she had in mind. The idea of greeting Vivian Leeds made her want to spend several days in town. She disliked the woman already, and she hadn't even met her.

She left Phillip in a small, exotic coffee shop on the mall while she floated through the plush women's department in the exclusive shop, dreaming of Blake seeing her in one expensive dress after another. She'd show him! She'd be the most beautiful woman he'd ever seen, and she'd make him stand back and take notice!

But when she tried on one of the elegant dresses she'd picked out, all she saw in the mirror was a little girl trying to play dress-up. She looked about fifteen. All the excitement drained out of her face. Her whole body seemed to slump as she stared at her reflection.

"It doesn't suit you, does it?" the pleasant blond saleswomen asked her.

Kathryn shook her head sadly. "It looked so beautiful on the model...."

"Because it was designed for a taller, thinner figure than yours," the statuesque older woman explained. "If I may suggest some styles...?"

"Oh, please!" Kathryn said, wide-eyed.

"Wait here."

The three dresses the woman brought back looked far less dramatic than those Kathryn had picked out. They were simple garments with no frills at all, and the colors were pale pastels—mint, taupe and a silky beige. But on Kathryn, they came to life. Combined with her black hair and green eyes, the mint was devastating. The taupe emphasized her rounded figure and darkened her eyes. The beige brought out her soft complexion and its simple lines gave her an elegance far beyond her years.

"And this is for evening," the woman said at last, bringing out a burgundy velvet gown with a deep V-neck and slits down both sides. It's a dream of a dress, Kathryn thought, studying her reflection in the mirror, her face glowing as she imagined Blake's reaction to this seductive style—the light went out of her suddenly when she remembered the warning he'd given her, about provoking him. But surely she had the right to wear what she pleased....

"Kathryn, we've got to go," Phillip called to her.

One expressive eyebrow went up, and her eyes danced mischievously. What would this gorgeous gown do to Phillip?

She opened the curtains and walked out. He stared at her, with lips slightly parted, his brown eyes stunned.

"Kathryn?" he asked, as if he didn't trust his eyes anymore.

"Yes, it's me," she assured him. "Oh, Phil, isn't it a dream?"

He nodded dubiously. "A dream."

"What's the matter?" she asked, going close to look up at him, while the saleswoman smiled secretively from a distance.

"Are you sure it's legal to wear something like that in public?" he asked.

She smiled. "Why not? It's very fashionable. Do you really like it?"

He caught his breath. "Honey, I love it. But Blake..."

She glared at him. "I'm grown. I keep having to remind Blake..."

"You won't have to remind him anymore if you wear that dress," he said, staring down at the soft, exposed curves of her breasts in the plunging neckline. "He'll be able to see for himself."

She tossed her long, waving hair defiantly. "I'll bet that actress wears more revealing clothes than this."

"She does," he agreed, "but her lifestyle is different from yours, kitten."

"You mean she sleeps with men, don't you, Phillip?" she persisted.

"Hush, for heaven's sake!" he said quickly, looking around to see if anyone was listening. "Remember where we are."

"But she does, doesn't she?" she kept on, glaring.

"I know you've been at it with Blake about your writer friend coming," Phillip told her quietly. "But don't think you'll retaliate by insulting his latest female acquisition. He'll cut you into little pieces, Kate."

She felt the rage welling up in her like rain catching in a vat. "I'm tired of Blake telling me how to live my life. I want to move into an apartment."

"Don't tell him yet," Phillip pleaded.

"I already have," she replied, her eyes sparkling with temper.

"And what did he say?"

"He said no, of course. He always says no. But it won't work anymore. I'm going to get a job, and an apartment, and you're going to help me," she added, with a mischievous glance upward.

"Oh, like hell I am!" he replied. "I'm not taking on Blake for you."

She stamped her small foot. "That's what's wrong with men today!"

His eyebrows went up amusedly. "What is?"

"That no one's brave enough to take on Blake for me! I'll bet Larry will," she added stubbornly.

"If he does, he'll wish he hadn't," Phillip said. "And if you buy that dress, Kathryn, I'm going away for the weekend." He made a mock shudder. "I can't stand the sight of blood."

"Blake won't do anything," she said smugly. "Not in front of his guests."

"Blake will do anything, any time, in front of anybody, and if you don't know that by now, you're even crazier then I thought you were." He shook his head.

"Give it up, Kathie. Blake's only trying to do what's best for you."

"That's beside the point, Phillip," she replied, smoothing the velvet under her slender fingers. "I don't want to spend the rest of my life being told what to do. Blake's not my keeper."

"If you go out after dark in that dress, you'll need one," he murmured, staring at her.

She leaned up and kissed his cheek. "You're a nice man."

"Kathryn, are you sure...?"

"Don't be such a worrywart," she told him. She motioned to the saleswoman. "I'll take all of them," she said with a smile. "And that green velvet one, as well."

Phillip frowned. "What green velvet one?"

"It's ever so much more daring than this," she lied, remembering the high halter neckline and soft lines of the other dress she'd tried on. "It doesn't have a back at all," she added in a wicked whisper.

"Lord help us!" Phillip said, lifting his eyes upward.

"Don't bother Him," Kate said, "He has wars and floods to worry about."

"And I have you," he groaned.

"Lucky man," she said, patting his cheek before she went to charge her purchases. "Come on. You have to sign the ticket."

"Whose name would you like me to sign on it?" he asked.

"Oh, silly!" she laughed.

* * *

She and Phillip had managed to sneak in the back way and dart upstairs to dress for dinner without being seen. Recklessly, Kathryn slid into the burgundy velvet dress after she had her bath, and tacked up her long hair in a seductively soft bun on top of her head with little curling wisps trailing down her blushing cheeks. She used only a little makeup—just enough to give her a mysterious look, a hint of sophistication. The woman looking back at her in the mirror bore no resemblance to the young girl who'd left that room the same day to go shopping.

Satisfied with what she saw, she added a touch of Givenchy perfume and sauntered downstairs. She heard voices coming from the living room, and Blake's was among them. She felt suddenly nervous, uneasy. That would never do. She lifted her head, baring the soft curve of her throat, and, gathering her courage, walked straight into the white-carpeted, blue-furnished room.

She noticed two things immediately: the possessive blonde clinging to Blake's sleeve like a parasite, and the sudden, blazing fury in Blake's eyes as he looked at Kathryn Mary.

"Oh, there you are, darl...ing," Maude said, her voice breaking on the word as she noticed the dress. "How...different you look, Kathryn," she added with a disapproving glance.

"Where did you get that dress?" Blake asked in a harsh, low voice.

She started to speak, then darted a glance at Phillip, who was burying his face in his hand. "Phillip bought it for me," she said in a rush.

"Kathryn!" Phillip groaned.

Blake smiled, like a hungry barracuda, Kathryn thought shakily. "I'll discuss this with you later, Phil."

"Could we make it after Kathryn's funeral?" Phillip asked, with a meaningful glance at Kathryn.

"Aren't you going to introduce me to your guests?" Kathryn asked brightly.

"Dick Leeds and his daughter, Vivian," Blake said, indicating a tall, white-haired man with twinkling blue eyes and the equally blue-eyed blonde at Blake's side. "This is Kathryn Mary."

"Kilpatrick," she added proudly. "I'm the youngest, next to Phillip."

"How do you do?" Dick Leeds asked pleasantly, and extended a thin hand to be shook. He smiled at her. "Not a Hamilton, then?" he asked.

"I'm a cousin," she explained. "Maude and the family took me in when my parents died, and brought me up."

"Apparently not too successfully," Blake said darkly, his eyes promising retribution as they seared a path down her body, lingering on the plunging neckline.

"If you don't stop picking on me, Blake," she said sweetly, accepting a glass of sherry from Phillip, "I'll hit you with my teddy bear."

Vivian Leeds didn't look amused, although her thin lips managed a smile. "How old are you, Miss Kilpatrick?" she asked listlessly.

"Much younger than you, Miss Leads, I'm sure," Kathryn replied with an equally false smile.

Phillip choked on his drink. "Uh, how was your trip, Viv?" he asked the blonde, quickly.

"Very nice, thanks," she replied, her eyes cutting a hole in Kathryn. "Lovely dress," she said. "What there is of it."

"This old rag?" Kathryn said haughtily, her eyes speaking volumes as they studied the rose silk gown the blonde was wearing. "It's warm, at least," she added. "I don't really care for these new fashions—some of them look more like nighties than dresses," she said pointedly.

Miss Leeds' face colored expressively, her blue eyes lighting like firecrackers.

"Let's eat," Maude said suddenly.

"Lead the way, Mother," Blake said. Amusement was vying with anger in his dark eyes, and just for an instant, amusement won. But then his dark gaze slid sideways to Kathryn, and the smile faded. His eyes curved over the creamy, exposed skin at her neckline, and she felt as if he had touched her. Her lips parted under a rush of breath, and he looked up suddenly and caught that expression on her young face. Something flared in his dark eyes, like a minor volcanic upheaval, and Kathryn knew that she was going to be in the middle of a war before the night was over. But she managed to return Blake's glare with bravado, and even smiled. If she was going to be the main course on his menu, she might as well enjoy the appetizer first.

Phillip dropped back beside her as they made their way into the dining room. "Feeling suicidal?" he asked under his breath. "He's blazing, and that sweet little smile didn't help."

"Revolutionaries can't afford to worry about tomorrow," she replied saucily. "Besides, Blake can't eat me."

"Can't he?" he asked, casting a wary glance toward his brother, who was glaring at them over Vivian's bright head.

"Phillip, you aren't really afraid of him, are you?" she teased. "After all, you're brothers."

"So," he reminded her, "were Cain and Abel."

"Don't worry, I'll protect you."

"Please don't," he asked mournfully. "Why did you have to tell him that I bought you that dress?"

"But, you did sign for it," she said innocently.

"I know, but buying it wasn't my idea."

"Be reasonable, Phil," she said soothingly. "If I'd told him it was my idea, he'd have gone straight for my throat."

He gave her a measuring look. "And having him go for mine was a better idea?"

She smiled. "From my point of view, it was," she laughed. "Oh, Phil, I'm sorry, really I am. I'll tell him the truth."

"If you get the chance," he muttered under his breath, nodding toward his brother.

Blake seated Vivian and then turned to hold out a chair for Kathryn. She approached it with the same aplomb as a condemned terrorist headed for the gallows.

"Nice party," she murmured under her breath as she sat down.

"And it's only beginning," he said with a smile that didn't reach his eyes. "Make one more snide remark to Vivian and I'll grind you into the carpet, Kathryn Mary."

She spared him a cool glance. "She started it," she said under her breath.

"Jealous?" he taunted softly.

Her eyes jerked up to his, blazing with green fire. "Of her?" she asked haughtily. "I'm not fifteen anymore," she said.

"Before the night's over, you're going to wish you were," he said softly. "I promise you."

The deep anger in his voice sent chills running all over her. Why did she have to open her mouth and challenge him again? Hadn't she had enough warning? She felt a surge of fear at what lay ahead. It seemed that she couldn't stop fighting Blake lately, and she wondered at her own temerity. Was she going mad?

One glance at his set face down the table from her was enough to make her want to run upstairs and bar the door.

Dinner was an ordeal. Vivian monopolized Blake to such an extent that he was hardly able to carry on a conversation with anyone else, but her cold blue eyes made frequent pilgrimages to Kathryn's quiet face. The animosity in them was freezing.

"You're not doing much for international relations," Phillip remarked as they retired to the living room for after-dinner drinks.

"Blake's doing enough for both of us," she replied, darting a cool glance toward the blonde, who was clinging to Blake's big, muscular arm as if he were a life raft. "He has bad taste," she said without thinking.

"I wouldn't say that," Phillip disagreed. His green eyes danced as they surveyed the blonde's graceful back. "She's pretty easy on the eyes."

"Is she?" she asked with magnificent disdain. "Frankly, she doesn't do a thing for me."

"Don't be sour," he said. "You forget why she's here, darling; remember the strike?"

"Oh, I remember," she told him. "But does Blake? I thought her father was the focal point."

"Part of it, at least," he said.

She stared up at him. "What do you mean, Phil?" she asked curiously.

He avoided her sharp eyes. "You'll know soon enough. Look, Mother's motioning to you."

Maude was showing some of her antique frames to Dick Leeds, but she left him with a smile and drew Kathryn aside.

"You're doing it again, my darling," she moaned, darting a wary glance in Blake's direction. "He's ready to chew nails. Kathryn, can't you manage not to antagonize him for just one evening? The Leedses are our guests, remember."

"They're Blake's guests," came the sullen reply.

"Well, it is Blake's house," Maude said with a placating smile. "Johnny left it all to him. He felt Blake would keep me from frittering it away."

"You wouldn't have," Kathryn protested.

Maude sighed. "Perhaps," she said wistfully. "But it's a moot point. You aren't improving Blake's disposition, you know."

"All I did was buy a new dress," she said defensively.

"It's much too old for you, Kathryn," she said quietly. "Phillip hasn't taken his eyes off you all evening, and every time he looks at you, Blake scowls more."

"Phillip and I aren't related, after all," Kathryn pointed out.

Maude smiled. "And there's no one I'd rather see him marry, you know that. But Blake doesn't approve, and he could make things very difficult for you."

She scowled. "He doesn't approve of any man I date," she grumbled.

Maude started to say something, but obviously thought better of it. "It will work itself out. Meanwhile, please at least be civil to Miss Leeds. It's terribly important that we make a good impression on them both. I can't tell you any more than that, but do trust me."

Kathryn sighed, "I will."

Maude patted Kathryn's slender shoulder. "Now be a dear, and help me entertain Dick. Blake is going to drive Vivian into King's Fort and show her how the city looks at night. She was curious, for some reason that escapes me."

It didn't escape Kathryn, and it didn't improve her mood, either. Especially when she watched Vivian and Blake go out the door without a backward glance. She wanted to pick up the priceless Tang dynasty vase in the hall and heave it at Blake's dark head. In the end, she consoled herself with the fact that at least she didn't have to face Blake until the morning. That was a blessing in itself.

Dick Leeds was interesting to talk to. She liked the elderly man, who seemed to have the same kind of steel in his makeup that Blake did. All too soon, he went upstairs to his room, pleading fatigue from the long trip. Maude followed suit with a sigh.

"Like Dick," she told Phillip and Kathryn, "I'm beginning to feel my age a little. Good night, children."

Phillip challenged Kathryn to a game of gin rummy after Maude went out the door, but she protested.

"You'll just beat me again," she pouted.

"I'll give myself a ten-point handicap," he promised.

"Well...just a couple of hands," she agreed finally.

He held out a chair for her at the small table by the darkened window. "Sit down, pigeon...I mean, partner," he grinned.

She smiled across the table at him. "Why can't Blake be like you?" she wondered absently as he shuffled the cards. "Friendly, and easy to get along with, and fun to be around...."

"He used to be, when you were younger," he answered, and his warm brown eyes twinkled. "It's only since you've started growing up that you think he's changed."

She stuck out her tongue at him. "I don't think, I know! He growls at me all the time."

"You light the fires under him, my sweet. Like tonight."

Her face closed up, like a fragile flower in a sudden chill. "I don't like her."

"And the feeling seems to be mutual. I don't think attractive women ever really like each other." He studied her unobtrusively. "But I have an idea that her dislike stems from your own. You've hardly been friendly toward her."

She drew in a defeated sigh. "You're right, I haven't," she admitted.

"Trying to get back at Blake?" he persisted.

"My arsenal is limited when it comes to fighting your brother," she sighed.

He laid down three cards in sequence and discarded. "That goes for all of us."

She held the cool cards up to her lips absently while she drew a card, looked at it, grimaced, and laid it down on the discard pile. "I don't see why I can't have an apartment," she said. Her full lips pouted against the cards. "I can get a job and pay for it."

"A job doing what?" he asked politely.

She glared at him. "That's the problem. Finishing school didn't prepare me for much of anything. I know," she said, brightening. "I'll advertise to be a rich man's mistress! I'm eminently qualified for that!"

Phillip buried his face in his hand. "Don't you dare say that to Blake when I'm in the room! He'll think I suggested it!"

She laughed at the expression on his face. Phillip was such fun, and such a gentleman. She was fonder of him than she liked to say. He was truly like the brother she wished she'd had. But Blake...she turned her attention back to her cards.

She was so caught up in the game of gin rummy that she forgot the time. She was one card short of winning the game when all of a sudden she heard the front door open and she froze in her seat.

"Oops," she murmured weakly.

Phillip smothered a grin at the look on her soft features. "Sounds like they're home," he commented, as

Vivian's high-pitched voice called good-night from the staircase.

Before she could reply, Blake, looking big, dark and formidable, came in the door. He glanced at the tableau they made as he slung his jacket onto a chair and tugged his tie loose, tossing it carelessly onto the jacket.

"Have a good time?" Phillip asked slyly, his sharp gaze not missing the smear of lipstick just visible on Blake's shirt collar.

Blake shrugged. He went to the bar and poured himself a jigger of whiskey, neat.

"Uh, I think I'd better get to bed," Phillip said, gauging Blake's mood with lightning precision. "Good night, all."

"I think I'll go up, too," Kathryn began hopefully, rising as Phillip made his hasty exit and disappeared into the hall.

Kathryn was only a step behind him when Blake's curt voice stopped her with her hand on the doorknob.

"Close the door," he said.

She started to go through it.

"From the inside," he added in a tone that was honeyed, yet vaguely threatening.

She drew a steadying breath and went back into the living room, closing the door reluctantly behind her. She leaned back against it, flashing a nervous glance at him.

"Did you have a nice drive?" she asked.

"Don't hedge," he growled. His angry eyes slid down her body in the velvet dress with its side slits and plunging neckline, and she felt as if his hands were touching her bare flesh.

"Dick's gone to bed. He's very nice," she murmured, trying to postpone the confrontation as long as possible. She'd seen Blake in plenty of bad tempers, but judging by the control she read in his face, this one was formidable. The courage she'd felt earlier, in company, dissolved now that she was alone with him.

"So is his daughter," he replied. "Not that you've taken the trouble to find out."

She shifted against the cold wood at her back. "She bites."

"So do you, honey," he replied, lifting his glass to his lips. "I want the truth, Kate. Did Phillip buy you that dress?"

She felt weary all of a sudden, defeated. Blake always seemed to win. "No," she admitted. "That is, he signed for it because I don't have a charge account, but Maude said herself that I needed some new clothes," she added defensively.

"I said the same thing. But I hadn't planned on your dressing like a Main Street prostitute."

"It's the style, Blake!" she shot at him.

"Almost exactly the same words you used after the Barrington's party," he reminded her. "And I told you the same thing that I'm telling you now. A dress like that raises a man's blood pressure by five points while it's still on the mannequin. On you…" He let his eyes speak for him, dark and sensuous as they caressed her.

"Vivian was wearing less," she replied weakly, feeling the heat in her cheeks. "I could almost see through *her* dress."

"Throwing stones?" he asked. "Your breasts are barely covered at all."

Her face went hot under the words, and she glared at him with outrage in her sparkling green eyes. "Oh, all right, I'll never wear the silly dress again, Blake! But I can't see what difference it makes to you what I wear!"

His eyes narrowed, and his hands tightened on the thick glass. "Can't you?"

She squared her small shoulders. "You're just being a tyrant again," she accused. Her hands slid down the sensuous burgundy velvet over her hips as she lifted her face defiantly. "What's the matter, Blake, do I disturb you?" she challenged. "Would you rather I wore my gym suit from high school?"

He set the glass down on the bar and strode toward her deliberately, his eyes blazing, his face harder than granite. She saw the purpose in his eyes and turned with a feeling of panic, grabbing for the doorknob. But the action was too late. He caught her and whirled her around with rough, hurting hands to hold her, struggling against the door.

Five

She stared up into the face of a stranger, and her voice caught in her throat. "Blake, you wouldn't...!" she burst out finally, frightened by what she read in his dark eyes.

He moved, and his big, warm body crushed her against the door. She felt the pressure of his hard, powerful thighs against hers, the metal of his belt buckle sharp in her stomach. There was the rustle of cloth against cloth as his hands caught her bare arms and stilled her struggles.

"Oh, wouldn't I?" he growled, as his eyes dropped to her tremulous lips.

Stunned by the sight of his dark, leonine face at such a disturbing proximity, she looked up at him helplessly until he suddenly crushed her soft mouth under his, forcing her head back under the merciless pressure.

She kept her mouth tightly closed, her body trembling with sudden fear at what Blake was asking of her. She stiffened, struggling instinctively, and his mouth twisted against hers to hold it in bondage, his teeth nipping her lower lip painfully.

A sob broke from her tight throat as she yielded to the merciless ardor that was years beyond her few experiences with men. Nothing that had gone before prepared her for the adult passion she felt in Blake, and it sparked a response that was mingled fear and shock. This was no boyfriend assaulting her senses. This was Blake. Blake, who taught her how to ride. Blake, who drove her to cheerleading practice and football games with her friend Nan. Blake, who was a confidant, a protector, and now . . .

He jerked his head up suddenly, surveying the damage to her swollen, bruised lips, her wounded eyes, her wildly flushed cheeks and disordered hair.

"You're . . . hurting me," she whispered brokenly. Her fingers went to her drooping coiffure, nervously, as tears washed her eyes.

His face seemed to harden as he looked down at her. His breath came hard and fast. His eyes glittered with unfathomable emotions.

"This is what happens when you throw that sweet young body at me," he said in a voice that cut. "I warned you before about flaunting it, and you wouldn't listen. Now, maybe I've managed to get through to you."

She drew in a sobbing breath, and the tiny sound seemed to disturb him. His eyes softened, just a little as they wandered over her face.

"Please let me go, Blake," she pleaded in a shaken whisper. "I swear, I'll wear sackcloth and ashes for the rest of my life!"

His heavy brows drew together and he let go of her arms to lean his hands on either side of her head against the door, pushing back a little to ease the crush of his powerful chest and thighs.

"Afraid?" he asked in a deep, lazy voice.

She swallowed hard, nodding, her eyes mesmerized by his.

He let his eyes move down to her swollen, cut lip as he bent toward her again. She felt his tongue brushing very softly against it, healing, tantalizing and she gasped again—but this time, not in pain.

He drew back and caught her eyes. The expression he found was one of curiosity, uncertainty. She met that searching gaze squarely and felt the breath sigh out of her body. Her heart went wild under the intensity of it. She wanted suddenly to reach up and bring his dark head back down again, to feel his mouth again. To open her lips and taste his. To kiss him hungrily, and hard, and feel his body against the length of hers as it had been, but not in anger this time.

His jaw went rigid. His eyes seemed to burst with light and darkness. Then, suddenly, she was free. He pushed away from her and turned to walk back to the bar. He poured himself another whiskey, and paused long enough to dash a jigger of brandy into a snifter for her before he moved back to the door where she stood frozen and handed it to her.

Wordlessly, he caught her free hand and drew her back to his desk with him. He perched against it, holding her in front of him while she nervously sipped the fiery amber liquid.

He threw down his own drink and put first his own glass, then hers, aside. He reached out to catch her by the waist, drawing her gently closer. He stared down at her flushed face for a long time before he spoke, in a silence heady with new emotions.

"Don't brood," he said, in a tone that carried echoes of her childhood. Blake's voice, gentle, soothing her when her world caved in. "The tactics may have been different, but it was only an argument. It's over."

She pretended a calm she didn't feel, and some of the tension went out of her shocked body. "That doesn't sound very much like an apology," she said, darting a shy glance up at him.

One eyebrow lifted. "I'm not going to apologize. You asked for that, Kathryn, and you know it."

She sighed shakily. "I know." Her eyes traced the powerful lines of his chest. "I didn't mean to say what I did."

"All you have to remember, little innocent one," he said indulgently, "is that verbal warfare brings a man's blood up. You can be provocative without even realizing it." He shook her gently. "Are you listening?"

"Yes." Her dark, curious eyes darted up to his for an instant. "You... I didn't think that you..." she stopped, trying to find words.

"There's no blood between us to protect you from me, Kate," he said in a deep quiet tone. "I'm not in my dotage, and I react like any normal man to the sight of a woman in a revealing dress. Phillip could have lost his head just as easily," he added gruffly.

She felt her heart pounding and caught her breath. "Perhaps,"she whispered. "But he would have been... gentle, I think."

He didn't argue the point. His big, warm hand tilted her face up to his quiet eyes. "Another of the many differences between Phillip and me, young Kate," he said. "I'm not a gentle lover. I like my women... practiced."

The flush made bright banners in her cheeks. "Do they get combat pay?" she asked with a hint of impudence and a wry smile as she touched her forefinger gingerly to her cut lip.

His lips turned up, and his dark eyes sparkled. It was as if there had never been a harsh scene to alienate them. "It works both ways, honey," he replied musingly. "Some women would have returned the compliment, with interest."

Her eyes looked deep into his. This, she thought dazedly, is getting interesting. "Women...bite men?" she asked in a whisper, as if it was a subject not fit for decent ears to hear.

"Yes," he whispered back. "And claw, and scream like banshees."

"I...I don't mean *then,*" she said. "I mean when... oh, never mind, you just want to make fun of me. I'll ask Phillip."

He chuckled softly. "Do you really think he's ever felt that kind of passion?" he asked.

She shrugged. "He's a man."

"Men are different," he reminded her. His eyes dropped to her mouth. "Poor little scrap, I did hurt you, didn't I?" he asked gently.

She drew away from him, and he relaxed his hold to free her. "It's all right," she murmured. "As you said, I did ask for it." Her eyes glanced off his. "You're . . . very sophisticated."

"And you're a delicious little innocent," he replied. "I didn't mean to be so brutal with you, but I do want to impress on you what you invite from a man with a dress like that." He smiled drily. "I've got a low boiling point, Kate, and I do recall warning you."

"I didn't think you were serious," she said with a sigh.

His dark eyes swept over her again. "Now you know better."

"And better," she agreed. She turned, almost knocking over Maude's priceless porcelain vase on its marble-topped table on the way out. "I'm taking back every dress I bought while there's still time."

"Kate, don't be ridiculous," he growled after her. "You know what I meant. I don't want you wearing dresses with necklines cut to the waist, that's all. You're still to much of a child to realize what you could be letting yourself in for."

She turned at the door with great dignity, her carriage so perfect that Mademoiselle Devres would have cheered. "I'm not a child anymore, Blake," she told him. "Am I?"

He turned away, bending his head to light a cigarette with steady hands. "When does that writer get here?"

She swallowed nervously. "Tomorrow morning." She watched him walk to the darkened window and draw the curtain aside to look out. His broad back was toward her and unexpectedly, she remembered how warm and sensuous it had felt under the palms of her hands.

"Aren't you going to tell me to call if off again?" she asked, testing him, feeling a flick of danger run through her that was madly exciting.

He stared at her across the room for a long moment before he answered. "At least I won't have to worry about you sneaking off to go to that convention with him while he's under my roof," he remarked carelessly. "And he'd have his work cut out to seduce you, from what I've seen tonight."

Her eyes flashed at him. "That's what you think!" she shot back.

He only laughed, softly, sensuously. "Before you flounce off, hugging your boundless attractions to your bare bosom, you might remember that I wasn't trying to seduce you. You ought to know by now that my taste doesn't run to oversexed adolescents. Not that you fall in that classification," he added with a mocking smile. "You're green for a young woman just shy of her twenty-first birthday."

That hurt, even more than the devastating taste of him as a lover. "Larry doesn't think so," she told him.

He lifted the cigarette to his hard mouth, his eyes laughing at her. "If I had his limited experience, I might agree with him."

That nudged a suspicion in the back of her mind. "What do you know about his experience?" she asked.

He studied her for a long, static silence. "Did you really think I'd let you go to Crete with him and that harebrained sister of his without checking them out thoroughly?"

Her face flamed. "You don't trust me, do you?"

"On the contrary, I trust you implicitly. But I don't trust men," he said arrogantly.

"You don't own me," she cried, infuriated by his calm sureness.

"Oh, go to bed before you set fire to my temper again," he growled at her.

"Gladly," she returned. She went out the door without even a good night, and then lay awake half the night worrying about it.

Her dreams were full of Blake that night. And when she woke to the rumble of thunder and the sound of raindrops, she had a vivid picture of herself lying in his big arms while his mouth burned on her bare skin. It was embarrassing enough to make her late for breakfast. She didn't think she could have looked at Blake without giving herself away.

But her worries were groundless. Blake had already left to go to the office when Kathryn came downstairs to find Vivian sitting by herself at the breakfast table.

"Good morning," Vivian said politely. Her delicate blond features were enhanced by her buttercup yellow blouse and skirt. She looked slim and ultrachic. She eyed Kathryn's jeans and roll-neck white sweater with disgust. "You don't believe in fashion, do you?" she asked.

"In my own home, no," she replied, reaching for cream to add to her steaming cup of coffee as Mrs.

Johnson hustled back and forth between the kitchen, adding to the already formidable breakfast dishes.

Vivian watched her add two teaspoons of sugar to her coffee. "Don't count calories either, do you?" She laughed.

"I don't need to," Kathryn said quietly, refusing to display her irritation. Where in the world were Maude and Phillip and Dick Leeds?

Vivian watched her raise the cup to her mouth, and her hawk eyes lit on the slightly raw lower lip, which was faintly throbbing this morning—a painful reminder of Blake's shocking intimacy.

The blonde's narrow eyes darted down to her plate as she nibbled at scrambled eggs. "You and Blake were downstairs together a long time last night," she said conversationally.

"We...had some things to discuss," Kathryn murmured, hating the memory of him that came back to haunt her with a vengeance. She was being forced to see Blake in a new, different way, and she wasn't at all sure that she wanted to. She was more afraid of him now than ever; a delicious, mushrooming fear that made her pulse race at just the thought of his mouth crushing hers. What would it have been like, she wondered reluctantly, if he hadn't been angry....

"You missed Blake this morning," Vivian remarked, her eyes strangely wary as she watched Kathryn spoon eggs and ham onto her plate. "He asked me particularly to come down straightaway when the alarm went off so that we could have breakfast together."

"How nice," came the stilted reply.

Kathryn's head was bent and she missed the faintly malicious smile that curled Vivian's full lips.

"He was anxious to leave before you came down," the blonde went on in a low, very cool voice. "I think he was afraid you might have read something more than he intended into what happened last night."

Kathryn's fork fumbled through her fingers and hit the china plate with a loud ringing sound. Her startled eyes jerked up. "W-what?" she faltered. "He *told* you?" she asked incredulously.

Vivian looked the picture of sophistication. "Of course, darling," she replied. "He was bristling with regrets, and I just let him talk. It was the dress, of course. Blake is too much a man not to be swayed by a half-naked woman."

"I was not . . . !"

"He makes love very well, don't you think?" Vivian asked with a secretive smile. "He's such a vibrant lover; so considerate and exciting . . ."

Kathryn's face was the color of red cabbage. She sipped her coffee, ignoring the blistering touch of it.

"You do understand that it mustn't be allowed to happen again?" the older woman asked softly, smiling at Kathryn coolly over her china cup. "I quite realize why Blake hasn't told you the true reason I came over here with my father, but . . ." she let her voice trail away insinuatingly.

Kathryn stared at her, feeling her secure, safe little world dissolving around her. It was like being buried alive. She could hardly breathe for the sudden sense of suffocation. "You mean . . . ?"

"If Blake hasn't told you, I can't," Vivian said confidingly. "He didn't want to make the announcement straight away, you know. Not until his family had a chance to get to know me."

Kathryn couldn't manage words. So that was how it was. Blake planned to marry at last, and this blond barracuda was going to swim off with him. And after last night, she'd actually thought... Her face shuttered. What did it matter, anyway? Blake had always been like a brother, despite his brutal ardor last night. And that had only been to warn her, he'd said so. He was afraid she'd read something into it, was he? She'd show him!

Vivian, seeing the look of despair that came into the young girl's face, hid a smile in her coffee cup as she drained it. "I see you understand," she remarked smugly. "You won't let Blake know that I said anything?" she asked with a worried look. "He'd be so unhappy with me. . . ."

"No, of course not," Kathryn said quietly. "Congratulations."

Vivian smiled sweetly. "I hope we're going to become great friends. And you mustn't think anything about what happened with Blake. He only wants to forget it, as you must. It was just a moment out of time, after all, nothing to be concerned about."

Of course not, Kathryn thought, feeling suddenly empty. She managed a bright smile, but fortunately the rest of the family chose that moment to join the two women, and she was able to bury her grief in conversation.

Kathryn had always liked the airport; it excited her to see the travelers with their bags and bright smiles, and she liked to sit and watch and speculate about

them. A long-legged young woman, tall and tanned
and blond, ran into the arms of a big, dark man and
burst into tears. Studying them as she waited for
Lawrence Donavan's plane to get in, Kathryn wondered if they were patching up a lovers' quarrel. They
must have been, because the man was kissing her as if
he never expected to see her again, and tears were
running unchecked down her pale cheeks. The emotion in that hungry kiss made her feel like a peeping
Tom, and she looked away. The depth of passion she
sensed in them was as alien to her as the Andes. She'd
never felt that kind of hunger for a man. The closest
to it that she could remember coming was when Blake
had kissed her the second time—that sensuous, aching touch that kindled fledgling responses in her un-
tried body. If he'd kissed her a third time...

A movement caught her eye and she rose from the
chair to find Larry Donavan coming toward her. She
ran into his outstretched arms and hugged him, lifting her face for a firm, affectionate kiss.

His blue eyes laughed down into hers under the
shock of red hair that fell rakishly across his brow.

"Miss me?" he teased.

She nodded, and the admission was genuine.
"Would I fight half my family to drive this distance to
pick you up if I hadn't?" she asked.

"I know. It is a pretty long drive, isn't it? I could
have caught a bus..."

"Don't be silly," she said, linking her hand with his
as they walked toward the baggage conveyor. "How
would you like a grand tour of Charleston before we
head home? Blake's guests got it, and you're just as
entitled...."

"Guests?" he echoed. "Have I come at an inopportune time?" he asked quietly.

"Blake's courting a labor union and a woman at the same time," she said with a trace of bitterness in her tone. "We'll simply keep out of the way. Phillip and Maude and I will take care of you, don't worry."

"Blake's the guardian, isn't he?" he asked, pausing to grab his bag from the conveyor as it moved past.

"That, and a distant cousin. The Hamiltons raised me," she murmured. "I'm afraid it isn't the best weather for a visit," she apologized, gesturing toward the rainy gray skies as they stepped outside and walked toward the parking lot. "It's been raining off and on all day and we're expecting some flooding before we're through. Hurricanes really get to us in the low country."

"How low is it?" he asked.

She leaned toward him, taking the cue. "It's so low that you have to look up to see the streets."

"Same old Kat," he teased, using his own nickname for her, and he hugged her close. "It's good to be down south again."

"You only say that because you're glad to get away from all that pollution," she told him.

He blinked at her. "Pollution? In Maine?" he asked incredulously.

She batted her eyelashes up at him. "Why, don't you all have smokestacks and chemical waste dumps and bodies floating in the river from gang wars?" she asked in her best drawl.

He laughed brightly. "Stereotypes?"

She grinned. "Didn't you believe that we wore white bedsheets to the grocery store and drank mint juleps for breakfast when you first met me?"

"I'd never known anyone from the south before," he defended himself as they walked toward her small foreign car. "In fact," he admitted, "this really is the first time I've spent any time here."

"You'll learn a lot," she told him. "For instance, that a lot of us believe in equality, that most of us can actually read and write, and that..."

The sky chose that particular moment to open up, and rain started pouring down on them in sheets. She fumbled with her keys, barely getting them into the car in time to avoid a soaking.

Brushing her damp hair back from her face, Kathryn put the small white Porsche into reverse and backed carefully out of the parking space. It wasn't only due to her drivers' training course that she was careful at the wheel. When Blake had given her this car for her birthday last year, he'd been a constant passenger for the first week, watching every move she made. When he talked she listened, too, because in his younger days, Blake had raced in Grand Prix competitions all over Europe.

She swung into gear and headed out of the parking lot onto the busy street.

"It's raining cats!" She laughed, peering through the windshield wipers as the rain shattered against the metal roof with deafening force. It was hard to see the other cars, despite their lights.

"Don't blame me." Larry laughed. "I didn't bring it with me."

"I hope it lets up," she said uneasily, remembering the two bridges they had to cross to get back to King's Fort and on to Greyoaks. When flash floods came, the bridges sometimes were underwater and impossible to cross.

She saw an opening and pulled smoothly out into it.

"I see palm trees!" Larry exclaimed.

"Where did you think you were—Antartica?" she teased, darting a glance at him. "They don't call us the Palmetto State for nothing. We have beaches in the low country, too, just like Florida."

He looked confused. "Low country?"

"The coastal plain is called that because... well, because it's low," she said finally. "Then there's the up country—but you won't see any of it this trip. King's Fort, where the family lives, is low country, too, even though it's an hour and a half away." She smiled apologetically. "I'm sorry we couldn't fly down to pick you up, but the big Cessna's having some part or other replaced. That's why Blake had to drive down for his guests. There's a company executive jet, too, but one of the vice-presidents had to fly down to another of the mills in Georgia."

He studied her profile. "Your family must own a lot of industries."

She shrugged. "Just three or four yarn mills and about five clothing manufacturing companies."

He lifted his eyes skyward. "Just, she says."

"Well, lots of Blake's friends own more," she explained. She headed straight down I-26 until she could exit and get onto Rutledge Avenue. "We'll go the long way around to the Battery, and I'll show you some of the landmarks on Meeting Street—if you can see them through the rain," she said drily.

"You know the city pretty well?" he asked, all eyes as they drove down the busy highway.

"I used to have an aunt here, and I stayed with her in the summer. I still like to drive down on weekends, for the night life."

She didn't mention that she'd never done it alone before, or that she was making this trip without Blake's knowledge or permission. Maude and Phillip had protested but nobody had ever stopped Kathryn except Blake, and they couldn't find him before she left. She could still see Vivian Leeds' smug expression, and her pride felt wounded. If he was involved with the blonde, he should never have touched Kathryn... but, then, she'd provoked him. He'd accused her of it, and she couldn't deny it. All she didn't know was why.

"I'd like to use this as a location for a book," he said after they reached the turnoff onto the Battery, with its stone sea wall, and drove along it to Old Charleston.

She smiled at his excited interest as he looked first out at the bay and then across her at the rows of stately old houses.

They passed the Lenwood Boulevard intersection and he peered through the slackening rain. "Do you know any of the history of these old houses?" he asked.

"Some of them. Just a second." They drove on down South Battery Street and she pointed to a white two-story antebellum house on the right with long, elegant porches. "That one dated back to the 1820's. It

was built on palmetto logs sunk in mud in an an-
tiearthquake design later used by Frank Lloyd Wright.
It was one of only a few homes to survive the 1886
Charleston earthquake that destroyed most of the
city.''

"How about that!" He laughed, gazing back toward the house enclosed by its neat white picket fence.

She gestured toward White Point Garden where a
small group of people were just disembarking from a
horse-drawn carriage. "There are several carriage
tours of the old part of town," she told him. "They're
fun. I'm just sorry we don't have time today, but,
then, it's not really the weather for it, either."

He sighed. "There wasn't a cloud in the sky when I
left home."

"That's life," she told him. "Look on the left over
there," she added when traffic let her turn onto
Meeting Street. "That first house was once owned by
one of the Middletons who owned Middleton Place
Gardens. The second house is built in Charleston
'double house' style—brick under cypress weather-
boarding. It's late eighteenth century."

"Lady, you know your architecture," he said with
grudging praise.

She laughed, relaxing in the plush leather seat. "Not
like Aunt Hattie did. She taught me. A little further
down, there's a good example of the Adams-style
construction—the Russell House. It's now the headquarters of the Historic Charleston Foundation."

He watched for it, and she caught a glimpse of
smiling appreciation in his eyes as they studied the
three-story building through its brick and wrought-
iron wall.

"I wish we had time to go through Market Street," she said regretfully as she gave her attention to traffic. "There's a place where you can get every kind of food at individual stalls, and there are all kinds of shops and little art galleries...." She sighed. "But I guess we'd better stop at a restaurant a little closer to home. The wind's getting up, and I don't think the rain's any closer to quitting."

"Maybe on the trip back," he said with a smile, and winked at her.

She smiled back, flicking the radio on to a local station. The music blared for a few seconds, and then the weather report came on. She listened with a face that grew more solemn by the minute. Flash flood warnings were being announced for the area around King's Fort as well as the rivers near Charleston.

"I hope you're not hungry," she murmured as she turned back into Rutledge Avenue. "We've got to get home, before that flooding covers the bridges."

"Sounds adventurous," he chuckled, watching her intense concentration as she merged into traffic.

"It is. Are you hungry?" she persisted gently.

"I was rather thinking along the lines of a chilled prawn cocktail," he admitted with a grin.

"I'll have Mrs. Johnson fix you one when we get home," she promised. "We keep it, fresh-frozen, because it's Blake's favorite dish."

He stared out the window at the gray, darkening skies, lit by stop lights and car lights. "Some of those trees are bending pretty low," he remarked.

"I've seen them bend almost to the ground during a hurricane," she recalled nervously. "That's what this is all about to be, I'm afraid. If I thought I could spare the time, I'd stop and call home. But I'm not going to risk it."

"You're the driver, honey," he said.

She smiled wryly. If Blake had been with her, he'd be at the wheel now, whether or not it was his car, taking over. She shifted in the seat. Comparisons were unfair, and she had no right to even be thinking about Blake now that he was practically engaged. But she couldn't help wondering what was going to happen when she got home. As Phillip had once said, Blake didn't particularly care how many people happened to be around if he lost his temper.

The rain followed them all the way to King's Fort, and despite Larry's periodic assurances, Kathryn couldn't help worrying. The little sports car, in spite of its brilliant engineering and design, was too light for some of the deep puddles of water they soared through. Once, Kathryn almost went into a mailbox as the car hydroplaned over the center line. She recovered it in time, but she was getting more nervous by the minute. There was no place to stop until they got to King's Fort, or she'd have given it up.

She gritted her teeth and drove on, refusing to let her passenger see how frightened she really was. If only Blake had been with her!

They were approaching the first river bridge now, and she leaned forward with anticipation, peering through the heavy rain as she tried to see if the bridge was still passable.

"How does it look?" he asked. "I think I can still see the road... I can!"

"Yes," she breathed, relieved. She geared down to get a better view of the rising water. It was already over the banks and only inches below the low bridge. A few more minutes…she concentrated on getting across and didn't think about it.

"Is it much further to the next bridge?" he asked.

"About twenty miles or so," she said tightly. He didn't say anything, but she knew he was thinking the same thing she was—that those few minutes might mean the difference between getting across or not.

There was almost no traffic on the road now. They only met two vehicles, and one of them was the state police.

"I hate to mention this," Larry said quietly. "But what if we can't get across the second bridge?"

She licked her dry lips. "We'll have to go back to King's Fort and spend the night in the hotel," she said, thinking ahead to Blake's fury when he caught up with her. "But the river shouldn't be that high yet," she said soothingly. "I think we can make it."

"Just in case," he asked with a speaking glance, "what kind of temper does your guardian have?"

She tightened her hands on the wheel without answering.

When they reached the long river bridge, her worst fears were confirmed. Two uniformed men were just putting up a roadblock.

She rolled down her window as one of them approached. He touched his hat respectfully. "Sorry, ma'am," he said quietly, "you'll have to detour back to King's Fort. The river's up over the bridge."

"But it's the only road to Greyoaks," she protested weakly, knowing no argument was going to open up the road.

The uniformed man smiled apologetically. "The Hamilton estate? Yes, ma'am, I'm afraid it is. But there's no way across until the water level drops. I'm sorry."

She sighed. "Well, I'll have to go into King's Fort and call home...."

"You're out of luck there, too," the officer said with a rueful grin. "The telephone lines are down. One way and another, it's been a rough day. I wish we could help."

She smiled. "Thanks anyway."

She rolled the window back up and hesitated just a minute before she put the small car into reverse, turned it neatly around, and started back toward King's Fort.

"I feel bad about this," Larry said gently.

"Oh, don't be silly," she replied with a smile, "it's all right. We'll just be...a little late getting home, that's all."

He studied her wan expression. "I'll explain it to him," he promised.

She nodded, but under her brave smile she felt like a naughty student on her way to the principal's office. Blake wasn't going to understand, and she sincerely hoped the river didn't go down until he cooled off.

Six

___

Kathryn pulled up in front of the King's Fort Inn and cut off the engine. She sat there for a minute with her hands tight on the wheel.

"Well, we tried," she said wryly, meeting Larry's sympathetic blue gaze. "I hope my insurance is paid up."

"Will he really be that mad?" he asked.

She drew in a hard breath. "I didn't have permission to come after you," she admitted. "I think I'm old enough to do without it. But Blake doesn't."

He patted her slender hand where it rested on the steering wheel. "I'll protect you," he promised, smiling.

She couldn't return the smile. The thought of Larry protecting her from Blake was almost comical.

The rain was still coming down as they ran into the hotel, and Kathryn held up her raincoat, making a tent over her wild, loosened hair. She laughed with exhilaration as they stopped under the awning to catch their breath.

He grinned down at her, his red hair unruly and beaded with rain. "Fancy meeting you here!"

"Not very fancy, I'm afraid." She laughed, putting a tentative hand up to her disorderly hair. "I must look like a witch."

He shook his head. "Lovely, as always."

"Thank you, kind sir." She darted a quick look at the hotel entrance. "It's the only hotel in town," she sighed, "and I'm sure we're going to cause some comment, but just ignore the stares and go ahead. We'll pretend we don't see any familiar faces."

"This town isn't all that small, surely," he remarked.

She smiled uncomfortably. "It's not. But, you see, the headquarters of the textile conglomerate is located here, and the family is fairly well known."

"I should have realized. Sorry."

"No need. Let's go in, shall we? You can get your bag later."

He followed her into the carpeted lobby. "What will you do for a change of clothes?" he asked.

She shrugged. "Do without, I suppose. Maybe in the..." Her voice trailed off, and she paled visibly.

Larry looked at her with a puzzled frown. She was staring at a big, dark man who was sitting in an armchair by the window reading a paper. He seemed vaguely weary, as if he'd been in that particular chair a long time. Even at a distance he looked threatening.

As Larry watched, he deliberately put down the paper and got to his feet, to saunter over toward them.

Larry knew without being told who the man was. Kathryn's young face was stiff with apprehension. "Blake, I presume?" he murmured under his breath.

Kathryn's fingers dug into her slacks, making indentations in the soft beige fabric. She couldn't get the words out.

Blake rammed his big hands into his pockets, towering over her, his face expressionless. "Ready to go home?" he asked curtly.

"How...did you find me?" she whispered.

His dark eyes swept over her face. "I could find you in New York City at rush hour," he said quietly. Those fierce eyes shot across to Larry's face, and the younger man fought the urge to back away. He thought he'd met every kind of personality in the book, but this man was something beyond his experience. Authority clung to him like the brown slacks that hugged his muscular thighs, like the red knit shirt that emphasized the powerful muscles of his chest and arms.

"Donavan, isn't it?" Blake asked in a cutting tone.

"Y-yes, sir." Larry felt like a boy again. There was something intimidating about Blake Hamilton, and he knew without being told that he hadn't made the best of first impressions.

"The bridge is underwater," Kathryn said softly.

"I know." He started toward the exit, leaving them to follow.

"What about my poor car?" Kathryn persisted.

"Lock it and leave it," he threw over his shoulder. "We'll send back for it when the river goes down."

Kathryn looked at Larry helplessly. He nodded, and left them in front of the hotel under the awning. "I'll get my suitcase out, and lock the car for you," he told her.

She stood beside Blake, miserable and shivering from the chill of the rain.

"Why?" he asked, the single blunt word making her want to cry.

She sucked in a steadying breath. "It was only a short drive."

"With hurricane warnings out," he growled, looking down at her with barely contained fury behind his half-closed eyelids.

She drew her eyes away. "How are we going to get home?" she asked weakly.

"I ought to let you and your boyfriend walk," he replied coldly, staring out at the traffic in the wet street.

She looked down at her wet canvas shoes and then back up at him. He was only wearing a lightweight jacket with his trousers, and no raincoat.

"Don't you have an umbrella?" she asked gently.

He shifted his big shoulders, still not looking at her. "I didn't take the time to look for it." His eyes glittered down at her, and his face hardened. "Have you any idea how long I've been sitting here wondering where you were?" he asked harshly.

She reached out and tentatively touched his sleeve. "I'm sorry, Blake, really I am. I wanted to call, but I was afraid to take the time...."

She suddenly noticed the new lines in his face, the bloodshot eyes. "Were you really worried?" she asked.

One big hand came out and ruffled her hair with rough affection. "What do you think?" he asked. Something in his face seemed to relax as he looked down into her soft eyes. "I've been out of my mind, Kate," he whispered, with such emotion in his voice that her heart seemed to lift up and fly.

"Blake..."

"Here I am!" Larry said merrily, joining them with his suitcase in his hand. "All locked up."

Kathryn folded her arms across her chest and tried to look calm. "How are we going to get across the river?" she asked Blake.

"I chartered a helicopter," he said with a wry smile.

She smiled. Leave it to Blake to make the most insurmountable problem simple.

Maude and Phillip had shared Blake's apprehension about the bad weather and Kathryn's absence, but they played it down. Vivian only shrugged when Kathryn told them about the rough trip home. She was much more interested in meeting another man to bat her false eyelashes at, Kathryn thought maliciously. The blonde was still glued to Blake and, remembering what was going on between them, Kathryn felt a twinge of pain. Blake had been worried about her, of course he had. But as his ward. Nothing more.

"You're very quiet tonight, darling," Phillip remarked when the rest of the family was gathered in the music room to hear Vivian play the grand piano. Kathryn had to admit that she was good. Larry, who played a little himself, sat and watched her with a rapt expression. It had been a bit much for Kathryn, after the rough afternoon. She had slipped out into the hall and gone into the deserted kitchen to pour herself a cup of coffee. Phillip had followed her.

Sitting, her slender hands contracted around the cup, she crossed her legs, making her beige silk dress swish with the motion.

"I like that dress," Phillip remarked, perching himself on the edge of the table facing her. "One of the new ones, isn't it?"

She smiled and nodded. "Larry liked it, too."

"I like Larry," he grinned. "He makes me feel mature and venerable."

Her eyebrows flew up. "He what?"

"He's young, isn't he?" he asked drily, eyeing her over his cup.

"Ouch," she murmured impishly.

He laughed at her. "You know what I mean, don't you? Beside him, Blake looks even more formidable than usual." The grin faded. "Did he cut you up?"

"Blake?" She shook her head. "Surprisingly, no. I guess I should have told him I was going in the first place."

"Maude finally reached him in Atlanta." He emptied his cup and let it dangle in his hands. "He flew to Charleston, you know. It was a devil of a risk, but he took the chance. You were headed home by then. He had the state troopers after you."

Her face went pale. "I didn't realize ...!"

"He'd been waiting three-quarters of an hour at the hotel when you got there," he added. "Sweating out every minute—along with the rest of us. Small cars are dangerous when it floods. I'm surprised he didn't really blow up. I imagine he felt like it."

She studied the coffee in her cup. "Yes, I imagine so," she whispered. Her eyes closed. She'd never have done it anyway if she hadn't been upset by what Vivian had told her at the breakfast table, but she couldn't tell Phillip about that. "It was a stupid thing to do."

"Just foolhardy," he corrected. "When are you going to stop fighting Blake?"

"When he lets go of me," she said curtly.

He only shook his head. "That could be a very long time...."

Greyoaks was imposing in the morning sunlight, and Kathryn reined up beside Larry to admire it.

She sighed. "You should see it in the spring when all the flowers are in bloom."

"I can imagine." His eyes swept over her slender body in her riding clothes. "You look completely at home on a horse."

She patted the Arabian mare's black mane. Sundance had been a little sluggish this morning, so she'd brought the mare instead. "I've been riding for a long time. Blake taught me," she added, laughing at the memories. "It was grueling, for both of us."

Larry sighed, studying the reins in his pale hands. "He doesn't like me."

"Blake?" She avoided his eyes. "He's hard to get close to," she said, knowing full well that wasn't completely true.

"If I planned to be here longer than three days," he admitted, "I think I'd buy a suit of armor. He makes me feel like an idiot."

"He's in the middle of labor disputes," she told him soothingly. "He and Dick Leeds are trying to work out some kind of agreement."

Larry smiled. "It looks like he's putting more effort into working on the daughter. A dish, isn't she? And talented, too."

Kathryn forced a smile onto her full lips. "Yes, she is."

"Are they engaged?" he asked with a sly glance. "I get a strong feeling that something's happening there."

"I think they are," she replied. "Let's head back, Larry. Mrs. Johnson hates to serve breakfast twice." She wheeled the mare and shot off ahead of him.

The question brought it all back. Of course they were engaged, and she couldn't understand why Blake was so concerned about keeping it a secret. The whole business made her angry. And Blake had told Vivian about... Her face flamed. She could never forgive him for that. And the conceit of the man, thinking that she was naive enough to read anything into that kiss. She'd put his treachery out of her mind yesterday, in the face of Blake's obvious concern for her safety. But now, with the danger over, it was burning holes in her temper. Damn Blake, anyway!

What you need, Kathryn Mary, she told herself as she leaned over the mare's black mane and gave her a pat on her head, is a place of your own!

She dismounted at the barn and waited for Larry to walk up to the house with her.

Blake and Vivian were the only ones at the breakfast table. Kathryn, smiling like a film star on display, clung to Larry's thin arm as they joined the others at the table.

"What a lovely ride," Kathryn sighed. She glanced at Vivian. "Do you like horses?" she asked.

"Can't stand them," Vivian said with a smile at Blake's taciturn face.

Kathryn's green eyes flashed, but she held onto her temper.

"The estate is very impressive," Larry remarked as he helped himself to bacon and eggs from the generous platters. "How many gardeners does it take to keep the grounds so neat?"

"Oh, Blake has three yard men, don't you, darling?" Vivian answered for him, leaning her muslin-clad shoulder briefly against his.

Kathryn wanted to sling scrambled eggs at her. She quickly lowered her eyes before any of her companions could read them.

"My parents have a garden about a fourth the size of yours," Larry continued, "without the gazebo. Dad's hobby is roses."

Blake lit a cigarette and leaned back in his chair to study the younger man with an unnerving intensity. "Do you grow flowers too?" he asked cuttingly.

"Blake!" Kathryn protested.

He didn't even glance at her. His whole attention was concentrated on Larry, who reddened and looked as if he might explode any minute. Despite his easy-going nature, he did have a temper, and it looked as if Blake was trying his best to make him lose it.

"Do you?" Blake persisted.

Larry put his cup down carefully. "I write books, Mr. Hamilton," he said tightly.

"What about?" came the lightning reply.

"Pompous asses, mostly," Larry grated.

Blake's dark eyes glittered dangerously. "Are you insinuating something, Donavan?"

"If the shoe fits..." Larry returned, his blue eyes icy.

"Stop it!" Kathryn burst out. She stood up, throwing her napkin onto the table. Her lower lip trembled, her eyes flashed. "Stop it, Blake!" she whispered furiously. "You've done nothing but pick on Larry since he got here. Do you have to...!"

"Be quiet," he said coldly.

She closed her lips as if he'd slapped her. "You're horrible, Blake," she whispered shakily. "Larry's a guest...."

"Not mine," he replied, glaring at Larry, who was standing now, too.

"You're right there," Larry replied gruffly. He turned to Kathryn. "Come and talk to me while I pack."

He left the room and Kathryn turned back at the doorway to glare at Blake. "If he leaves, I'll go with him, Blake," she told him furiously.

"You may think you will," he said in a soft, dangerous tone.

"We'll see about that," she choked, whirling.

Kathryn's pleas didn't deter Larry. He packed in record time and started to call a cab when Dick Leeds came out into the hall and stopped him.

"Vivian wants to do some shopping in Charleston," he said with a quiet smile, "and since the river's down, it's quite safe. Phillip's going to drive us, and you're welcome to ride along. We'd be happy to drop you at the airport."

"Thank you," Larry said. He reached down and pecked Kathryn lightly on the cheek. "Sorry, love. I'm very fond of you, but not fond enough to take on your guardian."

She stiffened. "I'm sorry it worked out like this. Give my best to Missy."

He nodded. "Goodbye."

She watched him walk away with a sense of loss. It had all happened so fast. Her head was still spinning with the suddenness of it. She tried to piece together Blake's unreasonable behavior. He'd done his best to break up her friendship with Larry from the beginning. But why? He had Vivian. Why did he begrudge Kathryn a boyfriend? She hated him. Somehow, she had to get out from under his thumb....

She stayed out of sight until they left. Blake wasn't to be found, and she thought he'd gone with the rest. Maude had tried to persuade her to come along, to Vivian's obvious irritation, but she'd refused. She couldn't have borne being shut up in the same car with Larry and Blake both.

She walked through the damp hedges to the gazebo. The grass and shrubs were still wet from the previous day's heavy rains, but inside the quiet confines of the little white building with its delicate latticework and ring of cushions, it was dry and cozy.

She sat down on the plush cushions and looked out over the cobblestone walks that led around and through the well-kept gardens. Although the azaleas and dogwoods that bloomed gloriously in the spring were not in season now, the roses gave the gardens a dash of color. The fragrance of the white ones was delicious. She closed her eyes and drank it in, along with the warm breeze that made the September day more like summer.

"Sulking?"

She jumped at the sound of Blake's deep, curt voice. Her startled eyes found him in the entrance of the small building, a smoking cigarette in his hand. He was wearing the same beige slacks and yellow knit shirt he'd had on at the breakfast table, and the same forbidding scowl.

She scowled back, curling her jodhper-clad leg under her slender body, tugging her white sweater down. "Haven't you done enough for one morning?" she asked angrily.

One dark eyebrow went up. "What have I done? I didn't ask him to leave."

"No," she agreed hotly. "You just made it impossible for him to stay and hold on to his pride."

He shrugged indifferently. "In any case, it's no great loss."

"To you," she added. "Your girlfriend is still here."

He eyed her carefully. "Yes," he said. "She is."

"Naturally. She's *your* guest."

He shouldered away from the entrance and walked toward her, stopping just in front of her. "Would you really want a man who was afraid of me?"

Her eyes shot up to his. "No," she admitted sharply. "I'd like one who'd beat the devil out of you."

A slow, mischievous smile touched his mouth. "Had any luck yet?"

She tore her gaze away, remembering Jack Harris and a string of others. "Why didn't you go with them? Vivian seemed to have taken a shine to Larry last night."

"Vivian's tastes are not necessarily mine."

Kathryn stared down at the dark green cushions, tracing a pattern on the one where she was sitting with a nervous finger.

"Why wouldn't you let him stay, Blake?" she asked bitterly. "He wasn't bothering you."

"He wasn't?" He finished the cigarette and flung it out on the cobblestones, where it lay smouldering briefly until the dampness doused it. "The damned young fool, letting you drive in that downpour! I should have broken both his legs!"

She gaped at him. "It was my car, he couldn't very well tell me to let him get behind the wheel!"

"I could," he replied gruffly. "And I would have. If I'd been with you, you'd never have left Charleston."

She couldn't repress a tiny smile: It was exactly what she'd been thinking on the way home. "There was a moment or two when I wish you had been," she said lightly.

He didn't reply, and when she looked up, it was to find his face strangely rigid.

"You shouldn't have worried," she added, aware of a new tension between them. "You taught me to drive, remember?"

"All I remember was that you were in danger in the company of a fool, a boy who didn't know how to take care of you," he said tightly. "If anything had happened to you, I'd have killed him."

He didn't raise his voice. But the words had as much impact as if he'd shouted them.

"What a violent thing to say," she laughed nervously.

He didn't smile. His dark eyes narrowed, spearing her with an intensity that made flames kindle in her blood. "I've always been violent about you. Are you just now noticing it?"

She gazed up at him quietly, stunned by the words, by the emotion in them, her lips slightly parted, her eyes curious and soft.

Blake leaned one big hand on the back of the seat over her shoulder and his eyes dropped to her soft mouth. The action had brought them closer; so close that she could smell the clean, masculine fragrance of soap and cologne, feel the warmth of his big body.

"Blake," she whispered, yielding without words, without thought, longing for him.

He bent his dark head and brushed his mouth against hers, a whisper of delicious sensation that quickened her pulse, her breathing. He drew back, and she lifted her finger to trace, tremulously, the hard sensuous curve of his mouth. Emotion trembled between them in the silence, broken only by the whispering breeze, and the distant sound of a songbird.

His lips moved, catching her exploring finger, and she felt the tip of his tongue moving softly against it. Her eyes looked straight into his, and she read the excitement in them.

He searched her flushed young face quietly. "Stand up, Kathryn," he said at last. "I want to feel you against me."

Like a sleepwalker, she obeyed him, letting him draw her so close that she could feel his powerful thighs pressing against hers, the muscles of his chest like a wall against her soft breasts.

His thumbs brushed against her mouth, and he studied it as if he needed to memorize it. "Are you afraid?" he asked in a strange, husky voice.

She shook her head, meeting his eyes with the hunger and need plain in her own. "Last time..."

"It's not going to be like last time," he breathed. "Kate...!" Her soft mouth parted eagerly as his lips met hers.

Her slender arms reached up around his neck, holding him, and she kissed him back feverishly, trying to show that she could be anything he wanted her to be.

His big hand tangled in the thick strands of hair at her nape, and his devouring mouth forced hers open even wider. He explored it with a deepening intimacy that made her tremble. With a sense of wonder she felt his hands at her back, sliding under her sweater and up to move caressingly against her silken skin.

"No bra?" he murmured against her mouth, and she could feel the amused smile that moved his lips.

She flushed at the intimacy of the question, and suddenly reached around to catch his wrists and hold them as he started to slide his exploring hands around under her arms.

"Blake..." she protested.

He chuckled softly and drew his hands away to replace them at her waist over the thick fabric. "You said you weren't afraid," he reminded her.

She lowered her eyes to his broad chest. "Must you make fun of me?" she asked miserably. "You know I'm not sophisticated."

"It's quite obvious," he laughed softly. "If you were, you would know better than to plaster yourself against a man when he kisses you. Ten years ago, I'm not sure I'd have been able to draw back."

She looked up, startled. "But in the movies..."

"Plastic people, contrived situations; this is real, Kathryn." He took her hand and pressed it inside the opening of his shirt against the hard, warm flesh and thick mat of hair. She felt the heavy rhythm of his heart. "Do you feel it?" he asked softly. "You make my blood run like a river in flood, Kate."

She was lost in his dark eyes, in the gentleness of his deep voice. Her fingers lingered inside his shirt, liking the feel of his muscular body, remembering suddenly and vividly the way he looked that night long ago with Jessica.

He seemed to read the thoughts in her mind. Abruptly he caught her hands and slid them under the shirt to lie against the broad, hard chest. Her fingers trembled on the hair-rough skin.

"I've never touched...anyone like this," she whispered, awed by the new longings surging through her body, making her tremble in his big arms. "I never wanted to, until now."

His lips brushed against her forehead, his breath warm and a little unsteady, while her curious fingers explored the powerful muscles.

She raised her eyes to Blake's. "I...Blake, I feel..."

His fingers pressed gently against her lips. "Kiss me," he whispered. "Don't think, don't talk. Just kiss me.'' His lips teased her delicately, softly, causing a surge of hunger that dragged a moan from her tight throat.

She went on tiptoe to help him, to tempt him, her lips parting under the lazy pressure of his mouth as he began to deepen the kiss. She felt his hands caressing her back, moving surely around her ribcage. But, this time, she didn't catch his wrists.

His thumbs edged out to trace the gentle slope of her high, firm breasts and she stiffened instinctively at the unfamiliar touch.

"It's all right," he whispered at her lips. "Don't pull away from me."

Her eyes opened, wide and curious and a little frightened. "It's . . . new," she whispered.

"Being touched?" he asked quietly. "Or being touched by me?"

"Both," she admitted.

His fingers moved higher, and he watched her face while they found the hard peaks and traced them tenderly, just before his hands swallowed the velvet softness and pressed against it with warm, sensuous motions.

"How does it feel, Kate?" he asked in a deep, honeyed tone. "Is it good?"

Her nails dug into his chest involuntarily as the magic worked on her, and she moaned softly.

"I shouldn't . . . let you," she whispered.

"No, you shouldn't," he agreed, moving closer. "Tell me to stop, Kate," he whispered. "Tell my you hate it."

"I . . . wish I could," she whispered. His mouth was on her closed eyelids, her nose, her high cheekbones, while his hands made wild shivers of sensation wash over her bare skin.

His mouth bit at hers tenderly in a succession of teasing kisses that made her want to cry out. "God, you're sweet," he whispered huskily. "As soft as a whisper where I touch you."

Her fingers tangled in the mat of hair over his strong chest. "I...dreamed about how it would be with you," she whispered shakily. "Ever since that night I saw you with Jessica, I've wondered..."

"I know," he whispered back. "I saw it in your eyes. That was what wrung me out so, Kate, because I wondered, too. But you were so damned young..."

She drew a deep, unsteady breath, lifting her body higher against his deft, sure hands. "Blake..." she moaned.

"What do you want?" His dark eyes burned into hers. "There's nothing you can't ask me, don't you know that? What do you want, Kate?"

Her body ached with the newness of wanting and she didn't know how to put into words what she needed. It had never been like this, never!

"I don't know how to say it," she admitted in a breathless whisper. "Blake...please..."

He bent, lifting her in his big arms without a word, and carried her to the cushioned seat that ringed the gazebo. Then he came down beside her with something in his hard dark face that was faintly shocking after all the years of banter and camaraderie and deep affection. She was just beginning to see Blake as a lover, and the effect it was having on her defied description. She looked up at him with all her confusion in her green eyes, and in her flushed, expectant face.

"I won't hurt you," he said softly.

"I know." She lifted her fingers to his hard, chiseled mouth and traced it gently. "I've never kissed a man lying down."

"Haven't you?" He smiled as he lifted himself to ease his formidable torso down onto her, so that they were thigh to thigh, hip to hip, breast to breast. She gasped at the intimate contact and her fingers dug into the rippling muscles of his shoulders.

His fingers cupped her face as he bent. "Am I too heavy, Kate?" he whispered against her soft mouth.

She flushed at the question, but she didn't look away. "No," she managed shakily.

He brushed his mouth across hers. "Pull your sweater up," he whispered.

"Blake..."

He kissed her closed eyelids. "You want it as much as I do," he breathed. "Pull it up, Kate...then help me pull up my shirt."

She looked into his eyes, trembling. She wanted him until she ached from head to toe, but he was suggesting an intimacy she'd never experienced before, and once it happened, there wouldn't be any going back.

"It's...I mean, I've never..." she stammered.

His thumbs brushed against the corners of her mouth while his tongue lightly traced the trembling line of her lips.

"Don't you want to feel me against you like that, Kate?" he whispered sensuously. "With nothing between us?"

She gasped against his invading mouth. Her eyes closed tightly. "Yes," she ground out, and even her voice trembled. "Oh, Blake yes, yes...!"

"Help me," he whispered huskily.

With trembling fingers, she lifted the hem of his yellow knit shirt and eased it up over the warm, hard muscles under their mat of crisp black hair, and her fingers savored the sensuous contact with him, while her heart pounded out a mad rhythm.

His mouth coaxed hers open, tasting it, gentling it, his fingers tenderly caressing her face.

"Now yours, love," he whispered softly. "There's nothing to be afraid of, nothing at all, I won't hurt you, I won't force you. Now, Kate..."

She looked into his darkening eyes while she slid the soft sweater up over her taut breasts and with a shuddering pleasure, she felt him ease down again until her taut nipples vanished into the dark pelt over his chest. She felt his body against hers in a contact that made magic in her mind and she gasped.

"My God, isn't it delicious?" he whispered tautly, shifting his powerful torso slowly, sensuously, across her breasts in the utter silence of the gazebo.

Her fingers hesitated on his hard collarbone, lightly touching him, feeling him. Her eyes widened as the intimacy sent her pulse racing, as her breath caught in her throat.

"You're...so warm," she whispered.

"A man being burned alive does feel warm," he replied half-humorously. He moved then, holding her eyes while his body eased completely onto hers.

"It's all right," he breathed, calming her as she stiffened involuntarily at the greater intimacy with his body. His hands stroked her hair lightly, his forearms taking the bulk of his weight. He studied her closely. "Now I can feel you completely," he whispered, "and you can feel me. We can't hide anything from each other when we touch like this, can we Kate? You know without words how much I want you, don't you?"

She flushed wildly as the exact meaning of his words got through to her, and she noticed for the first time all the differences between his body and hers.

Pleasure surged up in her like spring sap in a young tree as she sensed her own awakening to emotions and sensations that had lain dormant inside her, waiting for a catalyst.

Her fingers touched his face, his mouth, his arrogant nose, his thick dark brows, and when she breathed, she was made even more aware of the warmth and weight of his hair-roughened chest against the sensitive warmth of her bareness.

The weight of him crushed her yielding body down into the soft cushions and her arms went up to hold him even closer as he bent to take her mouth under his.

She opened her lips, her fingers tangling in his thick, cool hair as the kiss went on and on. His tongue darted into her mouth, demanding, tormenting, while his hands slid under her thighs and lifted her body up against his with a bruising pressure, until she was achingly aware of how much he wanted her.

She shifted restlessly under the crush of his body, and a hard groan tore out of his throat while he kissed her. A shudder ran the length of him.

"Don't do that," he whispered against her lips. "I may be past my first youth, but I can lose my head with you so easily it isn't funny."

She watched him, fascinated. "I ... I like the way it feels, to lie with you like this," she admitted in a whisper.

"My God, I like it, too," he groaned. "Kiss me, honey ... !"

His hungry ardor flared like wildfire between them. She stopped trying to understand and melted into him. It was glorious, the hungry crush of his mouth, the feel of his arms, the long, hard contact with his powerful body, the warmth of him that seemed to burn her everywhere they touched. She never wanted this kiss to end. She wanted to spend the rest of her life in his arms like this, holding him, loving him. Loving him!

He caught her wrists abruptly and tore her clinging hands away from his back. He looked down at her as if he'd been temporarily out of his mind and had only just realized what he was doing. He shook his dark head as if to clear it. With a violent movement he got to his feet and pulled his shirt down, keeping his back to Kathryn while she fumbled, embarrassed, with her sweater. She stared at his broad back incredulously. She'd forgotten what had happened just an hour ago, forgotten the anger and frustration she'd felt. In the shadow of Blake's blazing ardor she'd even forgotten Vivian. How could she have let him ... !

He turned, catching that expression of shock in her eyes, and something seemed to harden in his face, take the soft light out of his eyes. He smiled mockingly.

"Now tell me you miss Donavan," he said in a voice that cut through her heart like a razor.

She licked at the inside of her swollen lips, tasting the lingering touch of his mouth there, her eyes vulnerable, hurt.

"Was that why?" she asked in a sore whisper, stepping away from him.

He rammed his hands into his pockets. His face was harder than she could ever remember seeing it.

"Or was it...because you don't want another man to have me?" she asked painfully.

"I've got all the bodies I need, Kate," he said tightly. "I didn't raise you to take you into my bed the minute you came of age."

"But, just now..." she began hesitantly.

"I want you, all right," he admitted, scowling down at her. "I have for a long time. But just because I lost my head with you a minute ago, that doesn't mean I plan to do anything about it."

Of course not, how could he, when he planned to marry Vivian? "Don't worry," she said bitterly, getting to her feet. "I'm not going to 'read anything' into it this time either."

"What?"

"That's what you told Vivian, isn't it?" she asked in a broken voice, slanting a glance back at him as she stepped down into the garden. "That you were afraid I might 'read something' into what happened the other night? I'm not a child, Blake, I quite realize that men can be attracted physically by women they don't even like, much less love."

"Just what are you talking about?" he demanded, his eyes blazing.

"Vivian told me yesterday how much you regretted your actions the other night!" she threw at him.

The expression on his hard face puzzled her, if a fleeting shadow could be called that. "She told you that?" he asked.

She whirled. "No, I just made it up for the fun of it!"

"Kate...!"

"Don't call me Kate!" She glared back at him through her tears, missing the sudden glint in his dark eyes. "I hate you. And I'm going to get a job and my own apartment, and you can drag Vivian off into gazebos and make love to her! I don't ever want you to touch me again, Blake!"

"You will," he said in a strange, deep tone.

She turned and ran back toward the house as if invisible phantoms were chasing after her. She locked her bedroom door behind her and threw herself down onto the bed, venting the stored-up tears. She loved Blake. Not as she always had, as a protector, but newly, differently, as a man. She could barely believe it had happened, and she didn't want to admit it even in the privacy of her own mind. She loved Blake. And he was going to marry Vivian. Her eyes closed in pain. Vivian, living here, loving Blake, too, touching him, kissing that hard, beautiful mouth....

She groaned out loud with anguish. She'd have to get a job. There was no way around it now. She sat up, drying her tears. She'd start looking first thing in the morning, Blake or no Blake, and find something that she could do to make a living for herself. There was no way she could go on living under the same roof with Blake and his wife!

Seven

She was purposely late for breakfast, and when she got downstairs she glanced around quickly, hoping to find that Blake had already eaten.

Maude was just finishing a piece of toast across from Phillip, who was sipping his coffee. Blake, Dick Leeds and Vivian were nowhere in sight.

"My, aren't you dressed up," Maude commented, her approving glance resting on Kathryn's pretty beige suit and crepe de chine eggshell blouse with its neat bow. Her hair was drawn into a soft chignon, with wisping curls around her face, her feet encased in spiked-heel open-toed sandals in beige and brown. She looked the picture of working womanhood.

"Trendy-looking," Phillip added with a wink. "Where are you off to in your fine feathers, little bird?"

"I'm going to get a job," she said with a cool smile.

Maude choked on her toast and had to be thumped on the back by Phillip.

"A job?" she gasped. "Doing what, Kathryn?"

"It depends on what I can find," the younger woman said with a stubborn light in her green eyes. "Now, don't argue, Maude," she added, catching the quick disapproval in the pale, dark-eyed face.

"I wasn't going to, dear," Maude protested. "I was just going to ask how you planned to tell Blake."

"She already has," Blake told them, appearing in the doorway dressed in a becoming gray suit with a patterned tie that emphasized his darkness. "Let's go, Kate."

She sat there almost trembling with emotion, her wide green eyes pleading with him, even as she knew she wasn't going to fight. All her resolutions vanished when Blake confronted her. After yesterday, all the fight was gone, anyway. She didn't have the heart for it anymore.

"She hasn't had breakfast," Phillip observed.

"She'll learn to get downstairs in time, won't she?" Blake replied, and there was something vaguely menacing about the way he was looking at his younger brother.

Phillip grinned sheepishly. "Just an observation, big brother." He laughed.

Blake's dark eyes went to Kathryn, skimming over her possessively. "I said, let's go."

She got up, leaving a cup of fresh coffee and a plate of scrambled eggs behind her as she followed him out into the hall apprehensively.

"Where are we going?" she asked.

Both heavy brows went up. He opened the front door for her. "To work, of course."

"But, I don't have a job yet."

"Yes, you do."

"What as?" she asked.

"My secretary."

She followed him out to his dark sedan in a daze, only speaking when they were going down the driveway at Blake's usual fast pace.

"Did I hear you right?" she asked, and stared at his profile with unconcealed disbelief.

"You did." He took out his cigarette case and extracted a cigarette from it as he drove, leaning over to push in the cigarette lighter.

"But, Blake, I can't work for you," she protested.

His dark eyes scanned her face briefly. "Why not?"

"I can't type fast enough," she said, grasping at straws. Having to be near him all day, every day, would be more agony than ecstasy.

"You're about average, little one. You'll do." He lit his cigarette and pushed the lighter back in place. "You said you wanted a job," he reminded her.

She watched cars in the other lanes passing by them, not really seeing anything as she sat stiffly beside Blake.

"Where was Vivian this morning?" she asked quietly. "The two of you were out late last night."

"So we were," he said noncommittally.

"It's none of my business, of course," she said tightly, avoiding his eyes.

He only smiled, keeping his attention on the road.

* * *

The Hamilton Mills complex was located in a sprawling ground level facility in the city's huge industrial park, modern and landscaped. Kathryn had been inside the building many times, but never as an employee.

She followed Blake into his attractive carpeted office, where the dark furniture was complemented by elegant furnishings done in chocolates and creams. Her eye was caught and held by a portrait that spanned the length of the big leather sofa under it. She stared at the sweeping seascape, the sunset colors mingling with the clouds, the palm-lined beach a swath of white and silver. In the foreground were the shadowy outlines of a man and a woman.

"Like it?" he asked as he checked the messages on his desk.

She nodded. "It's St. Martin, isn't it?" she asked quietly. "I recognize that spot."

"You ought to. We shared a bottle of champagne under that spread of trees on your eighteenth birthday. I nearly had to carry you back to the beach house."

She laughed, remembering her own bubbling pleasure that night, Blake's company and the sound of the surf. They'd talked a lot, she recalled, and waded in the foaming surf, and drunk champagne, while Phillip and Maude visited one of the casinos and lost money.

"It was the best birthday party I ever had," she murmured. "I don't think we had a cross word the whole trip."

"Would you like to do it again?" he asked suddenly.

She turned. He was standing in front of his desk, his legs slightly apart, his hands on his lean hips.

"Now?" she asked.

"Next week. I've got some business in Haiti," he explained mysteriously. "I thought we might stay in St. Martin for a few days and I could go on to Haiti from there."

"Why Haiti?" she asked, curious.

"You don't have to come on that leg of the trip," he said with a finality that permitted no further questioning.

She studied the painting again. "We?" she asked in a bare shadow of her normal voice.

"Vivian and Dick, too," he admitted. "A last-ditch effort to get his cooperation."

"And hers?" she asked with more bitterness than she knew.

There was a long pause. "I thought you knew by now why she came along."

She dropped her eyes to the huge wood frame of the painting, feeling dead inside. So he was finally admitting it. "Yes," she whispered. "I know."

"Do you? I wonder," he murmured, scowling at her downcast face.

"Is anyone else coming?" she asked. "Phillip?"

"Phillip?" he said harshly. His face hardened. "What's going on between you two, Kathryn Mary?"

"Nothing," she said defensively. "We just enjoy each other's company, that's all."

Blake's dark eyes seemed to explode in flames. "By all means, we'll take Phillip. You'll have to have someone to play with!" His voice cut.

"I'm not a child, Blake," she said with quiet dignity.

"You're both children."

She squared her slender shoulders. "You didn't treat me like one yesterday!"

A slow, faint smile touched his hard mouth. "You didn't act like one." His bold, slow eyes sketched her body in the becoming suit.

She felt the color creeping into her cheeks at the words, remembering the feel of his warm chest, the hair-roughened texture of it against her breasts.

"Phillip," he scoffed, catching her eyes and holding them. "You'd burn him alive. You're too passionate for him. For Donavan, too."

"Blake!" she burst out, embarrassed.

"Well, it's true," he growled, his eyes narrowing on her face, darkening with memory. "I barely slept last night. I could feel your hands touching me...your body like silk, twisting against mine. You may be green, little girl, but you've got good instincts. When you finally stop running from passion, you'll be one hell of a woman."

"I'm not running..." she whispered involuntarily, before she realized what she was saying.

She stood there watching him, suddenly vulnerable, hungry as she remembered the touch of his hands against her bare skin and the violence of his emotion. She wanted to touch him. To hold him. To feel his mouth against hers.... He read the surge of longing accurately. His eyes darkened violently as he rose and came around the desk toward her. There was no pretense between them now; only a thread of shared hunger that was intense and demanding.

"You'd damned well better mean what I read in your eyes," he growled as he reached her, his big hands shooting out to catch her roughly by the waist and pull her close.

She gloried in the feel of his big, muscular body against the length of hers. Her face lifted to his and her heart floundered as her eyes met his from a distance of scant inches. His head started to bend, and she trembled.

His mouth was hungry, and it hurt. She reached up, clinging to him, while his lips parted hers and burrowed into them ardently.

"Blake," she whispered achingly.

His big hand moved up from her waist to cover her breast, taking its slight weight as his tongue shot into the warmth of her mouth.

"You're in my blood like slow poison, Kate," he whispered roughly. His fingers contracted, and he watched the helpless reaction on her flushed face. "I look at you, and all I can think about is how you feel under my hands. Do you remember how it was between us yesterday?" he whispered against her mouth. "Your breasts crushed against me and not a stitch of fabric to stop us from feeling each other's skin...."

"Oh, don't," she moaned helplessly. "It isn't fair...."

"Why isn't it?" he demanded. He lifted her until her eyes were on a level with his. "Tell me you didn't want what I did to you in the gazebo. Tell me you weren't aching every bit as much as I was when I let you go."

She couldn't, because she had wanted him, and it was in every line of her flushed face, the wide green eyes that searched his helplessly in the silence of the office.

"I'd like to take you to Martinique alone, do you know that?" he breathed huskily. "Just the two of us, Kate, and I'd lay you down in the sand in the darkness and taste every soft, sweet inch of your body with my lips."

Her breath caught at the passionate intensity in the words. "I...I wouldn't..."

"Like hell you wouldn't," he whispered. His mouth took hers hungrily, his hands slid down to grasp her hips and grind them sensuously into his until she cried out at the sensations it caused.

"Want me, Kate?" he taunted in a deep whisper. "God knows, I want you almost beyond bearing. It was a mistake for me to touch you the way I did. Now all I can think about is how much more of you I want. Kiss me, honey. Kiss me...."

She did, because at that moment it was all she wanted from life. The feel of him, the touch and taste and smell of him, Blake's big arms riveting her to every inch of his powerful body while his mouth took everything hers had to give. It seemed like a long time later when he finally raised his head to let his eyes blaze down into hers.

With a suddenness that was almost painful, the door swung open and Vivian's high-pitched voice shattered the crystal thread of emotion binding them.

"Well, hello," she said in her clear British accent. "I do hope I'm not interrupting anything?"

"Of course not," Blake said, turning to her with magnificent composure and a smile. "I promised you a tour, didn't I? Let's go, Kate," he said over his shoulder, "you come along, too."

She was still trembling, and she longed to refuse. But Vivian's eyes were already suspicious, and she didn't dare.

Blake escorted them through the huge manufacturing company, pointing out the main areas of interest—the training room where the new seamstresses were taught how to use the latest modern equipment; the pants line, where each sewing machine operator performed a different function in the manufacture of a pair of slacks; the cutting room, where huge bales of cloth were spread on long tables and cut by men with jigsaws through multiple layers of thickness. Kathryn remembered the terms peculiar to the garment industry from her childhood: "bundle boys" who carried the bundles of pattern pieces out to the sewers; "foreladies" who were the overseers for each group of seamstresses; "spreaders" who spread the cloth; "cutters" who cut it; and "inspectors" who were responsible for catching second and third quality garments before they could be shipped out as "firsts." Then there were the pressers and packers and the "lab lady" who washed test garments. Hundreds of sewing machines were running together in the room where the shirt line was located, and this section had button-holing machines as well as the other equipment found on the pants line. Kathryn's eye was caught by the brilliant colors.

"That shade of blue is lovely!" she exclaimed.

Blake chuckled. "I'll have to take you through the yarn mill sometime and show you how it's made. Bales of cotton go through a process that takes a rope of raw material and runs it through a volley of spindles in different rooms to produce a thread of yarn. We use cotton and rayon now. In the old days, the mill ran strictly on cotton."

"How interesting," Vivian said with little enthusiasm. "I've never actually been in a mill."

Kathryn gaped at her. This wasn't *her* first trip by a long shot. She was forever tagging along after Blake and Phillip in her younger days, because the whole process of making clothing had fascinated her. But she hadn't been in a yarn mill since her childhood, and she'd been too young to understand much of what she'd seen then.

"How many blouses come out of here in a week?" Kathryn asked, watching blouses in different states of readiness at each machine row as they walked past. She had to practically yell in Blake's ear to make him hear her above the noise.

"About ten thousand dozen," he told her, smiling at her shocked expression. "We've added a lot of new equipment here. We have over six hundred sewing machine operators in this plant, and it takes about a hundred and fifty thousand yards of material a week to keep these women busy."

Kathryn looked back the way they'd come. "The slacks... ?"

"That's a separate plant, honey," he reminded her, glancing toward the door that linked the two divisions. "We only have about three hundred machines on the pants line. Our biggest business here is blouses.''

"It's enormous!" she exclaimed.

Blake nodded. "We do a volume business. We have contracts with two of the biggest mail order houses, and you'll remember that we have our own chain of outlet stores across the country. It's a hell of a big operation."

"It must make lots of money," Vivian commented, and Kathryn saw dollar signs in the older woman's eyes.

Blake's eyebrow jerked, but he didn't reply.

When they finished the tour, Vivian persuaded Blake to take her out for coffee, and he left Kate with a Dictaphone full of letters to be typed. It rankled her that Vivian, who had gotten her breakfast at home, was being treated to coffee and doughnuts while Kathryn, who had been dragged away from her breakfast, got nothing. She was somewhat mollified a half hour later when Blake came back and set coffee in a Styrofoam cup and a packaged pastry in front of her on the desk.

"Breakfast," he said. "I seem to recall making you miss yours."

She smiled up at him, surprised but pleased, and her face lit up.

"Thanks, Blake," she said gently.

He shrugged his powerful shoulders and strode over to the dividing door between her office and his. "Any problems with the Dictaphone?" he asked over his shoulder.

"Only with your language," she remarked, tongue-in-cheek.

He lifted an amused eyebrow at her. "Don't expect to reform me, Kate."

"Oh, I don't know a woman brave enough to try, Blake," she said with angelic sweetness to his retreating back. Switching off the electric typewriter, she opened her steaming coffee.

It was almost quitting time when Phillip stopped by the office to see Blake. He leaned his hands on Kathryn's desk and grinned at her.

"Slaving away, I see," he teased lightly.

She sighed. "You don't know the half of it," she groaned. "I never realized how much correspondence it takes to keep a plant like this one going. Blake even writes to congressmen and state senators and the textile manufacturers association—by the way, I didn't realize he was president of it this year."

"See how much you're learning?" Phillip teased. He reached out a hand and tipped her chin up bending close to whisper, "Has Blake flicked you with his whip yet?"

Her eyes opened wide and she smiled. "Does he have one?" she whispered back.

It was pure bad luck that Blake should choose that moment to open his office door. He glared at Phillip so blackly that the younger man backed away from the desk and actually reddened.

Blake jerked his office door shut. "Take Kathryn home with you," he told his brother curtly. "Vivian and I are going out to supper."

And he left the office without even a backward glance, while Kathryn sat there with her heart in her shoes, wondering how Blake could have been so loving earlier in the day and so hateful now. What had she done? Or was it just that Blake was already feeling regrets?

The days fell into a pattern, Kathryn rode to work with Blake every morning, and back with him in the evenings. Although he was business-as-usual in his dealings with her, Vivian seemed to purple when Kathryn and Blake left together. The blonde did everything except lobby for a job of her own to try to take up Blake's free time. And she succeeded very well.

By Saturday, Kathryn was ready for some relaxation, and since Vivian had talked Blake into taking her by plane for a shopping trip to Atlanta, Kathryn asked Phillip to go with her to one of the new malls in town. The request seemed to irritate Blake, but Kathryn ignored his evident displeasure. After all, what right did he have to interfere with her life? He was too wrapped up in Vivian to care what she did. Even the thought of going to the islands with him was frightening now—although she knew she'd never be strong enough to renege on her promise to accompany him. She loved him too much, wanted to be with him too much, to refuse. He might marry Vivian, but at least Kathryn would have a few memories.

"You're walking me to death," Phillip groaned, hobbling with exaggeration to the nearest bench in the busy mall. He eased down with a stage sigh and a smile.

"We've only been in five shops," she reminded him. "You can't possibly be tired."

"Five shops, where you tried on fifteen outfits each," he corrected.

She plopped down beside him, sighing wearily. "Well, I'm depressed," she said. "I had to do something to cheer me up."

"I'm not depressed," he said with a sigh. "Why did I have to come along?"

"To carry the packages," she said sensibly.

"But Kathryn, love, you haven't bought anything."

"Yes, I have. In that little boutique we just came from."

His eyebrows lifted. "What?"

"This." She handed him a small sack containing a jeweler's box with a pair of dainty sapphire and diamond earrings inside. "Aren't they lovely? I charged them to Blake."

"Oh, no," he groaned, burying his face in his hands.

"Anyway, you can carry them," she said, "so you'll feel necessary."

"How will I ever survive all these honors you confer upon me?" he asked with mock humility.

"Don't be nasty," she chided, pushing against his shoulder with her own as they sat side by side. "I really am depressed, Phil."

He studied her dejected little face. "What's wrong kitten? Want me to slay a dragon for you?"

"Would you?" she asked hopefully, her green eyes wide. "You could sneak up on her while she's sleeping, and..."

"Your eyes need checking," he remarked, lifting an eyebrow at her as he folded his arms and leaned back against the wooden bench. "Vivian isn't a dragon."

"That's what you think," she muttered. "Wait until she's your sister-in-law and see if you still like her."

"Vivian? Marry Blake?" He sat up abruptly, staggered. "Where did you come by that piece of utter nonsense?"

"It isn't nonsense," she told him, sulking. "She's just his style. Beautiful, sophisticated and blond."

"That's his taste, all right. But do you really think he's got marriage on his mind?" he asked with a wry grin. "That *isn't* his style."

"Maybe she's something special," she grumbled, hating everything about the woman. She glared into space, hurting in ways she never had before. "She told me that Blake wanted her over here to meet us."

"I know. She's the power behind her father. She controls everything he does, or haven't you noticed her ordering him around?"

She shifted on the bench and crossed her legs. "Blake spends all his time with her. Don't tell me it's just for business reasons," she replied, smoothing the close-fitting designer jeans over her thighs. Her eyes dropped to her cream-colored cowboy boots and she grimaced at a scuff on the toe.

"You and I spend a lot of time together, too," he reminded her. "But we're just friends."

She sighed. "That's true."

"And Blake hates it."

Her eyes jerked up. "What?"

He grinned. "He's jealous," he laughed.

She went cherry pink and averted her gaze. "You're nuts!"

"Am I? He's crazily possessive about you. He always has been, but in the past few days I'm almost afraid to sit beside you when he's at home."

She felt her heart racing at the words. She hoped against hope that they were true, even while she knew they weren't. "He's just the domineering type," she corrected nervously.

"Really? Is that why he deliberately picked a fight with your boyfriend to send him packing?" Phillip eyed her narrowly. "When we got home from Charleston, Blake was gone and you were hiding in your room with a headache. What happened between you two while we were gone?"

The blush went all the way to her toes. She couldn't answer him.

"You light up when he walks into a room," he continued, smiling. "And he watches you when he thinks no one's noticing. Like a big, hungry panther with its eyes on a tasty young gazelle."

She hadn't known that, and her heart went wild. "Oh, Phil, does he, really?" she asked involuntarily, and everything she felt was in the starved look in the soft eyes she lifted to his.

He nodded quietly, studying her. "That's just what I thought," he said gently. "Adding your heart to the string he drags behind him, kitten?"

"Is it so obvious?" she sighed miserably. She turned her attention to the passersby.

"To me, because we've always been close," he replied. "I knew why you bought that sexy dress even before you did. You wanted to see what effect it would have on Blake. Dynamite, wasn't it, girl?" he asked knowingly, with a teasing smile.

She flushed wildly. "Do you hide behind the curtains?" she whispered, embarrassed by his perception.

"I'm not in my adolescence, Kate," he reminded her. "You and Blake have always been passionate with each other. You push him hard; it isn't hard to guess at the reaction you get. Blake's not a gentle man."

How little he knew his brother, she thought, her mind going back longingly to that lazy morning in the gazebo....

"Or is he?" he whispered, reading her dreamy expression.

She glared at him. "Don't pry."

"I'm not trying to mind your business," he said gently. "But I don't want to see you end up the loser. Blake's a very experienced man. He may be tempted by a bud about to blossom, but he's shy of nets. Don't try to cut your teeth on him. You might as well try to build a fence around the wind."

"What you really mean is that I can't compete with Her Ladyship," she threw at him.

"That's exactly what I mean," he said with gentle compassion. He patted her hand were it lay on the wood bench. "Kathryn, an experienced woman can attract a man in ways that an inexperienced one wouldn't even think of. I don't want to see you hurt. But you must know you're no competition for Vivian."

"Who said I was trying to be?" she asked. Her face shuttered. "You make Blake sound like a..."

"Blake is my brother," he reminded her. "And I'd do anything for him. But he's just noticed what a delicious little thing you've grown into, and he's lost his bearings. It won't take him long to find them, but that tiny space of time could be enough to destroy you." He squeezed her hand and grimaced. "Love him as a brother. But not as a man. I don't have to tell you how Blake feels about love."

She felt the life draining out of her. Her shoulders slumped, and she nodded weakly. "He doesn't believe in it," she whispered shakily.

"Blake wants one thing from a woman," he said. "And he can't have it from you."

She smiled wistfully. "He wouldn't take it even if I offered," she said quietly, darting a look at him.

"Not deliberately," he agreed. "But you could make him forget every scruple he has, little one. Or didn't you know that men are particularly vulnerable to women they want?"

She sighed softly. "And Blake being Blake, he'd marry me, wouldn't he? Even though he hated the idea of it, and me, he'd do the honorable thing."

"That's exactly what I mean." He held her hand gently. "Nothing would make me happier than to see you happily married to my brother. But I know Blake too well, and so do you. He's too much a cynic to change overnight."

"You don't think he could...care for a woman?" she asked haltingly.

He shrugged. "Blake is a private man. I've lived with him all my life, but there are depths to him that I've never been allowed to explore. Perhaps he's capable of love. But I think in a way he's afraid of it.

He's afraid of being vulnerable.'' He glanced at her with a dry smile. ''He may marry eventually to provide Greyoaks with an heir. He may even fall in love. I don't know.''

''You said he was possessive of me,'' she reminded him.

''Naturally, he's taken care of you half your life,'' he said. ''But what he really feels, no one knows.''

She bit her lower lip and nodded, turning away to stare at the pavement. ''You're right, of course.'' She forced a smile to her frozen face. ''Let's go get an ice-cream cone.''

He caught her arm gently and kept her from getting up. ''I'm sorry,'' he said suddenly. ''I didn't mean to hurt you.''

''What makes you think you have?'' she asked with a smile that was too bright.

''You're in love with him.''

She felt her face go white. She was only just beginning to admit that to herself. But, confronted with the accusation, she found she couldn't deny it. Her mouth tried to form words, but her tongue wouldn't cooperate.

He read the confusion in her face and stood up.

''Ice cream. Right. What flavor would you like, Kathy...vanilla or strawberry?''

It was only two days until Blake planned to fly them to St. Martin. The pace at the office was hectic. Kathryn took dictation until her fingers were numb, and Blake's temper, always formidable, seemed to be on a permanent hair trigger.

"You know damned well I don't use my middle initial in a signature," he growled at her, slamming the letters she'd just typed down on his desk violently. "Do them over!"

"If you don't like the way I do things," she complained tightly, "why don't you let Vivian come in and work for you?"

"She'd have been in tears by now," he admitted, with a faintly amused smile.

She straightened in the chair beside his desk, crossing her slender legs impatiently in the gray skirt that matched her silk blouse. "Afraid you might tarnish your shining armor?" she asked.

He studied her through a veil of smoke from his cigarette, his dark eyes thoughtful. "There isn't much danger of that happening with you, is there, Kate?" he asked quietly. "You know just about everything there is to know about me; my faults, my habits."

"Do I really know you at all, Blake?" she wondered absently. "Sometimes you seem very much a stranger."

He lifted his cigarette to his mouth. "Like that day in the gazebo, Kate?" he asked softly, watching the burst of color that shot into her face.

Her eyes darted back to her pad, and her heart ran away. "I don't know what you want from me anymore, Blake."

He got up and moved in front of her, leaning down to catch her chin in his big hand and lift her face up to his piercing gaze. "You're very young, Kathryn Mary."

"Oh, yes, compared to you, I'm a mere child," she returned.

"Little spitting kitten," he chided. Something wild and dangerous smoldering in his eyes. "Would you hiss and claw if I made love to you, Kathryn, or would you purr?"

She caught her breath sharply. "Neither!"

His eyes glittered down at her. "You don't think I could teach you to purr, Kate? Your mouth was wild under mine that day. I can still taste it, even now."

"I . . . didn't know what I was doing," she whispered weakly, embarrassed at the memory of her abandoned response.

"Neither did I, really," he murmured absently, watching her mouth with a disturbingly intense scrutiny. "I touched you and every sane thought went out of my head. All I wanted to do was make love to you until I stopped aching."

She caught her breath, meeting his eyes squarely. It was like the impact of lightning striking. It had been that way for her, too, but all he was admitting to was a purely physical attraction—just as Phillip had warned her. He'd lost his head out of desire, not love.

"Doesn't Vivian make you ache?" she asked in a tight voice, hurting with the certainty that what she felt for him was hopeless.

He searched her eyes quietly. "Not that way."

She dropped her gaze to her lap. "You can always find a woman, Blake," she choked.

He leaned down, placing his hands on either side of her against the chair arms, the curling smoke from his cigarette pungent in her nostrils.

"Not one like you, honey," he growled. "Or are you going to try to convince me that you've ever let another man touch you the way I did?"

She felt the heat creeping up from her throat, and her eyes riveted themselves to his tie, remembering the feel of his hands on her bare back, slightly rough, expertly caressing.

"You were afraid, because it was the first time. But if I'd insisted on making love to you, you wouldn't have stopped me. We both know that."

She felt the embarrassment, like a living thing, and she hated him for what he could do to her with words. He made her vulnerable. She'd never been vulnerable to any man before, it was new and disconcerting, and to cover her fears she sought refuge in temper.

"You flatter yourself, don't you?" she asked crisply, raising her sparkling eyes to his. "Maybe I was experimenting, Blake, did you think about that?" She watched the darkness grow in his eyes. "What makes you think I don't feel exactly that way with other men?"

"What other men?" he shot at her. "Phillip?"

She tore her eyes away and stared down at her pad blankly. There was suppressed fury in his voice, and she knew better than to deliberately goad him. If he touched her, she'd go crazy. It was her basic reaction to that vibrant masculinity that rippled in every hard muscle of his body. She was too vulnerable now, and the only way to keep him from seeing it was to make sure she kept him at arms' length.

"We'd better get this work out of the way," he said coolly, and sat down behind his desk again, idly crushing out his cigarette. "How about that shipment of poly-cotton we never received from our Georgia mill?" he asked quietly. "Check with the office there and find out if it was shipped. The spreaders will need it for the next cut.''

"Yes, sir," she replied in her best businesslike tone. "Anything else?"

"Yes," he said gruffly, watching her. "Send a dozen red roses to Vivian at the house."

That hit her like a ton of bricks, but she didn't even flinch. Methodically, she made a note on her pad and nodded. "One dozen, I'll call the florist right away. How would you like the card to read?"

He was still eyeing her. "Have them put, 'Thanks for last night' and sign it 'Blake.' Got that?"

"Got it," she replied. Her voice sounded vaguely strangled, but she kept the expression on her face. "Anything else?"

He swiveled his chair around to stare out the window. "No."

She went out and closed the door quietly behind her. Tears were welling in her eyes by the time she got back to her own desk.

Eight

"Just imagine, a week in St. Martin," Maude sighed, studying the list of chores she'd outlined for Mrs. Johnson and the daily maids while the family was away. "How sweet of Blake to take us all with him, especially when he's getting along so well with Vivian!"

"Oh, it's delightful," Kathryn agreed dully.

"They've hardly been apart at all," she sighed. "And they do make such a striking pair; Blake so dark and Vivian so fair... I think he's really serious this time." She clasped her hands together and beamed. "I'd love to plan a spring wedding. We could decorate the house with orchids...."

"Excuse me, Maude, but I really have to start getting my things together," Kathryn said brightly, rising from the sofa. "You don't mind?"

Maude was deep in her plans. "No, dear, go right ahead," she mumbled absently.

Kathryn went up the winding staircase, feeling dead inside. As she passed Vivian's room, her eye was caught by the vase full of red roses sitting on the dresser in full view of the door. Vivian had done that deliberately, no doubt, and Kathryn felt as if she'd been shot. At least Blake hadn't suspected how she felt about him. That would have been unbearable, especially since he was taking such a sudden and intense interest in the seductive blonde. They were going nightclubbing together, later that evening, and they'd been locked up in Blake's study ever since dinner. As it happened so many times since her return to Greyoaks, Kathryn sought out Phillip for companionship. And that seemed to catch Blake's attention in the most violent way.

The following morning he found Phillip sitting on her desk and he seemed to erupt.

"Don't you have anything to do, Phillip," he growled at his younger brother.

"Why, yes, I do," Phillip replied.

"Then why the hell don't you go and do it?" came the terse, irritable question.

Phillip stood erect, his hands in his pockets, and studied the bigger, older man quietly, frowning. "I was asking Kate to take in a movie with me tonight," he said. "Any objections?"

Blake's jaw tautened. "Make your dates at home. Not on my time."

"I do have an interest in the corporation," Phillip reminded him. "Just like all the other stockholders."

"Try acting like it," Blake said coldly. His eyes darted to Kathryn. "Bring your pad. I've got some letters to dictate." He went back into his office and roughly closed the door.

Phillip stared after him, not taking offense at all. He knew Blake too well. A slow smile flared on his lips. "Now, in a lesser man, I'd swear that was jealousy," he teased, eyeing Kathryn.

She stood up with a sigh, clutching her steno pad to her chest. "But not in a man with someone like Vivian practically engaged to him," she reminded him. "We'd better get to work before he gives us a pink slip."

He shrugged. "With the temper he's been in lately, I'm not sure it wouldn't be a relief."

"Speaking of relief," she said, lowering her voice, "you promised to help me look for an apartment."

"Not until we get back from St. Martin," he said stubbornly. "And only then if Blake's temper improves. I don't have a suicidal bone in my body, Kate, and I'm not taking on Blake for you."

She sighed. "You won't have to," she said bitterly. "He'll be glad to see me go now, and you know it."

He studied her. "Will he really?" he murmured.

"Kathryn!" Blake thundered over the intercom.

She flinched and hurried into his office.

He was sitting behind his desk, leaning back in his chair, and he glared at her when she walked in.

"From now on, don't encourage Phillip to waste time talking to you during working hours," he said without preamble, his eyes blazing. "I don't pay either of you to socialize."

She stared at him belligerently. "Do I have to have your permission to say good morning to him now?" she wanted to know.

"In this building, yes," he replied curtly. His dark eyes held hers fiercely. "You practically live in each other's pockets already. I shouldn't think it would work a hardship for you to spend just eight hours away from him!"

He whipped his chair forward and grabbed up a letter, his leonine face as hard as the oak desk under his powerful hands. She remembered without wanting to the warmth and tenderness of those hard fingers on her bare skin....

"Are you ready?" he asked curtly.

She sat down quickly, positioning her pad on her lap. "Any time you are," she said in her most professional tone.

For the rest of the day, Kathryn and Blake maintained a cool politeness between them that raised eyebrows among the staff. There had been numerous arguments, ever since Kathryn's appointment as his secretary, but this was different. Now they were avoiding each other completely. They didn't argue, because there was no contact between them.

"I say, have you and Blake had a falling out?" Vivian asked Kathryn that evening as she waited for Blake to change for their dinner date. "You've hardly spoken to each other for the past couple of days."

Kathryn, curled up on the sofa in her ivory-colored jumpsuit with a book, glanced at the older woman coolly. The blue Qiana dress the actress was wearing left nothing to the imagination, and even Kathryn had to admit it flattered her figure, her lovely face, and her elegantly coiffured blond hair. Just Blake's style, she thought bitterly.

"Not at all," Kathryn replied finally. "Blake and I were never close," she lied, remembering happier times when there was never a cross word between them, and Blake's eyes were tender.

"Oh, really?" Vivian probed. She smiled a little haughtily, primping at a mirror on the wall between two elegant bronze sconces. "I do hope you and he will get on together. Living in the same house, you know..." She let her voice trail away insinuatingly.

"Have you set a date?" Kathryn asked with careful unconcern.

"Not quite," the blonde replied. "But it won't be long."

"I'm delighted for both of you," she murmured as she stared blankly at her book.

"Are you ready, darling?" Vivian gushed as Blake came into the room. "I'm simply famished!"

"Let's go, then," he replied with a sensuous note in his voice that Kathryn didn't miss. But she didn't raise her eyes from the book, didn't look at him or speak to him. She felt dead, frozen. It wasn't until the door slammed behind them that she was able to relax. How fortunate, she thought, that Dick Leeds and Maude had also gone out for the night, and that she'd convinced Phillip to go to the movies alone. There was no one to watch her cry. Now, for certain, she'd have to leave Greyoaks. There was no way she could live in it with Vivian.

* * *

The following day dawned bright and sunny, perfect for the flight to St. Martin. Kathryn and Phillip were bringing up the rear. Vivian, in a stunning white lace pantsuit, was clinging to Blake's arm like ivy while Dick Leeds and Maude followed along deep in conversation. Kathryn was wearing a simple peasant dress in green and brown patterns that brought out the deep green of her eyes and set off her long, waving dark hair. She was dressed for comfort, not for style, and she knew she was no competition for the blonde. She wasn't even trying to be. She'd lost Blake, even though she'd never really had a chance to win him. There were too many years between them.

"You're tearing at my heart," Phillip said quietly, watching her as she watched Blake and Vivian.

She lifted her sad eyes to his. "Why?"

"I've never seen a woman love a man the way you love Blake," he replied quietly, with none of his usual gaiety.

She lifted her shoulders in a careless gesture. "I'll get over it," she murmured. "It...it's just going to take a little time, that's all. I'll land on my feet, Phil."

He caught her hand and held it gently as they walked toward the small jet owned by the corporation. "I honestly thought it was infatuation, at first," he admitted gently. "But I'm beginning to realize just how wrong I was. You'd do anything for him, wouldn't you? Even stand aside and watch him marry another woman, as long as he was happy."

Her long eyelashes curled down onto her cheeks. "Isn't that what love is all about?" she asked in a soft whisper. "I want him to be happy." Her eyes closed briefly. "I want everything for him."

He squeezed her hand. "Stiff upper lip, darling," he said under his breath. "Don't let him see you suffer."

She forced a laugh through her tight throat. "Oh, of course not," she said brightly. "We revolutionaries are very tough, you know."

"That's my girl. But why are you giving up the battle so soon?"

"Who said I was giving up?" she asked, glancing at him. "I've got the job I wanted, but not the apartment. Just wait until we come back!"

He chuckled. "That's my girl. I knew you could work it out."

"Of course we can," she said with a gleeful smile.

"We?" he asked, apprehensively.

"You know lots of people in real estate," she reminded him. "I'm sure you can find me something I can afford. In a good neighborhood."

The executive jet was roomy and comfortable, and as long as Kathryn didn't look out the window of the pressurized cabin, she was fine. She'd never gotten over the bouts with airsickness that were a carryover from her childhood, despite Blake's expert handling of the airplane.

Vivian was sitting in the co-pilot's seat, for which Kathryn was eternally grateful. She couldn't have borne her haughty company, her gloating smile.

"You look very pale, dear," Maude said sympathetically, reaching out to pat Kathryn's cold hand. "How about an airsick pill?"

"I've already had two," came the subdued reply. "All they do is make me dizzy."

"A spot of brandy might help," Dick Leeds suggested gently, as he appeared briefly beside her.

She shook her head, feeling even more nauseated. "I'll be all right," she assured them.

"Lie down for a while," Phillip said as the older passengers moved away. "Take off your shoes and just sleep," he coaxed, helping her stretch out in one of the plush, comfortable seats. "We'll be there before you know it."

They landed at Queen Juliana airport on Sint Maarten—the Dutch side of the divided island. As they stepped out onto the ground, the first thing Kathryn noticed was the hot, moist air that enveloped her. She stared at the blue skies and palm trees and the flags flying proudly at the terminal. She remembered the island with pleasure, as she had stayed many times at the family's villa.

A customs official took their immigration cards, and their passports, with a minimum of fuss. Blake obtained a rental car, and they were on their way.

"Where is your house?" Vivian asked, staring out at the red-roofed homes they passed as they drove along the paved road.

"On St. Martin," Blake replied as he drove. "The French side of the island; which is, by the way, very French. The Dutch side, which we're in now, tends to be more Americanized."

"It's confusing," Vivian laughed.

"Not really," Maude told her. "One gets used to it. The division is political as well as lingual, but the people are delightful on both sides of the island. And you'll love the shops in Marigot—that's very near our villa."

"And the restaurants," Phillip grinned. "You've never had better seafood."

"What do you like about it, darling?" Vivian asked Blake.

"The peace and quiet," he replied.

"Which you don't find much of during peak tourist season," Phillip laughed.

"Well, this is hurricane season, not tourist season," Maude said, shivering at the thought. "I do hope we don't run into any rough weather."

"Amen," Blake said with a faint smile. "I've got to fly over to Haiti on business while we're here."

"What for?" Vivian asked with blunt curiosity.

Blake gave her a lazy sidelong look. "I might have a woman stashed away there," he said.

It was the first time Kathryn had ever seen Vivian blush, and she made a good job of it. Her pale face turned a bright pink. "Oh, look, cattle!" she said quickly, gazing out the window toward a green meadow nestled between the mountains.

Blake only chuckled, concentrating on the road as they passed from the Dutch side of the island to the French.

Maude jumped as they hit a pothole. "Oh, you can always tell when we pass into St. Martin," she moaned. "The roads over here are just terrible!"

"Just like home, isn't it?" Phillip asked, winking at Kathryn.

"I think we have very good roads at home, Phillip," Maude said, "an excellent county commission and a superb road department. Remember, darling, I helped Jeff Brown get appointed to the state highway board, and I think he's done a fine job."

"Forgive me for that unthinking comment," Phillip pleaded. "Heaven forbid that I should sully the name...."

"Oh, do be quiet," Maude moaned. "Vivian, here's Marigot," she said, pointing out the window toward the bay where fishing boats dotted the Baie de Marigot past the powdery beach. There were red-roofed houses stretching all the way down the beach, thick in places, mingling with hotels. Kathryn felt a shiver of girlish excitement as they stopped at one of them minutes later. It was Maison Baie—roughly, Bay House—and her eyes lovingly traced the white stone building with its graceful wrought-iron balconies and breezeways and long windows. It, too, had the classic red roof, and carved wood doors.

"Is this yours?" Vivian asked, her eyes also taking in the graceful lines of the house and its colorful setting with palm trees, bougainvillea, and sea-grape trees further out on the powder-fine sand.

"Yes," Blake replied, cutting the engine. "Maison Baie. It's been in the family since my father was a boy, and the second generation of caretakers—a retired sea captain named Rouget and his wife—live here year round, looking after it."

"It's very pretty," Vivian said enthusiastically.

Kathryn stayed beside Phillip, feeling the coolness of the house wash over her as they walked inside. Rouget, a tall, thin man with white hair, came to meet them, welcoming them in his native French. Blake replied, his accent faultless, and Kathryn had to work to keep up with the translation. She'd forgotten just how French this side of the island really was. Her rusty attempts to speak the language had always amused Blake. Glancing at him, she wondered if anything she did would ever amuse him again.

The look on her young face was revealing, and Phillip drew her away before Blake could see it. She smiled at him gratefully as they left the spacious living room to settle into their respective rooms. Already she was hoping the visit would be a brief one.

That afternoon Vivian persuaded Blake to take her back to Marigot to look in the shops. Maude and Dick Leeds, deciding that the sun was a bit much, lounged on the balcony with chilled burgundy provided by Rouget. Kathryn spent the rest of the day lying quietly in bed, feeling out of sorts. The combination of the flight and the sultry, tropical climate had put her flat on her back. When night came, she was barely aware of Maude's fingers gently shaking her.

"Darling, we're going into Marigot to have seafood. Do you feel like coming with us?" she asked.

Kathryn sat up, surprised to find that the nausea and weariness were completely gone. "Of course," she said, smiling. "Just give me a minute to change...."

"What's wrong with what you have on?" Blake asked from the doorway, and she felt his dark eyes sliding up and down her slender body in the peasant dress that had ridden up above her knees while she rested. She pulled it down quickly and, smoothing it nervously, got to her feet.

"I...I suppose it would do, if we're not going anywhere fancy."

"The restaurant isn't formal, Kathryn," he said, moving inside the room. "Still queasy?" he added gently.

That soft note in his voice almost brought tears to her eyes. She turned away to pick up her brush. "No," she replied. "I'm all right. Just let me run a brush through my hair."

"Don't be long," Maude teased. "I feel as if I haven't eaten for days."

Kathryn nodded, expecting Blake to go, too. But he didn't. He closed the door quietly, an action that made Kathryn's heart go wild. She watched him in the mirror.

He moved up behind her, his dark eyes holding hers in the glass, so close that she could feel the blazing warmth of his big body. He was dressed in a red and white patterned tropical shirt, open at the throat, revealing a sensuous glimpse of curling dark hair and bronzed flesh. His slacks were white, hugging the powerful lines of his thighs. She could hardly drag her eyes away from him.

"Do you really feel up to this?" he asked quietly. "If you don't, I'll stay home with you."

The concern in his deep voice would have been heaven, if it had been meant differently. But it was the compassion of a man for a child, not of a man for his woman.

"I always get airsick," she reminded him dully. "I'm all right, Blake."

"Are you?" he asked tightly. "The light's gone out of you."

"It's been . . . a long week," she whispered unsteadily.

He nodded, dropping his narrow gaze to her long hair, her shoulders. His big hands went to her waist, testing the softness of her flesh through the thin dress, rough and vaguely caressing.

"I...I think we all needed a vacation," she laughed nervously. The feel of his hands made her heart turn over in her chest.

"Yes." He drew her slowly back against his big, hard-muscled body, so that she could feel his breath against her hair. "You're trembling," he said in a deep, lazy tone.

Her eyes closed. Her hands went involuntarily to rest on top of his as he slid them closer around her waist. "I know," she managed weakly.

His fingers contracted painfully. "Kate..."

She couldn't help herself. Her head dropped back against his broad chest and her body openly yielded to him. In the mirror, she watched his dark, broad hands move slowly, seductively up her waist until they cupped her high breasts over the green and brown pattern of the low-cut peasant dress. She let him touch her, helpless in his embrace, the hardness of his thighs pressing into the back of her legs as he moved even closer.

His dark eyes held hers in the mirror, watching her reaction. His cheek brushed against the top of her head, ruffling the soft dark hair while his fingers brushed and stroked, the action even more erotic because she could watch it happening.

Her fingers came up to rest on top of his, pressing them closer to the soft curves, while her heart threatened to choke her with its furious thudding.

His face moved down and she felt the heat of his lips at the side of her neck brushing, teasing, his tongue lightly tracing the line of it down to her shoulder.

"You smell of flowers," he whispered. His hands moved up and under the low neckline to surge down and capture her taut, bare breasts.

She moaned helplessly and bit her lip to stifle the sound that must have surely passed even through the thick stone walls of the house.

"I wish to God we were alone, Kate," he whispered huskily. "I'd lie down with you on that bed over there and before I was through, you'd be biting back more than one sweet moan. You'd be biting me," he whispered seductively, while his hands made magic on her aching body. "Clawing me, begging me to do more than touch your breasts."

"Blake..." she moaned, with a throb in her voice that broke the sound in the middle of his name.

She whirled in his arms, rising against his big body, her arms going around his neck, her lips parted and pleading.

"Kiss me," she whispered, trembling. "Blake, Blake, kiss me hard...!"

"How hard?" he whispered huskily as he bent. His mouth bit at hers sensuously, lightly bruising, open, taunting. "Like that?"

"No," she whispered. She went on tiptoe, her green eyes misty with mindless hunger, her lips parted as she caught his head and brought his open mouth down on hers. Her tongue darted into his mouth and she withdrew tauntingly just a half-breath away. "Like that...."

His mouth crushed hers, his tongue exploring the line of her lips, thrusting past them into the warm darkness of her mouth, his arms contracting so strongly that they brought the length of her body close enough to feel every hardening line of his.

"Do you...want me?" she whispered achingly.

"God in heaven, can't you feel it?" he ground out. "Stop asking silly questions...closer, Kate," he whispered. "Move your body against mine. Stroke it against me...."

She eased up on tiptoe. "Like this, Blake?" she whispered shakily.

His mouth bit at hers. "Harder than that," he murmured. "I can't feel you."

Trembling, she repeated the arousing action and felt a small shudder go through his powerful body. "Do you like this?" she managed in a stranger's seductive voice.

"Let me show you how much I like it," he whispered. He bent and lifted her off the floor, looking down into her green eyes as he started toward the huge mahogany posted bed against the wall.

Her arms clung to him, her lips answering the suddenly tender kisses he was brushing against her lips, her eyelids, her eyebrows, her cheeks. The chaste touch of his mouth was at odds with the heavy, hard shudder of his heartbeat against her body, the harsh sigh of his breath that betrayed the emotions he was experiencing.

"Are you going to make love to me?" she whispered against his lips, knowing in her heart even as she asked the question that she was going to give him everything he wanted.

"Do you want me to, Kate?" he whispered back. "Are you afraid?"

"How could I be afraid of you?" she managed in a tight voice. "When I..." Before she could get the confession out, before she could tell him how desperately she loved him, there was a sharp, harsh knock on the door, and he jerked involuntarily.

Vivian's abrasive voice called, "Blake, are you there? We're starving!"

"My God, so am I," he whispered, and the eyes that met Kathryn's as he set her back on her feet were blazing with unsatisfied desire.

She moved unsteadily away from him, her heart jerking wildly, her breath coming in uneven little gasps. She went back to the mirror and picked up a lipstick, applying it to her swollen mouth while Blake took a steadying breath and went to answer the door.

"I'm so hungry, darling," Vivian murmured with a smile, her hawklike eyes catching the slight swell of his lower lip, the unruly hair that Kathryn's fingers had tangled lightly. "Can't we go to dinner now that you're through talking to sweet little Kate?"

"I'm hungry myself," Kathryn said, avoiding Blake's eyes as she edged out of the door past him, managed a tight smile in Vivian's direction, and almost ran from the room. What in heaven's name had possessed her to allow Blake such liberties? Now the fat was really going to be in the fire. She had let him know how desperately she wanted him, and she was afraid that he'd take advantage of it. What Phillip had said was true—Blake could lose his head. If he did, he'd be gentleman enough to marry her. But she didn't want Blake on those terms. She only wanted his love, not a forced marriage. What was she going to do?

The little French restaurant was as familiar to Kathryn as Maison Baie, and she remembered the owners well—a French couple from Martinique who served the most delicious lobster soufflé and crepes flambées Kathryn had ever tasted. Her appetite came back the instant she saw the food, and Phillip's pleasant company at her elbow made it even more palatable.

She avoided Blake's piercing gaze all through the meal and when they got back to the house, she quickly excused herself and went to bed.

That night set the pattern for the next two days. Blake wore a perpetual scowl at Kathryn's nervous avoidance of him, and Phillip's efforts to play peacemaker met with violence on Blake's part. He stayed away during the day with Vivian, taking her on tours of nearby Saba and St. Eustatius—known to the locals as "Statla." But in the evenings he and the slinky blonde stayed close to home while he discussed the mill problem with Dick Leeds. It was at the end of one of those endless discussions that Kathryn accidentally came across him in the deserted hall upstairs.

His dark eyes narrowed angrily as she froze in front of him, on her way to change for supper in Marigot.

"Still running away from me?" he asked scathingly.

"I'm not running," she replied unsteadily.

"Like hell you're not," he returned gruffly. "You practically dive under things to keep out of my way lately. What's wrong, Kathryn, do you think you're so damned irresistible that I can't keep my hands off you?"

"Of course not!" she gasped.

"Then why go to so much trouble to avoid me?" he persisted.

She drew a slow, steady breath. "Phillip and I have been busy, that's all," she managed.

His face tightened. A cold, cruel smile touched his hard mouth. "Busy? So you finally decided to taste the wine, did you, honey?" His voice drew blood. "It's just as well. You're too much of a baby for me, Kathryn. I hate like hell to rob cradles!"

He turned on his heel and left her standing there.

She couldn't bear for Blake to think that about her, to look at her with eyes so full of contempt they made her shiver. But what could she do? The impact of his anger made her reckless and when the delicious white wine was passed around at the restaurant that night, she had more than her share of refills. Throwing caution to the wind, she sipped and swallowed until all her heartaches seemed to vanish. When Blake announced that he was flying to Haiti the next morning, she barely heard him. Her mind was far away, on pleasant thoughts.

"Honey, you're drunk," Phillip said with some concern when they got back to the villa. "Go to bed and sleep it off, huh?"

She smiled at him lazily. "I'm not sleepy."

"Pretend, before you give Vivian something else to laugh about," he asked softly. "And don't push Blake's temper any further tonight. I'm surprised he hasn't lectured you about the amount of wine you drank. He didn't like it, that's for sure.''

"Be a pal and stop preaching," she murmured, fanning herself with one hand. "It's so hot!"

"Feels like storm weather," he agreed. "Go to bed. You'll cool off."

She shrugged and, to Phillip's quiet relief, went up to her room before the others came inside the house.

Nine

But once she got into bed, she was only hotter. It was too sultry, to quiet, and her thoughts began to haunt her. Blake's harsh words came back like a persistent mosquito—too much of a baby, he said. Too much of a baby.

She tossed and turned until it became unbearable. Finally she got up, put on her brief white bikini and grabbed up a beach towel. If she couldn't sleep, she might as well cool off in the bay. Just the thought of the cold water made her feel better.

She made her way downstairs in the dark house with the ease of long practice, and walked a little unsteadily out onto the beach. Her bare feet smarted on the grainly pebbles until she reached the softer sand where the foaming surf curled lazily. The air was static, the beach completely deserted. She stood and the delicious scent of blooming flowers that merged with the tangy sea smell.

"What are you doing out here?" came a harsh, deep voice from the shelter of a nearby palm.

She watched Blake move into view in the moonlight, wearing a pair of white shorts and the same red and white patterned silk shirt he'd been wearing the other night. Only tonight it was unbuttoned all the way down his massive chest.

"I asked you a question," he said, and even in the moonlight she could see the boldness in his dark eyes as they sketched her slender body in its brief white covering. The way he was looking at her made her pulses pound.

"I came out for a swim," she said, very carefully enunciating each word. "I'm hot."

"Are you?"

Her eyes traced the hard lines of his body, lingering on his massive chest with its wedge of dark, curling hair that disappeared below his waistline. Her lips parted as she felt a surge of longing so great, it moved her toward him without her even being aware of it until she was close enough to touch him.

"Don't be angry with me," she pleaded in a husky voice. Her fingers went to his broad chest, touching the bronzed skin nervously, feeling the sensuous masculinity in those muscles that clenched under her soft touch.

"Don't," he said harshly, catching her hands roughly.

"Why not, Blake?" she asked recklessly. "Don't you like for me to touch you? I'm just a baby, remember," she taunted, moving her fingers under his deliberately. She could feel his heartbeat quicken until it was heavy and hard, hear the rough intake of his breath as she moved closer and let her body rest against his. The naked brush of her thighs against the hair-roughened muscles of his was intoxicating, and the feel of his hard chest against the softness of her body caused her to sigh.

"Blake," she whispered achingly. The alcohol she'd consumed made her uninhibited; she'd never been so dangerously relaxed with him before. But now she touched his shoulders and the muscles of his big arms in a desperate surge of longing, drowning in the nearness of him, the feel of his big, warm body under her exploring hands.

Her head moved forward, and she pressed her mouth against his chest, drinking in the tang of his cologne and the smell of some spicy soap on his bare skin.

He caught his breath sharply, and his hands suddenly gripped her bare waist. "Don't, Kate," he whispered roughly. "You'll make me do something we'll both regret. You don't know what you're doing to me!"

Her body moved sensuously against his, and she heard the hard groan that broke from his throat. "I know," she moaned, lifting her face to meet his blazing eyes. "Oh, Blake, love me!"

"On a public beach?" he growled huskily, before bending his head to take her mouth.

Her arms lifted around his neck, and his hands dropped to her thighs, lifting her body abruptly against his so that it was molded to every masculine line of him in a joining that tore a moan from her lips.

His fingers contracted, and she felt the shudder rip through his body with a force of a blow, felt the arms holding her begin to tremble as his mouth invaded hers, devouring it in the silence of the night.

They swayed together like palm trees in a hurricane, tasting, touching, burning with a hunger that seemed incapable of satisfaction. Her fingers buried themselves in his thick, dark hair, ruffling it as she yielded to the violent passion she'd aroused.

She felt his fingers at the strings that held her bikini top in place, and she was too lost in him to notice what was happening until she felt with a sense of wonder the curling hair of his chest against the bare softness of her own, and she cried out with pleasure.

"This is how it felt that day in the gazebo, isn't it, Kate?" he breathed roughly at her ear as he pressed her breasts against the thickness of dark hair that matted his muscular chest. "I want all of you against me like this, I want to lie down on the beach with you and let you feel every delicious difference between your body and mine."

Her thighs trembled where his broad fingers caressed them, drawing her hips to his. Her nails bit deeply into his hard back and she sobbed at the wave of emotion that trembled over her weak body.

"Kate, Kathy, sweet, sweet love," he whispered as his mouth touched her lips again and again, brief, hard kisses that aroused her almost beyond bearing so that she pressed even closer against his big, warm body and felt the shudder that went through it.

His mouth moved down her throat and her body arched as he found the thrust of her breasts and let his lips brush warmly, moistly, against flesh that had known no man's touch except his.

"Blake," she whispered achingly. I love you, she thought, I love you more than my own life, and if I have nothing else, I'll have this to remember when I'm old, and you and Vivian have children and I'm alone with my memories... Her fingers tangled in his hair and pressed his exploring mouth closer.

"God, you're soft," he breathed, lifting his head at last to move his mouth sensuously over hers. "Soft like silk, like velvet against my body... Kathy, I want you. I want you like I want air to breathe, I want to make love to you...." His mouth took hers again, deeply possessive, his arms swallowing her, rocking her while the waves pounded rhythmically against the white sand, the sound just penetrating her mind while she got drunker on pleasure than she ever had on wine.

"We've got to stop this," he groaned, dragging his mouth away to look down at her in the darkness that wasn't darkness at all, his eyes black and tortured as they met hers. "I can't take you here!"

Her hands ran lovingly over his hair-matted chest, feeling the roughness of it, the strength of those well-developed muscles. She wanted to touch all of him, every sensuous inch of him.

"We could go inside," she suggested in a husky whisper.

"Yes, we could," he said roughly. "And you'd wake in my arms hating me. Not like this, Kate. Damn it, not like this!"

He pushed her away, and for just an instant, his eyes possessed the small high curve of her breasts like a thirsty man gulping water. Then he swooped and retrieved the bikini top. He dropped it into her shaking hands and turned his back.

"Put it on," he said harshly. His fingers dug into his shirt pocket for his crushed cigarette package and matches. "Let me cool off for a minute. My God, Kate, do you see what you do to me?" he growled, half-laughing as his fingers fumbled with the cigarette.

She tied the top back in place with trembling fingers, avoiding his direct gaze. Out of the corner of her eye, she saw the orange tip of his cigarette glow suddenly as he took a draw from it.

"I'm sorry, Blake," she said miserably. "I...I didn't mean to...to..."

"It's all right, Kate," he said gently. "You had too much to drink, that's all."

Her eyes closed and she folded her arms around her trembling body. "I'm so ashamed," she ground out.

He stiffened. "Ashamed?"

She turned away. "I can't think what got into me," she laughed harshly. "Maybe it's my age, maybe I'm going through my second childhood."

"Or maybe you're just plain damned frustrated," he said, a whip in his deep voice. "Is that it, Kate? Can't Phillip give you what you need?"

Shocked, she turned, lifting her puzzled eyes to his across the distance. She'd never seen his face so hard. "What?"

He laughed shortly. "You make no secret of your preference for his company, honey," he reminded her. "But he isn't passionate. You're just finding that out, aren't you? Can't he give you what I can?"

"I don't...I don't feel that way about Phil," she stammered.

"Don't expect me to stand in for him again," he shot back. "I draw the line at being used for a damned substitute."

"But I wasn't...!"

He turned away. "Go back inside and sober up," he said, stripping off his shirt.

She stared after him, watching as he walked forward, flicking the cigarette away, and abruptly dived into the moonlit water.

Kathryn wanted desperately to follow him, to make him understand how she felt. To tell him that she loved him, not Phillip, that she'd give anything to be to him what Vivian was. But she knew he'd never listen to her in his present mood. He might never listen to her again, regardless of his mood. She wanted to hit herself for putting away all that wine. She'd killed Blake's respect for her, and along with it, every chance she'd ever had of making him love her. With a sigh she turned away and picked up her beach towel. She trailed it aimlessly behind her as she walked past the gnarled sea-grape trees back to the house, the flower-scented breeze making sultry whispers at her ear.

She overslept the next morning, and when she awoke it was with a bursting headache. She got to her feet to get a aspirin, glancing toward the rain-blasted window and the darkness of the clouds.

Phillip was the only one in the living room when she went downstairs.

"Where is everybody?" she asked, lifting a hand to her throbbing head as she sat down with the coffee she'd poured herself from the tray in front of the sofa.

"They drove Blake to the airport," he replied watching her closely. "He was bent on flying to Haiti today, despite the storm warnings. He left before this started; I guess they stopped to do some shopping on the way back."

Her eyes stared blankly out the window at the pouring rain, whipped by the wind. "It looks bad out there," she remarked, her heart aching when she remembered what had happened last night and why Blake might have decided to take a risk like this. Had she made him reckless? Had her stupidity caused him to lose his temper so badly that he had to get away from the island, from her, at any cost?

"Yes, it does," he said. He raised his cup of coffee to his lips, watching her over the rim of it. He sipped some of the hot liquid and then abruptly put the cup down with a clatter. "What happened?"

The question was so unexpected that she stared at him for several seconds before she spoke. "What?"

"What happened last night?" he asked again. "Blake looked like a thunderhead when he came downstairs this morning, and he didn't say a word all through breakfast. He didn't ask where you were, but he kept watching the stairs, as if he expected you to come down them any second. He looked like a starving man with his eye on a five-course meal."

Tears formed in her own eyes, ran down her cheeks. She put her cup down and buried her face in her hands, crying brokenly.

He sat down beside her and patted her awkwardly on the shoulder. "What did you do to him, Kathy?"

"I'd had too much to drink," she whispered through her fingers, "and he'd said I was a child—"

"So you went out to prove to him that you weren't," he said softly, smiling at her.

A nagging suspicion formed in the back of her mind and she raised her tear-wet eyes to his with the question in them.

"It's a very public beach, Kathryn Mary," he said with a mischievous grin. "And the moon was out."

"Oh, no," she whispered, going red. She buried her face in her hands a second time. "You saw us."

"Not only me," he replied drily. "Vivian. Watch yourself, little one, I got a look at her face before she stormed off upstairs."

She swallowed. "Did anyone else . . . ?"

He shook his head. "No. Mom and Dick were arguing politics. I'd taken Vivian for a stroll along the porch to see the view . . . and what a view we saw. Whew!"

The blush got hotter. "I could die," she moaned. "I could just die!"

"It's nothing to be embarrassed about," he said gently. "I'd give anything to have a woman care that much about me. And if you wondered how Blake really felt, I imagine you found out."

"I found out that he wants me," she replied miserably. "I knew that before. It's not enough, Phillip."

"How do you know that's all he feels?" he asked quietly. He leaned forward, studying the coffee table. "Blake's deep, Kathryn. He keeps everything to himself."

"I couldn't have faced him this morning," she said bitterly. "Not after what I did. Oh, Phillip, I'll never have another glass of wine as long as I live, I'll never touch another drop."

"Don't give up, girl," he said.

"Phillip, I don't have anything to give up," she reminded him.

"Don't you?" he asked, frowning. "I'm not so sure about that."

Vivian and Kathryn were left alone briefly while Maude supervised the evening meal and Dick and Phillip talked shop on the long porch. The rain had finally vanished, but the wind had only let up a little, and Kathryn couldn't help wondering if Blake was all right. He wasn't due back until the next morning, but that didn't stop her from worrying.

"You really did get smashed last night, didn't you?" Vivian asked, shooting a quick glance at Kathryn's subdued expression as she poured herself a small sherry at the bar.

Kathryn stiffened. "I'm not used to alcohol," she said defensively, eyeing the coffee cup she was holding.

"What a pity you had to overdo it," the blonde said with a pitying glance. "Blake was utterly disgusted."

Her face flamed. "Was he?" she choked.

"I saw you, of course," she sighed. "Poor man, he didn't stand a chance when you absolutely threw yourself at him like that. Any man would be... stirred," she added. Her eyes sharpened. "For my part, I'm furious with you. Blake and I... well, I've told you how things are. And I should think you'd have enough pride not to offer yourself to an engaged man.''

The coffee cup crashed to the floor. Kathryn got up and ran for the stairs. She couldn't bear to hear any more.

Blake was due by mid-morning, but when Phillip came back from the airport his face was grim.

"What's wrong? What happened?" Kathryn asked frantically.

"He left Haiti at daylight," Phillip said through tight lips. "And filed a flight plan. But he hasn't been heard from since takeoff." He caught her hand and squeezed it warmly. "They think he's gone down in some rough winds off the coast of Puerto Rico."

Ten

She couldn't remember a time in her life when she'd been so afraid. She paced. She worried. She cried. When Phillip finally took pity on all of them and agreed to let them wait it out at the airport, she hugged him out of sheer relief. At least they'd be a little closer to the communications network.

The airport wasn't crowded, but it wasn't as comfortable as the restaurant in the adjoining motel, so the five of them waited there. Vivian was worried, but it didn't deter her from flirting with Phillip or casting a wandering eye around the restaurant for interested looks. There were several Europeans staying in the motel, and a good many of the customers were men.

Kathryn had eyes for no one. Her worried gaze was fixed on her lap while she tried not to wonder how she could go through life without Blake. She'd never thought about that before. Blake had always seemed invincible, immortal. He was so strong and commanding, it didn't occur to her that he was as vulnerable as any other man. Now, she had to consider that possibility and it froze her very blood.

"I can't stand it," she whispered to Phillip, rising. "I'm going out to the airfield."

"Kathryn, it may be hours," he protested, walking with her as far as the door, only to cast a concerned look back at Maude, who was deep in conversation with Dick Leeds, her thin face drawn and taut with fear.

"I know," she said. She managed a wan little smile. "But if he...*when* he comes back," she corrected quickly, "I think one of us should be there."

He clenched her shoulders hard. His face was older, harder. "Kate, it's not definite that he's coming back. You've got to face that. His plane went down, that's absolutely all I know. The rescue crews are searching, but heaven only knows what they'll find!"

She bit her lower lip, hard, and her eyes were misty when she raised them, but her jaw was set stubbornly. "He's alive," she said. "I know he's alive, Phillip."

"Honey..." he began piteously.

"Do you think I'd still be breathing if Blake were dead?" she asked in a wild, choked whisper. "Do you think my heart would be beating?"

He closed his eyes momentarily, as if searching for words.

"I'm going outside," she said gently. She turned and left him there.

* * *

The skies were still gray, and the sun hadn't come out. She paced the apron with an impatient restlessness, starting every time she heard a sound that might be a plane.

Minutes later, Maude came out to join her, her thin arms folded, her eyes pale and troubled. "I wish we knew something," she murmured. "Just whether or not they think he could be alive."

"He's alive," Kathryn said confidently.

Maude studied the brave little face, and a dawning light came into her eyes. "I've been very dense, haven't I, Kathryn?" she asked gently, studying the younger woman's face.

Kathryn watched the ground, reddening. "I..."

Maude put an arm around her shoulders comfortingly. "Come in and have another cup of coffee. It won't make that much difference."

"They found him!" Phillip yelled from the doorway of the terminal, his face bright, his voice full of sunlight. "The rescue plane's on its way in now!"

"Oh, thank God," Maude murmured prayerfully.

Kathryn let the tears run silently down her face unashamedly. Blake was safe. He was alive. Even if she had to give him up to Vivian, if she never saw him again, it was enough to know he'd be on the same planet with her, alive. Alive, praise God, alive!

Maude stayed outside with her, while Phillip went back inside with the others after they'd all been told the news. Kathryn couldn't be budged, and Maude stood quietly with her, waiting. Minutes passed quietly until there came the drone of a twin-engine plane. It circled the landing strip and dropped down gently, its wheels making a squealing sound briefly, lifting, then settling onto the runway.

Kathryn watched the plane with tears shimmering in her eyes, until it stopped, the engine cut off, the door opened.

A big, dark man in an open-necked shirt stepped out of it, and Kathryn was running toward him before his feet ever touched the ground.

"Blake!" she screamed, oblivious to the other members of the family coming out of the terminal behind her. She ran like a frightened child seeking refuge, her face tormented, her legs flying against the skirt of her white sundress.

He opened his arms and caught her up against him, holding her while she ground her cheek against his broad chest and wept like a wind-tossed orphan.

"Oh, Blake," she whimpered, "they said you'd gone down, and we didn't know...oh, I'd have died with you! Blake, Blake...I'd have died with you, Blake," she whispered, over and over, her voice muffled, almost incoherent, her nails stabbing into his back as she clung to him.

His big arms tightened around her, his cheek scrubbing roughly against her forehead. "I'm all right," he said. "I'm fine, Kate."

She drew away a breath and looked up at him with tears streaming down her pale face, lines of weariness and worry making her look suddenly older.

He looked older, too, his face heavily lined, his dark eyes bloodshot as if he hadn't slept in a long time. She searched his beloved face, everything she felt for him showing plainly in her green eyes.

"I love you so," she whispered brokenly. "Oh, Blake, I love you so!"

He stood there frozen, staring down at her with eyes so dark they seemed black.

Embarrassed at having been so stupidly blunt, she tugged weakly at his arms and stepped back. "I...I'm sorry," she choked. "I...didn't mean to...to throw myself at you a second time. Vivian told me...how disgusted you were yesterday," she added in a whipped tone.

"Vivian told you what?" he asked in a strange husky whisper.

She stepped away from him, but she still clung helplessly to his big, warm hand, walking quietly beside him, the top of her head just coming to his chin, as they moved to join the others.

"It doesn't matter," she said with a painful smile. "It's all right."

"That's what you think!" he said in a voice she didn't recognize.

Vivian came running to meet him, shooting a poisonous glance at Kathryn. "Oh, Blake, darling! We were so worried!" she exclaimed, reaching up to kiss him full on the mouth. "How lovely that you're safe!"

Maude and Phillip echoed the greeting, Maude with tears misting her eyes.

"Close call?" Phillip asked with keen perception.

Blake nodded. "Too close. I wouldn't care to repeat it."

"What about the plane?" Maude asked gently.

"I'm glad it was insured," Blake replied with a faint smile. "I came down in the rain forest on Puerto Rico. The plane made it, barely, but I clipped off the wings."

Kathryn closed her eyes, seeing it in her mind.

"I'll buy you a drink," Phillip said. "You look like you could use one."

"A drink, a hot bath, and a bed," Blake agreed. He glanced at Kathryn as she moved away toward Phillip. She wouldn't meet his eyes.

"I... I'm going to pack," she murmured, turning away.

"Pack?" Blake asked gruffly. "Why?"

"I'm going home," she said proudly, letting her eyes meet his, only to glance off again. "I... I've had enough sun and sand. I don't like paradise... it's got too many serpents."

She turned toward the car. "Phillip, will you please drive me back to the house?" she asked with downcast eyes.

"Let Maude," he said, surprising her. "Would you mind, darling?" he asked his mother.

"No, not at all," Maude said, taking the younger girl's arm. "Come along, sweetheart. Vivian, Dick, are you coming?"

They declined, preferring to go with the men into the bar. Maude drove Kathryn home in a smothering silence.

"Don't go," Maude pleaded as Kathryn went upstairs to get her things together. "Not yet. Not today."

She turned at the head of the stairs with eyes so full of heartache they seemed to grow with it. "I can't stay here anymore," she replied softly. "I can't bear it.

I...I want to look for an apartment before he..." She turned and went on upstairs. The tears choked her voice out.

She had packed everything in her bags and had changed into a neat pin-striped blue blouse and white skirt for traveling when the door opened suddenly and Blake walked in.

She stared wide-eyed at him across the bed. He looked more relaxed, but he still needed a shave and sleep.

"I...I'm almost ready," she murmured, brushing back a wide swath of long, waving dark hair from her flushed cheek. "If Phillip could drive me..."

He leaned back against the closed door and watched her. He was wearing a white shirt open halfway down the front, with dark blue trousers. His thick hair was ruffled, his face hard, his eyes narrow and dark and searching.

"The Leedses are leaving," he said quietly.

"Oh, are they?" she murmured, staring down at the white coverlet. "For how long?"

"For good. I went to Haiti to sign a contract. I'm switching the London mill to Port au Prince," he replied.

She stared at him. "But, Vivian..."

"Kathryn, I brought her over because I knew she was the power behind her father," he said wearily. "I knew if I could convince her to meet my terms, she'd convince him. But you misread the situation completely, and I suppose it was partially my fault. I wanted you to misread it."

She glanced at him and away. "It doesn't matter now."

"Doesn't it?" he asked softly.

"I'm going to look for an apartment when I get home, Blake," she told him, lifting her flushed young face proudly. "I want to be by myself."

He searched her eyes. "You told me you loved me, Kathryn," he said quietly, watching the color flush into her cheeks at the impact of the words.

She swallowed nervously, and traced an idle pattern on the coverlet with her finger. "I...was upset," she faltered.

"Don't play games. Don't hedge. You said you loved me. How? As a big brother—a guardian—or as a lover, Kate?"

"You're confusing me!" she protested feverishly.

"You've confused me for a solid year," he said flatly. His eyes smoldered with reined emotion. "All I do lately is slam my head against a wall trying to get through to you."

She gaped at him. "I don't understand."

He jammed his hands in his pockets and leaned back against the door, letting his eyes trace the line of her body with an intimate thoroughness.

"You never have," he replied roughly.

Her soft eyes touched the worn, weary lines in his face. "Blake, you look so tired," she said gently. "Why don't you go to bed for a while?"

"Only with you, Kate," he said shortly, watching the color go back and forth in her cheeks. "Because I'm not going to close my eyes only to open them again and find you gone.

"Donavan," he growled. "And then Phillip. My own brother, and I hated him because he could get close to you and I couldn't. And you thought that I just *wanted* you!"

Her face opened like a bud in blossom, and she stiffened, barely breathing as she listened to his deep, harsh voice.

"Wanted you!" he repeated, eyes blazing, jaw tightening. "My God, I've been out of my mind wondering whom I substituted for that night on the beach, and all along…!" He drew a short breath. "How long had you planned to keep it from me, Kathryn?" he demanded. "Were you going to go home and lock it away inside you?"

Tears were misting her eyes. She moved to the foot of the bed and held onto the bedpost, smoothing over the silky mahogany. "Blake?" she whispered.

"You told Phillip that I had to be alive, because your heart was still beating," he said in a strange, husky voice. "It was that way with me over a year ago. As long as I'm still breathing, I know you are, because there is no way on earth I could stay alive without you!"

She ran to him blindly, seeing only a big, husky blur as she reached up to be folded against him in an embrace that all but crushed the breath from her slender body.

"Kiss me," he whispered shakily, bending to take her soft mouth under his. "Kathy, Kathy, I love you so…!" he ground out against her soft, eager lips.

They kissed wildly, hungrily, and she could feel the rhythm of steel drums in her bloodstream as the pressure of his mouth became deep and intimate, expertly demanding a response she gave without restraint.

He tore his mouth away finally and buried it against her soft throat. With a sense of wonder, she felt the big arms that were holding her tremble.

"I thought you hated me," she whispered, drowning in the unbelievable sensation of loving and being loved.

"For what?" he asked gruffly. "Trying to seduce me on the beach?"

"I wasn't," she protested weakly.

"It felt like it. You'll never know exactly how close to it you came."

"I loved you so," she whispered, "and I thought I'd lost you, and I wanted one perfect memory...."

"It was that," he said softly. His arms contracted lovingly. "I'll always see you the way you looked in the moonlight, with your skin like satin, glowing...."

"Blake!" she whispered, reddening.

"Don't be embarrassed," he said quietly. "Or ashamed. It was beautiful, Kate; every second of it was beautiful. It's going to be like that every time I touch you, for the rest of our lives."

She drew away and looked up at him. "That long. Will you marry me?"

"Yes."

He reached down and brushed her mouth with his, very gently—a seal on the promise. "I hope you like children," he murmured against her soft lips.

She smiled lazily. "How many do you want?"

"Let's get married next week and talk about it."

"Next week!" Her lips flew open. "Blake, I can't! The invitations, and I'll have to have a gown...!"

He stopped the flow of words with his mouth. Through a fog of sensation, she felt his hands moving slowly, expertly, on her soft body and she moaned.

He drew back a breath. "Next week," he whispered unsteadily.

Outside, the sunset was lending a rose glow to the bay, where fishing boats rocked gently at the shore. And in the orange and gold swirls of color on the horizon there was a promise of blue skies ahead.

*   *   *   *   *

BODY AND SOUL

Jennifer Greene

JENNIFER GREENE
lives on a centennial farm near Lake Michigan with her husband and two children. Before writing full-time, she worked as a personnel manager, college counselor and teacher.

Ms. Greene has won many awards for her category romances, and was named a winner of the RWA Rita Award and the *Romantic Times* Award for Best Series Author of 1988-1989.

Her upcoming Silhouette Books include *Just Like Old Times* (Silhouette Desire #728, August 1992) and *It Had To Be You,* (Silhouette Desire, *Man of the Month,* December 1992).

Jennifer Greene says, "I am delighted to be part of the tenth anniversary of Silhouette's Desire line. *Body and Soul* was my first book for Silhouette and my first Desire—so this is a personal anniversary for me, too. My thanks to Lucia and Isabel, for creating not only a wonderful series for me to write for, but for ten years of wonderful books to read."

Books by Jennifer Greene

Silhouette Desire

Body and Soul #263
Foolish Pleasure #293
Madam's Room #326
Dear Reader #350
Minx #366
Lady Be Good #385
Love Potion #421
The Castle Keep #439
Lady of the Island #463
Night of the Hunter #481
Dancing in the Dark #498
Heat Wave #553
Slow Dance #600
Night Light #619
Falconer #671

Silhouette Intimate Moments

Secrets #221
Devil's Night #305
Broken Blossom #345
Pink Topaz #418

Silhouette Books

Birds, Bees and Babies 1990
"Riley's Baby"

One

***

"Strip to the waist, please."

The face in front of Claire was gruesome. A faded scar zigzagged up the boy's cheek, his lip was split and the skin around his right eye was a mottled green and purple. His features were frozen in an expression of indifference, and dead eyes leveled on her, cold and black. Makowsky was seventeen.

Once he removed the blood-stained T-shirt, Claire's lips compressed, seeing the knife wound. The long deep gash above his right nipple was still oozing blood. Swiftly, Claire opened the triage cupboard and brought out gauze, antiseptic and a sterile suturing kit. "If I were your mother," she mentioned over her shoulder, "I'd turn you over my knee."

The boy said nothing, just glared at her with hostile eyes when she approached him. A switchblade knife was curled in his hand. As she cleaned the wound, he deliberately flicked it open.

"Can't you find anything better to do with your time than play around with street gangs?" Claire scolded. Leaning over him, she ignored the blade, working fast and efficiently. Although her tone was furious, her voice wasn't much louder than a murmur, and for a moment her dark-gray eyes raised compassionately to his. "This is going to hurt." She added softly, "Like hell, I'm afraid."

He didn't flinch when she poked the anesthetizing needle through the tender skin near his nipple. At least fifteen stitches, she judged. A little deeper, and the knife would have pierced his lung. He looked straight at the opposite wall when she started working.

"Aren't you tough?" she murmured ironically. "Real tough, Makowsky. Real macho. I'm real impressed. Except this is the third time I've seen you in the past three months, and I'm sick of your face." He didn't so much as flicker an eyelid to let her know he was listening. She continued to sew. "I told you the last time. You like this emergency room, fine, but there are hospitals closer to your own neighborhood. And if you get cut up like this again, you don't walk across town; you don't walk anywhere. Capeche?"

The boy's eyes glittered at her, his palm clenched tightly on the blade in his hand.

Eleven stitches done, four to go. "You hear me," she said firmly. "You can pull that big tough-cookie act on your street gang. It isn't worth beans to me."

When she was finished, five feet ten of scarred, solid muscle slid off the examining table. Standing, Makowsky presented a silent menacing image without half trying. Which reminded her, "And don't go scaring the nurses to death next time you come in here, either. If you haven't anything better to do than show off how tough you are, I'll put you to work emptying bedpans."

Still scolding, she watched while he tugged the torn and stained T-shirt over his head, dragged a leather jacket over his shoulder and swaggered to the door. When he was halfway through, she snapped, "Wait a minute."

His dead eyes focused back on her.

"Do you have cab fare home?" she asked swiftly.

For the first time since she'd met him, she saw a strange, almost human, expression cross his face. On anyone else, she would have called it a smile. He shook his head before striding out. "I never met anyone could talk as much as my mother," he said flatly. "Except maybe you."

The revolving door to the first-aid room couldn't slam, but it closed with a whoosh as he exited. Claire blew back a strand of ebony hair from her cheek. Her chin-length style normally swayed in thick smooth obedience, but this Friday night in February had been a frazzler. Two car accidents. A fire. One wife, badly beaten. And Makowsky.

All of it was typical emergency room business, particularly on a weekend. Claire was at her best in a crisis, but the Makowskys in life made her heart ache. She could patch him up, but she couldn't help him.

A fuzzy blond head with a nurse's cap popped around the door. Towering five inches over Claire, Janice had the look of an aging, bubble-gum-chewing cheerleader. But looks were misleading, and both women knew what an excellent doctor-nurse team they made.

"He's gone?"

"He's gone," Claire affirmed.

Janice pushed open the door, swiftly disposed of the wrinkled paper covering the examining table and started rolling a fresh layer over it. "I don't know how you handle that guy. He scares the wits out of me. He'd rather kill you than look at you, can't you see it?"

"The only one he's hurting is himself," Claire said crisply. "Can't you see that?"

Janice shook her head, clearly skeptical. "He can stay on his own side of town, as far as I'm concerned. I never understand how you keep your cool with patients like that."

"What's to keep cool?"

Janice gave her a wry look. "Never mind. You wouldn't understand. You're the only one on the floor who isn't glad it's nearly midnight, and I doubt very much you'd even blink if I announced World War Three. Even so, you must have noticed he had a blade?"

"Haven't I told you about my judo training?"

"You haven't had any judo training."

"True," Claire conceded wryly, and grinned when Janice chuckled. "Who's next, or did Barton cover him?"

"Dr. Barton's tied up, and room seven is all yours. I refuse to say more, except that I'll be delighted to take care of him myself if you want to take a break."

"I'm not tired."

"Pity," Janice said sadly.

"I take it he's single with all his teeth."

"On this one, I don't even care if he's single," Janice said fervently.

Claire burst out laughing as she headed for the hall. "Crisis, or have I got a minute?"

"He has an itty-bitty cut on his right hand. And I could easily hold his left hand while you—"

"I'll sic him on you for the paperwork," Claire promised and left.

Just past the Triage sign was the small staff lounge, where Claire ducked in to change lab coats. Washing her hands afterward, she glanced in the small spotless mirror above the basin. Dark-gray eyes stared back at her, reflecting intelligence and sensitivity. A smooth sweep of raven hair framed an oval face with delicate, almost fragile features. Her looks were more striking than beautiful, an issue that had never mattered to Claire one way or the other. She was more concerned that the shoulder seams of her white coat sagged on her small-boned frame. Getting a jacket from the laundry to fit her generally took a miracle.

She dried her hands with a wry smile. Maybe by her thirty-fourth birthday next week, she'd grow. There was always hope. Not that five feet four wasn't a respectable height, but she was tired of being the staff shrimp—something she was teased about often.

Winging back down the hall, she paused at the closed door to room seven, noted the name on Janice's quickly prepared chart and pushed open the door.

The woman in her promptly disappeared. She was one hundred percent doctor the minute she spotted the patient. The man was around thirty-five, extremely tall and lean. Too lean? His tuxedo jacket was tossed next to him on the examining table. In dark pants, cummerbund and a white formal shirt open at the throat, he clearly hadn't planned to spend his evening in the emergency room. Impatience and frustration were mapped in the scowl on his forehead.

Claire paid no more attention to his scowl than she did to his good-looking profile. A white linen cloth was draped around his hand. A small amount of blood was still seeping through, but not so much that she didn't have time to assess the patient's general state of health before attending to it. Moving forward, her lips curled in a reassuring smile. "Mr. Brannigan? I'm Dr. Barrett. I understand you cut your hand?"

"It's nothing," he assured her irritably. "I wouldn't have bothered to come at all, except that I couldn't get the bleeding stopped. It was the most stupid..." He was so annoyed with himself that it was a moment before he really looked at her. "I cut it with a cleaver," he said absently.

The last thing on Joel's mind was a woman, and if it had been, the taller, leggier type usually drew his eye. Still, her low soothing voice was like black velvet, and those soft dark eyes held him mesmerized.

It took an experienced eye to assess a figure all but swallowed in doctor's baggy whites. Joel had that experience. She wasn't too heavy or too thin, just curved on delectably feminine lines. Slim hands, a slight tilt to her nose, just the slightest stubborn lift to her chin... he liked everything he saw. And was amused to find her just as intently studying him, when she clearly didn't notice the man at all. Just the patient.

Claire noted the well-muscled arm when he was rolling up his sleeve. He might be lean, but he was clearly fit. Her glance wandered back to his eyes, for a moment diverted by their color. They weren't dark blue or light, just sort of…Irish blue. Wicked-colored blue. Not that she had any interest in his eyes beyond whether or not his pupils were dilated. With any injury there was the potential for shock.

His pupils appeared just fine; he was clearly focusing. On her. From the crown of her head to her white leather shoes, she felt the slow, experienced, distinctly male assessment. His eyes finally leveled back on hers, and she read the jury's verdict. Beddable.

Obviously, shock wasn't a problem.

"You cut it with a cleaver?" she repeated.

"Cutting onions."

Nodding sagely, she unwrapped his makeshift bandage and regarded the angry tear on the crease in his palm. If the cut wasn't huge, it was deep and clearly painful. She looked up again, this time more seriously studying him. He hadn't flinched when she touched the wound, indicating that he was no sissy where pain was concerned. Still, something about his pale color bothered her. "When you attacked the onions, did you suffer any other injuries?" she asked casually.

His eyes danced. "My pride. Probably irreparably."

She couldn't help but chuckle, until his left hand closed on her wrist. She didn't mind—Claire often used the medium of touch to offer reassurance. Still, she felt a quick momentary awareness that had nothing to do with the feelings of a doctor for her patient, and it rather startled her.

"What do you have in mind?" he asked her.

"Just a few stitches," she returned briskly. His thumb was on the pulse of her wrist, moving slowly across the blood-filled vein. "Mr. Brannigan," she said gently, "there's no need to be nervous."

"Nervous? The last time I was nervous I was six years old, with a broken window behind me and my dad standing in front of me. *Not* smiling."

"Hmmm." Mentally she acknowledged that he didn't look the nervous type, and she doubted that he'd have patience with those who were. Character lines were grooved between his brows and around his eyes, lines of a man who'd battled with life and didn't back down. Still, the faintly ashen sheen of his complexion continued to perplex her. And he wasn't letting go of her hand. "This won't be nearly as tough to face," she promised him wryly. "Believe me, it'll only take a minute or two. Some prefer sitting, some lying down. Whichever you find more comfortable."

He didn't bother to answer, establishing clearly enough what he thought of lying down for the simple procedure. Slowly, his hand dropped from her wrist. "You're sure it's worth the fuss of sewing up? Now that the bleeding's stopped, I feel enough like an idiot for taking up your time as it is."

"Not that it's that bad, but yes, I really think it needs a few stitches. Any injury to the palm is hard to heal, and this one's fairly deep." She washed her hands a second time, and then whisked a suture kit from the triage cupboard. Automatically keeping her back to the patient, she filled a hypodermic needle with anesthetic, squeezed a little from the tip and set it on the tray behind her. Perching on a stool, she scooted closer, dragging the rolling tray with her. Laying his open palm on a sterile cloth on her lap, she started gently cleaning the wound.

"Do you always work the evening shift?"

"Almost always. I'm a night person and always have been."

"Why an emergency room instead of private practice?"

Expecting questions, Claire only smiled. Patients inevitably talked off the top of their heads when they were nervous. They never meant anything by it, and anything that kept the patient distracted was to Claire's advantage.

Once the wound was clean, she reached behind her for the hypodermic, still talking in her low soothing way. "I tried private practice for two years, but frankly, this just seems to be my niche. The night hours, the constant challenge, the real need for skilled medical people in crisis situations... What do you do, Mr. Brannigan?" She looked up only because of a doctor's second instincts.

Sound instincts. His eyes focused on the needle, and his face abruptly turned from pale gray to chalk. One hundred ninety pounds of deadweight surged toward her so fast she barely had time to set down the syringe. The wheels of her stool spun back, and she instinctively grabbed for the patient. For an instant they were both in midair. The next moment, she was squeezed in a sandwich between hard linoleum floor and man. All the air gushed out of her lungs as if she'd been hit by a linebacker.

Gingerly, she tried to move, assessing him first for damages, then her. Brannigan was fine. She'd instinctively jammed his head to her chest in the fall. She wasn't faring so well, however. Her bottom smarted, she couldn't breathe under his weight and one of her legs was crushed.

"Janice!" Her voice was loud but deliberately calm. There was no excuse for alarming other patients, and if Janice didn't know that certain tone in her voice by now... She managed to release her leg from his punishing weight, check his wound for reopening and grab for the pulse on his wrist.

By the time Janice's face appeared at the door, Joel Brannigan was passed out between her splayed legs, and Claire was looking irritable.

"Good Lord. I admit I fell for him, but *you*? And if you're in that kind of mood, wouldn't a bed be more comfortable?" Her teasing was superficial; Janice instantly scurried over to kneel by Claire, reaching for the unconscious man. "Maybe I'd better call the orderly—"

"Skip it," Claire ordered swiftly. "Just hand me the hypodermic."

"Pardon?"

"We have a baby on our hands where needles are concerned. I should have picked up on it when I first saw him. Just hold him still for me, will you? I'll manage the shot, and *then* we'll worry about getting him back on the table."

"If it's just a faint, he might not stay out that long."

"Pray," Claire suggested wryly.

She'd barely managed the shot before he came to, and then he made a devil of a problem, trying to groggily push both women out of the way so he could stand up. In spite of his actions, the women managed to get him back up on the table with his head between his knees. Claire sneaked a grin over his head at Janice, when they both heard a trail of very low, very distinct four-letter words.

"I think he's better," Janice whispered dryly.

"I am *fine*. And trying hard to apologize, if you'll both let me up."

Janice looked at Claire. "Still need me? There's a patient in nine—"

Claire nodded. "We'll be fine."

Those blue eyes glaring at her didn't appear to agree. "Dammit. Did I knock you down? Are you hurt?"

"No problem," Claire said soothingly.

"You're sure?"

Actually, everything wasn't exactly hunky-dory. At the best of times, the palm was an awkward place to stitch, and now she knew better than to let him see the suturing needle. Mulling over the problem, she finally backed against the examining table, perched securely against his side, and drew his right arm under hers so that she could lay his palm in her lap. The position wasn't exactly a standard medical procedure, but flexibility was a key word in an emergency room. His palm was secure and out of his sight, the only two things that mattered.

"No shots, that's done," she promised over his shoulder. Truthfully, she was rather pleased with him. Most men would have had a macho fit over a faint. His first concern had been her. Sweet, really. Rare being more the point. "All you have to do is lie still for a minute. Will you do that for me?"

Cotton wool seemed to have invaded his throat. At least the world had stopped turning green. Regardless, his awareness could never be so foggy that he couldn't feel her slim little fanny leaned into his side. A curved feminine spine was in front of him, with a silk swirl of ebony hair on top. And if his hand had no feeling, his wrist did. That wrist was lying between her thighs. He cleared the cotton wool from his throat without all that much effort. "I think," he murmured, "that there's a hell of a lot I'd be willing to do with you."

Claire's eyebrows shot up in surprise. Most people didn't recover that fast from a faint, but she'd already had the sneaky feeling that this man was an exception to a lot of rules. Gently sliding the curved needle under his skin, she drew up the silk thread and tied the first stitch. "Feel anything?" she asked casually.

"Your hips against my ribs. Nice hips," he complimented. "And I think I'm going to need mouth to mouth resuscitation after this. What time do you get off?"

"Midnight. And behave yourself." Two more stitches were done. An outstanding job, if she said so herself.

"You're beautiful," he mentioned.

"Thank you."

"I get the feeling you saved me from a cracked head or worse. By Chinese tradition, when you save a life, it's yours."

"Just stay away from cleavers in the future and we'll call it even."

"Move your fanny back just a little. You'll be more comfortable."

There, he succeeded in making her head swivel around. Those dark eyes pounced hard on his. Feminine, beautiful eyes. Her face was softer than cream, and she didn't need lipstick. Her mouth was beautifully shaped, and colored a rich crimson on its own.

"Are you going to behave?" she questioned mildly.

"I don't think so." Particularly when he could see she wasn't the least irritated. Her lips were trying to hold back a smile. He had a wish—almost a need—to see her laugh. "It takes a great deal to throw you, doesn't it?"

"You don't seriously think you're the first patient who's ever fainted on me? *Most*—" she scolded "—at least wait until they've seen my needle technique."

"I'll make it up to you. You can show me your other techniques after you get off work. Your bedside manner, for instance."

"Hmmm." She turned back around to finish the stitching. "Can you feel any pressure?" she asked crisply.

"All kinds. But believe me, my hand is happy between your..." He added immediately, "How married are you?"

"Has anyone ever accused you of having a one-track mind?"

He chuckled, delighted with her. Nothing appeared to upset her equilibrium. Perhaps that was exactly what most attracted him. "You didn't answer my question."

"You didn't answer mine."

Finished, Claire immediately stood up and pushed aside the table cart. In spite of herself, she knew her face was a little flushed. It didn't help when the tall giant righted himself and kept staring at her. A boyish shock of hair flopped on his forehead, which almost made him look as if he were an innocent teenager. *That* man hadn't been innocent in diapers, Claire thought.

He glanced at her handiwork with a disparaging frown. "This is it? Don't I get a bandage? Some big heavy white thing to make it official?"

She shook her head. "You get nothing else, Mr. Brannigan, but orders to keep it clean and dry, and to show up back here—or at your own doctor's—in a week to have the stitches out."

"Joel," he corrected.

"Joel then."

"Peroxide? First-aid cream? *Nothing?*"

"Just keep it uncovered."

Watching him slowly raise his legs to the side, she made certain his balance was back and that the unnatural pallor was gone. Once her doctor's instincts had been satisfied, she let a little helpless feminine curiosity take over.

She saw the harmless smile but didn't buy it. He had the most wicked eyes she'd ever seen. They weren't just bedroom eyes, that blue invited a woman to do it anywhere.

Dark bushy eyebrows arched over his eyes. Squared-off cheekbones and a small scar near his jaw made for a rough look, not in keeping with the tux. The etched lines of experience on his brow were trophies of tough

times, real pain. He wasn't an easy man to read. The
lines, the sassy eyes, the sophisticated attire—none of
them seemed to go together. Added to that, he was an
intimidating six feet two, and never mind that he was
a little lean.

She found herself staring, woman to man, until she
became abruptly aware that those blue eyes were
glinting knowingly down at her. Just that quickly, the
look of humor was gone and his features turned still.
"Coffee?" he said quietly.

She shook her head.

"That was a serious invitation, you know—assum-
ing you wouldn't bring your needles along."

"I always bring my needles along. I poke people
for a living, if you haven't already guessed." He
was...disturbing her. Swiftly she moved to open the
door. "No more dizziness?"

He ignored the question, just looked at her. "I
think," he said in a low voice, "that you and I are going to run into each other again."

He was gone. Claire wasn't aware she was holding
her breath until it all left her lungs in a single whoosh.
Her lips curled in a reluctant smile. The grin turned
into a throaty chuckle. Swiftly she cleaned up the
minimal debris from his stitching.

She saw more naked men in a week than most
women saw in a lifetime, but it had been a very long
time since she'd felt that tickle of awareness, that idiotic little glow that came from flirting with a good-
looking man.

He wasn't the first man who'd tried to divert himself from the threat of pain by flirting with her. To
take it seriously would have been ridiculous.

Besides, she'd liked him. She liked his blue eyes and his sass and she liked his lazy smile. When she heard the faint whine of an ambulance in the distance, her grin died and Joel Brannigan fled from her mind. She had work to do.

Two

___

"Aunt Claire?"

The tiny whisper barely filtered through the luscious waves of sleep. Claire shifted lethargically, burrowing her head just a little deeper under the pillow.

The pillow lifted. "Aunt Claire, are you *still* asleep?"

Claire's eyes opened groggily, on a pair of strawberry-blond pigtails and two disarmingly innocent blue eyes. "I've been waiting my entire life for you to wake up," the four-year-old mentioned. "I made pancakes and bacon. Watched television. Helped Grandma get dressed. Washed all the dishes. Gee. It's practically bedtime again."

"Is it?" Claire murmured. By the clock hands next to the bed, it was just after 7:00 A.M. Yawning, Claire adjusted the pillow and tried to force her eyes to stay open. "You made the pancakes and bacon, did you?"

"Completely by myself," her niece assured her. She slugged a pair of minuscule fists in her overall pockets. "We also had a robber this morning. Scared Grandma half to death, until I chased him off. He took my favorite dolls and two other toys." The urchin sighed. "I guess I'll just have to live without. Unless someone has time to go shopping with me today."

"That's all he took, toys?" Claire asked gravely.

Dot nodded. "You should have seen him. He had purple glasses and a big white beard and two guns."

"Did he now?"

A quelling "Dot?" echoed through the hall. By the time Claire's mother opened the bedroom door, the room was utterly still except for the quivering lump of bottom sticking up under Claire's comforter.

Nora Barrett viewed the lump under the covers with two fists perched on her hips. Giving Claire a look, she said loudly, "I told Dot that if she even came *near* your room before nine o'clock this morning, she was going to get a ruler on her backside."

"Haven't seen her," Claire said blandly.

"If you do happen to run into her, you can tell her from me that she's in trouble. Working the late hours you do, you need your sleep, and even four-year-olds are old enough to learn a little consideration."

"Mmmm," Claire offered responsively.

Nora viewed the lump again. "If you think there's a chance you could still doze off..."

Claire shook her head with a grin. "Don't worry about it, Mom."

"You're really awake?"

"Yes." Guessing what was coming, Claire affectionately watched her mother plop at the foot of the bed. Nearing sixty, Nora still had her daughters' raven-dark hair and smooth complexion. She also attacked life at a lickety-split pace. Since Jedd Barrett's death ten years before, Nora's first love was her house; following that she tutored music and French, gardened, belonged to endless clubs and cared for Dot. The problem was that she occasionally tried to do those things all at the same time.

"I had a little mishap," Nora began.

"How bad?"

"I went to heat up water in the kettle this morning and didn't notice it was empty. Bad enough that it burned the bottom of the kettle..." Nora peeked at her daughter cautiously but should have known there would be no scold from Claire. "Anyway, it seemed to do something to the stove. The burner element went *prrft*. I'm afraid to turn it on."

"I'll take care of it."

"And while you're in the kitchen..." Nora added nervously.

Claire yawned. The warm bundle snuggling next to her under the covers was poking an elbow in her ribs. She rearranged the comforter and gave the urchin a peekhole for air. A huge grin beamed back at her. "What else?" she asked her mother.

"Something happened to the brass lamp—"

"In the *kitchen*?"

"No, in the living room. When I ran over the cord with the vacuum cleaner, I took it into the kitchen to see if I could fix it," Nora explained.

"I'm getting the feeling I'd better get out of bed," Claire mentioned to the ceiling.

"I don't want to rush you," her mother said worriedly. "And I don't want you all tired out for your date tonight. It's rare enough you get an evening off— *Walter!*" A howling bloodhound turned the corner to the bedroom on a skid, and after two unsuccessful tries managed to lurch up on Claire's bed. His huge wrinkled jowls were contorted with worry, hopelessness clearly visible in his sagging eyes. Claire petted him soothingly, hearing a fire siren in the distance. "It'll be over in a minute," she assured the frantic dog.

"This place is getting worse than a madhouse," her mother complained. "Walter, get off Claire's bed this instant."

The hound buried his sad eyes in Claire's lap, as if the rest of him were equally hidden.

"If you would all clear out," Claire suggested calmly, "I promise to get up and moving. One lamp, one stove, one shopping expedition, one run in the park—"

The dog raised his head expectantly. Claire nodded to him. "Out, now. All."

The exodus was more lingering than hurried, but expecting anything else was wishful thinking. As Claire pulled off her nightshirt, she wondered vaguely how easily a woman could conduct a nice illicit affair in this house. The chaos was so constant that she doubted anyone would notice if she brought a man home to bed. The problem was more finding a man willing to be awakened by inventive four-year-olds and disaster-prone mothers and howling dogs. Her sister

Sandy, Dot's mother, was also a member of the household, and Sandy generally contributed even more emotional hysteria.

Noting a fresh layer of snow on the huge oak in the yard, Claire pulled on burgundy-colored wool pants and a matching sweater. Padding barefoot to the window, she pressed her nose to the glass, like a child. She loved fresh snow. And she loved the two huge oaks in the yard, the wrought-iron gate leading up to their stone house and the old neighborhood in North Chicago where she'd lived all her life.

Still, it was past time she moved out, reestablished her own place. Two days ago she'd turned thirty-four. Since then she'd felt an odd restlessness she couldn't seem to shake. For a woman who fiercely valued privacy and independence, she'd lived long enough without both.

She'd been home for four years, ever since her divorce was final. That same year Sandy had also moved back, with a fierce chip on her shoulder and an illegitimate bundle named Dot. Claire's staying had been less choice than circumstance. She'd been kept busy loving her little niece who needed affection so badly, wading through her mother's crises and soothing her sister, who was still trying to pay back every man alive for the one who'd left her stranded.

Between her family and her work there'd been no time for a man. Only this birthday seemed to have hit her hard. Was she really content to lead a nun's existence for the rest of her life? And though her family would lead her to believe otherwise, Claire knew they could cope without her.

Most days.

Restlessness fled from her mind as she entered the kitchen a few minutes later. Calmly peeling back a banana while holding Dot on her lap, she called the electric company about the stove. The radio belted out rock for cover noise—rock being her mother's favorite—and TV blared from the other room.

Later, over a cup of coffee, she took pliers to the lamp's frayed cord, intermittently removing rainbow stickers from the dog's back where Dot had decorated him. When Nora started swinging a mop like a lethal weapon, Claire moved her repair project to the top of the kitchen table.

"You're taking forever," Dot announced sadly from the doorway.

"The stores aren't even going to open for another hour," Claire explained.

"I've got a list if you're going to the grocery," Nora said.

Claire sighed. She really had high hopes of buying a new cocoa-colored blouse to go with her winter-white suit, but it could wait. And so, she thought fleetingly, would a man in her life.

Steve had been good looking and warm, loving and smart. Claire had adored him. Two years into the marriage, she discovered he loved her too much. He was jealous of her job, her family and any man who looked at her twice. The arguments had been painful, and Claire kept disbelieving anything so good could go so wrong.

The relationship *had* been good in the beginning, right up until the time Steve put a ring on her finger. The commitment made the difference. Suddenly any claim to privacy was misunderstood; he expected to know every thought she had, where she was every minute. Steve made the mistake of taking a swing at her one night, over the idiotic issue of whether her male patients took off their clothes when she examined them. That was the end of the marriage.

All her life she'd believed herself to be a loving, caring person. Rationally Claire knew she'd done all she could to save her marriage. But deep down she feared Steve had been right when he'd accused her of being incapable of the kind of commitment a wedding ring demanded.

And she'd rather smother at home than go through another broken marriage.

Shivering, Claire pushed through the revolving glass doors of the Falk building. Tugging off her gloves, she pocketed them and glanced around. The high-rise building was one of Chicago's newer convention centers, and only a three-block walk from University Hospital. Marble floors and crystal chandeliers dominated the lobby, and the whole place reeked of expensiveness.

Not her normal watering place. With a wry smile, she paced toward the elevator. Ralph had insisted on this belated birthday dinner, but she doubted he'd guessed the cost. If it had been anyone else but a good friend, she would have told him to forget it.

She punched the Up button and slipped out of her heavy winter coat while she waited for the elevator to arrive. The doors opened. Claire took a step and then halted, her mouth suddenly drier than cactus in full sun.

The doors closed again while she was still standing there, biting her lip irritably. Foolishness, claustrophobia. It would have been different if she'd been locked in a closet as a kid, but she hadn't the least excuse for her fear of closed-in places. Actually, elevators and closets had never bothered her until about four years ago.

And she was far too adult to let them bother her now, much less walk up twenty-three flights of stairs because her throat was dry. She jabbed the button again with her thumb, arranged the coat on her arm and absently fussed with a spot of lint on her cuff. Her dress was white angora, and draped in gentle folds from the snug collar to her knees, a simple style that covered everything it showed off. Normally she plucked it from her closet whenever she needed a mood boost.

It wasn't working. Her mood took a dismal turn the moment the elevator doors slid open again. Taking a long determined breath, she forced herself to step into the empty cubicle. The doors closed on her like the sound of doom. *Idiot, Claire*, she thought to herself.

Her stomach lurched on that first upward surge. A fan was pouring in heat from a ceiling vent, and she had a fleeting memory of a movie where the villains poured nerve gas in through the elevator vents. She could immediately smell nerve gas. *Shape up, Claire.*

The elevator stopped two floors up to let in a tall man in a tuxedo. Again, the upward surge attacked her stomach, but this time she was distracted by her companion. She hadn't forgotten him, perhaps because he'd fainted on her in such inglorious fashion in the emergency room. Or perhaps...because he was just the kind of man who lingered in a woman's mind.

Joel made to push his floor button, and then turned around when he saw twenty-three was already lit up. Surprise hit him less than simple pleasure. For two weeks, he'd found himself studying women, looking for one with those same beautiful dark eyes.

He might have known she'd have no equal.

His eyes took a leisurely tour from her head to her toes. A rough day abruptly turned promising.

He hadn't forgotten any of her features. Her face had character as well as beauty. Thick black eyelashes, delicately arched brows, a slash of red lipstick on her mouth, which she didn't really need... But it was the look of sensitivity and wit that captivated him. The lady cared about life but wasn't about to let it mow her down. He'd never yet been attracted to a woman who couldn't hold her own.

Below her neck, other details demanded his attention. The color of her dress should have promoted pure, virginal images. It failed. Next to her dark hair and cream coloring, white was strikingly alluring, and the clinging angora molded delectably over gentle but unmistakable curves. Slim legs led down to a ridiculously frivolous pair of strappy leather sandals.

How could he have been such a fool as to let her walk away the first time?

Leaning back, he leveled a lazy grin in her direction. "Is *that* what happens when you take off your coat? I hate to tell you this, Doc, but that figure is dangerous."

"Watch it. I carry needles in my back pocket," she said gravely.

He chuckled. "You also do very good work. The hand's all but healed." He lifted his palm for her to see the neat line of pink in the top crease. "You coming up to meet my cleaver?"

"Pardon?"

"Are you going to the Top Hat on the twenty-third floor?"

She smiled. "Belated birthday dinner I've been dragged into," she admitted. "My date's waiting for me."

Joel's expression didn't change. When a man grew up on the South Side of Chicago, he learned to expect shadows coming out of the corners. Shadows were challenges, not obstacles.

Claire felt that same delicious little feminine awareness she'd felt when she first met him. He should feel like a stranger, but he didn't. Still, she could barely hold a conversation, not now. The four walls were fast closing in on her. Oh, for an earthquake or a tornado, she thought dismally. Anything but an elevator.

". . . he a close friend?"

She didn't answer, because the elevator gave a sedate lurch when the illuminated numbers beside the floor buttons registered 23. She could no more have stopped herself from bolting for the doors than breathing. Only the doors didn't open.

Joel frowned, punched the Open Door button and waited another few seconds. "Nothing to worry about," he said lightly. "We've been calling this elevator Fussy Gussy ever since she was installed." Drawing a key from his pocket, he inserted it into the gold panel above the floor numbers. When the panel opened, he reached in for a small black telephone.

Claire vaguely heard him clipping out an order. She was too busy swallowing to really listen. To quell the thickening lump in her throat, she glanced frantically around the tiny cubicle for an escape route. The elevator was carpeted halfway up and paneled in scrolled pecan to the ceiling. The escape hatch at the top didn't appear large enough for a dog to get through. *If* one could reach that high. Was it her imagination, or was there suddenly less air?

"Doc?"

"Hmmm?" Her eyes swiveled back to the lean giant. The groove between his eyes deepened as he stared at her, and she was again struck by how incongruous the elegant tux was next to those paganly wicked eyes.

"Something tells me you feel about elevators the way I feel about needles," he said dryly. "They'll have the doors open in a few minutes. I guarantee it."

"Yes." She could feel the color leaving her face. There *was* less air.

"There's plenty of air," he said quietly.

"Yes." The Robert Frost poem about fire and ice zipped through her mind. She'd take either. Just not smothering.

"You're not seriously frightened?"

"Of course not." Nothing threw Claire. Anyone could tell him that. Only her palms suddenly turned slick as butter as she stared at the door.

"Are you going to faint on me?" he murmured. Faster than the blink of an eye, he uncoiled from his lazy slouch and crossed the single step to reach her. His hands curled firmly on her shoulders. "Are you listening to me?"

"Yes." Sort of. His closeness helped. In a way. Her eyes focused on the starched frilled shirt in front of her. His chest was hard and lean beneath it. Like ballast. And like ballast, she felt his body heat, standing that close. The warmth of him was distinctly male, and helplessly distracting.

"We'll be out of here in five minutes. There's a backup ventilating system even if all the power went out, which it hasn't. Fussy Gussy's just a stubborn lady, nothing more than that. No serious mechanical flaws, just a little gear that drags in her door mechanism when she's in a bad mood. Nothing dangerous." He added wryly. "Are you listening?"

"Yes," she said absently.

"We were just discussing elephants climbing trees."

"Yes," she agreed.

He sighed. And then stopped breathing, as he watched his own fingers gently comb through her hair, wanting to soothe her . . . or just wanting the excuse to touch her? Like black silk, the strands draped and curled around his fingers.

His eyes darkened, turned broody. Gently, his thumb urged her chin up. Her eyes met his, hers infinitely soft. Young-soft. Vulnerable in a way he'd already guessed she rarely showed. Don't you dare take advantage, growled his conscience. "Doc?" he murmured.

"Hmmm?" She seemed to feel sleepy, lethargic, infinitely lazy. Was it because there was no air or because of the way he refused to stop looking at her.

"Have you ever had to try out a rather unconventional cure to heal a patient?"

Her mind tried to focus on the unexpected question. "Yes, of course—"

"Because I'm looking for an excuse to kiss you silly. And that," he murmured, "is the best one I can come up with."

His mouth hovered low and then gently shaped to her parted lips. Vaguely Claire was aware that he'd given her those few seconds to tell him no. That fast, it was too late.

His mouth was warm, soft, inviting. She didn't need his life history to know he'd coaxed a woman before, and was an expert at persuasion. Claire reached for reason in a brain too cloudy to care. It had been incredibly long since a man dared to kiss her like this. The heady sensation of dizziness suddenly had nothing to do with claustrophobia. A long-buried need surfaced, nameless and incredibly powerful. Sensuality? Loneliness? The need to just feel wanted again?

Deliciously wanted. She felt her purse sliding down her arm, heard it flop to the floor. He dropped her coat. Before her arms lifted to wind around his neck, his lips had homed on hers again. This time the smooth pressure of his mouth was no longer teasing, but bold, demanding.

There were clothes between them, but nothing to stop the seal he so effortlessly made of their bodies. Brannigan's brand, she thought helplessly, and felt like a licked stamp, ready to send. She'd have to stop all this terrible nonsense in a minute. Where was her common sense? You'd think she was seventeen again, believing in love and in a frantic rush to experience it.

He wasn't a soft man. His chest was ungiving muscle, his thighs lean and taut. Tension and power were part of his build. The only hint of softness came from his mouth, and those even lips kept moving over hers, flirting with desire, teasing with promises that just . . . weren't possible.

"Joel," she breathed against him protestingly. It was time to climb back to real life.

"You remembered my name." He sounded surprised and definitely approving. His breath hovered over hers, his mint, hers now mint as well. "The color's also back in your face. The cure worked," he whispered wryly. "Only I've forgotten what we were trying to cure. Are you going to open your mouth for me?"

Would a mother leave her child alone in a candy store?

Claire opened her mouth with the obvious answer, and found his tongue slipping in, intimately warm, smooth and damp. That tongue traced the back of her teeth, then wandered to her soft inner cheek.

Air was leaving her lungs at an alarming rate. He wasn't about to be content with a simple kiss, and she was old enough to know better than to play with fire. Unfortunately, her bones were metamorphosing into marshmallows.

His right hand was no less limber than his left, in spite of his recent injury. Both slid slowly over the soft angora fabric, from the length of her spine to that hollow dip at her waist, to where her hips flared out in feminine softness. She lost more air, in one shocked rush, when one by one she could feel his fingers gen-

tly denting her bottom, molding her to the saddle between his splayed legs.

Her cheeks flushed. She pulled back, her arms
nervously dropping to their sides. For a few moments, he'd almost made her forget a lot of things.
Maybe she'd wanted to forget. Maybe she'd wanted to
be touched by a man who clearly knew a woman's
body, where to touch, where to tease. To feel totally
out of control, to fiercely desire and be desired.

There were still no excuses for letting something go
too far, when she knew she was unwilling to follow
through. A moment's strong impulse didn't change a
lifetime lesson. Claire had been closed in by intimacy
before.

Joel's breath was uneven, and his heart thudded in
his chest. No woman had affected him so strangely in
a very long while. For a moment he'd forgotten time
and place. His palm reached up, just wanting to touch
her. He smoothed back her hair, a gentling, soothing
caress, nothing more.

Claire's face lifted. His hand dropped to his side.
Desire etched his features in stern lines, and she had
the sudden fleeting intuition that this was a man who
rarely played, no matter how often he would have
others believe he did. He wasn't a man to be toyed
with, because he wouldn't allow it, and he was worth
more.

Confused, she found herself staring at his face, un-
certain what she was feeling or what she could possibly say.

The elevator doors jerked open, startling her. "Mr.
Brannigan?" a voice said.

Joel smoothly retrieved her coat and purse and handed them to her as he exchanged a brisk word with the harried-looking man in a maintenance uniform. For a moment his only thought was to shield her from anyone else's eyes. "How many times does this thing have to be repaired before you get it right?"

"We thought the last time—"

"I'm not suggesting you're personally to blame. I am suggesting that your crew stay tonight until there's no possibility of that elevator malfunctioning again."

His voice was assured, commanding. Nothing left of the tender softness she'd heard moments before. Disoriented, Claire stepped from the elevator, and half stumbled. Joel's arm immediately supported her elbow.

"The lady all right?" asked the whiskered man.

"The lady's just fine. Wait here, if you will..." Joel steered her around the corner from prying eyes and halted abruptly. His authoritative frown quickly disappeared and a lazy grin took its place. He couldn't help it. She looked utterly delectable with her mussed hair and red-crushed lips. "You *are* all right?" he murmured.

"Yes." She flushed. Claire, act your age, she thought helplessly.

"The ladies' room is that way." He motioned. "Believe me, you couldn't look more beautiful, but I have a feeling you might want to repair a few damages before you meet your...date."

Reality came down with a bump. She straightened. "Listen. I think you may have misunderstood—"

He shook his head. "Believe me, I know when a woman is kissing me back." His mouth crooked in a teasing smile. "I'll make sure you and your date have a very entertaining dinner," he promised.

"Now, wait a minute," Claire said irritably.

But he was gone, wandering off toward the maintenance man, his hand lazily slung in his tux pocket, and his stride lithe and free.

Three

———

According to the mirror in the ladies' room, Claire wasn't wearing any lipstick, but her lips were red and swollen looking. In addition, her hair looked as if she'd just gotten out of bed and her dress had hand-prints in intimate places.

On closer inspection, she found the handprints were imaginary. Her body might still be able to *feel* Joel Brannigan's hands, but they didn't show.

Brushed, blushed and reperfumed, she walked out of the ladies' room at a crisp, efficient pace, suitable for a thirty-four-year-old woman doctor who never lost control of her life. Her head was still slightly fuzzy but it was clearing. She should be ashamed of herself for responding so ridiculously to a near-stranger. She also should be embarrassed. Actually, Claire was both, but she was also slightly amused.

She'd been on a vestal virgin perch for four years. Maybe it was time someone knocked her off.

She spotted Ralph immediately, standing by the maître d'. His gleaming scalp was like a beacon. Though he was younger than Claire by a year, his hair was thinning out in a neat circle at the top of his head. In a few years he'd resemble a medieval monk; at the moment he resembled a solid teddy bear. His stocky frame was clothed in a dark suit that almost managed to look unwrinkled, and his easy grin lit up as she pounced on him for an affectionate hug. "Thought you'd never get here," he scolded.

"I thought you'd skip out the minute you saw the prices," Claire teased lightly.
It's your birthday. If I'd let you pick the restaurant, we'd have ended up in a deli."

"What's wrong with a deli? And as far as birthdays go, number seven is sacred, but your thirty-fourth is a nothing."

A waiter led them to the table Ralph had reserved, and they both opened gold-rimmed menus. Claire took one look and peeked at him over the top. "I told you we'd be better off at a deli. You just bought into that practice, for heaven's sakes—"

"Hush, and pray that a lot of mothers bring their children in for vaccinations next week."

Claire convinced herself she was relaxed. Ralph was just... Ralph. As comfortable as old shoes and a Morris chair. Divorced two years before, he'd often shared a lunch and dinner with her. His specialty was pediatrics, Claire's second love after emergency service, and the two were inevitably content to talk shop for hours.

She refused to think about elevators and tall men with blue promises in their eyes. So she'd flipped out for one twenty-minute period in her life? It wasn't likely to happen again. She settled back, determined to enjoy.

Within a year of opening, the Top Hat had gained an incredible reputation in Chicago. Claire could see why. For openers, the menu included a variety of unusual cosmopolitan choices, from Greek to Persian to French to Russian.

And the decor of the place was irresistible. The restaurant wasn't one room but several. A bar was decorated pub style, where a mellow singer crooned seductive love songs for couples on the minuscule dance floor. A second room was lit from behind stained glass; hanging greenery and a fountain made it into a tropical garden. An Italian bistro was available behind swinging doors.

Ralph had reserved a table in the long narrow room overlooking Lake Michigan. The carpeting was red plush, the silver gleamed and the tablecloths were a scarlet damask. A single candle flickered from each table, bedded in pewter.

Floor-to-ceiling windows caught the black diamonds of the ice on the lake. One couldn't see the city itself. One didn't have to. The mesmerizing brilliance of a city that came alive at night was all reflected on the water. To Claire, there was no other place like Chicago and there never could be. On State Street, you found the best of theater and the worst of pornography, side by side. On Michigan Avenue, you could buy shoes from $6.95 to $1200 a pair. Throughout the city people wore tennis shoes with minks; old walked with young; Italian with Hungarian; rich with poor. Jazz, blues, country, symphony, rock, the oldest of love songs . . . music was the lifeblood of the city.

"Are we awake?" Ralph questioned gently.

Claire, her chin cupped in her palm, leveled her eyes away from the window back to Ralph. "Sorry. Woolgathering."

A humorous frown drew his uneven brows half together. "You have an odd look in your eyes tonight. I have this continual fear that you're going to go and do something stupid like fall in love, and then I'll lose my dinner companion."

She chuckled. "*Not* likely," she assured him.

"You think not? Every once in a while I get the feeling you have a secret romantic streak."

"No one could be a doctor for long and still believe in hearts and flowers," she said dryly.

"So cynical?"

Claire shrugged. "Resigned," she corrected lightly. "Reality's good enough; I'll take life as it is. I once gave all that other stuff a whirl, but I'll never do it again."

The waiter appeared, standing politely by their table. "The owner suggested you might like a little wine before dinner. Compliments of the house." He bent over to pour them both a glass of Bernard-Massard Kir Royal, and left the open bottle in a chilled sterling-silver urn.

Once the man was gone, Ralph took a sip of the sparkling wine and glanced curiously at Claire.

"Don't ask me," she said lightly. But she knew. Shivers of terrible premonitions crept up her spine as she lightly sipped the wine. The clues had been obvious, of course: Joel's tux, that he'd called the maintenance man by name, that he'd exited on the floor the restaurant was on. She just hadn't previously put those little details together. It didn't matter that he owned the place, but she was fighting a fierce mental battle trying to pretend a few kisses in an elevator were inconsequential. As long as she never ran into him again, she knew she could succeed. Knowing he was close by made that impossible.

Ralph was still looking at her. "I think," she said casually, "it was a man I once patched up in the emergency room. Ralph?"

"Hmmm. This wine is delicious."

"Yes. You know, we really don't have to eat here. I'd be just as happy to go to a deli. You just bought into that practice; I know you're paying alimony—"

"We're staying," Ralph announced. "I love this place."

Claire felt like throwing herself in the nearest chair. Unfortunately, she was already comfortably sitting. So he's around, she thought. Big deal.

Ralph kept peeking at her with peculiar studying looks. Darn it, were those handprints showing? Claire felt obliged to chatter, which was easy enough. They wandered into shoptalk and stayed there. She was almost relaxed again, until she heard a husky bass voice from behind her.

"Joel Brannigan." A long, distinctively familiar arm stretched across the table to Ralph. "I hope you enjoyed the wine? And I thought I might offer you a few specialties of the house for your dinner. We're old friends, aren't we...?" He waited an imperceptible moment, impossibly mischievous eyes on Claire.

"Claire," she supplied dryly.

Ralph looked bewildered when she gave her name. "*Old* friends?"

"I collapsed on Dr. Barrett in an emergency room once. One of several things I doubt that she's forgiven me for. I hoped I could make it up to her with dinner." His smile was winsomely boyish, making Ralph automatically chuckle, man to man. As Ralph introduced himself, Joel seated his long frame in the red leather chair between them. Behind him, like the devil's sidekick, was a waiter rapidly opening serving dishes. Oysters on the half shell appeared first, then a Mediterranean salad.

Joel suggested lamb cooked in nectarines, a Persian dish, for Claire. Chicken saltimbocca was chosen by Ralph. When dinner was served, both men were chatting like old friends. Ralph, ever gregarious, loved meeting new people.

"The place is jumping," he complimented. "Heard it's only been open a year?"

"A little longer than that. Another will be opening in San Francisco next year if this one continues to do well."

"Can't imagine why it wouldn't." Ralph swallowed, and took another sip of wine. "How'd you happen to get into the restaurant business, if you don't mind my asking?" He grinned. "Claire's always telling me I can't mind my own business. I think it comes from working with kids all day. They inevitably ask whatever they want off the top of their heads."

Joel smiled lazily in return. "I don't mind your question. I got into this line of work through law school."

"Pardon?"

Joel chuckled. "Law school. From the time I was a kid I earned my way through school as a short-order cook. The wages improved as I worked my way up from hamburger havens and into serious restaurant work. By the time I passed the bar, I discovered there was a bigger fortune to be had washing dishes. The Ruby Plate was my first place—it's still going, but the Top Hat's my real baby."

Stop it, Claire felt like saying. He was looking at Ralph, but talking to her. She could feel it. And he wasn't touching her, but it was there again. A purely elemental sexual awareness. Maybe it had been allowable when she'd felt weak as a kitten in the elevator, but it wasn't acceptable now. She wasn't a giddy seventeen-year-old but a grown woman, a serious and responsible woman.

Ralph was halfway through a dissertation on pediatrics when he inexplicably started coughing. "Peppe—"

Frowning, Joel surged up from his chair to thump him on the back. He raised his fingers in the air and snapped; a waiter rushed over. "Too much pepper? I don't believe this. Bring the gentleman another dinner immediately."

"No nee—" Ralph choked.

"There's every need. Listen. You just relax for a few minutes and I'll have a new dinner brought here immediately. In the meantime, if you don't mind I'll steal Claire for a dance in the other room."

Ralph's eyes were watering like an open faucet. One arm frantically motioned them away as he grabbed for a glass of water with the other.

"Not if you mind, of course," Joel said genially.

"Go," Ralph said hoarsely. "Please. Just g—"

Joel's fingers lightly closed on Claire's wrist. She stood up immediately, and like a lamb led to the slaughter followed Joel into the bar.

The dance floor was crowded; the pub-style bar tumbled over with people relaxing on a Friday night. A sultry singer in red satin was belting out the best of blues, and as Joel paused at the edge of the dance floor and turned around, Claire stood stock-still and favored him with a vitriolic stare.

"You did that deliberately."

"What?" Such innocent eyes.

"Put pepper in Ralph's dinner."

"Doc," he murmured, "I've worked like hell to build up the culinary reputation of this place in the past year. You really think I would have risked tossing it down the drain for a dance I could have asked for anyway?"

Claire paused in momentary indecision, which was a mistake. Joel immediately slipped both arms around her waist, and started moving to the music. "I have to go back," she said unhappily.

"Not for one dance, you don't."

"Joel." She stopped dead again. "When I come with a man, I leave with him. No exceptions. And the only reason I followed you out here was to tell you that . . . I know you must have misunderstood my behavior in the elevator. But really . . ."

She was so miserable. She also didn't know how to dance. Joel slowed his step with a smile, wrapping his arms around her so she couldn't falter, making it easier for her to follow him. He'd already figured out that he could never admit to spiking Ralph's dinner with pepper. He'd only been reduced to that sleight of hand when he realized Claire was determined to ignore him all evening.

At least for the moment he had the advantage. Claire hadn't ever run into a dirty infighter who'd grown up on the South Side of Chicago before. "Take it easy, Doc," he said mildly. "Your Ralph really didn't mind about this dance, you know. He was embarrassed, and all but begging to be left alone for a few minutes."

"This isn't right," she said mutinously.

It might not be right, but Joel already guessed Claire was an intelligent woman. One dance was not worth starting a battle over, no matter how much she wanted to fight. In response to her momentary acquiescence, his hands loosened at her waist, and his limbs picked up the natural rhythm of the love song.

Lorene caught his eye, her voluptuous body displayed in red satin, her lashes fluttering in his direction as she sang. The invitation had been extended to him before. When he'd first been divorced, he'd played around enough to know that waking up with a stranger was asking for loneliness.

It might not show, but he was as wary of love as the lady in his arms. Her eyes, her laughter, her sensuality, her natural manner when he'd first met her—so much drew him, when he hadn't expected to be drawn again into a love web. He'd invited huge risks all his life, but it had been a long time since he'd opened himself up to real hurt. He intuitively knew that the small package in his arms could seriously hurt him. But he wasn't letting her go.

The dance floor was dark and private. Other people crushed against them, yet barely seemed to exist. Claire's cheek lay against his shoulder, gently forced there by his coaxing hand.

The man enfolding her in his own private cocoon was a commodity Claire hadn't run into before. Ralphs she knew how to deal with. Flirts, hustlers and cheaters she'd run into, and one man who had broken her heart in a marriage gone wrong. Never before had she met a stranger who stirred her like this one.

It was only physical, she consoled herself. "Sex-starved divorcée" was a sordid epitaph, but for heaven's sakes, wasn't it an accurate one? After all this time, maybe her hormones were getting just a little carried away. But as she felt Joel's lips whisper in her hair, and his hands slide lazily down her back in sensual rhythm, she had the terrible thought that these kinds of reasons wouldn't wash. She'd felt it in the elevator and she was feeling it now. Something in his hands made her believe in love songs again. Something in the way he lifted his head to look at her made her think of the lights on the lake, the loneliness of black diamonds, a city of millions where two people existed on their own island.

"I'm going to see you again," he murmured.

"No." She tried to sound forceful, but her voice came out breathless and low.

"We're going to make love," he whispered. "I want you, Claire. More than I've wanted any woman in a very long time."

She shook her head helplessly. The song ended, and Claire tried to draw free. Joel's hands tightened at her waist. "One more."

"No!"

He looked at her, and she flushed but didn't look away. He could feel the tension in her fragile limbs. Very gently he once again draped her arms on his shoulders, holding eye-to-eye contact until she shook her head with a fierce sigh and laid her cheek in the crook of his neck. He closed his eyes, lips pressing approval in her hair as the music started.

Claire felt as if someone had tossed her into a stormy sea. Her arms tightened around his neck as if Joel was a ballast in a safe harbor. Her finger tentatively stroked the thick dark hair at his nape. He liked that. She could feel the sudden thud of his heart against hers, and felt a rush of pleasure that she was entirely unprepared for.

Nothing seemed real. She never drank, so perhaps it was the two glasses of wine, but she felt as if someone else was on that dark dance floor. Someone who was deliciously aware of two bodies courting each other where no one else could see. Her breasts crushed against his chest, her softness introducing itself to his unyielding flesh. Thigh flirted with thigh, stomach with stomach. The rhythm was slow and the ritual ancient. The man would have her know the feel of him, the smell of him, the difference between her body and his. The woman naturally touched, then retreated, and touched again, each time wooed closer.

Her breasts suddenly ached, as if they were full and huge, when she was small in build. How could that happen? It was only a dance, Claire reminded herself. Yet wanting stole through her body like a slow, seeping drug. She felt his shirt and imagined his skin. She felt his hand on her spine, and could feel the imprint on bare flesh.

Foolishness. Magic. Craziness. Her mother liked to say that Claire could knit during an earthquake and never miss a stitch. Nothing threw Claire...except closed-in spaces. She was too smart and too experienced in life to invite trouble. Yet her body was swaying against his, inviting trouble. She could feel his arousal growing against her, and she desperately wanted this man, and no other, inside of her. None of the dozens of men she'd dated since her divorce. Just this man. Now.

The music would stop soon and she'd go back to Ralph. This was a nice safe restaurant, with people everywhere, and there seemed no terrible harm in dancing. She felt warm, feminine, aroused, sensual, small and just a tiny bit insane. Wariness was there, but so was wonder in wanting a stranger this much.

His lips nuzzled her forehead. "Doc," he murmured gently, "did you just discover fire?"

"Mmmm."

"You can either pull back a little, or find yourself being made love to on the dance floor."

She smiled up at him. He shook his head.

"You're asking for trouble," he murmured lazily.

"I couldn't be," she assured him. She never asked for trouble, because on an emotional level she'd been hurt too badly. But she'd misjudged the man, because his small amused smile died, and before she'd gathered lethargic wits together his mouth had covered hers.

Her head reeled back from the pressure of his mouth. Desire, like the soft texture of silk, became something raw. Naked. His hands tightened on her hips and he drew her up to him, hard.

Music disappeared; soft lights disappeared; other dancers disappeared. His lips crushed on hers and her heart was suddenly pounding. The game was over. The man was real.

When his head finally lifted, she saw his face looking as if it were carved in granite, his eyes sparkled like blue diamonds of wanting. He clearly didn't give a damn if the whole world saw.

When had the song ended? The singer was nowhere in sight, and the other people had already filtered back to their tables. Claire suddenly wrenched free, whirling mindlessly for the door.

As she ran past crowded tables and black-coated waiters bearing steaming trays, all she could think of was escape. Ralph glanced up from an empty plate as she approached, beaming genially at her.

"You can't imagine the tremendous meal I've had. I swear there must have been seven courses; I've never seen anything like it in my life. I tried to make them wait for you, but they just kept bringing the food."

So normal. When her heart was having hysterics. "Ralph, I have a terrible headache," she said quietly. "I hate to do this, but if you wouldn't mind taking me home?"

"Of course, honey. For heaven's sake, what's wrong? You never have headaches."

He was so nice, but so slow. The waiter refused payment, insisting the dinner had been taken care of by the owner, but Ralph persisted in arguing. Claire had her coat on and her purse in hand as she glanced frantically around.

Joel was gone. Nowhere in sight.

She still couldn't breathe until they'd left the place, and then she had to face that wretched elevator. Ralph, good sport that he was, agreed the stairs would be good exercise and never once hinted that she was behaving slightly off the wall.

They soon made it out to the cold street. Chicago wasn't named the Windy City on a whim, and the wind never died down. It whipped in and around the skyscrapers, grabbing at her coat and Ralph's, making them both laugh as they battled through it to Ralph's car.

"We'll have to eat there again," Ralph told her. "Particularly if you can get a free dinner on the house each time," he added wryly.

The dinner, she wanted to tell him, hadn't exactly been free.

She couldn't sleep. She wandered around her rose and cream bedroom in the dark, her hands clutching an old woolen robe closed, pacing back and forth.

Her mother and Dot were asleep in the rooms next to hers. Sandy rarely came home as early as midnight. Everything was normal: the winter moon stealing in the windows in gentle shadow, her bookshelves, stashed with well-thumbed texts, her closet, with neatly hung clothes, the perfume bottles on her dresser. Everything was the same.

Except her brass bed was empty, and there was no point in tossing and turning when she couldn't possibly sleep.

An affair. Would it be so terrible? Then why did you run, accused her mind. She'd bolted from the place as if it had been burning.

She felt burning. She'd run for the obvious reasons. Joel didn't have to say it for her to understand that he wanted to possess her, body and soul. Steve had been a pussycat to Joel's tiger.

Never, she thought. Never that way again. Never where she lost control, where a man would take her over, own her, swallow her up until she lost herself and became an appendage of someone else. Maybe an affair, someday. But not with Joel.

Four

———

"Morning," Claire murmured sleepily from the kitchen doorway.

Both her mother and sister were fussing with bacon at the stove. "Good morning!" Nora beamed back. "How was your dinner with Ralph?"

"Terrific, thanks."

"Where did you go?" Sandy asked.

Pouring herself a cup of coffee, Claire gave an abridged version of her evening to the two. From the other room, she could hear the loud noise of Saturday-morning cartoons on TV. Walter was laid out in a dead sprawl on the kitchen floor.

There was absolutely nothing here to remind Claire of a tall dark-haired man if she didn't let it.

"You went out with Roger last night?" she asked her sister.

Before Sandy could answer, Nora said flatly, "She got in at four. I know because I heard her."

Sandy sighed and folded a lacy robe around her chest as she reached for her coffee. "Contrary to what Mom thinks I was doing until four in the morning, I was busy breaking it off," she informed Claire, but her voice carried deliberately to Nora.

"I don't know whether that's good news or bad," Nora said crisply. "The way you've been going through men these past few years, you're going to use up Chicago's male population before the year's over."

"I can always move to New York."

"You two could at least wait until after breakfast before you start arguing," Claire interjected mildly. She viewed them with slightly exasperated eyes. Though the three Barrett women had the same dark hair and slight frames, their temperaments might as well have been from different planets. Sandy and her mother loved to rewrangle old arguments.

"You need to quit playing around and find a husband," Nora persisted to Sandy.

"Husbands are plentifully available. Finding single men is the tough problem."

"Sandy! You haven't—"

"No, she hasn't," Claire interjected firmly, with a look for her sister. The bickering stopped when Dot appeared in the doorway, her huge blue eyes focused hopefully on her mother.

"Does anybody think this is a good day for the zoo?" she inquired.

Sandy laughed. "It's the middle of the winter, nut. Of course not."

Dot's eyes quickly lost their hopeful look. "I knew that," she said softly. "I just heard they had a giant panda bear bigger than a skyscraper, and I thought—"

Sandy stood up, scowling down at her daughter. "You know that's not true, and I talked to you about telling stories. Now scoot. Back to your cartoons."

Dot's shoulders slumped dejectedly, and tiny hands slid into the pockets of her overalls as she ambled back into the other room. When Sandy left to get dressed, Claire and her mother exchanged glances.

"I can live with her affairs," Nora said in a low voice. "She's a grown woman, and I have to believe she's been raised right; sooner or later she'll come to her senses again. But when I see the way she treats that child..."

"She isn't having half the affairs she'd have you worry about, Mom." Claire calmly moved to the stove to save her mother's forgotten bacon. "If you noticed, she only dates men who have the same red hair and blue eyes that Dot has."

"You mean men who look like Greg." Nora shook her head despairingly. "She hasn't been the same since he left her. She used to laugh all the time, not be so selfish.... Damn!" Her elbow knocked a container of sugar from the kitchen table. White crystals sprayed everywhere.

Nora's klutzy streak accelerated whenever she was worried. "I'll get it," Claire said soothingly. "Just sit down." The bloodhound slithered over on his belly to lap up the sugar on the floor, making an ungainly mass for Claire to wipe around. "And as for Dot, Mom, we'll take care of her."

"We're not the same as her own mother."

"I know that," Claire said soberly, and straightened, ignoring the hound licking at her hand. "But in fact, I've thought about taking Dot away from her."

"What?" Nora raised startled eyebrows.

Claire moved back to the stove, lifting the crisp bacon slices onto paper towels. "It's not Dot's fault she looks so much like her father," Claire said quietly. "Maybe if I took her away for a while, Sandy would see what she's doing. I don't mean a permanent move—although if it came to that I would. I meant more just moving away for a year, getting a job with another hospital—I've had offers. Working the evening shift, I'd have to hire a baby-sitter, but I'd still be with her most of the day.... What's wrong?"

"How long have you been thinking about this?"

Claire shrugged. "Weeks. I don't know. Why?"

"Because it's so like you to be so concerned," Nora said softly, her lips curved in a loving smile. She shook her head. "I don't want to see it come to that—"

"Neither do I. For my sister's sake."

"For yours as well," Nora corrected. "I swear you'd give the shirt off your back to help someone else. No matter what the sacrifice."

"Are you joking? Haven't you noticed I've turned into a selfish old bird these past few years?" The bacon done, Claire whirled around to clean up the rest of the sugar, only to see Dot's woebegone face reappear in the doorway.

"Where's Mom?" she asked dejectedly.

"Don't know. But I was planning on a walk to the children's zoo after breakfast, if I could find someone to go with me," Claire said lightly.

"I'd go with you!" Dot immediately volunteered.

"It'll be cold," Claire warned.

"I don't care!"

"Does anyone in this household want scrambled eggs? I've been trying to make breakfast for an hour. It's already past eight," Nora noticed.

The mood of the house changed abruptly. Dot scurried to set the table, singing as she went from chair to chair. Walter started to howl in unison. Nora turned up the radio for a favorite song and started cracking eggs over a sizzling frying pan. Claire went to her room and hurried into old corduroy jeans and a bulky mauve sweater. By the time she returned to the kitchen the noise was so deafening that no one heard the doorbell.

Stepping over the dog, Claire made it to the door in one breathless rush. When she opened it, she was momentarily so shocked she couldn't say anything.

Cold air wafted around Joel, who stood tall and silent as he looked at her. Wearing a sheepskin jacket over jeans, his collar was pulled high, but his cheeks were red with cold and snow glistened in his hair. He was a dominantly male presence in a household of women.

And then he smiled. "Good morning," he murmured.

"Who's there?" Nora called from behind her.

"Who's there? Who's there?" chanted Dot.

Joel's eyes never left Claire's. Like a sponge, he absorbed the look of her face without makeup, her casual sweater and cords and that instant vulnerable wariness in her eyes—so swiftly masked. "I thought there might be a good chance I'd catch you home on a Saturday morning," he said quietly. "Claire, I needed to see you again."

Eyes wide with curiosity, Nora's head appeared over Claire's shoulder. "For heaven's sakes, come in. It's colder than a stone out there. We've got coffee. Claire, don't just stand there..."

Claire moved, somewhat mechanically, feeling a moment's pity for him. Joel had no idea what he was getting into. Once he identified himself as a friend he didn't have much of a chance. Nora cracked three more eggs, poured him coffee, ordered him not to sit where there was spilled sugar, and made steady conversation about life, the weather, and women mayors.

Dot offered him a hand to shake, and then settled Indian style on the chair next to him, occasionally mentioning that he was tall, that she had two cabbage patches he could play with, and did he know they were raising a live bear in their back yard?

Walter raised enough energy to lurch to a sitting position, laid a wrinkled head on Joel's knee and closed his eyes again.

Claire raised her eyes helplessly to the ceiling. Her family just wasn't shy. Although Joel didn't appear overwhelmed, she thought he should be.

He also shouldn't be here. Like someone had suddenly turned on an additional heater, she felt her skin feel over-warm. Her thoughts scattered as she recalled dreams of a seductive dance floor, but this was a blue and white chintz kitchen, bright, noisy, and in no way conducive to erotic thoughts. The look in Joel's eyes should be banned. Couldn't he see that her mother and a child were present?

Her heart told her she was ridiculously glad to see him. Her mind told her she should have locked the back door the moment she saw him standing there.

Joel politely raised his voice over the din. "I had in mind stealing Claire for the morning if she didn't have anything else planned," he told Nora.

"Sorry," Dot said instantly. "Aunt Claire's going to the zoo this morning. She promised, cross heart and hope to die."

"Now, she didn't either, Dot," Nora scolded gently. "And Claire can take you to the zoo any old time. For that matter, if you really want to go, I could take you—"

"She promised," Dot insisted. "Didn't you, Claire?"

"Aunt Claire," Nora corrected, and then whirled around. "Oh my heavens, the eggs!"

Claire jumped to her mother's rescue. She disposed of the eggs, forbade Nora to go near the stove and hurriedly whipped up pancake batter for the group. That group seemed to include Joel, who appeared installed at the kitchen table as if born there. Claire watched as first Dot, then her mother and later Sandy, who appeared just as breakfast was being served, fell under the spell of Joel's charm.

Silently Claire lifted four pancakes onto his plate, knowing it was a mistake. Food was energy, and Joel clearly had enough of that without giving him more.

"Did you hear that?" Dot shouted. "Joel's going to the zoo with us!"

"Mr. Brannigan," Nora corrected, "and if you don't calm down and behave properly, you're not going anywhere, young lady."

"He likes pandas. Did you know that, Aunt Claire? He likes monkeys, too. And he says it isn't too cold, either."

"Does he?" Claire's eyes met Joel's over the chaos, hers their darkest gray, wary, assessing. *Maybe,* hers said tentatively.

A slow lazy smile spread over his features.

Lincoln Park was nearly empty of people, primarily because most Chicagoans had more sense than to wander around on a freezing morning in February. Dot, bundled in a bright red snowsuit, was riding astride Joel's shoulders. "Lions now," she ordered imperiously, as they left the penguin house.

Joel glanced up. "Don't tell me. That's completely on the other side of the park."

"Please, Joel?"

He shook his head at her winsome plea, and muttered to Claire, "I hope you're planning on enrolling her in a convent before she's eleven. She swings those eyelashes like a vamp now."

"Have you considered putting her down so she could walk?" Claire asked blandly.

Joel looked appalled. "She doesn't want to walk."

"Joel likes me up here," Dot explained. "Don't you, Joel?"

"Of course I do, poppet." He added dryly. "Do you know how much you weigh?"

"Forty-seven hundred pounds."

"Exactly what I would have guessed."

By one o'clock they'd zigzagged the entire length of the park twice, seeing every exhibit that was open in the winter. Joel bought a trayful of chili dogs, popcorn and drinks from a vendor, and the three devoured the junk food from a park bench.

Afterward, Dot sprang off to pounce on ice cracks on the pavement, and Joel haphazardly strewed popcorn to a growing group of pigeons at his feet. A soporific laziness seemed to have claimed Claire, at least until Dot meandered back. Claire adjusted her red angora hat and scarf, stuffed her hands back into mittens and walked with the two of them.

Dot alternately raced ahead and fell behind, occasionally bringing them treasures: two pine cones, a branch shaped like an L, three stones. Joel dutifully raved over each, and pocketed them as treasures.

Except for claiming Claire's arm as they walked, he never let on by touch or action that he had any interest in the day beyond entertaining a four-year-old child and acting like a saint.

As they finally started the long walk back to the car, she caught the first hint of mischief in his eyes when he turned back to her. "See?"

"See what?"

"See how harmless I am? Have I once grabbed you?" He added abruptly, "How long do I have to stay on all this good behavior?"

She couldn't help but chuckle. "For another hour. When you can take us home so I can change clothes and go to work," she said dryly.

"Then we've got a lot to cover in an hour," he murmured. He rearranged her scarf, which was perfectly all right the way it was, and retucked her hair under her angora hat. And then looked at her.

Claire's household had knocked him for a loop. He had planned to steal her away for a quiet cup of coffee somewhere. Instead, he'd been subjected to a feminine onslaught. Claire moved through the chaos with sylvan grace, a serene island—his island.

He hadn't fallen in love in years. One minute he felt like laughing at himself, the next he doubted his sanity. Regardless, he'd been sure if he just saw her again he'd be able to put his feelings back in perspective.

It wasn't working. At first, Claire had tried being stiff and quiet with him, but that couldn't last. Laughter was too much part of her, and he loved making her laugh, loved the looks of affection she lavished on her niece, loved her cheeks and nose turning red from the cold. She was too natural to wear a mask for long. She was natural munching on hot dogs and making faces for the polar bear. He knew damn well she'd be natural in his life.

"What is all this we have to cover in the next hour?" Claire asked wryly.

"That I wasn't after a short night of fun and games, if that's what you were thinking."

Claire's eyes immediately searched for Dot, and he saw the quick color that climbed her cheeks.

"She didn't hear. She's off looking for a four-leaf clover for me."

"It's February," Claire objected.

"Which is why it should take her a while." He linked an arm through hers as they started walking again, and motioned to the spot of red snowsuit in the distance. "I've always wanted one of those. Exactly that brand."

"You're old enough to have half a dozen kids."

"I was married for five years, but my ex-wife didn't want children."

"Joel," Claire said abruptly. "I'm not asking."

"Hush. I'm busy building trust," he scolded. Exasperated eyes turned to him, but he shoved her hat down over her eyes and kept talking. "I married Nancy when I was in law school. She liked the idea of marrying a lawyer, but she was willing to settle for marriage with a high-class restaurant owner. The problem was that I couldn't play dress-up all the time. I like making money just fine, but when I'm at home, I'd rather drink beer than champagne, I'll fix a peanut butter sandwich instead of beef bourguignonne and I wear jeans with holes in them."

"Joel—"

"I believe I made her life hell. So she was a little bit of a snob—that's not a crime but I made out like it was. I was too young and too stubborn and probably damned insensitive."

"Shut up, will you?" Claire said cheerfully. "This isn't any of my business." She'd stopped dead, her eyes averted to the distant woods where Dot was playing.

Firmly, gently, his gloved hand turned her chin back to face him. "I don't want a glitter lady, I had one. For that matter, I've had my share of quick affairs. What I want, Claire, is a woman I can talk to. Laugh with. Fight with, and still know she'll be there the next day. I want a woman who's comfortable sometimes with just silence. Do you know what I'm talking about?"

"Yes," she said breathlessly. His gloved hands were cupping her face, holding her still. All she could see were his blue eyes, bright, clear and so intense.

"No games, Claire. I won't play games with you. Do you hear me?"

"Yes."

He sighed, and touched her nose with his gloved finger. "More importantly, do you believe me?"

"What I believe," Claire said slowly, "is that you're a bad case of heartache running around on two legs."

"Lunch. Wednesday."

To accept was to let him into her life, and she understood that. She searched his face, wishing she could know answers ahead of time. All she really saw was a stubborn chin and more dazzling glints in his eyes. He knew damn well he'd gained ground. "How much time do I have to think about this?" she hedged.

"Three more seconds."

"Yes, then, to *one* lunch," she said irritably.

An unholy grin wreathed his features. "Race you to Dot?"

"Pardon?" Just a second ago they'd been talking about crisis issues. Like lunches.

"Let's see how out of shape you are, Doc."

He naturally won the race, with legs practically twice the length of hers, and he'd also stolen a head start. With an arm strangling her neck and another holding Dot's hand, he led them out of the park. He made the mistake of trying to talk to Claire once on the ride home. Dot promptly interrupted with another of her stories, and that was the end of that.

Joel parked in front of the house. Dot promptly bounced off Claire's lap and out of the passenger door, backtracked to crawl in for a hug from Joel and immediately hurried out again to tell Grandma about the polar bears.

By the time Claire had climbed out of the car, Joel was at her side. She hesitated, and then smiled. "If the household doesn't intimidate you too much, you're welcome to come in for coffee. I only have a half hour before I need to get ready for work, but we probably could both use a quick cup to warm up."

"Thanks, but I don't want coffee."

No, she knew exactly what he wanted even before he reached out for her. For a moment his lips were cold. He'd slipped off his gloves and his palms cupped her face, pushing back her hair.

Her own lips were so chilled they were almost numb, yet feeling returned subtly, stealthily. And his tongue inside her mouth was as warm as fire.

Outside, there was an old neighborhood of stone houses and wrought-iron gates, of huge oaks and elms, limbs gnarled and stark with dripping snow. A car went by, then another. A winter sun rayed down a watery glaze; slush curved on the pavement.

They could have been in the tropics. Her arms wound around his neck, and she simply let the feeling happen. He made the slush and the cold and the lonely emptiness disappear, and he wasn't really doing a thing but kissing her senseless. Coats and scarves and hats were in their way. Everything was in their way. Her mouth moved on his, her tongue inviting love play, and her hands slipped down over his shoulders, his back, trying to find the man through his clothes.

"It would be warm enough, in the snow," he murmured.

"The devil it would be," she whispered back.

"I'd keep you warm."

"You'd have to be on the bottom." She flushed the minute she said it, and she might have known he'd pick up on the intimate implication. His head jerked back, and a small smile played on his mouth.

"We'll try it that way, and any other position you like. Whenever you want. Even now if you'd like."

"Brannigan. My mother is in the house. She's probably watching."

"I don't care if the whole neighborhood is watching." He took a nip out of her ear, then her neck, then gradually worked his lips around her jawline, back up to her mouth again. Her knees were turning into tinsel. His hands slid under her coat and she could sense his sudden impatience, a man's impatience.

She could feel a matching woman's impatience in every pulse beat in her body. She'd only agreed to a lunch, not an affair. But she knew better. The man would take the mile. She'd said yes to possible heartache, on the very faint desperate hope that he might be a different kind of man, a man she could love and be loved by, and who wouldn't push her into corners.

Maybe... He pushed off her hat; it fell to the ground and she couldn't seem to care. His lips whispered into her hair, trailing over her temples, her eyelids. In a very cold world, his breath was impossibly warm.

"I wouldn't do that if I were you."

The tiny soprano startled both of them. Both glanced down to Dot. Standing with her mittens in her snowsuit pockets, her tone was conversational. "My aunt doesn't like that," she informed Joel.

"She doesn't like what, honey?" Joel strove to make his voice normal.

"People kissing her like that except me. Aunt Claire says that's the best kind of kisses, when you hold on tight and love hard. But she doesn't like it from other people.''

"Dot. Go back in to Grandma," Claire ordered briskly.

Dot nodded, and took a step toward the house, but turned a serious face back to Joel. "I'm just telling you. Nobody kisses her that way but me. I thought you should know."

"Thanks, poppet."

In a moment, the front door slammed, letting them both know Dot was in the house. Joel paid no attention, watching the color rise and fall in Claire's face. "I think the little one was accidentally telling me that there hasn't been a man in your life in a long time," he said quietly.

She smiled brilliantly. "You've already heard her tell a million stories. Dot is extremely inventive."

"How long, Claire?"

"If you'd like coffee . . ." Her tone was bland.

"I'll see you Wednesday. Noon."

He drove off, while she was still standing on the sidewalk. Her toes were freezing, her lips as warm as coals. She couldn't seem to move. In an instant, she was going to go in the house and murder her niece.

In the meantime, she felt shaken. Joel saw too much. He knew too much, too soon. She hadn't known him long enough to trust him.

She just, badly, wanted to.

Five
───

"Isn't that *adorable*?" Nora said from the living-room window.

"What?" Snapping a red leather button earring on her ear, Claire appeared from her bedroom.

"Joel's here."

Claire stopped dead. "He can't be. It's only a quarter after eleven."

"Well, he is, and he has the most *adorable* car."

Claire fled back out of sight, and returned hopping as she put on one red sandal in midstride, then the other. Her black silk blouse and winter-white skirt had seemed too plain until she found the red trims to spruce it up. Or was the outfit too formal? How was she supposed to know how to dress when she didn't even know where he was taking her?

"Your other earring," Nora reminded her calmly. "And you can't go out in those sandals in this weather."

"The sidewalks are dry." Claire ran back to fetch the missing earring as she heard the thumping knock at the front door.

"I'll get it," Nora said. "Give you a chance to catch your breath for a second or two."

Claire nodded gratefully, until she heard Joel's gentle low greeting and Nora's immediate, "Joel, don't you think she should wear boots?"

Without blinking an eye, Joel kissed Nora's cheek in greeting, and ordered behind him, "Claire, wear your boots."

With a wry look for both of them, Claire grabbed her coat and escaped out the door. Joel's lithe stride caught up with her only seconds later, but when she turned to greet him, he was staring gravely at her feet.

"Those are the most frivolous-looking things I've seen in a while. Do they stay on by gravity or force of will?"

"Force of will."

"I should have guessed that, knowing you."

"Are we just going to skip hello and start right in?" Claire asked mildly. After a late night's work and too little sleep, Claire hadn't had the time to worry about this lunch. Or maybe it was just too late to worry at all. She was half inclined to kill Joel for being nearly an hour early; other than that a very natural smile had helplessly formed the minute she saw him.

He hadn't made much effort to look dangerous, so it obviously came naturally. On someone else the gray cord jacket and dark pants would have seemed innoc-

uous. On Joel, dark colors only restrained the sexu-
ality that came with the man. Leashing a cougar, one
still had a cougar, and that not quite civilized spark of
don't-give-a-damn was in his eyes. When they reached
his car, however, those devilishly unfathomable eyes
abruptly added a boyish vulnerability.

She gathered the car was his baby and promptly
rallied. "How *dare* you expose her to slushy streets?"
she scolded.

"Nineteen thirty-five Cord Winchester Sedan.
Completely original."

"Ah," she said knowledgeably.

"She's been stuck in a garage all winter, but I
thought you'd better meet each other. She's your only
important competition."

Claire figured he'd spent hours wondering how to
subtly tell her that there weren't any other women
wandering through his life at that moment. But there
was no time to mull that over. Freezing to death in the
brisk wind, she wandered with deliberate slowness
around the car, patting the rolling bumpers, com-
menting loudly on chrome, the long sleek style and the
pearl-gray paint.

"I'm impressed," she finished finally.

His throaty laughter filled the quiet street. The lady
clearly didn't know a steering wheel from a camshaft.
"What you are is freezing your fanny off. In." He
opened the door, motioning her inside with a grin.
"You really are a good sport, Doc."

She climbed onto the white leather seat and waited
patiently for him to come around. As he slipped the
key in the lock, she murmured, "Whew. Passed that
test."

He started the engine, played with the heater, fiddled with the rearview mirror and then smoothly leaned over to claim a kiss. "Good morning, Claire."

His lips lingered only a moment before he straightened again, but he couldn't possibly have waited longer to touch her. He adored her legs in the frivolous sandals, and the irreverent spark in her eyes was all Claire. So was the warmth of her mouth and the promise of sensuality that touched her features when he kissed her. He doubted she had any idea how much he wanted her at that moment.

"I only agreed to a lunch," Claire mentioned casually.

"Unfortunate."

"Pardon?"

"Nothing." He smiled warmly at her.

He'd spent a great deal of time deciding where to take her. He wanted her alone. He wanted her totally at his mercy, but also hoped to have her feel completely at ease. Not altogether the easiest of requirements to fulfill.

As he parked the car, Claire stared in surprise. The weathered sign read Shar-Su'un; the unpretentious building could have used a paint job. They weren't in the best part of town.

"Now, don't judge until you've been inside," Joel admonished. With a palm at the small of her back, he ushered her inside, where he took her coat and then bent over to take off his shoes. "Custom of the house," he murmured.

Claire left her sandals next to his. A very tiny man in black Oriental attire offered them both white paper slippers, but neither took him up on it. Padding be-

hind the waiter in stocking feet, Claire glanced back
with an inquisitive look for Joel. Was this place on the
level?

She saw no tables at all, and as far as she could tell
the building was made up of a series of halls. The
gentleman led them up a narrow set of stairs before he
stopped at a tall screened door and bowed.

Claire hesitated and then bowed back. The man
beamed at her. A moment later she felt transported to
another world.

The tiny room was carpeted in gold, with thick gold
cushions on the floor surrounding a low, black lac-
quered table. A mural of gold-tipped swallows at sun-
rise had been painted on two walls. In the corner a
bonsai tree spread its delicate branches over a minia-
ture fountain, lit with tiny white lights from beneath.

Although Claire was somewhat unnerved to be in a
room no larger than a closet, she was still enchanted.

"You like it?"

"I love it," she corrected, and sank down on a
cushion, her legs to the side. Smiling, she watched Joel
wrestle with a position to accommodate his long legs.
He finally settled Indian style next to her, which put
her within touching distance if she so much as
breathed. His eyes rested momentarily on hers, as
warm as the Caribbean in the sun, endless blue and
fathomless.

She glanced away. We're going to keep this light,
Claire, she told herself. Just keep it light, have a good
time....

"Are you going to trust me to order for you?"

"Maybe in the next life." She'd eaten Japanese before. Raw fish wasn't her favorite.

"No courage?" Joel teased.

You don't know the half of it, she thought darkly. But Joel proved so comfortable to be with she found her guard slipping helplessly. Each course was served by their tiny waiter, who came in on soundless slippers, stayed to ensure they were pleased and left silently. While Claire had ordered standard fare, she was intrigued by the artful arrangement of dishes placed in front of Joel.

He raised a fork with a morsel of food on it to her lips. "Just try," he coaxed.

"Exactly what is it?"

He shook his head. "You'll have to take the risk."

She did, and after swallowing the delectable tidbit, regarded the rest of the dishes in front of him in a more favorable light. Joel chuckled, moving his plates closer to hers. "Doc's learning that danger can be delicious," he teased.

"Now, don't be smug. What is this?"

He wouldn't tell her, but he did freely talk about himself as they finished lunch. By the time Claire was bending over to pour tea from a delicate enamel teapot, Joel leaned back against the wall with a cushion behind him, his long legs stretched under the table.

"Who would have guessed you'd like octopus?" he asked lightly.

By that time, Claire really didn't want to know exactly what she'd enjoyed so much. "I've eaten all of your lunch," she said guiltily.

"With the appetite of a lumberjack," he teased.

They bantered lazily, but Claire's mind was more on some of the things he'd told her.

Joel had grown up in one of Chicago's ethnic neighborhoods. His mother had deserted before he'd started school, and his father wasn't much into working. By the time he was ten, Joel had lied his way into his first job at a hamburger place. He'd bused and washed dishes—and that way managed to feed himself.

From those beginnings to a man who owned two successful restaurants had been a long haul. He didn't talk much of it, but said enough to let Claire realize that he'd learned to use his fists before he'd learned to use his head. She now saw that he'd risen by sheer guts, anger and determination.

Claire also guessed that he was a lonely man.

Sipping from the tiny cup of tea, Claire felt a mix of pain and empathy for the man next to her, although she was careful not to show it. Joel hadn't told her his story to gain her sympathy, nor did he want it. He wanted something else from her entirely, and every time he looked at her she knew what it was.

Perhaps it was the sweet tea flowing down her throat, perhaps the magical fountain in the corner and the feeling that the two of them were isolated in their own private world in this little room... but her heart kept telling her she wanted the same thing. To lean back, to curl up next to him on the cushions, to block out her own lonely past and simply let closeness happen.

"You're very good at making me talk," Joel said quietly.

She poured him a second cup of tea. "I wanted to listen."

He motioned her to lean back against him. "I want to listen as well."

"To what?"

"Claire. You know damn well what," he scolded. He pushed a cushion against the wall next to him.

Claire hesitated and then leaned back, uncoiling her legs and stretching them out beneath the table next to his. If the waiter had walked in, he wouldn't have thought anything amiss. It was only Claire who suddenly had rampant strange thoughts, about the look of his muscular long legs next to her slim ones. About male and female.

"You want a quick life synopsis?" she asked.

"For openers."

She set down her cup of tea and leaned back again. "My life hasn't been like yours," she said quietly. "I've always had it easy, Joel. I've always been loved, I've never wanted for anything I needed. My dad was a professor at the University of Chicago and I adored him. The only unbearable thing I've had to live through was his death. I don't think anything—ever— could hurt like that again."

He drew up a knee, leaning an elbow on it so he could look at her, watching the play of subtle corner lights on the silken strands of her hair. "Med school was so easy?"

"No." She half smiled, closing her eyes. "But I wanted it that much."

"You always wanted to be a doctor?"

"My mother can tell you about the time I was four and dragged home a pigeon with a hurt wing from Michigan Avenue." She added wryly, "Stubbornness is a family trait. Barretts aren't very good at changing their minds once they're committed to something."

He was silent a minute, listening to the lady's soft voice. This particular Barrett was committed to being a giver, and there was the slightest trace of hesitancy in her mellow tone. He guessed she wasn't used to talking or thinking about herself. "You're being stingy," he murmured.

"Pardon?"

"Where's the rest of the synopsis? Like moving right up to more recent times?" Very slowly, he stretched out an arm, and very naturally drew her into the crook of his shoulder.

Claire's eyes closed helplessly. His arm around her was nothing, really. Just a simple touch, with no sexual connotations. They were only two people relaxing for a few quiet moments after a filling meal. Nothing was going to happen in a restaurant.

Still, she could feel the warmth of his arm through her silk blouse. The heat of his side, and the strength of the man. When her eyes opened again, she was suddenly aware of how long she'd been sitting in a tiny closed room without feeling oppressed by it.

"Share," he ordered. "Talk to me."

"Joel—"

"You patch up people for a living. You make them whole. I've seen you with your family, and it's the same thing." He flicked up her chin, looking at her. "I learned to take risks young, but not like the ones you take. I'm not afraid of losing a fight or a fortune, but those things are separate from feelings. You must risk losing part of yourself, caring for people day by day."

"It's not like that," she said softly.

"Then tell me what it is like."

She kept staring at his face. His chin was clean-shaven, soft and smooth, and shaped in a most determined square. Joel's face got a certain look-at-me-and-no-one-else look when he wanted something. He had it now. His fingers were gently fingering through her hair, as soothing as a whisper, but demand was in that chin and in piercing blue eyes intent on hers.

She started telling him about her sister, because nothing else seemed to come into her head. He wanted her to share something that mattered. She wasn't ready to give him that intimacy of trust and doubted he cared an ounce about Sandy's story, but it was the closest she could come to showing him she was a most imperfect human being who hurt when she failed at healing. Caring had its own risks.

"Sandy fell in love with a man named Greg Barker five years ago. She'd just started in the advertising firm where he worked—Sandy's good, she's wonderfully artistic—and he was her boss. When he was offered a job in the east, he took it, leaving her high and dry and three months pregnant."

"Did he know?" Joel questioned.

Claire shook her head. "She said it was over before that. He didn't love her; there was already another woman involved. Sandy didn't take it just hard—she's let it destroy her."

"In what way?"

"She dates any man who asks her—who has red hair and blue eyes like Greg. Only she doesn't see that that's what she's doing...and she takes it out on Dot." Claire's eyes clouded. "It's not physical abuse, it's emotional. Sandy would never physically harm Dot, but she gives her no attention, no love, no affection. Mom and I can only make up for so much, and unless my sister changes, I have to believe Dot would be better off away from her. In fact, I've thought long and often of moving and taking Dot to live with me.''

Silently, Joel stroked her cheek with the pad of his thumb. Claire looked up at him. ''You have a foolish image of me if you think I very effectively fix people. I don't have any idea how to help my sister. There are times I'd like to shake her and times I'd like to hold her.'' She hesitated. ''I've never easily taken risks, Joel. People overlap in life. You touch one, you touch another. I could become extremely angry with Sandy—but then she might take it out on Dot. Every time I touch a patient, I have to be aware that one bodily system overlaps another. You can heal one, and cripple another.''

''Do you know the name of the company in the east where this Greg Barker works?'' Joel asked idly.

''Pardon?'' She was desperately trying to tell him that she wasn't as quick to take risks as he was. Not risks of the heart. But she *was* willing to share part of her life, a slice of the pie if he didn't demand too much.

''Do you know the name of the company?''

''I . . . Fankin and somebody, I think. Why?''

''Because,'' Joel said gently, ''you're correct, little one. Our worlds have been very different. In mine, when you're in an intolerable situation, you face it. There is no other choice. It's a risk that has to be taken. There's no guarantee it would help Dot, but it sounds very much as if your sister needs to see this man again, to get him out of her system one way or another.''

Claire considered the thought. Until Joel tugged at her shoulder and she raised dark gray eyes full on his blue ones.

"You want me to find him for you?"

"I don't even know if that's possible," she said absently. His eyes were like sky, in a closed-in room.

"We'll see." He would try. Greg Barker didn't matter to him, but proving something to Claire did. Reaching out for life was a choice always worth taking. "In the meantime…" He turned her hand, so that her palm was facing him, and very slowly he drew a finger down its first long crease, so lightly that she felt a tickle shiver down her spine. "We see a very long lifeline here. Of a lady who is willing to talk about other people at length, but rarely herself. We're going to have to take care of that." He glanced at her. "We also see a very long wealth line."

"That would be nice."

Very gravely he continued to study her palm, his thumb gently stroking the sensitive flesh. "You got lots of spankings as a child."

"You have a Romany background as well as Irish?"

He nodded, with a scolding look to admonish her interruption. "All of them deserved." Her fingers wanted to curl up, but his forefinger laid them open again. "Actually, you should have gotten a few more."

"I'm not sure I like this fortune," Claire remarked dryly, but her voice was oddly breathless.

"You'll save billions of people."

"Billions?"

"Give or take. You like spindly shoes. You have wonderful legs."

"How long," Claire drawled dryly, "have you been a palm reader?"

"Years, child." Joel's brows drew up in a fierce scowl. "I need silence for concentration."

"Sorry." He stroked the rampant pulse in her wrist, his touch so light she was sure he didn't know what he was doing to her.

"You stayed out all night after your senior prom—"

"I did not."

"Hush. *Almost* all night."

"Brannigan. I had the flu."

"I see it now," he adjusted immediately. "You stayed *up* all night your senior prom night. Not out, up. Psychics don't always get it *exactly* right the first time, you know."

"Even allowing for that, you're pretty hoaxy," Claire mentioned.

"Did I just hear sass from the peanut gallery?"

"No, sir."

Joel dropped her hand. He held her instead with his eyes, blue focused directly on gray. "I see a man," he said quietly. "A man who hurt you very badly...."

Her smile died. She couldn't have said what happened exactly. A valve closed in her brain, and she suddenly felt the claustrophobia of four walls. His game wasn't a game. He'd known where he was going from the beginning, and he wanted to know too much, too fast.

She'd felt the sensation before. A man who'd pushed her against the wall, who wanted to own her mind and who wasn't content being loved with her heart. A man who insatiably demanded more.

Rushing sensations of smothering clogged her head, making her feel half-faint and disorienting her as she leaned forward.

"Claire..."

"I made a mistake, coming here with you." She groped for her purse, and forced herself to face him. Her face was white, and she tried to smile but couldn't keep it. "I'm sorry," she said in a soft voice. "Sorrier than you know, Joel. Please believe that."

"Wait!"

"Thank you for the lunch," she said abruptly. She managed a reasonably sedate walk to the door before her feet picked up speed.

It was foolish but suddenly she couldn't breathe. Hurrying through the narrow halls only made it worse. Low ceilings and walls were closing in on her everywhere, and the only thought in her head was finding air.

She could hear the pound of footsteps behind her, but they weren't as fast as her own. Joel couldn't possibly move as fast as she did, he wasn't driven by these crazy demons. *I don't believe you're acting like such a fool,* she thought with shame. But she couldn't stop running.

She snatched her shoes and coat and hauled in huge lungfuls of air as her stocking feet hit the cold dry pavement. The day was so bright, it stung her eyes, bringing tears.

Bless Chicago, there were always cruising taxis in the downtown area. She hailed one, climbed in, slammed the yellow door, closed her eyes and never looked back.

Wednesday nights were usually quiet in the emergency room, but not this one. Before nine o'clock, there were injuries from a six-car pileup on the Dan Ryan Expressway, a leg to be set, a fire victim and a child suffering from flu and dehydration. Claire's voice stayed calm, her manner remained efficient and caring.

She hadn't changed. As always, her emotions cut off and her mind went on full power when she was working. She had never shown up for work when she wasn't prepared to give her whole self to her patients, and tonight was no exception.

No one could have guessed to look at her that she'd acted like a neurotic, irrational nut earlier. Janice would have instantly said something if she'd seen anything different in her performance. Instead, there was the usual, "Get out of here and get some dinner before it's midnight, for God's sake."

The staff cafeteria was in the building across the street, a quick dash over—no one ever bothered with a coat. Claire filled her plate, settled next to three other doctors at a corner table and then picked at her food.

She was still full from dreadful things like octopus and squid. She drank a cup of tea, but it wasn't Japanese green tea. She was sitting on a chair, not cushions. And there wasn't a blue-eyed man anywhere around who wanted...too much.

Call him, scolded a voice in her head. You owe him that. To tell him it was your fault, not his....

Her beeper went off halfway through dinner. The other doctors at the table gave her a sympathetic grimace. Janice was waiting for her in a side room, a rare frantic look in her eyes when Claire hurried in. The woman on the examining table had a huge extended belly and was panting to beat the band.

"No time to get her upstairs. The head's crowning. But it's the cord—I think it's tangled around the baby's neck—Baker's tied up with a heart patient in two. Her blood pressure's climbing, and she doesn't speak a word of English. I can't..."

Janice calmed when Claire started talking. The woman was tiny, dark-eyed and terrified. Claire didn't know a word of Spanish, but she murmured a steady stream of low-voiced orders to her. Not to push. It would hurt; she had to find the cord, but it would be over soon. The baby would be fine; relax; relax....

A boy.

There was nothing else like the sound of a newborn's scream for life. That slippery smallness, that warm throbbing pulse of life, so tiny, so real, so determined to make himself heard. Claire felt Janice watching her, smiling, when she held the baby just a moment longer than necessary. The child had to be cleaned, the mother attended to, before the two bundles were sent up to the obstetrics ward.

"I need a coffee," Janice said feelingly when it was all over. "What is this? A simple Wednesday night, and all hell's broken loose." She sighed. "I was so scared we'd lose her. Sorry I panicked like that."

"No one expects you to be perfect, you know."

"For once, you looked a little ruffled yourself. Not that it showed to the patient. Still..." She grinned suddenly. "I hate to tell you this, Doc, but you look downright disheveled at the moment. A miracle!"

"Thanks. Go take your break and get out of my sight, would you?"

At midnight the next shift took over, and Claire headed for the showers, dropping her tired whites in the laundry on the way. Afterward, she redressed in her black silk blouse, white skirt and terribly frivolous red sandals. Belting her winter coat, she let herself out the door and paused abruptly.

She'd taken a taxi to the hospital and was without a car. The darkness above was like a black blanket that hovered just above the skyscrapers. The streets of Chicago were never completely dark and Claire started walking.

She often headed north and walked the two miles home. This time she veered west. It was three blocks to the Falk building.

Her mind had focused entirely on her work for the past eight hours. That was the way it should be, the only way it could be if she were to be a good doctor. For eight hours she'd put her heart at bay. Her life was devoted to saving people, not hurting them.

And the thought of hurting Joel went against every grain. Joel had done nothing but try to share and ask her into his life. He shouldn't be the one to pay because she ran into her own personal brick walls. She owed him an apology and an explanation.

The Falk building was open. Claire took a moment to glare at the elevator and then marched for the stairs. She was muttering any number of unrepeatable names by the time she'd climbed to the sixth floor, none of them flattering and all of them referring to herself and people who have foolish phobias about closed-in places.

She rested at the tenth floor. And sat at the seventeenth. By the twenty-third floor, her right upper thigh had developed a charley horse, and she could only walk by slinging her purse over her shoulder and bending over with her hands clutching her thigh.

It was 2:00 A.M. as she turned the corner to the Top Hat. She felt like an emotional and physical cripple and the sign on the door said Closed.

Six

Ignoring the sign, Claire tested the door and discovered it unlocked. Gingerly she peeked in. Only a faint light picked up the gleam of silverware and freshly starched tablecloths. The main dining room was ghostly quiet and empty.

Limping, she wandered toward the vague sound of voices in the bar, and hestitated in the doorway. Two men were sitting in the far booth, nursing a drink and talking low. The bartender was behind the leather bar, polishing glasses, a tall rail of a man with Ben Franklin glasses and a curly fluff of white hair. He glanced up when he noticed her. "We're technically closed, honey, but if you just want a quick one..." He motioned her in.

Gratefully she maneuvered as far as the bar stool, and then collapsed. Beneath the counter, her fingers impatiently kneaded the pulled muscle in her thigh. "Would you know if Mr. Brannigan is still here?" she questioned.

"Sure. In the back somewhere. Want me to call him for you?"

She shook her head. She was here to see Joel, but she didn't want to show up on a stretcher. Anyone who tried to take the bar stool away from her at the moment wasn't likely to live long. The next time an athlete showed up with muscle cramp in her emergency room, he was getting top priority over everyone except cardiac arrests.

The bartender cocked his head. "What's your poison?"

"Nothing, reall—well, water?" she asked desperately.

"Water?" The bartender tested out the word as if it were unfamiliar.

"It's not something you have to mix, Willie; it comes directly from the tap. The clear stuff," drawled a lazy voice behind her.

Claire's head whipped around, to find the sultry singer she'd noticed the week before. Lorene was dressed in sapphire and skin, primarily skin. Her dress had more slits than fabric and showed off a flawless figure, accented further when she climbed on the bar stool next to Claire with a friendly nod. "What'd you do to your leg?"

"Would you believe it doesn't like to climb stairs?"

Lorene nodded. "I get shin splints after working in heels all night. You're the doc, aren't you?"

"Pardon?"

"I saw you the night you were dancing with Joel." Lorene took a small sip from the glass in her hand and nodded a thank-you to Willie. "Since Joel doesn't usually dance with any of the customers, I asked him who you were—that's how I knew you were a doctor. University Hospital?"

"Yes." The pain in her thigh was easing. Claire drew a long breath, studying the other woman curiously.

"You're probably wondering why he told me, but Joel always answers a question you ask flat out. When I first worked here, I thought that was a blessing. Now I think he does it on purpose. Half the time when people ask questions, they don't want to know the answers."

Claire half smiled. "I never thought of that."

"If you worked here, you'd know that one no-show and you're out. He's not much on little white lies, either. On the other hand, you got a problem and he's there, no criticism, no judgments made. I've seen him fuss with a sauce in the kitchen like a fussy old hen. I've also seen him deck a customer who caused a lady trouble without a moment's hesitation. And you're wondering why on earth I'm telling you this stuff."

Claire chuckled. "Yes."

"How's the leg?"

"I think...fine now."

The brunette slid off the bar stool. "Well, come on then. I'll take you to Joel."

Claire followed Lorene through a black door behind the bar. Beyond, a dark hall was carpeted in pale blue, so plush it cushioned the sound of their footsteps. Three closed doors led off the hall; Lorene rapped on the last one, and then moved aside with a sleepy grin for Claire. "I make a play for him every Saturday night. I always have and always will, but nobody better say I'm not fair to the competition. Good luck, honey."

Lorene rapped once more, opened the office door and then disappeared in the same direction she'd come. Claire stared after her thoughtfully, wondered vaguely how and why any man would turn down those lush invitations, then peeked cautiously into Joel's office.

If it was an office. Blue carpeting led up to a computer terminal on the left, which looked efficient enough, but next to it was bunk a bed. Her eyes trailed from the bed to the huge scatter pillows on the carpet to a long low coffee table covered with money. She blinked.

Joel was sitting Indian style between stacks of greenbacks, his feet bare and his white tuxedo shirt opened halfway down his chest. His hair looked wind-whipped and his lazy grin...well. If he was irritated that she'd run out on him at lunch, it certainly didn't show, nor did he appear the least surprised to see her. He motioned her closer with a handful of Hamiltons, looking impossibly like a cross between mischievous boy and dangerous gangster. "'Bout time you got here. For God's sake, help me."

"This is your *office*?"

"You mean the beds?" He grinned. "This is combination first-aid station, quality control room, getting fired and hired room and counting money vault. I haven't got time to sit in a regular office just so I can look good." He motioned her down again. "Want tens or twenties to count?"

She still didn't move foward. "Joel, it looks like you have a fortune there!"

"Gross not net, more's the pity. I hate this part of my job with a passion. Each register has to come up with its nightly balance, but every once in a while I pull a double-check before the night deposit. Keeps my people on their toes, but there's nothing filthier than counting money. You'd better roll up your sleeves."

He knew exactly why she'd come. Claire wasn't the type to let herself get away with running. He also guessed from the rare look of nervousness in her eyes that she was about to apologize and split—something he wasn't about to let happen.

"Grab a pillow," he suggested.

"Joel," she started out helplessly. Maybe if they could have started out with hello and how are you, the conversation would be going easier. "Look. I owe you an apo—"

"Did you take the elevator?" he interrupted, handing her a stack of tens. "You put the faces all the same, and then just count."

She moved forward reluctantly, and just as reluctantly knelt down on the other side of his money-laden table. "I—no. I took the stairs."

"I'll have to move the restaurant down to the ground floor."

"That would help," she said dryly.

"And we won't try lunches in closed-in spaces again."

"Which is what I came to talk to you about. It was a wonderful lunch, and I didn't mean to cut out on you like tha—"

"Thirsty?"

"I—no."

"Not even water? Lemonade? At two o'clock in the morning, there's nothing better than lemonade."

By the time she finished one stack of tens, she tried slightly raising her voice, since he didn't seem to be hearing a word she said. "What am I supposed to do with these now?"

"Wrap 'em." He handed her a narrow tan band. "It licks at one end."

"Thank you." She licked, wrapped and reached for the next pile, arranging her legs under her more comfortably.

"Want to see the rest of the restaurant after this?"

"Yes. I mean maybe." She gave him a wry look. Enough was enough. He clearly didn't want to hear what she'd come to say. Just for fun, she said it anyway. "I'm not going to sleep with you, Joel."

He didn't even blink. "Any men faint on you tonight?"

She hesitated, and then answered. "Nope. I poked a few with needles, though."

"And?"

"And delivered a baby."

When they finished counting, Joel absently piled the stacks of bills in the open leather briefcase next to him, but his eyes were half on Claire. Her eyes had turned luminous the minute she'd mentioned the baby. She clearly loved delivering them.

He could picture her delivering babies, just as he could picture her dealing with accident victims. Either way she would be cool and calm, her emotions controlled until she had the time to release them in private. Through hooded eyes he watched her. She'd made her point. They both knew it. Claire wasn't going to ruffle because he hadn't commented. She only ruffled in closed-in spaces.

"Want to come see my freezer?" he asked conversationally.

"No."

He sighed. "You have to see my kitchen."

To her amusement he put on socks and shoes for the event, and led her through every nook and cranny of the restaurant. Claire didn't know what she expected, but it wasn't a liquor room larger than her bedroom, and freezers that could surely have fed the city through a siege. His kitchen was an arsenal of contraptions and had tools for every culinary need; he even showed her his cleaver drawer.

She kept watching him, on one hand absorbing the massive organization required to run a restaurant of this size, on the other hand not in the least surprised. All of it suited Joel. He knew all seventy-five of his people, and he knew what was in the back corners of every drawer. He didn't do things halfway.

She wasn't exactly sure why she was still trailing after him, but she was. He was easy to talk to and a night owl like her. After a full night's work, she was exhausted, but not sleep-tired. She could see Joel gradually unwinding the same way she did after a stressful evening.

In her heart, she was increasingly aware that she didn't want to shut him out of her life. Every time he made her laugh, he was growing on her. He was so incredibly easy to be with...at least when he wasn't touching. Was it so impossible, a simple friendship? Finding a rare person she could talk to at three in the morning?

And by the time Joel finished his tour it was three. The only lights left on were the ones he was turning off behind them. "Are we going to have to walk down all those stairs, or can you handle the elevator?"

"You can take the elevator," she assured him, as she gathered up her coat.

"What we'll take is a deck of cards. A few games of poker will take your mind off the trip down."

It was a crazy idea, but it worked. Every five floors, he stopped the elevator for a hand of poker. He was a merciless player, and she'd lost thirty-seven cents before they reached the ground floor. She managed to keep her composure until they reached the bottom, although her legs felt as if she'd run the marathon and lost. Her charley horse had also decided to knot up again, which didn't make it easy to fake a smooth walk onto the open street.

A brisk wind immediately surrounded them, slashing open their coats, lifting their hair. It was brighter on the open street than it had been in the lobby. Chicago liked its night lights. Joel's face was shadowed in light and darkness as he turned to her, a faint smile on his mouth. "Did you drive or walk from the hospital?"

"I walked, but I can get a cab."

He said nothing, surprising her. She'd expected something to intimate his unwillingness for her to go home alone. She knew that he'd heard her short statement of intent. But he'd also looked at her for the past two hours in a way that warmed.

Or burned. Depending on the viewpoint. Claire had already decided that she was doomed to feel hot-blooded around Joel. When he still did nothing, she hailed the first yellow cab that turned the corner.

"Well..." She turned to him with a polite good-night kind of smile, only to find him flanking her climb into the cab.

Before she could breathe, he'd handed the driver a bill and ordered a meandering drive through the city. "Don't fuss," he murmured as he settled next to her. "I have to check out my city at night."

"But you have your car."

"Of course I have my car. You can't see the city when you're driving yourself, and I'll go back to my car after we get you home. You're not ready for bed, are you?"

The question seemed to take her remarkably off balance. Joel smiled. He'd intended her to hear the double entendre in his voice. She wasn't ready for bed.

Tonight.

"Tuck. Right here." He motioned to the vacant hollow between his stretched-out arm and his body. "We're going home to two lonely beds sooner or later. Foolishness. Let's at least take advantage of a cuddle."

Claire's eyes whipped to the cabdriver. He was negotiating an innocuous turn. "It isn't foolishness," she whispered irritably.

"If you try that 'just be friends' routine on me, I'll take you over my knee. You know better. You also know exactly where we're headed." Since she was sitting so rigid she was shivering; he hauled her closer, tucking her exactly where he wanted, stretching out his legs with languid ease.

When her cheek brushed against his shoulder, she closed her eyes, and at that exact moment knew they would be lovers. "We're not going to be lovers," she whispered.

"Yes, we are."

"I don't know you well enough—"

"Yes, you do."

The man was exhausting. She should have known he wouldn't fight back until he had the advantage. And now he had the advantage. Weariness was suddenly hitting her like a steamroller. She was cold, and her limbs wanted to lock around Joel's warm body and just secure themselves there. He smelled strong and male, and his bristled cheek was nuzzling her forehead.

All night she'd battled for life against death in the emergency room. It was what she wanted to do. She took pride when she did it well, pride she was willing to share with no one. But when it was over, there was something incredibly seductive in having a man to lean against, to just be held. The feeling of vulnerability was strange, unfamiliar, a little frightening. She was used to being strong. She wasn't used to a man who valued that strength, and yet allowed her moments of softness as well.

"Joel."

"Hmmm?"

The city lights were blinking on and off, on and off, every time they turned a corner. Skyscrapers disappeared when the cabdriver navigated toward the lake, and there were her lonely black diamonds again. At night, one could believe the lake went on forever. Like a certain kind of loneliness.

"I'm an extremely selfish woman," she informed him quietly, her cheek still resting in the hollow of his shoulder.

Joel fingered a strand of her hair; a faint smile that she didn't see hovered on his mouth. Claire was the least selfish woman he'd ever met. "You think so?"

"I know so. I've fought hard to live my life my own way, and I won't give those rights up for anyone."

"You sound very sure that having a relationship means giving up those rights," he said idly.

"I am sure. I've been there." She tilted her head up to face him, her voice low and vibrant. "You want an affair, Joel? If you want to take me back to your place right now, I'll go with you. As long as you understand it's not for the long term. No strings, that's the label of the times anyway, isn't it?"

He traced the line of her jaw with his finger. "Awfully brave talk," he murmured, "for a lady I'm willing to bet has never had a one-night stand in her life."

"I am trying to be honest with you."

"And I'll be just as honest with you. No. Not short and sweet. Not with you. I already told you that." His eyes leveled on hers, not blue in that shadowed darkness but endlessly dark, bright, searing.

She shivered. They were there suddenly, all the foolish things: they hadn't needed to say hello and how are you, he seemed to have anticipated her words before she'd even said them, her body naturally relaxed next to him, when a sane, rational woman would be sitting on the other side of the cab, huddled sensibly against the window. The signs told her what she already knew. She was becoming abysmally attached to his obstinate tenor, to his sexy eyes, to just being with him.

She had to say something, to bring it all back in perspective again. While she was groping for the words, he murmured, "Which leg?"

"Pardon?"

"Which leg has the muscle cramp."

"I never once said I had a muscle cramp."

"As a doctor you should know that a charley horse never goes away until you've worked it out. Where is it, Claire?"

"As a doctor," she assured him, "I can diagnose my own physical ailments, Joel."

The cabdriver peered at her through his rearview mirror. Claire smiled brightly for him. In the meantime, Joel had leaned over her, and his palm was gently skimming over the back of her stockinged calf.

By the time his palm had reached the hem of her skirt, the color in her face had to be scarlet, and thankfully concealed by the darkness. "Front of your thigh or back?" he questioned.

The cabdriver's eyes whipped again to his mirror. Claire waggled a repressive hello at him with her fingers. "Don't," she hissed to Joel.

His palm slid between stocking and slip, forcing her to hold her breath. He glanced up, dark eyes intent on hers. "It's going to hurt to work it out, you know."

That wasn't what she was worried about.

She leaned back helplessly as his hand completely disappeared under her skirt. His palm climbing her thigh was creating havoc with her temperature. All the heat in her body rushed to her thigh, leaving her palms cold and trembly. It hurt like the devil when he touched the muscle knot but she barely noticed. It might not have been so bad if she'd worn panty hose, but it was one of those days she'd opted for garter belt and stockings. Which meant that his warm smooth hand was pressing directly on intimate flesh.

Efficiently he unhooked the garter, parted the stocking. There was no hesitation. He could have done it for a living. "You're going to have to relax," he scolded. "You're only making it worse."

A man's hand was buried under her skirt in a public cab and she was supposed to relax?

"Claire. I mean it. Just forget all that and relax."

He kneaded the huge knot, working it out with the roll of his palm. Claire bit down on her lip, disbelieving how much it hurt, and then it was done. Joel refastened the garter as expertly as he'd unfastened it.

His hand slid back out. He readjusted her skirt, kissed her forehead with lips as warm as silk and leaned back against the seat again. "Better?"

Her mouth was still dry. "Yes."

"A warm—not a hot—bath. And no more stairs for a few hours."

"Thanks, Doc," she said dryly.

He shot her a look, just before he gave the driver her address.

"Joel?"

"Hmmm?"

"Nothing." That he'd hurt her seemed to be her undoing. His touch had been gentle, firm and completely asexual. She hadn't felt so totally unnerved in an age. She knew Joel wanted her, and she also knew the man had been fooling around her upper thigh with only one thought in his mind, and it wasn't sex. Just . . . caring. Even if he had to hurt her to show it.

"You still want to talk?" he murmured. When he turned, streetlights flashed on the white of his forehead, then his face was in darkness. All she could see were his eyes, intently trying to read the expression in her own. His lazy smile vanished, and his voice suddenly came out low and thick. "Hell, no, you don't want to talk."

Slowly his lips came down on hers. His hand slipped inside her coat and glided smoothly, surely, over breast, ribs and hips, anchoring her possessively closer.

The cab stopped. There was total silence except for the gently revving engine. His mouth moved soundlessly over hers, tasting hungrily, seducing the sweetness from her lips. Her limbs surged toward him, hands climbing his shoulders, clenching in his hair. The streetlights were bright; she closed her eyes.

Magic. The damned man had magic. A ripple of fierce, sharp wanting ached through her, so strong she felt lost in it. His tongue thrust in her mouth, stretched to its limit and withdrew.

Beneath her coat, his palm cupped her breast, kneading it almost roughly. Even through layers of clothes he could feel the nipple tauten, and her fingers suddenly clench in his hair. Her quickened breath felt so sweet against his cheek.

His mouth covered that soft murmur that was for him alone. Slowly his hand left her breast to trail up to the pulse of her throat, that vulnerable pulse of life that throbbed under the stroke of his thumb. She *was* vulnerable. He wanted her to know it, to feel it, to memorize exactly how it was between them.

He knew, if she didn't at the moment, that it would be a long time before he touched her again. Claire was not going to have that quick affair she said she wanted. To push her was to lose her; he'd discovered that when she ran out on him at lunch.

He wasn't about to risk losing her, but for the patience that was going to be required of him, the lady was going to have to pay, just a little.

Over and over his mouth claimed hers, not allowing her breath, not giving her a moment to recover from the spiraling sensual whirlpool his tongue and hands created. So dark, so private that world. Like a bird, she felt trapped, wanting to soar, yet not wanting to be freed from the lush promise of captivity at the same time.

"You want I should drive around the city again?"

"Shut up," Joel suggested peaceably to the cabdriver.

"Okay by me."

Joel wasn't paying him any attention, but Claire had shivered violently when she heard the sound of the cabdriver's voice. Joel brushed her hair back from her face, closed her coat, touched lips to hers again and never once closed his eyes on the restless darkness in her own. "I'll pick you up after your shift tomorrow."

She could barely talk. "No." Quickly, cruelly, she remembered where she was.

"And don't walk the city alone at night again."

"Joel. Short term, only. And only if you're sure that's what you want."

"You're off at twelve?"

"You're not listening to me."

"True. Are you off at twelve?"

Irritably Claire jerked forward, pushed the handle of the door and let herself out. Joel said nothing, just trailed her to the house. Her head bent as she fumbled for her key. Her hands weren't steady. He could see that.

He loved her for those trembling hands. He waited patiently, until she had her key in the lock and had pushed the door open, before he walked back to the cab. The driver didn't say a word to him the entire ride back.

Seven

When Claire left the emergency room the next night, Joel was waiting for her. For a moment she said nothing, and just stood there glaring at him.

A siren screamed in the distance; mist floated in from the lake. He would remember those details later. At the time he considered gathering her up and kissing that stubborn look off her face. Instead, he glared right back in total silence, communicating without question that, if necessary, on certain occasions he was willing to stand on deserted street corners in the middle of the night for the next hundred years.

As it happened, it wasn't necessary.

"Damn you," she said finally.

He accepted the accolade with a throaty chuckle, and so the pattern was set. By the time February turned to March, they were both experts on Chicago

streets at three A.M. Some nights they walked the
lakeshore; some they wandered through the enter-
tainment district; some nights they window-shopped
on Michigan Avenue. Other times they jammed their
hands in their pockets and said nothing at all, just set
a direction and walked.

Very carefully Joel avoided touching her. He just
learned. She liked to walk fast, not slow. She always
wore a scarf around her throat; the scarf was too long
and he inevitably had to rewind it around her neck
before it caught on something.

They passed few people at those hours, but those
they did were usually yawning and bleary-eyed,
trudging wearily to an unknown destination. Claire's
step was as brisk as spring; her laughter was low-
pitched and throaty. She took delicious pleasure from
simply breathing and being alive. She loved walking.
She loved the silence of the late night.

She was a disaster when she lost a patient. Joel had
to guess what had happened the first time; she didn't
tell him. She walked out of the hospital with her head
high and her face white, and she walked very fast, not
talking, her body stiff and brittle next to his.

That was the only night Joel nearly faltered. All he
wanted to do was wrap her up, take her home and
make love to her until that aching strain left her face.
He didn't. He knew Claire too well by then. Death was
part of her job that she had to deal with every day, and
it was critical to her pride that she be able to cope.

Instead he'd walked her legs off that night, from the
Sears Tower to the Water Tower and back again, all in
silence, and at an exhausting pace designed to wear her
out. But she didn't tire until nearly five in the morn-

ing, and in all those hours they'd barely exchanged a word. She'd complained once about her tired feet, but he didn't pay any attention. He didn't take her home until that look was gone from her eyes and she was almost silly from weariness.

He knew what to do after that, how to judge her mood by her expression when he picked her up. On days she delivered babies she wasn't above cavorting in the streets, teasing him unmercifully, demanding munchies that he learned to carry in his pocket—chocolate was her downfall, cashews her second failing.

On certain days she wore anger like a protective shell. Unnecessary accidents, people who needlessly hurt each other, neglected children—he knew when she'd had those to contend with at work. She'd fly out of the hospital at a brisk pace. She'd look for any excuse for an argument and her tongue had the lash of a whip. But if she expected him to run for cover because she had a bit of temper, she was doomed to disappointment. After a brisk walk he'd hear that sigh. He always smiled then, well aware what was coming. For the rest of the evening, she'd make him talk about himself, her questions insatiable, thought-provoking, probing. He could cheerfully have strangled her for some of the things she demanded knowing. God in heaven, she knew about the pack of gum he'd stolen when he was five years old and she knew about the first girl he'd made love to when he was fourteen, a disastrous experience.

Joel answered every question she had, but very carefully asked none in return. He'd figured out that her ex-husband had been an overpossessive bastard who'd taught Claire that love was squeezing the body and soul from a person. His ex-wife had been from the same mold, which was exactly how he understood where Claire was coming from.

Oddly, he gained an increased understanding of what their respective ex-spouses had felt, because he, too, wanted Claire, body and soul. He couldn't even deny the elements of possessiveness in those feelings of love. He didn't want another man near her. He didn't want another man to see her face light up with laughter under a faint streetlight, her mouth full of cashews and her lips touched with their salty residue. He didn't want another man to rearrange the scarf around her neck. He didn't want another man to see that haunted, vulnerable look in her eyes when she was fighting to deal with the loss of a patient, her eyes too damned dry to cry when he knew she needed to.

There was a difference, though, in his feelings over those of their respective ex-mates. He didn't want to change Claire and he didn't want to smother her. He just wanted to love her, and more and more he was shaken by how powerfully explosive that desire grew.

"The thing is, Mom, you've got to stop using the garbage disposal as a wastebasket."

"I *didn't*. It was just one of those bread wrapper things. I figured it was tiny enough to go down."

Claire, kneeling on the counter with her head buried in the sink, muttered, "No more bread wrapper things!"

"I won't."

"Not even one."

Nora leaned over the counter, looking worried and, hopefully, helpful. "Are you crabby this morning?" She sounded as if the possibility were utterly impossible.

Claire gritted her teeth, trying to make the allen wrench turn the screw or nut or whatever the thing was in there that didn't want to turn. "*Yes*. I am crabby. In fact, I'm close to downright mad. This whole family seems to assume I'm a part-time plumber and carpenter. What really kills me is that you know—at least used to know—as much about this stuff as I do. I refuse to have you all dependent on me this way...."

Nora nodded thoughtfully. "I think I see," she said cheerfully. "You're angry at *me*, because *you're* the one who's been spoiling us for the past few years?"

There was a short silence. "I'm going to have to think about that comment for a few minutes," came the muffled voice from the depths of the garbage disposal.

"You do that, dear. Do you want me to turn it on?"

"*No!*"

Nora jerked back. "I'm going to make you a cup of coffee," she said loudly. "That'll perk you up."

Claire sat back on her heels, looking perky enough. Her red-checked shirt was rolled up at the cuffs, and tucked into a trim pair of navy cords. Her hairstyle was new as of yesterday. It wasn't a drastic change; her hair still curled under slightly and swirled at her cheekbones, but now there were spikes of bangs on her forehead.

Other changes included a whiff of spicy perfume around her throat and wrists, and a little more attention to makeup than she usually bothered with. It had recently occurred to Claire that over the past few years, she just might have let herself go. Not taken enough pride in her appearance, not fussed to make herself as attractive as she could be.

The little changes were only for herself, and had nothing to do with Joel...in fact, she was pleased as punch that Joel was keeping his hands to himself. For the first time in her life she'd found a man she could love as a friend. She could actually give-and-take talk to Joel. She could play with and laugh with him, and he didn't try to take her over. She could be totally natural with him.

Their time together had been irreplaceably special, only it was slightly disconcerting for a man to make it very clear he wanted you, and then never make a single pass. Maybe once he'd gotten to know her, he'd no longer felt the attraction. Maybe he'd discovered she was just ordinary looking, drab, a sexually unappealing woman.

Then why the devil couldn't *she* stop feeling the chemistry? She wanted their friendship. But over the past few weeks, when his hand had accidentally touched her shoulder, or the small of her back, or her own hand, she'd felt a voltage overload that would have threatened the stability of Hoover Dam.

Claire's well-ordered world was tipping, and she was *not* happy. Frowning, she bent over and gave the screw one last furious turn with the allen wrench. Success! It budged. With a deliriously relieved sigh, she sat back again, ran the water and turned on the disposal.

It gave its normal, gruesome grating noise. Dot and Nora offered a round of applause from the other side of the kitchen. Walter started howling, and the noise momentarily blocked out the sound of a rap on the door.

Joel turned the knob, now knowing better than to wait for anyone in the household to hear him. Dot immediately hurled herself at him, and Nora followed directly thereafter.

Claire rocked back on her heels, smiling in spite of herself. Before he'd even considered taking off his coat, he saved the whistling kettle from overflowing, whisked Dot in his arms and went over to the cupboard, allowing her to remove his favorite mug.

"I came to take my favorite girl out to lunch," he told Dot.

"Me?"

"You. At my place. If you want to come."

"Sure, Joel!"

"Mr. Brannigan," Nora automatically corrected.

He got his coffee and seated himself, listening to a double conversation about the movie Nora had seen the night before and the elephant Dot had recently purchased on a trip to Africa.

The moment he had the chance his eyes skimmed over Claire. Her feet were delectably bare. He noticed the new fringe of bangs on her forehead, the movement of her breasts beneath the soft flannel shirt, the sexy curve of fanny outlined in her jeans and the soft natural red of her lips.

His reaction was immediate and physical, and he decided it wasn't wise to take off his coat after all. Somehow he didn't think Claire's mother would approve of the bulge in the front of his jeans at the moment. He flashed a familiar, easygoing smile in Claire's direction.

"How come you want me to go to lunch with you?" Dot, perched on the table facing him, bit down on a cookie.

"No reason. Just seemed like a good idea for some company on a Saturday morning."

"But Aunt Claire hasn't seen where you live, either."

"Aunt Claire might not want to see my place."

"Did you ask her?"

"Aunt Claire..." Joel drawled. "Do you want to come home with us for peanut butter sandwiches?" Before she had the chance to answer, he whispered to Dot, "Hustle off and ask your mother if it's okay if you can go."

Dot raised her tiny eyebrows. "Why? She never cares what I do. She won't even notice if I'm gone."

The tiniest silence invaded the kitchen. Then Claire rushed over and planted a kiss on the urchin's forehead. "That's not true, darling," she said lightly. "Your mom cares very much. Everybody just shows caring in different ways."

Her eyes met Joel's, mirroring her distress for Dot. On another level entirely, she noted the spark of vibrance in his eyes, the brawny shoulders in his sheepskin jacket, the male aura he brought in with him that always made her feel so utterly dwarfed and ridiculously feminine.

He didn't seem to notice her new hairstyle, much less pay any more attention to her than to Dot.

In short order, she pulled on her wool socks, heavy shoes and jacket. A month before, she'd have thought twice before accepting an invitation to the wolf's den.

Now, she had the depressing thought that she'd have been safe even without Dot's chaperonage.

Dot and Joel popped out through the door first, leaving her to trail after them lickety-split. She was left to open her own car door, and invited to the back seat while the other two took the front.

For two cents, though, she'd kiss him for the attention he paid to Dot. The little girl was eating up his attentions, absorbing them like a sponge. Joel was careful to keep the relationship casual, as if he knew how badly Dot could be hurt by a male figure in her life who couldn't be there permanently, but he extended love and laughter to the little one in a way that warmed Claire's heart.

For a buck, she'd also kill him. She was distinctly being treated like a friend. Hell's bells, she'd hardly been neutered.

And she hated sitting in the back seat.

Joel and Dot finished the mad race up the nine flights of stairs first, then both waited patiently for Claire to make a panting third. "We could have beat her even if she took the elevator, couldn't we have, Joel?" Dot said smugly.

"Now, the only thing we don't tease your aunt about is elevators, sweet." Joel turned the key, opened the door and ushered the two of them in. "How about if we let Claire just relax and wander around a little, while you and I make lunch?"

"A surprise?" Dot pleaded.

"A total surprise," Joel agreed. "And your aunt may not come into the kitchen until we've finished."

From the corner of his eye, he could see Claire's increasingly unsettled expression, before he disappeared into the kitchen with the four-year-old. Behind the closed door, he chuckled aloud, making Dot look at him curiously.

It wasn't something he could exactly explain to the youngster, but the lamb had willingly come to the wolf's den.

Claire dropped her jacket on a chair, flicked her hair back and looked around. She glanced once at the closed door to the kitchen with a rueful grimace, and then shrugged.

Being ignored had at least one side benefit. For a month a little bug of feminine curiosity had been driving her nuts, wondering what Joel's place looked like. His condo was on the ninth floor of a contemporary high rise, overlooking the Chicago River. That much, perhaps, she'd expected. Joel loved the city, and it was no surprise he lived in its heart.

His living-room furnishings rather startled her, though. He'd paid no decorator for a perfectionist decor. She wandered, touching things absently.

The huge room was a contrast of textures from the richness of thick cream-colored carpet to the roughness of stuccoed walls. The corner fireplace was stone; around it were shelves in soft polished teak. The huge couch was a summer-leaf green, with cushions so thick a woman could drown in them. Old blended with new. He had one of those TV screens that took up an entire wall, but on his bookshelves he had old editions, a group of pewter sculptures and—good heavens—an honest-to-goodness etching collection.

Her fingers drew back as if burned. Slinging them more safely in her pocket, Claire decided she would politely sit and wait for the other two. And then promptly got up and wandered toward the bathroom, not because she was giving in to any more curiosity but because her hair needed a brush.

She brushed and rebrushed, looking around. Behind her was a sunken tub, scarlet red, big enough for two if not three. A hedonist's dream. Huge red towels looked softer than blankets, and each would certainly have wrapped around her twice. Shoving the brush back in her purse, she hesitated, for some idiotic reason not wanting to leave the room. It smelled so much like Joel, like his soap and shampoo and after-shave. She had a sudden terrible craving to know what brand of toothpaste he used, and wondered vaguely what was wrong with her lately. The details of Joel's personal life were none of her business. Only lovesick teenagers had obsessive needs to know those itty-bitty things.

The craving persisted. To divert herself, she stepped on his scale and nearly choked when the scale talked to her. "See a doctor immediately," droned the voice. "You have lost eighty-three pounds since yesterday."

Flushed, she fled from the bathroom, again glancing toward the kitchen. The door was still closed. She relaxed. No more snooping, Claire, she thought.

Between the doors to the bathroom and the living room was a half-open door; she didn't step in, just looked. This was his office, with a desk, papers piled everywhere, and machines from a computer to a calculator. He worked too hard, she reflected absently, then she jumped when she heard Joel's voice from behind her.

Her head whipped around to see him bearing down on her with a four-year-old in tow. His eyes had a flash of sheer wicked amusement, a glint of something private and fleeting passing between them that startled Claire. The next instant, he was murmuring about Dot. "We're eating in the bedroom. Your niece has informed me that she's never allowed to get crumbs in bed. In this house, she's allowed to get crumbs in bed."

"Ah." Claire nodded sagely, following the two of them to the far door. "You know, you told me to look around," she said uncomfortably. "I hope you didn't mind?"

"Course he doesn't mind, Aunt Claire," Dot scolded with a giggle. "That's why he brought us here, to see everything. I love it," she told Joel. "So does Aunt Claire. You want us to come live with you here?"

"I..." Joel cleared his throat. "Your grandma would miss you too much."

"She could come, too."

Claire figured Joel could handle his way around most women, even persuasive four-year-old ones. She left him to it, staring in surprise at his bedroom. The carpet was scarlet and a huge bed took up the center of the room. That was all there was. A bed. Mirrored closets evidently hid his clothes and everything else. French doors led to a balcony overlooking the river, which would have drawn her attention at any other time. As it was, all that filled her vision was that bed. And in a moment the huge tray in the middle of it,

followed by a reclining Joel and an urchin sitting Indian style.

"Come on," Dot said impatiently.

The spread looked like scarlet velvet, and most unused to crumbs. Furthermore, there was very little
room for Claire to sit where she wasn't touching Joel.
She slipped off her shoes and gingerly climbed on, not
wanting to spill the three glasses of lemonade on the
tray. Joel regarded her with dancing eyes, his stocking foot patting her fanny closer.

"You're going to fall sitting that close to the edge,"
he said mildly.

"This is . . . quite a lunch," she said dryly.

A bowl of mixed cashews and raisins appeared to be
the main course. Glistening wet red grapes were the
appetizer. Tiny pieces of bread had been haphazardly
adorned with cheeses—Dot style, Claire suspected.
"Sbrinz is Swiss," Joel told her. "The kashkaval is a
salty, Yugoslav cheese. Gorgonzola's Italian, the
samsoe's Danish; Gouda's Dutch. And of course Brie.
Dot told me she's sick to death of eating food that's
good for her, so we went for a junk-food lunch."

He knew very well it wasn't a junk-food lunch. She
wondered whether he also knew that his ankle was
pressing against her bottom, and then thought irritably, of course he knew. It just meant nothing to him.

"Don't worry about crumbs," Dot piped up.

"I won't."

"You have to try everything. If you don't like it, you
can go in the bathroom and spit it out, but you have
to try everything." Dot flopped on her stomach, her
cheeks bulging. "I think that's a lot better rule than
having to finish everything on your plate no matter

what. Nobody should have to finish broccoli, Joel says.''

"In his house, we live by Joel's rules. In our house, we live by Grandma's rules," Claire said mildly.

"Joel has other rules. Want to hear?"

"Definitely."

"Nobody touches his knife drawer."

"A good rule."

"You can jump on the couch as long as your shoes are off."

"Another good rule."

"You can open any cupboard and look at anything you want and he doesn't care how many questions you have. He says that's an important rule. That there's no question you can't ask." Dot dribbled another handful of nuts and raisins into her mouth. "And there's another important rule. Before you start to cry after you spill a glass of lemonade, you have to give him a hug."

Claire asked gravely, "How many hugs did you have to give Joel?"

"Three."

"Was Joel crying?"

"What?"

"Nothing, poppet." Do you want me to mop your floor, she mouthed at him.

No, he mouthed back. Halfway through the meal, Dot wandered off to explore, coming back every minute or two to grab another handful of food. "I found him," Joel told her quietly, when the child was out of hearing range.

"Who?"

"Dot's father. He's moved twice from the address where your sister believed he was living. It took some time to track him down." Joel dusted the crumbs from his hands onto the tray. "Minnesota. Unmarried. Doing well for himself."

For a moment she felt overwhelmed. She'd forgotten his offer to do that. She was touched by the trouble he'd gone to and bewildered at what to do with the information now that she had it. For a moment, she even forgot that she hadn't asked a man's opinion on anything in years. "You really think it would help if she saw him again?"

"Has the situation gotten better between Dot and your sister?"

Claire shook her head sadly. "She seems determined to let a mistake with one man affect her whole life. She's smart enough to know better than that, but..."

Her voice trailed off. Joel thought roughly that Claire, too, was smart enough to know better than to let one man's mistakes haunt her. Only "smart enough" had nothing to do with emotions. "From everything you've told me, it's past time your sister tried to lay her ghosts," Joel asked quietly. "What can she lose?"

After a moment, Claire said, "Nothing." And added sadly, "But she has a daughter to lose if nothing changes."

"You're still thinking of taking the child away?"

She nodded. "Legally if I have to," she said unhappily.

"Maybe you will have to," he said gently, "but it could just be that Sandy'll turn herself around if she has to face what's really been bothering her. I think it's worth a try, Claire, but no matter what…stop it. The worrying about Dot. She'll be fine. That child will never hurt for love as long as you're in her world.''

There was something in his face, a fierce look of protective tenderness—but it was gone, so quickly. He moved, averting his eyes as he put the lunch tray on the carpet. Before he'd straightened up Dot had popped back into the room, bounded to the bed and attacked him. Joel was ticklish. Claire wasn't quite sure how she was cajoled into joining them…actually, Joel demanded that she save him.

She wasn't so inclined. Dot held his hands while she skimmed fingers up and down his sides. The situation deteriorated badly. His arm snaked out to grab her, and before she could protest she was flat on her stomach with a wallop of a spank on her backside. Dot thought that hilarious. She thought it even more hilarious when Joel flipped her over, straddled her thighs, and ordered Dot to hold her hands above her head so he could tickle her.

Only he didn't tickle her. Claire was laughing, breathless, so were the other two. Her blouse had untucked and her hair was disheveled, her lipstick worn off and she was pleading in gasps for mercy.

Only like a clock suddenly ticked in slow motion, she saw only Joel's eyes for a few seconds. She felt the weight of him on her thighs. She saw him leaning over her, her breasts protruding up for him as Dot held her hands, and she saw his eyes, devil blue, inches from hers.

In that instant, she knew exactly how it would be if he made love with her. The weight of him. The feel of the mattress beneath her, the disheveled look to his hair and the flush on his face and that searing blue in his eyes.

The moment was gone. Dot, disappointed, lamented loudly that he'd failed to tickle Claire silly as the two traipsed to the kitchen with the lunch tray. Glancing at her watch with slightly shaky hands, Claire hurriedly joined the clean-up crew. Both she and Joel had their heaviest work days on Saturdays, and now they would both be late.

Less than ten minutes later the three were in their coats, and at the door, Joel put his hand on the knob and then shook his head. "I've got one more important rule I forgot to tell you about," he told Dot.

"What?"

"I get a kiss for lunch or nobody gets to leave."

Dot, giggling, threw herself in his arms, and planted a resounding smack on his cheek. "You want two?"

"When they're that good, yes."

He got two. Dot slid down and then looked expectantly at Claire. "Hurry up," she prodded.

Claire, smiling, shoved her purse to her shoulder and lifted her arms to Joel's neck. Only Joel didn't return the smile. And when she would have laid gentle lips against his, she felt her neck reel back from the quick pressure of his mouth.

For a month he hadn't touched her. For a month she'd dreamed of magic and there it was again, that sweet ache, his special taste, that promise of incredibly delicious wicked sensuality. Her fingers tightened at his nape; her eyes helplessly closed. Darkness enfolded her.

It was over too fast, far too fast. Joel lifted his head, and said mildly to Dot, "Was that good enough, or does she have to do it again?"

"She can't help it if she can't kiss as good as me," Dot told him.

"True."

Had he felt a damn thing, or was it a game? Claire ran a rough hand through her hair on the way to his car, feeling disoriented and restless.

"Is it okay with you if I ask Aunt Claire to come over next Tuesday to watch a football game?" Joel asked Dot.

"I hate football."

"That's why I thought I'd just ask your Aunt Claire."

"Aunt Claire," Claire mentioned, "happens to like football. Only it's a little difficult to watch at the end of March."

"Not with a VCR. The Super Bowl. I taped it because I was working—"

"I was working, too."

"Tuesday's Aunt Claire's day off," Dot mentioned.

"Exactly why I thought she'd consider it." Joel's eyes met hers in the rearview mirror.

"Fine," Claire said. There was no reason at all for her voice to sound irritated. She loved football. She also, to her dismay, loved Joel.

And no man, ever, had confused her as much as this one did.

Eight

―――

"Brannigan, I swear you're an overgrown child."

Joel violently shook the pan on the stove to the rhythm of kernels popping. "You can't watch the Super Bowl without Coors and popcorn," he insisted.

Claire shook her head in despair. "And to think when I first saw you I thought you were this suave, debonair, sophisticated man."

"I fainted all over you when you first saw me."

"The first minute I saw you, you were wearing a tux and still looking fairly cool. Now look at you."

He ignored her comment and grinned. A holey black sweatshirt stretched over his shoulders, matched by a renegade pair of jeans that were so faded they should have made the ragbag. "I noticed the lady was in a real formal mood herself."

"You can't watch the Super Bowl with your shoes on," she informed him loftily.

"Socks either?"

She was too busy to answer. As fast as the popcorn popped its last kernel Joel was pouring it in a bowl. She'd barely added the melted butter and collected two beers before Joel was headed toward the living room. Seconds later they were both stretched out on the carpet, pillows stashed behind them and the bowl perched between. Joel flipped the remote-control switch at his side, and abruptly the five-foot screen on the wall was alive with muscular gorillas in football jerseys and helmets.

Claire sighed with contentment. Her dad had taught her a love of football, and when he was alive the two of them had invariably spent Sunday afternoons in front of a screen with their feet up, back-seat coaching at the top of their lungs. These days she rarely caught a game because of her working hours, and she missed those times—not the sport so much as the ambience of a Sunday afternoon. Joel was clearly a man like her father—Miami hadn't finished their third play before he was on his feet swearing at them.

Chuckling, she munched on popcorn, her eyes dancing. Flipping the lid on a Coors, she took a long draft, and then folded her arms loosely behind her head. "Five bucks on Montana," she said lightly.

"We already know the outcome of the game," Joel growled.

"I think you should have gotten hold of a different game. Obviously, you're not going to survive Miami's downfall. How could you possibly not back Montana, anyway?" Her eyes darkened as she spotted her favorite quarterback fumbling the ball. "Dammit. Where the hell is that coach? Of all the stupid plays to call—"

Joel burst out laughing. "You tell 'em, tiger."

"I'm tempted," she said darkly.

He instantly pictured her, big as a minute, barefoot, in snug jeans and a delectably soft yellow angora sweater, scolding a team of brawny football players. "I have no doubts that you could sway the team to your way of thinking," he agreed dryly.

She was totally relaxed, Claire at her most touchable. She hadn't balked for an instant over the invitation to spend a lazy afternoon alone with him in his apartment. He'd carefully not bought firecrackers or champagne for the event, but the temptation had been there. Her trust had not been easy to win.

Sprawling back down beside her, he removed the popcorn bowl from between them, and matched her crossed knee with his crossed knee. Her bare foot wagged like a puppy's tail whenever the game picked up excitement. He grew less interested in the players' antics than in Claire.

Her face flushed when she was excited. Her eyes brightened. Her breasts, draped so alluringly in the soft sweater, rose and fell with quick breaths. When she jammed her hands in her pockets, those breasts were squeezed together. When she threw an arm behind her neck, they pouted up for him. When she lay absolutely flat—in despair over one of Montana's rare bumbles—those breasts disappeared in the folds of her sweater. And when he hooked an arm around her shoulder, she leaned willingly back against him, where he had a much better view of her breasts altogether. And her hips. And her legs.

Claire's eyes stayed riveted to the screen, but her attention kept wandering to the man. Whether in motion or sitting still, he always made her conscious of his maleness. Joel was sure—of himself, and of his world.

She'd seen the world through his eyes for weeks. Nothing threw him. He was a man with whom one could be quiet. A man to enjoy a rousing argument. A man who could reach across a room with a smile.

A man she'd fallen in love with. Something she'd sworn she'd never do again.

Tucked up against him, she could feel her body growing warm and aware. Every once in a while his finger lifted to sift absently through her hair. Since that touch was in her hair, she wasn't absolutely sure why she felt it in between her thighs. She couldn't seem to stop looking at his thighs. Like rock, the long corded muscles; she was sure they would be hair covered. When she'd seen his chest through the open throat of a shirt, he'd had a healthy spray of curly dark hair. Bristly to the touch?

Her eyes unwillingly strayed back down his chest to where his sweatshirt ended up in jeans. The faded denim didn't fit tightly, but it snugly outlined his long muscular legs. The room wasn't brightly lit; Joel had drawn the drapes against the afternoon sun before he'd started the game. Colors flashed on and off on the screen with each fast-moving play; those colors illuminated the most intimate masculinity in his jeans, then left it in shadow.

The room was suddenly unbearably hot. "If the Dophins would quit trying to pass..." she muttered with frustration.

"Claire."

"Hmmm."

"The Dolphins haven't had the ball in three plays."

She tilted her face up, expecting to see a teasing smile on Joel's face. There was no smile. And when had the room suddenly become so quiet? The game was still blaring, but it seemed to be coming from a long distance away.

His eyes filled her vision, as blue as the hottest flame. That fast, her intuition picked up three facts of life. That his no-touch policy the past month had been a game, that his patience was over and that...he'd won.

An unconscious shiver rippled up and down her spine. Joel had clearly played a master game. He'd waited until it was too late for her. Too late to brush off her feelings for him as a fast affair. Too late to play it light, too late to pretend she was only caught up in an impulse of sexual feelings alone.

Her heart was suddenly beating three times faster than usual. He was much, much more of a dirty player than she'd given him credit for.

His first kiss seemed to be an apology for that. His lips coaxed hers, skimmed over their softly reddened shape, whispery soft, inviting.

In her head, she damned him a dozen times over, but her body seemed to have an entirely different reaction. Her lips had missed that special taste of him, and molded greedily beneath his. Like feast after famine, her senses absorbed the feel of the man close, and demanded more. It had been so long and she'd forgotten that his tongue was dangerous. His tongue made her...forget things.

Joel slowly, almost reluctantly, raised his head. His eyes seared hers, searching her features. One by one he stole the pillows behind her head and tossed them out of reach. His hand reached back to a VCR switch, and suddenly there was total silence.

Bright colors from the screen still reflected on his features, features drawn with a fierce effort at self-control, mirroring need and want. There was no sound, just the look on his face. And those pagan eyes.

He leaned over her, large hands cupping her face, pushing back her hair. Claire felt as if she'd been asleep for four years. Joel had wakened her into a drowsy state of awareness from the moment she met him, but it had still been dreamlike, a flirtation with danger, a tease with longing. This wasn't a dream, but the reality. And she still couldn't believe how fast her heart was beating.

"Don't you dare tell me you don't want this," he said lowly.

"I never said I didn't want you," she responded helplessly.

He shook his head. "And you know damn well that I need more than that," he whispered fiercely. "I want *all* of you, Claire, and that, sweetheart, is exactly what you're going to give me...what we're going to give each other."

His mouth covered hers, so roughly that her head reeled back. He slid his hands down her back, pulling her close, his palms cupping her bottom and cradling her to his thighs. His lips left hers only to explore her neck and throat, the softness of her hair.

A small sound escaped her lips. He slid a leg between hers, anchoring her, rubbing between her jeaned thighs. Pushing up her sweater, he changed their rhythm from fast to infinitely slow, taking time to caress the satin-smooth flat of her stomach, and then her ribs, so small, so fragile. When he reached behind her to flick open the catch of her bra, he was looking at her eyes.

Her whole face was flushed, her eyes turned sleepy. They both heard the sound of that tiny catch unsnapping. He was still looking in her eyes when his palms pushed open the fragile wisp of lace, when her breasts were bared for his touch.

"Stop," she murmured.

"Stop what?"

"Stop...looking at me."

He shook his head. His finger found the pulse of her rapidly beating heart. That same finger trailed a lethargic circle around her right breast, then her left. Through the sense of touch, not sight, he found both tiny peaked nipples. He teased both between thumb and forefinger, watching Claire's pupils dilate. Such exquisitely small breasts, infinitely firm and tender. They barely fit his palm, yet when his hand covered one, kneading the pearl-soft flesh in his hand, she restlessly closed her eyes.

He heard a murmured garble that sounded vaguely like "Damn you, Brannigan." He didn't smile. Leaning over, he shifted lower, lashing a tongue on those tender pink tips. God, she was sensitive.

Her nipples were tiny rose tips, tight in arousal, tighter yet when he rubbed his teeth against them. Claire's spine arched, and he heard a rush of air escape her lungs.

His fingers slid beneath the waistband of her jeans, and she tensed.

"Sssh." He raised up to kiss the pulse at her throat, then wandered back to her mouth. "We're not going to hurry. I'm not going to rush you, Claire. I just want to see your skin. All of you. Don't fight me."

"I wasn't," she whispered back. "I was just..." Her voice trailed into a small tremulous laugh, reflecting a shyness that wasn't at all like Claire. "You'd think I'd never done this before. I... It isn't supposed to...feel like this."

He smiled then, a faint slash of tenderness on his mouth. "We haven't even started, foolish one."

He didn't understand. She didn't...make love like that. Touch was a good thing; sexual feelings were a good thing. But not some fierce, terrible out-of-control wanting. He shed her sweater while murmuring to her. Then his sweatshirt, then her jeans. He kissed the skin he uncovered.

That was when she started trembling. It wasn't the near-nakedness. It was after he skimmed off her jeans, when she felt his lips on her ankles, climbing up her calves, the touch of his tongue on her thighs. "Joel—"

He wanted too much. Intimacies that had never occurred to her, emotions she'd never felt with anyone else. She reached for him blindly, needing to stay the wild surge of dizzying sensations that flooded her head out of control.

Her hands touched his chest, and her fingers were suddenly sifting through the curling hairs, then rushing over his skin. He came back up to her mouth. Her hands were already caught up in the knowing of him, and the feel of her bare breasts against his warm skin only fanned flames already lapping at her senses with the speed of a forest fire.

She'd wanted him forever. And damn it, he knew. The more she touched, the more he rewarded her with long, flaming kisses. When her hands slid down to his jeans, she heard his harsh intake of breath.

He took them off, and it was her turn to breathe harshly. His skin was all dark gold. She saw the power of the man, the ripple of sinew beneath smooth flesh, the hard strength of him. She felt a lick of delicious fear, which only intensified when he slid back down beside her. He kissed her, once, gently on the lips. His hands cupped her face.

"I won't hurt you," he whispered.

"I know that." She couldn't stop herself from raising a hand, letting a single finger slowly trace the grave lines of his face. He was so beautiful. And so full of wanting. She was so scared without having the least idea why.

The rough feel of carpet beneath her contrasted to the endless softness of his tongue, the silken caress of his hands. Restlessly she surged beneath his probing fingers, her hands seeking to find and caress him with the same seductive power, feeling inadequate, feeling she could never match the soaring desire he invoked in her. Every part of her ached. Her eyes and hands and legs. Her heart. Her soul.

"Joel..."

He was a stranger, a fierce primitive warrior poised over her with a golden slick body, his breath harsh, his power over her absolute. She could see the moisture on his mouth from the intimate kiss she'd allowed no man. She could see the small damp bruise on his shoulder, the mark of her teeth that she hadn't been able to control. And when he surged inside her body, filling that feminine hollow, she let out a low, fierce moan of yearning, as pagan and abandoned as Eve.

His palms raised her hips, and he drove inside her, filling her again, deeper this time, and then deeper again. "Look at me," he whispered.

Glazed eyes sought his mindlessly.

"So tight, so warm," he murmured. "Do you know how long I've wanted to be inside you?"

Her lashes darted down.

"No," he whispered. "Don't look away. I want to watch you. I want you to see how good you feel to me, and I want to watch you cry out...."

He kept whispering, wonderful, terrible things. Intimate things. No one had ever told her such things. No man had ever made her feel so uniquely desirable, so desperately wanted. Her skin was so heated, too hot.

Tension kept climbing, centered in her most feminine part. She felt...invaded, conquered. He wasn't just making love to her body, but also to her mind, her soul. He touched her wanton core; he sapped inhibitions and left her weak and clinging.

She heard herself murmuring his name, over and over. Light and darkness. Color like rainbows, the surge of thunder-clotted clouds, and then release, like a torrent of spring-cooled rain. Claire was bewildered to find tears in her eyes that Joel was kissing away. "You never believed it would be less between us, did you?" he murmured.

It was still dark, but that muzzy predawn dark. Lying on her side, Claire slid an arm from beneath Joel's body to silently pull the sheet up over his shoulders. He'd covered her in the night, but neglected to cover himself.

Sitting up, she studied him with love for endless minutes. She could see his night-darkened chin, his broad forehead, the rumpled sheen of his hair.

Her heart was pounding a lonely drumbeat, insistent, despairing. The last thing she wanted to do was get up and leave him, but it was exactly what she knew she had to do.

After they'd made love the first time, Joel had made dinner and brought it back to the living room. They hadn't eaten it, and she couldn't even remember what he'd fixed.

She could remember very clearly when he'd carried her into the bedroom. Twice and then a third time they'd made love, and in between Joel had served wine, toasting her in the darkness, making her laugh. She'd never imagined a lover like him, both earthy and sensual, tender and savage. He gave...everything.

And demanded everything in return.

Eyes still closed, she could feel soreness in her most feminine part. She could still feel the whisker-burn on her breasts, the reddened spot on her throat where he'd nuzzled too roughly. Worse, she knew he had marks she'd made on his body. Marks she'd never in her life made on a man.

The last time she'd been so sleepy she would have sworn there was nothing left to give or take. She'd been so wrong. He knew exactly where to touch, how to tease with beguiling tenderness, how to suddenly, roughly turn into a pagan, demanding lover. And he'd taught her to touch him back the same way. Joel had encouraged her, whispering, approving... she could still hear her own voice cry out that last time. And Joel's exultant laughter, before they'd both slept.

Slowly she edged from the bed, dragging a hand through her hair. For hours now she'd lain in the darkness, a nameless panic gripping and twisting her heart. He'd whispered that she should have known how it would be between them.

She had known. Making love, Joel had claimed her, body and soul. She loved him with her whole heart. And felt such despair.

She silently slipped on her clothes in the darkness. Dragging on her coat in the unlit living room, she let herself out of his apartment.

She'd drowned and gone to hell once before, for a man who wasn't worth half of Joel, a man who never asked half of what Joel demanded. Making love was only part of it. She knew Joel saw that as a beginning.

All she could remember was how she felt after the divorce, as if she'd lost herself, as if "Claire" were a parcel she'd forgotten on a bench somewhere. She couldn't forget how commitment made a man turn possessive, and Joel had been fiercely possessive in his loving.

Shadows chased her down the lonely flights of stairs. Shadows of inadequacy, that no matter how much she gave before, it had never been enough. Feelings of being cornered, and of being closed in.

A rare blur of tears clouded her eyes when she finally walked out onto the silent street.

"Good heavens, you're up early." Nora yawned from the kitchen doorway.

"Hmmm. Coffee's ready, and French toast is on the way." Claire's voice was deliberately cheerful, but she quickly turned her face from her mother's shrewd gaze. Nora was one of those mothers who could spot circles under the eyes as fast as she could diagnose measles.

A few minutes later the kitchen spilled over with noise. Claire was thankfully too busy to think. Wednesday was a nursery-school day for Dot; she showed up in the kitchen with a polka-dotted sweater and striped pants, and started wailing at the top of her lungs when Nora insisted she change.

Walter lifted his head and started howling in sympathy. Sandy appeared in the doorway, her eyes sleepy but well made-up. She was dressed for work in a smart red wool suit that didn't handle a cup of coffee spilled on it well.

"Mother!"

Nora had been too busy studying her elder daughter to watch what she was doing. Now she looked at Sandy with a stricken face.

Claire dispensed kisses to Dot, poured a second cup of coffee and urged her new midnight-blue dress on her sister, diverted her mother to the stove and the French toast and patted the bloodhound.

First crisis averted. She was surviving, Claire kept telling herself. He wouldn't miss her. There'd be a woman somewhere who could give Joel exactly what he wanted and needed.

The thought of any other woman with Joel made her violently ill, but it wasn't a joke. To let it go on any longer would only have made her feel worse. She was already in love with him, but she couldn't try and live that way, not again. Love had looked beautiful the first time around, too—in the beginning.

"Claire..." Nora started to say, but was interrupted when Dot returned in a red plaid blouse to match her purple-striped sweater. Then Sandy returned from the bedroom wearing a full slip and muttering about cleaning bills. The French toast was burning when the backdoor opened.

Joel hadn't shaved. He'd managed a rapid shower and change of clothes, and unlike Claire he'd had all of three hours' sleep.

She gathered at first glimpse that he was furious. His brows were furrowed together and there was a silence to his face. A stoniness, which made her spine stiffen and something thick clot in her throat.

"Joel!" Dot flung herself at him. "Make them stop making me change clothes! You know I look beautiful!"

He just stood there, glaring at Claire. "I want to know what the hell happened," he said in a low voice.

"I..." Flustered, she looked away. How on earth was she supposed to answer him, anyway? Nora had removed the French toast and left the griddle on the open flame. Smoke was whispering out from beneath it. Sandy was trying to chase after Dot to change her

clothes again, and to put a sweater on over her slip at
the same time. Walter stepped in as Dot's defender,
and Sandy tripped over him and cannoned into Joel.
Nora was standing there with two cups of coffee ready
to offer one to Joel.

"Claire!"

Now what on earth did the man expect her to do,
talk above the chaos? She saved the griddle, turned
down the flame and listened to her sister's litany
against the moaning bloodhound hiding under the table. All the time her heart was tripping over itself,
trying to find words. There were no words. Only a
child giggling with Nora chasing her, and breakfast
still to be made.

"Where's Joel?" Dot demanded.

"Mr. Brannigan," corrected Nora wearily.

Claire lifted her head, her face white. He was gone.

He *had* expected her to answer him over the chaos.
He'd expected her to value their relationship over
anything else, to just ignore her entire life.

It wasn't reasonable. He wasn't a reasonable man.

"Where did he go, Claire?" Sandy asked bewil-
deredly. "A moment ago he was right here, I was just
about to tell him about my—"

"Honey. What is wrong?" Nora asked gently.

"Where's Joel? Where's Joel?" chanted Dot.

Out of her life. That was all, just . . . out of her life.
Claire stood stock-still, feeling pain rush over her in an
enveloping cloud. Then she grabbed her coat.

Nine

A brisk wind whipped at her hair as she rushed out the back door. Joel was backing out of the drive and into the street at racing speed. She saw his iron features through the windshield and thought he wasn't going to stop...until she heard the sudden screech of brakes.

Fear of loss drowned instantly in a fury of relief. Claire barreled around the front of his car. Before he'd rolled down the window halfway, she was leaning in, her gray eyes snapping. "You could have waited thirty-seven seconds! You could see the whole house was in an uproar—"

"What I could see is that you were hiding behind a pile of noise." Blue eyes seared hers, colder than an iceberg. "I don't have time for games, Claire, I told you that before."

"Well, aren't you holier than a saint? You set me up last night, Brannigan," Claire accused. "You did it with popcorn and football instead of champagne and soft lights, but you still set me up. You knew well I wasn't expecting—"

"To make love? You should have been. Regardless, get in."

One car honked behind them, then two. Claire glared at both drivers, feeling confused, out of breath and miserable.

"Get in, Claire."

He leaned over to open the passenger door. She hesitated, and then hustled around the front of the car. She climbed in stiffly, her temper reduced to nerves by his dark-eyed stare. "I was wrong, running out on you," she said uncomfortably, her voice low.

"Yes."

"It wasn't that last night wasn't special."

"Last night was damn well more than special. And you know it."

"I'm trying to apologize. Quit snapping at me."

"For some strange reason, I don't purr when I'm mad."

But Claire could see that his anger was fading. From the possessive looks he shot her it seemed to be enough that she was in the car and with him. Which was not to say he looked necessarily...manageable. "So don't purr. You still don't have to growl. And where on earth are you driving?"

"The same place I would have taken you this morning if we'd woken up together. Wednesday mornings I have a commitment that it's past time you knew about. Now why did you leave?"

She couldn't very well think when he was pelting questions at her. The words escaped with a slight feminine roar. "Because I was scared witless. Why else do you think I would have left in the middle of the night?"

"If you were scared witless, you should have woken me up and said, 'Brannigan, I'm scared witless. Let's talk about this.' Not run off and let me worry to death about what happened to you when I woke up and found you gone."

Abruptly, Claire's heart stopped racing. "Brannigan, I was scared witless, let's talk about this," she repeated dutifully, but her tone was unhappy and she stared unseeing at the skyscrapers whizzing past them. "Joel. I didn't want to hurt you, any more than I wanted to stay around and be hurt. And I felt that was what would happen if I stayed."

"What would have happened is that we'd have made love again this morning."

She flashed him a glance. "I didn't mean that."

"No, honey, I know you didn't." The anger left Joel's voice. He said quietly, "I hold a few old-fashioned values very strongly. I think you know that. I protect my own. What I have, I keep. Claire, I want a woman to belong to me, in the traditional way." He hesitated. "To me, those values are part of loving, the way a man loves a woman."

She closed her eyes, leaning her head back against the soft upholstery. "Love isn't always a pretty word, Joel. I learned a long time ago not to let myself 'belong' to anyone."

He fell silent for a moment. "I don't think you learned that. I think someone taught you that."

"Is there a difference?"

"Yes." Joel's voice turned deceivingly light, his tone barely audible. "Remind me to murder your ex-husband if I ever meet up with him, would you, Claire?"

"Pardon?"

Joel stopped the car. "This will unfortunately have to wait. Believe me, we're not through talking."

Claire was momentarily distracted when she noticed where they were—a deserted alley on the wrong side of town. The three-story brick building might have been a school at one time. Tenements surrounded it. Factory haze hung like clouds over threadbare wash hanging from open windows; trash and debris huddled around the curbs. The morning had a springtime feel in the breeze, but not here. The look of poverty was the look of a six-year-old darting in front of cars, risking his life, not caring.

The minute Joel stepped out of the car, a sullen-faced teenager moved out of the shadows. Money was exchanged. Claire understood that the boy was being paid to baby-sit Joel's car while they went inside. Tossing Joel a questioning glance, she felt his palm at the small of her back, propelling her forward.

Once inside the building, they climbed down a wide set of stairs. If the building wasn't condemned, it should have been. The walls were stained, cracked, and peeling paint. The linoleum was pitted, and old school lockers hung off their hinges.

When Joel opened the far door, the sound of raucous laughter startled her after the silence of the long corridor. The gym had seen better days, but the basketball hoops at both ends looked brand-new. There

were at least fifteen kids, all dressed in jeans and
sneakers and worn T-shirts. Sixteen appeared to be the
average age, though they had that dead-eyed, street-
wise hostility in their eyes of children who'd been
adults since they were born. A basketball was winging its way across the court, and the play stopped only
when Joel was spotted. The teenagers promptly
swarmed him.

"Hey, man. You're late."

"Who's the chick?"

"This your woman, man?"

Joel was setting the bag down he'd brought in with
him, and taking off his jacket. "This is Claire," he
introduced swiftly. "You ever see her in this part of
town, you make sure no one messes with her."

"Like no sweat."

"Your woman, huh?"

Briefly Joel glanced at her, his expression deadpan.
For the first time all morning, Claire almost laughed.
The boys were of an age. Two flicked out afro combs
in honor of the introduction. Another stood with feet
apart, crotch jutted out. Claire tried to look suitably
impressed by their manliness. All she could think of
was that they desperately belonged in school.

"You ready to work out?" he demanded.

"Hey, we been ready all morning. You're the one
who's late."

"Snake here, he's got a pretty fancy lay-up to show
you."

"Talk's cheap," Joel said curtly.

Claire, deserted, climbed several tiers of the
bleachers while the play started. Perching elbows on
knees, she watched with her chin cupped on two fists.

If her heart were still full of conflicting emotions, this clearly wasn't the time to sort them out.

The boys played basketball as if it were a war. Joel was their general. Within fifteen minutes T-shirts were stripped and tossed on the bench one by one, and bodies returned to the court to sweat in earnest. Unfamiliar with basketball, Claire didn't pick up the subtler points of the game. She could figure out enough to know Joel was working them to death.

He was also swearing, bullying and yelling at them. Before the hour was done, faces were glistening and chests were heaving from the exertion. By the time Joel ordered the boys to the showers, she couldn't imagine why they looked at him with such adoration.

Joel ambled toward the bleachers, wiping his damp forehead with the arm of his sweatshirt, breathing every bit as hard as his charges. Claire adored him at that particular moment. Very few would have touched those kids with a ten-foot pole.

"What'd you think?" Joel demanded.

"You were mean to them," she accused.

"Your ears burning?"

"I've heard the words before."

He grinned. "Not usually yelled at the top of the lungs, I expect." He glanced at his watch. "Give me five minutes to take a shower. I promise, no more—"

He didn't make it to the shower before kids started filtering back out of the locker room. She watched curiously as each came up to Joel, pulled out some kind of book or magazine from their pockets and waited while Joel marked something in a small black book.

With her chin cupped in her hands, she studied him. Like the boys, he'd removed his sweatshirt. Clean sweat glimmered on his shoulders and forehead, like oil on dark gold. She'd loved watching him in play, moving across the court with the grace of a silent cat, all swift-moving masculine grace. She had a sudden vagrant fantasy of Joel seducing her in the bleachers, his whole body smooth and slippery, her whole body smooth and slippery.... Her eyes trailed the give-me-five salute he gave the last boy, and she sighed.

The man roused lascivious daydreams even when surrounded by a dozen hoodlums.

Too late, her mind whispered. Even if you know it can't end well, your heart should have known it was too late to run.

When the last boy had left the gym, Joel flicked his pen closed and pocketed it, walking toward Claire. "By any remote chance, do you have five more minutes of patience left so I could still get that shower?"

Her lips curled in a smile. "You haven't heard me complaining yet, have you?"

"It doesn't usually take so long," he apologized.

"Brannigan, I'm perfectly content here," she assured him.

"Five..." He started to promise again, and stopped with a sudden wayward grin. "Come on. There're a few people on the second floor upstairs, where they're putting together a kind of halfway house for runaways. Regardless, there's no one anywhere around down here. You can come in with me." He reached for her hand.

She shook her head. "You're out of your mind. I'm not going in a men's locker room."

It seemed she was. Even though he locked the door, there was something about a female invading such a distinctly male sanctum that made her nervous. Particularly when Joel deserted her with a "Make yourself at home. I've got to get a towel—and do a quick cleanup after the devils."

"What were you doing, with the books and magazines?" she called after him. Pushing her hands in her pockets, she wandered a little. One room simply held rows of lockers, another was a small office and the third simply held a dozen showers, all in the open without private stalls. Someone had recently put a fresh coat of paint on the place. She had the sneaky suspicion it was Joel. And though the smells were distinctly warm, damp and male, there was no staleness or old sweat odors. The floor was old cement and pitted, but clean.

"The kids have to read the equivalent of a book a week or they don't get to play," Joel answered her from behind a locker partition. "Half the time they bring in girlie magazines. I don't care as long as they master the printed page. Most of them dropped out in ninth grade without being able to get through Dick and Jane."

"Why?" she asked simply.

"Why what?"

"Why are you involved?"

Except for a white towel draped on his shoulders, Joel walked around the corner stark naked, and frowning. "I meant to get you a chair from the office."

"I don't need one. And you didn't answer my question." She chuckled when he tossed the towel at her head, and peeled it off. "Brannigan!"

He was already in the open shower room, flicking on the closest set of faucets. "To answer your question...in case you have any illusions left as to my illustrious background, this is it. My neighborhood. Where I grew up."

A small lump formed in her throat. She had a sudden image of a very young Joel, a lonely frightened boy wandering those dangerous streets outside. She'd patched knife wounds from this neighborhood. She'd seen addicts, and children who'd never had the chance to be young.

The hot water pelted down in a triangular stream. Joel ducked under, lathering his head in a cloud of steam. Leaning her cheek against the cool, smooth wall, Claire watched him. He had a scar on his back, white and faded. She'd felt it in the night before, but never asked him how he'd gotten it.

The rest of his body was sleek and hard. Intuitively Claire guessed it would always be that way. Toughness was a defense he'd learned early, weakness something he'd never tolerate in himself. For others, Joel could be patient, understanding and gentle. But who had ever taken care of Joel?

Barely a few minutes had passed before he flipped off the water. His head was dripping, water streaming from his long limbs, blinding his eyes. Claire stepped forward to hand him the towel, and instead found she was using it herself to wipe the water from his face.

When he could see again, his eyes snapped open on hers, gleaming blue. "Personal service?"

Her eyes shifted away from his. She went behind him, using the towel on his neck and shoulders. "No one can dry their own back."

"I've been drying my own back since my first shower."

"You've undoubtedly been arguing since you could first talk, that's for sure."

"I'm not," Joel said quietly, "arguing."

No, Claire thought absently. He was standing absolutely still while she dried his back. It took a long time. Amazing, that she could name every vertebra, every muscle, every nerve and blood vessel in the back, and she felt she was getting her first lesson in anatomy. The man was beautiful. The wide sweep of his shoulders, the power of his lean muscles sheathed in smooth, cool flesh...

Joel turned, stealing the towel from her hands. At the rate she was going he was nearly dry anyway, and as he finished the job, he looked at her.

"No," she said swiftly.

He tossed the towel down.

"No, Joel. You're crazy. We're in a *locker room*."

"I liked the way you dried my back."

"I can see that." Color climbed her cheeks. Good heavens, the man became turned on at just the slightest touch. "I'll go out and wait until you get dressed—"

"Honey. The only thing in that direction is urinals."

Her faint pink cheeks turned tomato-red. Claire stopped backing up abruptly, and propped her hands in her pockets, looking casual. "Now listen. We're two adult people."

"Exactly." He took another step forward.

"Joel!"

"What?"

"I don't trust the look in your eyes."

"You're responsible. Now you pay the price."

He meant no more than to claim a kiss, to tease more laughter from her. But then she passionately responded, her hands sliding up around his bare neck, her lips parting expectantly. She shouldn't have done that. She shouldn't have murmured under his nuzzling mouth; her eyes shouldn't have dilated with loving softness.

"Your skin is cold," she whispered.

"So warm me." Her Windbreaker was half unzipped; he undid the rest and pushed it off her shoulders. A soft yellow sweater was under it, tucked into her jeans. When his mouth lowered on hers, she leaned back against the wall for balance. He pushed up the sweater, and reached the soft bare skin of her stomach.

She was no longer smiling, and her face had turned pale. "Joel . . ." Her voice was breathless.

"You belong to me. In the oldest way a woman can belong to a man," he whispered. "That's what you think you're afraid of, Claire."

He skimmed the sweater over her head and then bent down, his lips roaming in her hair, her temples, down to her throat. "You think I don't know what it is to be smothered, sweet. But I do. When I showed you those kids today, I was showing you kids that are closed in by their whole world. I've been closed in. I've been in relationships where I was the only one doing the compromising. I love you, Claire, but loving you doesn't mean I want to own you. Wanting—needing—you to belong to me is something else completely.''

His palm slid up from her waist. A finger discovered the front catch of her bra and unsnapped it. A breast tumbled into his palm, as if waiting for the gentle kneading it promptly received.

Her breath caught in her throat. They were in a locker room, she reminded herself. Stark white walls. Nowhere to lie down.

But the barrenness of their surroundings was in direct contrast to the lush reality of Joel's presence. His cool smooth flesh, warming beneath her hands. The feel of his muscles contracting wherever she touched, the power of his wanting affecting her feminine senses. She wanted to believe that there was a difference between belonging to him and possessiveness.

It was very difficult to think that anything could be wrong when he touched her. Her breasts firmed under his hands. The soft flesh felt tight and hot. The tiny button nipples burned as they grazed against his cooler chest.

His hands unsnapped her jeans zipper, then slipped inside to bare flesh, molding her to him. She already knew that he was aroused. She just hadn't felt how much. Her fingers clenched in his hair and she rubbed deliberately against him. If Joel could be crazy, so could she. She wooed his mouth back to hers, nibbled his lips the way he'd nibbled hers, tasted and sipped and savored and darted her tongue inside.

A thousand things were in her head, none an awareness of a silent cold locker room. She'd nearly lost him, and whatever hesitations she had about a permanent commitment, she already knew she'd half die before losing Joel. And the man himself, a man who'd grown up in such poverty and loneliness. If he refused to admit it, she still saw. How many times had he had the chance to be simply lighthearted?

Her hands turned teasing, lightly skimming his sides, fingertips dancing around his thighs. She broke off the kiss, and traced a delicate pattern with her tongue on his throat, down into his flat nipples nestled in crisp dark hair.

"Claire." His tone was distinctly guttural.

Her smile was sinful. Immoral bliss, knowing she was responsible for the smoky look in his eyes. "Don't you Claire me. You started this."

"I admit that. But if you continue to touch me that way—"

"I'm going to continue to touch you that way." She had to stand on tiptoe, to trace the line of the shell of his ear with her tongue. The man was irritatingly tall.

And her knees were becoming irritatingly weak. More so, when Joel pushed down her jeans. A wisp of silk panties was lost with them. For a moment she stared with a degree of detachment at the pile of the clothes on the cement floor. They seemed to be hers. "Joel?"

A fierce raw ache filled her when his hands stroked intimate territory. The tables were being turned. Closing her eyes, she had the terrible feeling she had already lost control. "Joel, this seemed like a good idea...."

"Hmmm?"

"But there's nowhere...it isn't possible."

His head tilted back, eyes dark, his features harsh
under fluorescent light...except for the sudden trace
of a smile. "Between a man and a woman, there's very
little that isn't possible," he whispered. "Tell me what
you want, Claire."

She shook her head.

"Tell me."

She couldn't. She wanted a thousand things from
Joel, none of which she believed she could have. It was
a sane rational world; she bore the scars. A moment
of spring fever didn't change that.

His lips came down on hers yet again, this time in an
endless drugging kiss. As her arms swept helplessly
around him, she felt his hands on her hips, lifting her.
For a moment she was suspended in midair, then his
smooth warm heat slid inside her feminine core. A low
moan of surprise and pleasure escaped her lips.

Her legs wrapped around him instinctively; her back
grazed against the cool smooth wall for balance. "You
can't..."

"You're mine, Claire. Try and tell me that isn't
what you want."

She couldn't. She couldn't tell him anything. The
moment had been full of play, adventuresome and
loving, but it was suddenly something else. Their lips
were clinging as if the end of the world were close. She
was trembling all over.

With his hands on her hips, he moved her in that
ancient love rhythm. She'd known nothing like it before. Their eyes were inches from each other. She
could see the moisture dot his forehead, the strain he
bore from holding her weight, the fierce blue of his

eyes. Her cheek fell to his shoulder, and she felt his lips
whispering in her hair, on her temples.

"So sweet," he murmured. "So much fire. Let go,
Claire. Let it happen. Let me love you...."

Her fingers tangled in his hair, and she'd never felt
more vulnerable in her life. She could feel his body
tighten, and soared like a swallow let free, her spine
arching back, her legs wrapped tightly around him. A
splash of sky, and then Joel's fierce kiss.

Slowly, he lifted her up and then down until her feet
touched ground. "No tears," he whispered.

"I wasn't crying," she lied.

He dried the crystal under her right eye with his
thumb, then her left, then just held her close.

In time, she realized how tightly she was holding
him. "Brannigan?"

"Hmmm?"

"We really have to get out of here before someone
catches us."

"You should have thought of that before, Doc."

"This was crazy." Claire reached for her jeans. Her
voice still sounded shaky. "You must be a bad influence. Actually, I knew that the minute I saw you...."

He pushed the jeans from her hands and leveled one
last kiss on her mouth. When he lifted his head, she
saw the darkness in his eyes, the sudden tense silence
in his expression. "I love you," he said quietly, "body
and soul, Claire. I need and want you the same way.
Don't try to pretend it's less than that."

I love you body and soul. The words echoed in her
head all through her working hours in the emergency

room. It was a quiet night. Two car accidents. An old woman with arthritis.

In between were long spaces of silence, when all she could do was think about Joel. It seemed so simple. She'd never loved anyone more. Her heart swelled around him. She'd seen him angry, tired and tense. She'd seen him loving and tender. She'd seen the man sleeping and she knew exactly what a powerfully sexual being he could be awake.

She loved all of him, the good and the bad, but she couldn't misunderstand the warning he'd given her. He wanted a commitment, he would take nothing less.

For four years she'd told herself she didn't believe in that kind of love. Not violets-in-spring kind of love, not all or nothing passion, not this obsessive desire to always be within touching distance, not rainbows.

Joel was waiting for her after work. She couldn't help but smile at him. He looked wretchedly tired, with huge circles under his eyes. She knew she looked no better. He drove in silence until they reached her driveway.

When he stopped the car, she leaned over, eyes soft, and pressed a single kiss on his lips. "If there was any question in your mind... I love you, too," she murmured. "And I'm trying to lay my ghosts. Would you be patient a little longer?"

His hand reached out, enclosed hers. A moment later she left the car, entered her silent house, shed her shoes and crashed on the bed for the next twelve hours.

Ten

For days Claire had spent every spare minute with Joel. On Saturday morning, she was almost disoriented to wake up in her own bed, much less to waken to a pint-size contralto whispering, "Aunt Claire. Aunt Claire. We need a doctor."

Claire's eyes desperately wanted to stay closed. "Sweetheart. We've discussed this," she murmured groggily. "You're not going to die from the bruise on your knee."

"It isn't knees, it's Mommy." Dot shook her head in a classic adult expression of despair. "There isn't even blood, but she's crying so hard. I told her it was nothing. I took her the whole box of bandages, but she closed the door and told me not to tell anybody."

Claire had sat up the moment she heard the word "crying," and was already reaching for her robe.

"Okay, poppet. We'll take care of her," she said calmly.

"You can't tell her I told you."

"You know I won't."

"I could get you some bandages." Dot was trailing Claire down the hall to the far bedroom.

Claire knocked once, gently, and then opened her sister's door. The room was in darkness except for the huddled figure on the bed. Claire took one look, felt her heart turn over and gave a soothing smile to her niece. "I'll fix her up in a jiffy, but this is one of those rare times I'll have to do it without you, sweet. Do you know where Grandma is?"

"Sure. She's in the basement, doing wash." Dot confided, "I had to sort all the clothes for her."

"She needs you," Claire agreed. "Would you do me a favor, honey?"

"Sure."

"I want you to go find Grandma and help her every bit that you can for the next hour. Don't even leave her for a minute, okay?"

"Why?" Dot's eyes grew wide.

"It's a secret," Claire whispered. "And it'll earn you a chocolate ice cream cone at the end of it."

"All right."

Dot flew off, and Claire quietly re-entered Sandy's bedroom, closing the door behind her. Her sister's face was buried in a pillow, but nothing could totally muffle the sound of sobbing. Sheets and blankets were tossed every whichway; clothes were strewed on the floor. Claire leaned over the huddled form, putting her hand on her sister's shoulder.

"Just . . . go away. Please."

"No." Claire said it simply, then put both arms around her sister, forcing her tearstained face around.

Sandy gave a muffled sound and then lurched up, burying her face in Claire's shoulder. "God, I've been so stupid. All this time..."

"Tell me." Claire held on, brushing back her sister's hair as she would have for a child.

"Greg came back. I didn't tell you or Mom or anyone, but he called me at work and I went out with him last night and..." Sandy drew back, rubbing her fingers across her eyes. Her breath was hiccuppy, catching every time she tried to talk. "All this time I loved him. All this time I kept thinking that he'd be sorry, that he'd see what we had, that he'd come back. All this time I thought I'd throw it in his face and show him how happy I was without him...but really I wanted him back. I always wanted him back. There was never anyone else...."

"I know, hon." Claire sighed, and leaned back on her elbows. Sandy huddled by the headboard, her knees drawn up, her face a mess, her fingers fluttering in nervous trembling.

"I couldn't even believe he was in town. I mean, why now? And it was all so perfect at first, just like it used to be. We laughed, and he took me to a restaurant we used to like...." Her voice broke, then gained momentum again. "And then it all changed. I told him about Dot. You know what he said?"

"What?"

"He was angry. Not angry that I hadn't told him at the time, but angry that I didn't have an abortion way back then." Sandy's voice rose to a hysterical pitch. "An abortion? For my Dot?"

"Easy," Claire said soothingly.

"It's his *daughter*. He didn't even care. He got this worried look on his face as if he thought I was going to ask him for money. Money!" Sandy hissed. "All this time. All this time I've been carrying a torch for that man; all this time I've let that man affect my life. For *nothing*. I don't want him. I don't even like him. I thought, you lose, buster. You'll never see your daughter tell a tall tale, you'll never see her all pink-cheeked in sleep, you'll never see her clutching onto one of her dolls and telling it to eat peas. Dammit. Peas. You think that's stupid—"

"No," Claire whispered.

"I love my daughter," Sandy said fiercely.

"I know you do."

Sandy covered her face with her hands. "You think I don't know how badly I've messed up with her? She's worth so much. Anything. My life. I knew that from the day she was born, only it always hurt so much to look at her; she always reminded me..." Sandy wiped her eyes again. "How could I have been so blind for so long? To let the past take over the present . . . to keep an open book on what should have been shut . . ."

For just an instant, Claire stiffened. A very old private hurt simmered to the surface, and glittered in her soft gray eyes. For so long, how easy it had been to criticize Sandy, when she was guilty of the same crime. Hadn't she, too, let one man from the past color her whole world?

They talked longer, before Claire quietly slipped off the bed and left her sister alone for a while. Tears were in her eyes as she went back to her own room, quickly dressed and went back in search of Dot and her mother.

Nora was at the kitchen table, coloring. Dot was playing teacher. Claire automatically smiled, but over the child's head she met her mother's worried eyes. Nora knew something serious was wrong.

"Did you find out what hurt Mommy?" Dot piped up.

"Sure did," Claire said brightly.

"She's not crying anymore?"

"Nope. Everything's going to be fine." Claire said it to Nora, who gave a huge sigh in relief.

"I'd better go check on her then." Dot slid off the stool. "Grandma, you finish up that picture. This time see if you can stay in the lines."

"Hold it, Tonto." Claire whisked up the tot before she reached the door and swung her up in her arms. "We have an ice cream cone to buy, if you remember. And after we eat it, believe me, I just have the feeling your mom's going to be very anxious to see you."

By ten o'clock, Joel's staff had figured out that it was wise to stay out of his way. An irritable frown hadn't left his brow in hours. Saturday nights were always an exercise in chaos, but this one was worse than most.

His chefs had decided it was a good night to show temperament over the issue of a cranberry-ginger sauce. Since Harry and Geraldine regularly threatened to quit over who was the superior cook, Joel was used to handling them. Both required daily doses of appreciation and lauds for their efforts, and both deserved it. It was just one of those nights when he would have preferred to knock both their heads together and have done with it.

Lorene had called in sick. The substitute singer was packing in customers at the bar in her see-through dress, but she had the voice of a flat hen.

A waiter had dumped a full tray of dinners in the middle of the restaurant.

The maître d's wife was pregnant. That in itself was fine, except George had been confusing reservations for two days now, ever since he'd heard about the baby. Customers stacked up waiting for tables that should have been ready for them did not make Joel happy.

They'd run out of bourbon, requiring a quick purchase run. Since Joel controlled the entire liquor supply, he had only himself to blame for that, which only made him feel more irritable.

By ten, he had a raw gnawing headache. Only to ask for more punishment did he decide to poke his nose once again in the kitchen, on his way back to his office. Pushing open the revolving door, his eyes scanned over gleaming appliances, busy waiters, and Harry and Geraldine...chattering in sudden remarkable harmony.

The source of that harmony was seated on the counter, dressed in whites with her feet swinging. Claire had a pastry in one hand and a chicken bone in the other, and her cheeks were stuffed.

For the first time in hours, Joel felt a lazy, relaxed grin forming on his face.

"This isn't my fault," Claire managed to say, swallowing hastily. "I came here to see you. I could only grab an hour for my dinner break, and when Harry

heard that he dragged me in here. Both of them—"
she motioned darkly to the beaming chefs "—claimed
I was a skinny excuse for a woman who needed fat-
tening up."

"You know what she eats on her dinner hour?"
Harry scowled to Joel.

"I know."

As fast as she had a napkin whisked on her hands
and lips, Joel was lifting her down from the counter.
She had barely a minute to register the private gleam
in his eyes. There was no question he was having a
rough night—or that he was in no mood for a crowd.
The speed with which he grabbed her hand was almost . . . embarrassing.

"You are both extremely wonderful cooks in spite
of your insults," she told the two on exiting. "The best
food I've ever tasted. He's paying you fairly?"

The swinging door closed on the sound of their
laughter. His office door closed seconds later, with the
two of them inside. Abruptly, Joel backed Claire
against a wall, and chained her in with arms on both
sides of her, leaning down to her upraised face. "Are
you expecting a kiss hello?"

"Why else do you think I came here? And considering I have to be back at the hospital in twenty-three
minutes, you'd better make it fast."

He obliged, taking a tender bite of her neck.

"Lips, Brannigan."

"In a minute. I'll work my way up there."

In time, he raised his head. Her eyes were shimmering by that time, her fingers holding onto his shoulder for balance. "There's no time for that and you

know it," she scolded breathlessly. "Besides, can't you see I look like a sack? Where's your taste in women?"

He fingered her starched white coat. "Right inside this sack."

Claire shook her head. "You could almost make me believe that you're trainable."

"I'll 'trainable' you."

"In the meantime, sir—" Claire popped out from under his arm "—the real reason I'm here is to deliver a major thank-you where my sister is concerned."

"She saw her Greg?"

Claire shot him a wry look, as she bent to fill two mugs with coffee from his ever-brewing pot in the corner. "You know darn well she saw Greg. You set it up."

He ignored that. "What happened?" Easing down into a chair, he stretched his legs and motioned her to his lap.

She shook her head with a scolding grin. She knew how he ran the place; people walked into his office all the time. "What happened is that Sandy ended a relationship that was and always would have been bad for her. As far as her relationship with Dot...Rome isn't built in a day. Sandy's got a lot to make up for, but if you could have heard how she talked about her, seen Sandy trying to play a simple game of blocks this afternoon...those two belong together." Claire slugged her hands in her pockets. "It'll take time," she said simply, "but I believe my sister will end up a good mother. You were right. Sandy needed to see Greg again. And you were also right, someone should have taken direct action a long time ago. Brannigan?"

"Hmmm?" He could feel a chuckle starting just from the expression on her face.

"I can't *stand* men who are always right."

He motioned her to his lap again. She declined, her features turning suddenly serious, her voice low. "Know something? You didn't go through all the trouble of finding Greg for my sister's sake."

"Didn't I?"

"You wanted me to see something, didn't you... that she wasn't the only Barrett woman letting the past intrude on her present relationships."

The silence didn't last five seconds. "So..." Joel drawled. "Did you manage to take the elevator up here or the stairs again?"

Her eyes held his a moment longer, then dropped. "Stairs." Claire sighed. "I know, neurotic. You've never said a word but you must have thought it. You don't have to tell me that; it's just that every time I near an elevator, I see pillows piling toward my face, threatening to smother me."

"Almost every time I see you, I think of pillows too," he assured her, and watched a faint color climb her cheeks.

The phone rang. When he reached over to grab it, he grabbed Claire as well, propelling her back on his lap as he answered the call from the bar. Once he hung up, he scolded, "Don't start complaining now. You said you came here to give me a thank-you. I'm just making it easier on you."

That was the entire problem with the man. There were certain things Joel could make seem incredibly easy. Loving him, for one. Forgetting that she'd even had a past, was another. Winding her arms around his neck, she accepted kiss after kiss. They started on her eyelids, wandered to her cheeks, then strayed back to her lips again. "Stop," she murmured.

"Why?"

"This is supposed to be my thank-you. Not yours. I'm perfectly capable of delivering it my own way."

He appeared skeptical. She had to show him. She couldn't show him properly without undoing two buttons of his shirt, and then three. Her small palm slid inside, loving the feel of his warm flesh as she layered her lips on top of his, exploring exactly what her smaller tongue could do against his larger one.

Beneath her Joel shifted uncomfortably. She could feel his arousal pressed against her, and shifted herself.

"Doc," he murmured, "you're going to pay for this."

"Do you feel thoroughly thanked?"

"Actually..."

Actually, she forgot entirely about time and place until she heard a discreet cough behind them. Blinking as she looked up, she saw George, Joel's head waiter, staring with fascination out toward the window. With a grin she bounded off Joel's lap, grabbed her coat from the far chair and pecked George's cheek in passing. "Having a good night, George?"

"Great night, Claire. Did I tell you my wife's pregnant?"

"George! That's wonderful!"

Joel's phone rang again.

She heard, "You. Come back here!" and calmly kept going after a wink of congratulations for George. Dr. Barton had agreed to cover her for the dinner hour, but in emergency service that wasn't really a fair thing to ask. She was due back, and knew Joel had his hands full as well.

A gently euphoric mood stayed with Claire until eleven o'clock, when a dozen casualties were brought in simultaneously from a fire in a local motel. The halls and examining rooms suddenly filled up faster than the staff could handle them. Most of the victims were suffering no more than superficial cuts and bruises, but two had collapsed ... and the child playing with matches who had started it all was badly burned. Claire didn't even look at the clock until one in the morning.

By the time she pushed open the hospital doors to leave, it was closer to two. Her mood was subdued and she was bone-weary. Discovering a steady, dismal rain didn't help.

When Joel stepped out of the shadows, she managed the first smile she'd had since she'd left him at dinner. "You haven't been waiting out here all this time? You know I don't expect you on a Saturday."

"It seemed a good night for a walk."

Again, she felt a smile forming, the night's traumas fading from her mind. Slipping an arm around his waist, she felt the fine mist of rain on her face but no longer resented it.

"You need a hat."

He stopped, long enough to find a forgotten scarf in her raincoat pocket. She watched him tie it on her head. His fingers were clumsy, and terribly gentle. His hair was plastered to his head and he'd forgotten to button his own raincoat. When he finished with her scarf, she started redressing him.

"You ran out on me," he reminded her. "I'm not forgiving you."

"Oh, well." She finished the top button and pulled his collar around his neck.

"If you'd been there five more minutes without interruption..."

She chuckled, again curling her arm around his waist as they started walking. "I can't help it if you can't control your baser primitive impulses."

"We are only walking," Joel said in an injured tone, "because I can't trust your impulses in a car."

"We are walking," Claire informed him, "because you took one look at my face and decided I had a terrible night. Mind reading is one of your more upsetting qualities. We always walk when I have a terrible night."

"What was it, Claire?"

"A child burned." She swallowed. "She'll be all right. It's just..." She felt Joel squeeze her shoulders, and abruptly leveled him a smile. "Where's my cashews?"

He dug a crumpled bag from his pocket.

"Thank God."

"You're going to get fat on those."

"After we fatten me up, we'll start on you. We have to get you off cheeses and vegetables and meats and get you into some serious junk food."

"Are you sure you have a medical degree?"

"Top of my class."

"Goes to show you what the medical profession is coming to."

The rain kept falling. They walked the lakeshore before heading inland toward her house. The lake was black and still, accepting the tiny drops of rain without sound. A mile into their walk, Claire noticed vaguely that their voices had lowered, that they were increasingly talking irrelevant nonsense, that they were both damp and getting cold...and that she couldn't remember being happier.

Nothing mattered when she was with him. All day she'd been sifting through a dozen old memories. Joel was nothing like her ex-husband. She'd never loved Steve with an ounce of the passion or intensity she loved Joel. It was time to put the past to rest. Joel had never shown in thought or action that he was overly possessive.

Yes, but isn't that the point? a small voice reminded her. It was beautiful before—in the beginning. A man doesn't change until after you've made the commitment.

But that wary little voice just didn't understand. The world had seemed dismally gray when she left the hospital, and now it wasn't at all. The rain made puddles that dazzled under streetlights. Street lamps were shrouded in golden halos. The air smelled washed clean, and the sky was as black and soft as silk. What made the difference was the man beside her.

"Stop that," Joel murmured.

"Stop what?"

"Looking at me that way. I've decided you need a good night's rest, and until I've got you in my bed full-time that means I've got to send you home alone occasionally."

"I'm not sleeping well alone recently."

"I don't sleep at all," Joel growled.

Smiling, she reached up on tiptoe to kiss him. "I suppose that's another less than subtle hint that I'll be responsible for your failing health unless I marry you?"

He must have seen the change in her face, because he stopped still, searching her eyes. So silent he was, his features so grave, his eyes blue diamonds. "Don't tease. Not on this."

"I wasn't teasing." She took a breath, fingering his collar with suddenly unsteady fingers. "If you've changed your mind, of course—"

From the way he gathered her up and crushed the life out of her, she knew he hadn't changed his mind. Doubts were put aside. This had to be right. It wasn't the moment, or the time and place, for doubts. Just for kisses in the rain.

They walked on, her head on his shoulder, both feeling a mixture of exhilaration and total exhaustion. It was long past three when they reached her backdoor. Neither wanted to be anywhere but together, but Claire had promised her family an outing early in the morning. She and Joel postponed the separation another fifteen minutes, trying to argue about nothing.

"I should have driven. You're cold."

"I didn't want to drive; I needed to walk. And I'll be warm soon enough. And you could take my car back, so you don't have that walk—"

"I don't want your car. I want you."

They dallied another fifteen minutes, necking, whispering promises for another night, another time.

Both were so tired they were giddy; neither wanted to give in. "Come in," she coaxed.

"You know better."

"I could just make coffee. I wasn't suggesting anything else."

"If I come in for coffee, your mother will find us both in your bed tomorrow morning. You want that?"

"You're certainly making a lot of rash assumptions about your irresistible sex appeal."

"When you've got it, flaunt it."

"I thought that's what I was inviting you to do."

He swatted her fanny, sending her in.

"You're a cold and unfeeling man, Brannigan. I can't imagine why I love you."

He was unimpressed by the insult. She sighed, locking the door, then peered out at him one last time, hating the look of his lonely figure walking down the street. A huge yawn nevertheless escaped her lips.

"Claire."

She whirled around in the faint kitchen light, to find her mother in the doorway. Nora shook her curlered head. "When it's gotten so bad that you walk in the rain without knowing or caring," Nora said sagely, "it's past time you married the man."

"Yes," Claire said simply. She shivered suddenly, and told herself it was only because the night had been so cold.

Eleven

Frowning, Claire leaned over the bathroom counter to brush on eyeshadow and mascara. She stood back to review the results.

Dramatic. Definitely more sultry than her usual mode. Regardless, it was tough dredging up enthusiasm for an obligatory hospital personnel party. Dr. Hunter had been named new chief of staff, which was fine, but Claire wasn't inclined to waste a rare Monday night off standing around with a martini in her hand.

"Let's see," Dot piped up from behind her.

Claire obediently turned.

Dot looked her up and down, with such an adult catlike scrutiny that Claire smiled. "Beautiful," the four-year-old judged. "Not as beautiful as my mom, but you can't help that, Aunt Claire." She paused. "Purple eyeshadow would help."

"Purple doesn't go too well with green, sweet."

"Purple goes with everything," Dot corrected her, and trailed Claire back to the bedroom. "You know, I'd be glad to go with you to this party, but Mom and I are making popcorn tonight."

"Much more important," Claire agreed gravely, as she pulled a dress from its hanger and stepped into it. The gown was emerald-colored, raw silk, with full feminine sleeves that buttoned tight at the cuff, and a low square neckline that set off her great-grandmother's green garnet. Very sexy, she thought glumly to herself as she surveyed the finished product in the mirror.

Her off-mood was inexplicable. Everything had been going wonderfully for almost two weeks. Her sister's laughter rang through the house as it hadn't in years; Dot couldn't keep a grin off her face. Claire's work was the challenge and reward it always was. Joel's lovemaking the day before...well...

Claire's eyes softened as she sprayed perfume on her wrists and throat. That man could turn on a turnip. When given a woman to work with, he had no equal. For the past week, one would think he had nothing in his head but making her feel infinitely desirable, incomparably beautiful and insatiably sexy.

"I hear the bell," Dot announced. "Want me to let Joel in?"

"Would you, poppet?" She gave one last rueful glance at the mirror, aware her pulse had quickened even before she saw him. Slipping on heels, she snatched a beaded evening purse and white cashmere cape, and then just stood there a moment.

Joel would make a boring evening sparkle for her, she already knew that. It didn't matter where they were or what they did, from walking for miles in jeans to eating exotic dinners in formal clothes.

The unsettled mood still wouldn't leave her. The day before, after they'd made love, Joel had pressed for a wedding date. Preferably tomorrow. She felt exactly as he did, that there was no point in waiting. Neither enjoyed her leaving to go home after making love; Claire wanted his child; she wanted her things next to his in the closet...and to feel that threat of being closed in was absurd.

And she didn't feel it, she convinced herself. She just felt uneasy.

Joel's knowing eyes traveled head to toe, approved, lusted after and had her laughing even before they exited the house. "In a lousy mood, hmmm?" he murmured gravely. "We'll go off in a corner and play poker if the party's that bad, you know."

She shook her head, loving the look of him in a dark suit. His hair looked brushed by midnight; his blue eyes were snapping. "You don't realize how awful this is going to be," she told him. "You have to stand around for three hours and do nothing but discuss hospital politics. You're fed nothing but martinis, which have to be the most dreadful drink that was ever invented. And half the wives expect you to know what charitable organization they're working on, or you'll get a nose in the air."

"Are you trying to subtly tell me that I'd better come up with a great-aunt belonging to the D.A.R.?"

Joel deliberately straightened his tie when they got into the car.

"You laugh now. You'll be yawning in a half hour."

"I could liven up the group with stories of my street gang days."

He had her more cheerful by the time they arrived at the townhouse. If he didn't know the cause of her rare unsettled mood, he guessed part of it. Claire liked one on one with people and felt nervous in a crowd.

"I just never know what to say to these people," she murmured when he took the white cape from her shoulders inside.

And immediately proved herself wrong. Joel watched, proud of her, as various doctors and their wives came over to affectionately greet her. She might hate the attention, but her colleagues clearly appreciated her.

She was separated from him in a matter of minutes. Joel didn't mind. Like the oil man in winter, the bar operated on a keep-filled basis. The townhouse was tastefully furnished with Queen Anne antiques, and he wandered through admiring them. Strangers identified him with Claire and immediately introduced themselves; he didn't lack for conversation and could hold his own in a crowd. A few guests, as Claire had said, were distinctly fuddy duddies. Most were well-informed, caring people, with a slight disproportion of men over women.

For the first half hour, he kept an eye on Claire. For the next half hour he kept an eye on the men, since most of them seemed to gravitate in her direction at one time or another. His mood altered abruptly. Doctors were supposed to be paragons of good breeding;

he'd never guessed she worked with such a den of wolves. Before that hour had passed, he saw several kisses delivered to Claire.

She returned to his side many times in the next half hour, still holding the same martini she'd started with...and was whisked away as fast as she'd arrived. A doctor he knew damn well was married—he *looked* married—dragged Claire off to a corner to discuss some medical technique. Joel might not know medicine but he knew techniques just fine.

The color green started with his shoes and slowly filled him up until he was brimming with it. He was slightly inclined to stand on a table and announce she was his.

No one showed the least inclination to leave at nine, the time the cocktail party was supposed to be over. By nine-ten he saw Claire swiftly trying to make her way to him, her eyes sparkling with good humor, her silk dress caressing her figure with every movement she made. She grabbed his arm and whispered, "Can we bump this pop stand? We've been good long enough."

She expected a quick comeback, but Joel didn't give her one. Still smiling, she said a rapid succession of goodbyes while Joel fetched her cape. A few moments later they were outside on an absolutely wonderful spring night.

The air was tantalizing with that special drug of spring. Leaves were popping, rustling like new paper. Daffodils and hyacinths smelled heady and sweet from their flower beds. "You were an angel to put up with two hours of that nonsense," she told Joel as they got into the car.

"Hmmm."

Claire, suddenly aware of Joel's taciturn silence, asked "What's wrong?"

"Nothing."

She stared at him for a moment, startled at the marble set to his features, the stiff way he drove. "Something is," she said quietly.

Joel fell silent. "You looked beautiful tonight."

"Thank you. Only why am I getting the impression that's a criticism instead of a compliment?"

"It was a compliment, obviously." He shot her a smile that didn't quite meet his eyes. "Beautiful is rather an inadequate word, for that matter. Delectable, alluring, enticing..."

Claire leaned back her head, smiling, watching him. "You're in an extravagant mood? But then I saw the doctors' wives hanging all over you half the time we were there. You were by far the sexiest man there, and I was afraid you were going to have your ego irreparably enlarged by the time I got back to you."

"And was yours?" Joel asked smoothly.

"Pardon?"

"Did tonight feed your feminine ego? I noticed there wasn't a man there who wasn't drooling over the neckline of your dress."

Claire turned to ice. She heard the jealousy in Joel's voice, and felt as if a ghost had just slapped her on the face. "I don't believe my neckline is overly low," she said slowly.

"I didn't say it was."

"You seemed to imply I was...teasing other men."

"No. I was implying that you attracted other men. Which you do, and which is natural, with your looks and personality. Oh hell." Joel sighed, grabbing at the

tie around his neck to loosen it. "That comment was
out of line. Just give me a minute, would you? Jealousy hit me hard, watching other men continually
fawn over you. The way that newly married chief of
staff looked at you, I wanted to deck him."

Claire considered telling him that she'd been working with that married man for the last five years, and
that he'd never made a pass. But she didn't. Instead
she simply closed her eyes tight for a moment, and felt
sick. Déjà vu hit hard. She'd been in the same spot
before, where she had to explain her every action,
where every conversation with a male member of the
human species was suspect.

"Claire?"

She opened her eyes, to find Joel frowning at her,
the car stopped at a stoplight near her house.

"I would like to get out," she said clearly.

"What?"

"Out. Now." She didn't wait, just pulled the door
handle and pelted out of the car. Her heels clicked on
the pavement. Her lungs hauled in air, and she suddenly felt as if she couldn't get enough.

Behind her, she heard the squeak of brakes, a car
door slam, a man's footsteps racing behind her. Joel's
hands circled her shoulders, whirled her around.
"What the hell is going on?" he demanded fiercely. "I
was jealous. It's not the prettiest emotion, but it's a
fairly human one. I meant no lack of faith in you—"

"Not now maybe," she said wearily.

"What's that supposed to mean?"

"Joel." She shook her head helplessly, trying to
blink back the tears. "It always starts that way, with

little things. Only then it just gets worse. It's no good. I won't be ... smothered again."

"Wait a minute," he growled. The street lamp glowed on his face, all white, stark, sharp lines. "No games, lady. Cards on the table. I don't like seeing other men touch you. Is that a crime?"

"No," she said bitterly. "It's perfectly natural. Exactly the problem. Leave me alone, would you, Joel?"

She started walking, when his hand circled her wrist. The feeling of being handcuffed raised the taste of copper in her mouth. His words came out short and clipped. "Listen," he said flatly. "And listen good. You're of age, you can handle yourself. You've got the judgment to separate wolves from friends, and I trust that judgment. I didn't attend that party to interfere and I wouldn't have. A man who can't hold his own woman except with force or threats isn't worth much. Either there's love and trust or there isn't. I have that love and trust for you."

When she said nothing, his words came out harsh and fast. "I'm a very human man, Claire. I never said I was more. Humans are an imperfect species. If you expect me to feel nothing when another man puts his arm around you—that will never happen. That's not trying to put chains around your neck, it's simply an expression of feeling. Dammit, are you really so unforgiving?"

Tears suddenly fell freely. "Let me go," she said softly.

"No."

"Joel. Let me alone. You're hurting me—"

Abruptly he released her wrists.

"I love you," she said swiftly. "But it's not enough. Maybe I am unforgiving. Maybe I can't love enough back. All I know for sure is that I'm just as human as you are, just as imperfect. And I can't live with that constant fear of being closed in." Abruptly she swiveled around and started walking, her head high, tears flowing down her cheeks.

He didn't follow her or call out. She could feel him standing there, alone under the streetlight, his eyes searing her back. She didn't hear him start his car. She crossed the street to the last block where her house was, and kept walking. She wanted to reach up and wipe the tears from her face, but was too proud. He'd see the gesture.

A huge lock turned on the empty heart in her chest. She'd known it would happen from the beginning. Men understood all about independence until they had a commitment. Then the possessive games began. She'd only fooled herself, thinking it would be different with Joel.

God, she hurt. The only thing that kept her world from splintering in a thousand pieces was knowing it could never happen again. There would never be another man after Joel.

For the next few days Dot crawled on Claire's lap, offering fierce warm hugs for no reason at all. Walter followed her from room to room whenever she was home, determined to lean against her whenever she sat down. At work, Janice started bringing her homemade soup for breaks.

A week later, Claire's sister stopped in the doorway to her bedroom on a Sunday morning. Sandy had her hands in her robe pockets, her cheek pressed against the doorframe. "You know," she said slowly, "you've kept this family together ever since Dad died. You've seen us all through thick and thin. Every once in a while, you could let a few of us help you back. Can't you talk, Sis?"

A week after that Nora closed the doors of the kitchen, served Claire hot tea and gradually added six spoonfuls of sugar until the cup of tea was reduced to mud. "Have I ever told you how often your father and I argued?" she asked conversationally. "You can't really love someone without learning how to fight with them. If a relationship always went smooth as glass, you'd be bored to bits. I mean, I would be bored to bits, of course. We're not talking about you."

Since Claire was smiling, and carrying on all her normal responsibilities, she couldn't quite figure out how they all knew. Makeup hid the shadows under her eyes. Anyone could have a sudden plunge in appetite. She was hardly acting like a moping child; she had too much pride.

Midnights were the worst times. It was coming out of the hospital doors and finding no one there. She kept telling herself that if she got to the point where she stopped looking for him, the rest would fall into place again. Only she couldn't seem to get to that point. She searched for him every night. And Joel just wasn't there.

"Just keep calm," Claire said firmly. "I'll find it. It's just going to take me a minute." She again aimed the flashlight at the fusebox, and glanced back to her audience. Sitting on an old table in the basement,

Nora, Sandy and Dot were lined up like patient schoolchildren. The bloodhound was next to them. All were looking at her expectantly, knowing she'd find the fuse that affected the kitchen light upstairs.

Their house was old, with the kind of fuses that had little windows and metal clips. If all the fuses had been marked the job would have been simple. They weren't. Claire needed to find the one with the broken metal clip, only none of them looked broken.

"You should all know how to do this yourselves," Claire said irritably, which effectively stalled the household from panic for another fifteen seconds. For the zillionth time, she whisked the flashlight across the twenty fuses.

The sound of footsteps on the stairs made everyone except the dog freeze. He hurled himself in a frightened mass for Claire.

Biting her lip, she flicked up the flashlight to the intruder's face, and instantly dropped it. "Damn. Double damn. Triple damn...." She groped on the floor, her heart ticking like a watch gone mad. It was Joel, his face white under that sudden flash of light, his eyes blue and searing like hollow flame. He looked exhausted. And beautiful. The loneliness of the past few weeks ached through her body like an incurable disease.

"I've got it," he murmured and grabbed the rolling flashlight. Shoulder to shoulder, he leaned next to Claire, facing the fusebox. "Looks like we've got a pretty critical audience there?" he questioned in a low voice.

She couldn't seem to catch her breath. "I...yes."

"We may have to try these out one by one."

"Yes."

Swiftly he substituted new fuses for old, waiting to see if the light flicked on in the kitchen. Claire stood in absolute stillness beside him, staring at the fuses as if she'd never conceived of anything so fascinating. On the sixth try, the light in the kitchen reflected down the stairway, and a roar of applause sounded behind them. Just as quickly, the four bolted for the stairs without a single glance back except for Dot, who muttered a "Hi, Joel!" before her mother snatched her up and carted her the rest of the way to the kitchen.

"But why can't I—" echoed from the distance until the door to the kitchen was firmly closed.

"There must be some reason they want us locked in this basement," Joel murmured dryly. He tossed the broken fuse in his hand absently, the motion as lazy and easy as the eyes that flicked enigmatically to hers. "Take it easy, Claire," he said quietly. "I didn't come here to talk or pressure you. I only came here because of your claustrophobia."

Something in Claire sparked and then died. "Pardon?"

"There's a cure. Something that's been very successful. If you can spare an hour, I would suggest that you give it a chance."

She couldn't seem to think. "An hour..."

"I don't see how it could possibly hurt you to try." Joel's eyes looked hard and distant, his tone almost formal.

Hesitantly, she said finally, "All right."

Upstairs, she went to the front hall for a spring jacket while Joel waited in the kitchen. "I'm going out for a while," she mentioned in general.

"All right, Claire."

"All right, Claire."

"Okeydoke, Aunt Claire."

The voices were in unison, all faces wreathed in innocent smiles. Claire considered killing the lot of them. Her cheeks red, she followed Joel to his car, but he didn't say anything. Actually he didn't say anything until they reached his place, where she felt a moment's trepidation.

"We have to go up to my office," he told her.

Trepidation was replaced by a terrible feeling of disappointment. His office. Of course.

She couldn't think of anything she was less interested in at the moment than her claustrophobia, but she couldn't seem to talk. Her eyes were glued to him. She was within touching distance, hearing distance, smelling distance. Principles didn't seem to mean much when she was that close to him again.

She wanted to apologize, to take back her harsh words the night of the party. She wanted to explain that she was capable of being totally irrational on that certain subject. Probably because she was an idiot. It didn't matter why, not any more. She wanted to ask his patience through a few squabbles and fights that would undoubtedly still happen because of her idiocy, and she wanted to assure him that she would get over it in time. These past two weeks she'd learned something terribly painful. Running from hurt was no escape from it, because life wasn't much worth breathing without him.

But she said nothing, because her throat was full, and she was afraid that if she bridged past she'd cry. Maybe... in a few minutes. Or maybe... if he'd just look more approachable. Joel had that distant look of a man who'd been through war, and the formal shell around him was stiffer than steel. He was being friendly, cool, quiet. If there was a man of passion underneath that, she was terribly afraid he was unwilling for her to see it again.

"Stairs..." He urged her up, and then didn't say a word as she mounted nine sets of them, with him trailing behind her. She waited while he unlocked his place, and then he motioned her in. "You know where the office is."

She nodded, and started walking there. She stopped in the doorway, rather startled at the look of the room. Suits and shirts still on their hangers were strewed on desk and chairs. She glanced back, but Joel moved forward without looking at her.

"Do you think you can manage to trust me for a good ten minutes?" he asked evenly.

"Dammit. Of course," she said irritably.

A wisp of a smile barely turned the corner of his lips. "Good. In here, then."

The door looked part of the paneling, until he swung it open. Never having guessed there was a room beyond the office, she stepped forward curiously. Too late, she was inside and heard Joel close the door with the two of them inside.

"What is this?" she demanded lowly.

The walk-in closet was windowless, and except for cream-colored carpeting and a lightbulb, totally empty. She didn't need a minute and a half before the walls starting closing in.

"You said you'd trust me for a few minutes," Joel reminded her.

"I do trust you."

"And do you love me?"

She could suddenly see three of Joel through prisms of tears. "Yes. *Yes!*" She added in a desperate rush, "Joel. Get me out of here so we can talk."

"In a minute."

His arms reached out and plucked her from that terribly cold place. She was clinging even before his mouth layered on hers. She was terribly afraid he could taste the metal in her mouth, that taste of fear. It had nothing to do with her fear of closed-in places.

He didn't seem to notice, or maybe the smooth sweep of his tongue simply drowned that taste with his own. From her toes to her fingertips she could feel the distinctive man-strength that was Joel.

Rough hands urgently pushed open the buttons of her blouse, unsnapped her bra, flipped open the snap of her jeans. The man was in a hurry. A shiver vibrated through Claire, from the look in his eyes. The look was fierce, almost savage, all demand, no asking permission.

"Touch me," he whispered. "Now, Claire."

The easiest thing he could possibly have asked her to do. His skin...she'd missed the warmth and texture of his skin. She'd missed the flow of muscle in his upper arms and shoulders when she ran her hands there; she'd missed the concave flat of his stomach, the thud of his heart under her palm.

These things belonged to her. Body and soul this man was hers, and hers alone. She'd never understood possessiveness before, but she knew it now, and reveled in it. Where she touched, his flesh grew warmer; his muscles tightened; his breathing changed. All for her. By the time she worked down to the snap on his jeans, she no longer had any clothes on. He had far too many. Not for long.

Carpet suddenly cushioned her back. She couldn't remember falling. "Look around you," Joel whispered.

She looked the only place that mattered, and saw his eyes, full of love, a fierce desperate blue. His head ducked down, his mouth nuzzling the soft flesh of her neck, trailing down to the hollow between breasts. His palm slid down to the silken hair between her thighs as his tongue swirled her nipples, making them ache, making them hurt with longing.

"Joel—"

"You know where you are?"

Of course she knew where she was. With him. But not close enough yet. "I'm sorry," she whispered. "I'm so sorry, Joel. I was wrong. No, I don't expect you to be perfect. For that matter, I would have reacted exactly the same way if I saw you kissing another woman, even if she was one hundred two years old...."

He didn't seem to be listening. Her eyes closed and her neck arched back, helplessly drawn from the words she wanted to say to a world where words had no meaning.

Only the senses—touch and taste and hearing—had meaning. Only...Joel. And for a man who'd shown no more patience than the devil a few moments before, he suddenly turned lazy and lingering. Her hand skidded down his sides, slippery, hot, urging him to take her.

In time, he shifted her beneath him. As he drove into her, her first muffled gasp of pleasure was drowned in his mouth.

There seemed no end. Ripples and waves of heat flowed and ebbed, all in a fierce welcomed rhythm. Her skin grew slick, so did his. Fire and ice turned one, in a fierce, violent explosion ... of softness.

"Are you going to open your eyes?" Joel whispered.

Claire smiled and snuggled closer before her lashes shuttered to half mast. She would have felt disoriented if Joel's arms hadn't been around her. A harsh lightbulb from the ceiling half blinded her; she could reach out and touch three of four walls.

"Why," she murmured dryly, "are we in a closet?"

"To prove something to you." Joel's fingers pushed back her hair, combed through the disheveled strands. "When we're together, sweet, you don't feel closed in. I had to prove it to you. That it's different for you and me. I don't give a damn how it was for you and anyone else. This is us, Claire. I had to try one last time to prove the difference to you, to make you see it."

"I saw," she whispered. "Joel—"

"I don't want to make demands on you," he interrupted swiftly. "Your job does that; your family does that. That's never what I wanted from a woman, and never what I'd do to you. I want to be the man you want to come home to, to get away from just those kinds of emotional demands. I want to be the man you feel free to be yourself with. Where all the pressures go away, and you just feel..."

"Loved?" She arched her head back, staring at him with luminous eyes. "I feel loved, Joel, body and soul. And I love you that same way."

"Be sure," he whispered.

"I'm sure."

"Be sure *long* term. I'm talking gray hair and rockers now."

A soft smile curled her lips. "If you want to see how fast I'll marry you, Brannigan," she whispered, "see how fast you can get me out of this closet."

Joel sat up. A teasing frown arched his brows. "I thought we'd cured that claustrophobia. Because if we didn't..."

Laughing, she pulled him back down beside her.

*   *   *   *   *

TO MEET AGAIN

Lass Small

To Paul Lutus,
who programmed the Apple Writer II
quite brilliantly,
with my thanks.

And
to all the user groups
with their proud hackers
who share their knowledge,
card expansions and
innovations so generously.

And especially to
Fort Wayne Apple Computer
Users Group—
an impressed salute.

LASS SMALL

finds living on this planet at this time a fascinating experience. People are amazing. She thinks that to be the teller of tales of people, places and things is absolutely marvelous.

Her upcoming Silhouette Books include a series about the Fabulous Brown Brothers, starting with *A Restless Man* (Silhouette Desire #736, August 1992) and continuing with *Two Halves* in October 1992 and *Beware of Widows* in December 1992.

Lass Small says, "It still amazes me to hold my published books, and to receive letters from readers. I am highly honored to be one in this celebration for Silhouette Desire's tenth anniversary. Isabel, Lucia and Karen—here's to the next ten years!"

Books by Lass Small

Sihouette Desire

Tangled Web #241
To Meet Again #322
Stolen Day #341
Possibles #356
Intrusive Man #373
To Love Again #397
Blindman's Bluff #413
*Goldilocks and the Behr #437
*Hide and Seek #453
*Red Rover #491
*Odd Man Out #505
*Tagged #534
Contact #548
Wrong Address, Right Place #569
Not Easy #578
The Loner #594
Four Dollars and Fifty-One Cents #613
*No Trespassing Allowed #638
The Molly Q #655
'Twas the Night #684
*Dominic #697

*Lambert Series

Silhouette Romance

An Irritating Man #444
Snow Bird #521

Silhouette Books

Silhouette Christmas Stories 1989
''Voice of the Turtles''

One

It all began with a package of gum. None of it would
have happened if Laura Fullerton hadn't decided she
needed a specific kind if she was going to fly. She'd
found her ears tended to block. However, Laura was
at O'Hare Airport, there in Chicago, before she remembered the gum. That's when she ran into Tabitha,
who'd been a sorority sister when they were at Indiana University in Bloomington. It was the first step.

"Laura!" Tabby called as if they were friends.

Laura turned about, vaguely recalling the voice,
knowing whoever it was had to be an acquaintance.
Calling her by name was an unarguable clue.

The aptly named Tabby was deliberately thin, and
she was wearing a designer travel jump suit that looked
smashing with her black hair and green eyes. It was a
discreet golden color. She looked like the cover of

Vogue in the days when women were being posed to resemble animals.

In contrast, Laura had on a smart navy business suit with a crisp shirt blouse, and her blond hair was in an efficient knot at the back of her head. Her walking shoes revealed she was not so new to air travel that she wasn't aware of the walking done in terminals.

"Where're you heading?" Tabby's teeth were normal; one always expected them to be small and feline.

"Columbia, South Carolina, via Atlanta."

"Oh, good. Give me your ticket and I'll switch your reservations—you'll still make your connection—and we can travel as far as Atlanta together."

Laura dredged up a smile.

So on that April day, the two women—who had only Greek letters in common—were sitting side by side in Chicago's O'Hare, that hub of world travel, waiting for their plane.

"How amazing to run into you." Tabby's green eyes studied her companion with the nonlethal interest of a well-fed cat. Tabby knew Laura had to be thirty, only a year young...uh older than Tabby. Tabby was avoiding thirty and had adjusted her age three times now. She noted Laura was still as slender as she'd been at eighteen and her hair looked suspiciously the same blond. Was it actually sun streaked? Or done cleverly so? And Laura's eyes hadn't ever been that blue. Were they really that color? Contacts were quite incredible these days, and a lot of people wore them to change or deepen the color of their eyes.

They talked rather inanely, for they were strangers, and Laura had been looking around at all the people striding purposefully, shuffling in lines, hurrying or waiting. "Ah, Tab, this life is remarkable. I've seen people I haven't seen in years. It seems to me everyone flies. Doesn't anyone just go to an office, work all day and go home at night? Does the whole world spend their lives flying from place to place?"

"You'll get used to it. The food isn't as good as it once was."

"How long have you been living this way, Tabitha?"

"For about—uh—since college. I was graduated young. Skipped a couple of grades . . . early on."

"You were always precocious," Laura commented dryly.

"Laura, do you wear contacts?"

"No. Why?"

"Don't you wear glasses at all?"

"No. Not yet. I come from a family of eagle-eyed people."

"Amazing." Tabby wasn't convinced.

"Do you know who I ran into last week? You'll never guess. She was a Tri Delt. Never mind guessing, I'll tell you. Ann Thompson!"

"Ann Thompson?" Tabby tasted the name. "Who's Ann Thompson?"

"Don't you remember? She married George Miller."

"I never knew any Ann Thompson. What'd she look like?"

"She's—"

The speaker came on: "Passengers for Miami flight—"

"That's us," Tabby said, rising.

"Atlanta, Jacksonville and Miami," the interrupted voice droned on.

They gathered their things and moved toward the line.

"Ann Thompson..." Tabby still chewed on that name trying to place her. It wasn't unusual for Tabby to have trouble recalling a woman.

"Ann Thompson... Miller," Laura added.

Then the second step in Laura's destiny occurred. Out of the crowd a man's voice intruded as he questioned, "Laura?"

"Pete? Why, hello!" Laura laughed as he leaned to kiss her. That flustered her, for she wasn't yet one of the kissing "hello" greeters.

He said cheerfully, "I only recently heard you and Tom split years ago. I'm just surprised it lasted as long as it did."

What was Laura supposed to reply to that? She hurried into chatter. "Tab, you remember Peter Watkins?"

Tabby remembered men and enthused, "Oh, yes! Hel*lo*!"

Her smile turned Cheshire briefly, to fade as Laura asked, "How's Molly?"

"Molly plus two babies." Peter dug for pictures.

It was comparatively easy to arrange their seats on board so that Peter was between them, and the talk was quick and animated until Peter asked, "Have you heard about Tanner? Or do you remember him?"

"Tanner? I remember him!" Tabby said in a perfectly normal way as though nothing had changed.

But Laura's face went still and cautious as if she realized it was the third step. "What about Tanner?"

"He was in a hell of a wreck. Completely totaled his Porsche. There wasn't any part that wasn't destroyed or at least bent." Pete shook his head.

"What about...Tanner?" Laura's breath was caught in her chest and her face was frozen. Her jaw didn't work right and her eyes weren't focused. The sounds around her were dimmed by a roaring in her ears and she saw Tanner quite clearly. He'd been tall, long-limbed, with dark tumbled hair and blue, blue eyes.

As from a distance, Laura heard Pete's reply, "Tanner? Oh, he's okay. He's down north of Myrtle Beach, at his parents' summer place. Been there awhile and probably will be for some time. He was given a leave of absence to recover. I doubt he'll ever get over losing..."

Laura gasped.

"...that Porsche. It was the perfect car. Was. That's the crucial word. What a mess. I saw pictures. Isn't it just like Tanner to have pictures of its demise? I've never seen a man so wrapped up in anything. Actually—" Pete slowly shook his head and his laugh was ironic "—it took them almost an hour getting him out of it. He was *really* 'wrapped up' in it. He'll probably have it burned, and spread the ashes on his place out in the wilds of lower Manhattan Island."

"New York?" Tabby frowned carefully.

"If you've ever been there, you know there's nothing wilder than New York." Peter was logical. "Tanner's family own some land there. It's under buildings, of course." He laughed, carried away by his imagination. "Some of the concrete jungle."

Laura's voice sounded faintly, "Is he...all right?"

"I haven't seen him. Charlie showed me the pictures of the car. Do you remember Charlie? I run into him a couple of times a year, here and there. He's a church *deacon*! Can you believe that? Charlie! Sells insurance. Last time I saw Charlie was in Denver. Do you suppose our whole class is flying around somewhere?"

"Yes." Laura could believe that. She was still in shock and impatient to find a way to bring Peter back to talking about Tanner.

"What are you doing now, Laura? Flying for pleasure or profit. What was your major?"

"She does paintings for lobbies." Tabby smiled at Peter for no more reason than the fact she always smiled at men.

"Oh." Pete had no idea what lobby paintings meant, and he wasn't terribly interested.

Laura elaborated, "I was an art major and I've done lobby paintings, but recently I've expanded. There's a group planning a chain of leisure houses. The chairman had seen some of my work and he's allowing me to try for the decoration contract. It's my first expansion project."

Pete nodded without a whole lot of interest and inquired, "Are you ladies going on to Miami?"

"I am." Tabby licked her lips to freshen her smile.

"No." Laura still wasn't focused. "My presentation is in Columbia, South Carolina."

"Hey! If you have time, you ought to drop over to the coast and see old Tanner. He's all alone down there."

"Tanner has never been alone in all his life." Laura's voice was just a little stiff.

Pete grinned. "He is now. He was getting burned out as it was. He was older than the rest of us, if you recall. His stretch in Nam put him in with us kids. Go over and say hello. He'll be grateful. The Moran place is easy to find. Just go north of Myrtle Beach out past Ocean Boulevard. It's a big old gray clapboard house. You can't miss it. Give him my regards and take a bouquet—here's the money." Pete slid his wallet out of his inside jacket pocket and removed a bill. "Give him this bouquet for his *Porsche*! He'll love it. I'll call him and tell him I'm sending a proxy to visit. Okay? Here's his address. You can just show up."

Laura took the bill, but she was almost reluctant to commit herself to going. Should she? Should she go down and see Tanner again? The chatter continued between Pete and Tabby, and Laura must have contributed her share, but she was thinking of Tanner. She could go and see him. But should she?

Still occupied with the thought, Laura said good-bye to Pete and Tabby in Atlanta. She was aware that she was leaving Pete alone with Tabby, and the danger to Pete that entailed. But he was thirty, and he loved his wife and babies. He'd been flying around alone for years. He could take care of himself.

After that brief splinter of concern, her mind went back to The Question: Should she? How would it be to see Tanner again? How badly had he been hurt? And all through her presentation before the attentive board of directors, a corner of her mind was questioning: Should she?

She was still debating when she rented the car. By the time she was driving east on Highway 20 it occurred to her the debate was somewhat redundant. She was going.

Tanner. Just the name was enough to give the inside of her stomach deeply erotic shimmerings. She remembered when she first saw him around campus at I.U. in Bloomington, Indiana, and assumed he was a professor. He stood out even in the thirty-thousand-student maelstrom. He was older, smoother, he made all the other guys she knew look like high school visitors. Tanner.

He'd passed her one day as she crossed the shallow, narrow stream that divided the campus and was called the Jordan River, and he'd winked at her. She was immobilized. She turned like some kind of zombie programmed to simply trail along after him but he walked on with his long stride. She spent all day coaxing her nervous system to recovery.

That was the only time she'd ever seen him alone. He was always with other people. Laughing. He drew people like a magnet. Careless, easy, his smile so lazy and knowing. His dark hair mussed, his blue eyes amused by the world and everything in it.

Tanner would always wink at Laura when he saw her. Even surrounded by all those fawning women, he would wink at her. And it was like a kiss. It was a private thing just between them. She'd yearned over the idea of him. At night lying on her sagging mattress in the sorority house, listening to her roommate breathe in untroubled sleep, Laura would think about Tanner.

She'd met him so casually. There had been no heralding horns, no drum roll. She'd been standing with—who was it?—and Tanner had come up behind her. Then she had heard his actual voice and he'd said, "Well, hello. And who is this?"

She only remembered seeing his blue eyes with their incredible lashes looking down at her. Had she ever acknowledged the introduction? Probably not. She'd been stunned. Tanner shouldn't happen to a young, innocent woman. She had been too stupid to know what to do about him. She'd fumbled it. Botched her chance. But that's silly, she thought. She'd never had any real chance with Tanner.

He'd kissed her. That was what wrecked her whole facade of sophistication. Tanner's kiss had ruined her forever for any other man. So why was she driving through South Carolina in order to see him? Because she needed to confront this strange spell that had lingered for all these years. She would find out it had been a fantasy, and then she would be free of him. She needed to do this for her own sake. A dream can be a pleasant interlude for idle moments, or it can be crippling, making all other men seem lesser.

From the time she'd met him, she'd been helpless. An idiot. After that brief first meeting, he'd touched her shoulder as he left. He probably knew what chaos was racketing around in her body, and he escaped while he could still get away from her. He realized that if she'd ever managed to get her fingers unclutched from her stack of books, she'd have clutched them into him.

After that she noticed women always presumed too much around Tanner. They always had their hands on him. He didn't appear to mind. He was kind. He allowed it. They obviously needed it somehow. She thought they were all disgusting. Poor Tanner. But then she saw that he winked at others the same way he winked at her. It was like a casual smile to him. The wink was meaningless.

When he asked her out the first time, she'd just said yes to Mike. She went back to the sorority house and cried. But she knew that if she had gone with Tanner, she would have given him her soul. It was better to be safe with Mike than to get on the merry-go-round of madness that sharing time with Tanner would have done to her. Then Tanner graduated and was gone forever.

After she broke up with Mike, Tom asked her out, and she was already engaged to Tom when Tanner came back on campus to visit. He said he'd just heard she'd broken up with Mike and would she go with him? So she lost her only other chance to be with Tanner.

She'd had some bitter days. But Tom was sweet and she married him. Tanner had come to South Bend for the wedding. Quiet. Serious. He'd kissed her in the receiving line, and that was probably what ruined the honeymoon. Tom, well, that was all past.

She wondered if Tanner had ever married. He had to be thirty-five. How had he survived all these years? How had he survived Nam so unblemished? And now he'd survived a terrible wreck. What would it be like to see him again?

Would seeing him cure her? Or would it wreck her completely? She was light-years older now. Surely she would be able to speak and move when she was with him this time? She was a mature woman, capable of business presentations, good in her field, competent to cope with any situation. She had become used to directing other people and helping them to understand how things should look. She could communicate calmly under almost any circumstances and keep her head. What would seeing Tanner do to her?

What if he didn't know her from Adam...Eve. Pete hadn't told Tanner *who* was coming to see him. Only a proxy. Would Tanner stand there and look beyond her for the surprise? What was she doing driving now down Highway 501 in South Carolina all these years later, chasing a dream? A memory? A "might have been"?

Laura stopped at a florist in Myrtle Beach and bought a bouquet of red carnations with some fern. An anonymous arrangement, good for any occasion, she had decided. After that there was no reason to put it off, and she drove north on Ocean Boulevard and on out of town to the Moran "cottage."

She arrived toward evening. The house appeared to be on the highest knoll around where, unperturbed, it looked out on the great Atlantic Ocean. The palms rustled in their restless way as they strained the wind. The sky was overcast and the water curled in white horses that thundered onto the shore. The ocean. She had never been on a coast before.

In getting out of the car, she found she was a little stiff from sitting so immobile and tense while driving to Tanner. She stood straight, allowing her muscles time to adjust as she looked around. The house was gray clapboard with deep porches and wide windows that were open to the winds. There were spring's tulips carefully nurtured in beds around and about. And of course there was sand.

She took up the green, tissue-wrapped bouquet from Pete and went up onto the porch, deliberately making noise with her heels on the wooden steps and across the porch.

Had he heard the car? Would he be curious? Was he watching? She looked around at the view from the porch as if seeing him wasn't urgent, and as if her insides weren't trembling with her anticipation. She tried to appear as if this was a lark for her to come down here and see Tanner Moran.

She heard the door open and turned with a slight smile. So he *had* been watching. She saw he was dressed in soft, casual cottons, as he opened the screen, and he walked with one crutch. He came out, watching her, but he wasn't smiling. She was sure he didn't remember her.

"Hello, Tanner." He was even more devastating! Good Lord, what was she doing here?

"Laura." He said the name only.

"You do remember me." She managed her hostess smile, mutilating the flowers' stems between her two hands.

"Vividly."

"You look just the same."

"A bit battered. You look . . . I can't believe you're here." His voice was soft. His face was still serious. There were laugh lines that were pale in his tan, to emphasize the fact that he wasn't smiling. Why was he so serious?

"I saw Pete on the plane from Chicago. He said you were here, so I drove over from Columbia. How are you?"

"Fine."

How inane. "Pete sent these to your *Porsche*." She laughed awkwardly and held out the flowers.

He took them, still watching her, and said, "Thank you."

They just stood there. She wasn't sure what she should do. He hadn't invited her inside. He probably had a harem ensconced in there and didn't want this interruption.

"Come inside." It was as if he was only then conscious that he was host.

"Well . . ." She shouldn't be too quick to go inside. She was bent on being casual.

"You drove down from Columbia? What were you doing there?" He held the door for her and she went on in.

The rooms distracted her from his questions. From the big center hall she could judge the house was larger than she'd first thought. Through doors she could peek into unused rooms where the furniture was draped with cotton dust covers for protection against the salt air, dust and sand. "This is perfect." She looked around. "Marvelous."

"It's like old silver and the patina of scratches that enhances it." He looked only at her. "The long years of living here have given the house a coating of love."

His word choice surprised her, she looked at him and her eyes then clung to him.

His marvelous deep voice went on like velvet, "We're the fourth generation to live in this house. My great grandparents bought it so all the grandchildren and their children could get together in the summers. This house is saturated with all the laughter and quarrels and gossip of a whole lot of relatives. Think what it could tell if it could talk." He grinned then. "You can see I've been alone for a while."

"I like the idea of all those lives linked here."

His eyes were steady on her. "Me too." Then he moved as if he'd caught himself staring and he asked, "And how is Tom?"

"He was fine, the last I heard."

"When was that?" He'd gone still again.

"Oh, three . . . no, four or so years ago. We were divorced after a couple of years."

"I hadn't known. I'd heard you were in business but no one ever mentioned a divorce. Have you remarried?" He watched her.

"No. Are you married?"

"No."

They both moved as if to break the tension. It must be her tension. Why would he be tense? He took Pete's flowers into the kitchen, and she trailed along as she'd longed to do all those years ago. He put the bouquet into an empty peanut butter jar and added water.

"I can't make the stairs but I can give you a tour of the lower floor. It's nicely laid out. Come and see." So he showed her around the rooms. The windows and doors were left open so that air moved and the place wouldn't be stale and musty. He walked, limping, supported by the crutch.

Being an artist, she naturally looked at the pictures on the walls. He told where they'd come from or who had painted them. They were almost all of the sea, palms, the house, sailboats or any combination thereof and were done by family members. All were charming and of a very wide range of talents.

Other than the pictures, the house primarily was colors to her. Fabrics were a new interest so those were noticed. She appreciated the rug lying like a jewel on the floor of the library, but flinched over the sand that it must endure in a beach house. The view out over the porch was magnificent and a sailboat rode the waves as if on cue.

For something to fill the silence, which she found awkward, but mainly to hear his voice again, she asked, "Where do you live ordinarily?"

"Wherever I'm working."

"Oh." She tried another tack. "Do you sail?"

"Not lately. Are you a sailor?"

"No." When they talked she had the excuse to look at him.

"You get seasick?" He smiled just a little.

"I've never tried sailing. I'm a landlubber. A prairie woman."

"We'll have to give you a taste while you're here. You can stay awhile? You're not due anywhere soon?"

"Well..."

"You would rescue me from terminal boredom." He was serious again.

"I can't believe you would ever be bored."

"I just discovered that I have been."

What did he mean by that?

"I can hold the door for you and carry your things across the porch, but stairs still throw me. I'm sorry."

"I have muscles." She grinned at him. He wanted her to stay with him?

"Muscles, huh? Don't intimidate me."

She laughed, putting her head back and enjoying the release from tension. Why had she been tense? He did want her to stay with him.

"You'd probably like a shower and more comfortable clothes? You did bring some knockabout clothes? If you didn't, we have a guest closet of almost anything, nothing designer but all well-worn, soft, broken in. You can dig through those."

How easily he assumed she would stay with him. Why not? It was a hospitable house, geared to provide for any oversight. There was certainly room enough, with casual, extra clothing in a guest closet . . . and the host was Tanner.

She wasn't sure she wanted to be that scruffy with him. She wanted to look pretty for him. But she would investigate the closet. There might be something wickedly intriguing. Something soft and sensual. In a guest closet? Come on, Laura, don't be silly.

Two

Tanner was still assimilating the fact: Laura Fullerton was actually here with him! She was real. He watched her as if she could disappear if he took his eyes from her for more than a brief second. It was unbelievable that she could be there, in that house and with him. He felt he shouldn't question it too closely, she might vanish. "Never doubt, accept." That's what his dad had always said.

How could any female look the way she did? Like a fragile princess in a tower. A lady. This was a dream. He didn't know quite how he should go about being alone with Laura Fullerton. He'd never had the chance when they were at I.U. There always seemed to be men around her. Male Neanderthals with their knuckles dragging and saliva dripping from their pointed teeth.

He smiled as he felt his own teeth pointing and his arms lengthening so his own knuckles would drag if she stayed around. She hadn't yet rejected his invitation to stay with him for a while. Would she? My God. If... All he had to do was remember which leg he was limping on.

She wouldn't let him carry her suitcase across the porch. "If you'll just hold the door?" Then she hesitated in the center hall, not knowing where she would go. She put down her bag and turned toward Tanner.

"I have one of the cooks' rooms at the back." He smiled. "Or," he said dismissively, "You can have any of the north rooms, those facing the top of the stairs. And there are the maids' rooms in the attic. No one else is here, so you have a wide selection."

He didn't want to crowd her in any way or have her feel threatened. He wanted her to feel as if whatever she did, it was by her own choice. That she was in control.

As he suspected, Laura was oddly uneasy. She'd never been in any situation even similar to this one, and she wasn't exactly sure how she should act, so she rushed into words: "In all of my life, I've never been on a coast."

He made his voice casual and a little slow. "You never went to Florida on spring break?"

Unknowingly she gave him an insight to her thinking. "I was quite strictly raised." There was a slight, telling pause before she went on. "Spring break I helped spring-clean at home. My parents said that provided enough of a change. Actually it was fun. We had a good time. I have three sisters and we're all very close in age. They're cheerful. They all pitch in and work hard."

"I met them at your wedding."

"Oh, yes. I'd forgotten."

"I'm an only child."

"How horrible for you."

He smiled a little. "There were all these cousins." He gestured to indicate the big old house so often filled with relatives.

"Yes. Well, I'll go on up." But still she hesitated.

"Sorry I can't help."

Again she chattered, "I can handle it. I've learned to travel with only the essentials. Suitcase gallantry is apparently a thing of the past. I'll never forget a strong young man, carrying his little overnight bag, allowing me to struggle along with two weekenders and a garment bag in the Dayton airport. I send thoughts his way every now and then."

"He probably doesn't connect his rotten luck with his rudeness to you and probably a lot of other people, if he could have been so unkind to you." Tanner's tone was regretful because he hadn't been there to help her.

"That was my first trip. Perhaps his acting as ungentlemanly as he did was a lesson. Since then I've never taken more than *I* can handle alone. But I still don't like him. I think it was his smile. I would have learned anyway, when I found I had too much to carry by myself and help is so chancy."

She smiled at Tanner, and with nothing else to delay her commitment—to actually going up the stairs and selecting a room—she quite bravely lifted her suitcase and carried it up the steps.

With that action she had selected the course of her life. It seemed to her at the time, that she was doing something from which there was no retreat. She was choosing to do this rash thing. She was going to stay with Tanner, and... She couldn't think beyond the fact that she would be there with him. That was enough for now.

He stood watching her hips as she climbed the stairs. Lovely. He'd boxed himself in. He'd expected her to take one of the cooks' rooms downstairs. He'd said he couldn't climb stairs, but that wasn't quite true.

He called to Laura, "The guest closet is one of the middle ones by the front bath. See it?"

"This one? Towels. This one. I found it."

He measured his walk and the crutch thump carefully, for the sound in case she listened, as he went to the kitchen. It was a good thing the freezer was kept stocked. He heard the pipes rattle as she showered. He leaned against the counter and, with the predictable body reaction, "saw" her naked in that upstairs bathroom, and his mind "watched" her hands wash her body.

She was here in this house, and they were alone. She was going to stay with him. There was the chance he would make love with her. He groaned and turned to lean on his hands, spread apart on the counter, and he shook his head before he straightened and took deep breaths.

It was Laura, long ago, who'd inadvertently helped him hone the math rotes of tables and formulas he'd been forced to use to distract his mind from her.

* * *

He'd chopped the salad with a meat cleaver, thawed two steaks in the microwave and had charcoal smoldering in the grill out on the kitchen deck, when he heard her light steps coming down the back stair to the kitchen.

She called, "Brace yourself!"

He turned with an almost breathless anticipation, his grin beginning.

She opened the door at the bottom of the stairs and jumped down to spread her arms, as she exclaimed, "Ta-daaa!" She was a little overanimated in her effort to be casual.

She wore a man's shirt belted at the waist with a tie. It looked very much as if that was *all* she wore. And his mind became very busy when she lifted the shirttails to expose purple running shorts that fit. So he didn't have a cardiac arrest after all. His grin broadened, mostly over his own reaction to her, but she thought he was being very nice and friendly.

"What can I do?" She immediately took in his preparation. "The table?"

"We don't eat out of the skillet?" He pretended surprise.

"Tacky," she pronounced haughtily as she dug into drawers and opened cabinets to find what was needed.

"I should have known you were running around loose long ago. I might have recovered faster."

Rather sassily she inquired, "Been coping with ptomaine from eating from unwashed skillets?"

"I am meticulous. I *always* wash my eating utensils. I like your hair up that way."

"I couldn't find any more pins."

"I'll go up later and see if I can't find some some-where."

"I thought you couldn't climb stairs." She paused to look at him.

"While carrying suitcases," he reminded her quite cleverly and smiled only a little as if being polite.

"I see." She gave him a careful look.

They ate on the deck on a round metal table where they'd put Pete's flowers. The table was rather bat-tered but handy, and it fit perfectly in one corner of the deck where the rail benches met. Trees grew close to the deck and their branches were a leafy shade for those using it, but they could still see through the trunks of the trees to the ocean. It was a lovely set-ting.

He scorched the steaks and she took hers back and cooked it. He couldn't understand what was revolting about all the succulent juices that collected on his plate or why she averted her eyes. He thought that was funny.

She enjoyed the chopped salad and savored the Tanner Moran dressing. When she questioned him about the ingredients, he tried to remember what he'd put into it. The variety of spices and herbs he men-tioned was outrageous. She was not quite sure if she should believe him. He was astonished she'd doubt him.

In describing the dressing, Tanner would take up a tiny bit of the lettuce, then he'd squint his eyes and move his tongue around his lips as he considered what was in the dressing.

She watched his tongue. She wasn't thinking about ingredients for a salad dressing; she thought about his tongue on her. How shocking.

After they had eaten, she found half a fresh apple pie in the refrigerator. "Do you bake?"

"No, there's a nice little lady, a neighbor, who looks in on me now and then." His face was bland.

"We have neighbors like that in South Bend." She busily cut wedges and added some vanilla ice cream. Leaning on his crutch, he held the door as she carried their desserts out to the metal table. With the first bite she was impressed. "Your neighbor is a jewel." She closed her eyes and made a very throaty sound of relishing the pie.

"She's very helpful." He smiled as the fine hair on his back rose along his spine while he listened to her sound of enjoyment. My God, would she react to him that way?

"I think I need to know her secrets."

"I . . . would doubt she'd share them with you." He was more amused than the words warranted.

She chose to take his statement at face value. "I know cooks like that. They'll give you the recipe all right and just neglect to give a vital ingredient so yours turns out rotten. I'm not a natural cook."

"You cooked the bloody hell out of that steak."

She nodded judiciously. "Aptly chosen words."

"I'm quick," he agreed.

"Are you? I only remember all the people who crowded around you in school. And how disillusioning it was when I found out you winked at everyone. You haven't winked at me since I got here."

"I'm saving it for effect."

"Really?" She gave him a careful look. "A whammy?"

"A try."

"I'll have to brace myself." She turned her attention back to the pie.

"I intend to catch you unaware."

"Warned?"

"Anticipation?"

"Now, Tanner..." She stopped and looked at him again.

"Did I ever tell you that no one has ever said my name the way you do?"

"Tanner?"

"The first time you said it about knocked me sideways."

"You patted my shoulder."

"I kissed you," he corrected. "But you didn't kiss me back."

"I'd never met anyone like you." Her tone was very serious. "You just kissed me without any warning. I wasn't prepared."

"You have to be warned?" He moved a bit closer and watched her pupils expand. She didn't move away. He leaned over and gently kissed her lips. "Hello, Laura." His voice was low and reedy with desire.

She swallowed and opened her eyes, but he kissed her again, wrecking his entire nervous system, pointing his teeth and allowing his lengthening arms to wind around her twice.

"Tanner..." But she slowly shook her head and her eyes were very serious. "Don't make a move on me yet."

There was the "yet." He took a deep breath and said, "Hold very still and don't say anything exciting."

"Exciting? Like what?"

"Oh, you know: hello, or how are you, or it's going to rain...anything like that."

She grinned and made a scoffing sound.

"Your lips move when you speak and I think of them moving under mine." He was completely serious. If he'd been only flirtatious, it wouldn't have been so unsettling to her.

Self-conscious, she quickly licked her lips then looked at him and parted them to protest she hadn't meant anything by doing that, but he kissed her again.

"Now, Tanner..."

And of course he replied, "Great!" and shoved the table back to rise. He had to remember to reach for the crutch.

"No!" she protested.

"I'll probably go stark, staring mad with you around here." He grinned. "And I can't even jog."

"Awwww."

"I find sympathy erotic."

She gave him a companionable swat to the shoulder and said, "Stiff upper lip and all that sort of rot, old man."

But she sent him into a rumble of laughter that he fought to control.

"You silly," she said with a commendable show of casual tolerance as she got up.

Handling the crutch quite easily, he helped carry their dishes into the kitchen to add to the dishwasher. "Thank God you arrived."

She glanced at him in quick inquiry.

"Alone, I could never fill the dishwasher." He grinned. "You thought I was going to say something else, didn't you."

"Well, the state of the dishwasher hadn't really occurred to me as being a problem to discuss."

"I never dreamed you would divorce. I thought when you married it would be for life."

"Me, too." She started the dishwasher. "What about you? I can't understand why you've never married."

"I've been too busy. Too involved in...rather complicated...operations in...apprehending... uh...tricky people. White-collar crimes."

Replying was obviously a courtesy to her, but he really didn't want to talk about it. He was giving minimal information and wouldn't volunteer much on his own. There was a thoughtful silence before she asked cautiously, "What do you do for a living?"

"I investigate strange occurrences."

"Like...?"

"Oh, like money where there shouldn't be any. Strange traffic patterns. People in odd places. That sort of thing."

"Dangerous work?"

"Rarely."

She had expected him to say no. "What do you mean...rarely?"

"For the most part citizens are law abiding, then there are those who choose to be clever. When they're caught it's like Monopoly—they go to jail or forfeit a bundle. No big deal. They tried it but got caught.

White-collar crimes. On occasion, someone will have real criminal reactions: they weren't guilty, they were *caught*, and they get mad at the catcher. That can be very, very nasty.''

"This wreck you were in . . .''

"It's being investigated quite carefully.''

"By whom?''

"My organization.''

She guessed. "You'd rather I not pry?''

"There's nothing to tell.''

"I . . . see." She leaned against the counter and they were silent for a minute or two. Soberly she said, "I'm surprised that I'm here. I shock me a little.''

"I remember the first time I saw you at I.U. crossing our River Jordan, and you were wearing a blue shirtwaist when all the other girls were in shorts or jeans. And my dreams were filled with you. The one class I had with you—ethics, for God's sake—I never heard one word of that class. I sat two rows back and one seat over from you so I could feast my eyes on you. My eyes consumed you and you didn't even know it.''

"Tanner," she cautioned.

"Just take it easy. You will let me kiss you goodnight?''

"I'm not sure that would be wise.''

His eyes crinkled. "I can control myself. I'm a mature adult. You needn't be afraid of me.''

"No blundering into the wrong bedroom looking for the bathroom in the middle of the night?''

"Promise." He held up his right hand in solemn pledge.

"Well, when it's bedtime, I'll let you kiss me good-night." With her agreement, there was a shimmer of anticipation at the thought of his kiss.

He suggested, "We could practice."

She was briefly startled, then she gave him an amused, chiding look.

He argued, "If I only get one good-night kiss, what if I louse it up? That could ruin my whole evening! We ought to practice." He was completely logical.

"Tanner—" she shook her head and sighed a bit broadly "—you're really pushing it."

"Oh yes."

"Cut it out."

He slumped very dispiritedly.

"Have you tried the stage?"

"Oh, was the dejection well-done? I've really never needed to practice." He gave her a sly and foxy look that made her laugh.

He remembered the crutch as they went into the living room. There was a folding card table, beautifully made of cherry wood. On it lay a partially done jigsaw puzzle. Laura was drawn to it. And they spent almost an hour slowly fitting pieces, until she yawned too many times.

Reluctantly she said, "It's been a long day and I must go to sleep."

"Good. Now I get my kiss."

She grinned at him. "You really shouldn't just leap into such an experience, you should approach it gradually. Kiss my hand the first night, then my cheek..."

"Let's read ahead a week or two."

"My mother always said nothing worthwhile is ever accomplished in a hurry. Everything takes time."

"Yes."

"Would you like to kiss me now?"

"Will it count against the good-night kiss?"

"It would *be* the good-night kiss."

He watched her with narrowed, suspicious eyes that held humor. "By any chance are you working as a part of a revenge group that I've helped corner somewhere along the way?"

She agreed airily and invented a mob. "Maxie and Bugsy and uh..."

"I knew it." He played along with her imagination. "They must have hunted you down knowing it was fated that I had a good-night kiss long overdue. What did they bribe you with to come here to torture me this way?"

"Rubies, emeralds and pearls?"

"Don't you believe them. They had to give it all back. With fines. They won't be solvent enough for this kind of caper for years yet."

Having said all that about honor, it amused him to drag the crutch over to use as help in rising. He did it well. Then he reached out a hand and tugged Laura to her feet. "I have to lean against the wall," he told her. "Because I want to hold you with both arms."

She bought it. He propped the crutch nearby, not overdoing it, and then took her into his arms. Quite easily he had reminded her he'd been badly injured and her sympathy had been touched. He pulled her closer, feeling her against him. Relishing her there. His strong hands moved on her back and up her sides in a very insidious way.

He hugged her, prolonging it exquisitely, making her wait. Making her aware of him. Making her aware of herself and her reaction to him. He was merciless. He had no idea how long he could keep her there in that house with him, and he had to use any opportunity that came his way.

He figured if he wasn't going to sleep that night, then neither was she. Deliberately he brushed his lips over hers. She lifted hers to return his kiss, but he drew back an inch to say, "I had to be sure they were there. Since I get only one, I'd hate to blunder and miss entirely."

She didn't break position and left her mouth where it was. She hadn't really listened to his words. She was being distracted by the shimmer of tiny, pulsing thrills.

He ran his evening's beard down her cheek and under her ear. His hot breath rasped in his throat and she felt it almost roar in her ear as he said urgently, "I lost your mouth. Is it around here?"

Somehow she managed to form the words: "Over here." Her own breathing was unsteady. He had her completely concentrated on him. The sensations that flickered through her body were electric in her reaction to him. How clever he was. She wanted more of him.

He whiskered the side of her throat in his search for her mouth, and his hands moved on her back. He braced his legs apart and pulled her closer, his hands went down her back and he drew her tightly to him.

It was then he finally got around to kissing her. The kiss concentrated Laura's attention to the need he'd built in her. She was a shambles. Her lips clung to his as he tried to ease from the kiss and it continued long past what had been her deadline. He was wickedly pleased.

But worse, he insisted on breaking off the kiss. He even helped her to stand away from him. He loosened her resisting arms from around his shoulders and held her reaching hands politely between them. Then he lifted them and kissed them. He explained, "The first night and hand kissing. Do I get to still kiss hands tomorrow? Or only cheeks by then?" And he grinned at her.

She replied something unintelligible as she swallowed with some difficulty.

He patted her bottom as he started her up the stairs. She hesitated and looked back, but he only said, "Good night, Laura."

She said, "Ummm."

He was jubilant. His conscience didn't even twinge.

Three

——

It wasn't until after she was in bed, lying there in the dark room, that Laura really became aware of her surroundings. She'd scrubbed her teeth, braided her hair into two pigtails and changed into her night wear of T-shirt and panties before she began to realize how big the house was . . . and how isolated.

At that point her awareness lay in hearing sounds that were different for her. First to capture her attention were the unusual ones of the surf and the palms rustling and rattling in the almost constant breezes. Other sounds reminded her that the house was old and wooden, and the creaking was like a ship groaning through a gentle sea.

She was too tired to allow her imagination to interpret any of the other sounds. She shunned the possibility that the old house could well be haunted. She did permit herself some questioning as to why she was where she was. The Fullertons' daughter, Laura, doing this rash and reckless thing?

To be here alone with a man she hadn't seen in seven years, well, actually six years, nine months and twelve days. How interesting—how telling—that she couldn't remember how long it had been since she'd last seen her ex-husband, but she could remember exactly how long since she'd last seen Tanner. It was the day she married Tom Bligh, and Tanner Moran had ruined her honeymoon with his reception line kiss.

How could a human man kiss so perfectly? Her body wasn't curious about analysis, it just craved more. She moved restlessly under the onslaught of reaction that flickered like summer lightning in her passion-drugged cells. There had to be something genetic about his talent. What if scientists could splice a gene to duplicate Tanner's talent for kissing? Nobody would get anything else done.

Life, however, consisted of more than just reaction to kisses. She really didn't know Tanner well enough to have committed herself to visiting him alone in this enormous summer house. He could have changed.

His kisses hadn't. But what about his character? She had changed since she knew him; perhaps he had, too. The years between twenty-five and thirty-five were the years that molded character. How old was he exactly? She went to sleep trying to figure that out.

Her body's senses had lain there smoldering like coals lightly covered with the ash of hidden fire. The wind of her dreams stirred the ash covering and allowed the oxygen of her imagination to feed the dormant embers and blow it again to flame.

She made restless sounds and movements as the longing intensified but the dream-Tanner was elusive. How unkind of him to tease and torment her.

There was a loud bang. It couldn't be a car's backfire, not on that deserted road. A shot? It must have been a door slamming. Whatever it was, it brought her almost to the surface of her dream state, and in the brief rousing, she thought she heard a woman's laugh. But she ignored that puzzle as she tried to sink back into her alluring fantasy. In searching again for her dream, she slid into deeper, restful sleep.

Tanner waited for her to sleep. Her bed had squeaked with her entry, and his longing for her flamed vividly. He almost put the crutch aside and only just avoided pacing—and disturbing that creaky floor. He again took up the crutch and moved with its sound to his room. He put it by the bed before he released the window screen, slid over the sill, to the ground, melted into the night, and walked carefully with his healing muscles.

He didn't yet run. He'd been promised that the time would come when he would run again. How ironic to have been a year in Nam, without a scratch, to almost be wiped out in a car wreck. How miraculous to have survived that incredible wreck without brain damage. Not only did he survive but, as bad as the damage to him was, he would heal. He had a little metal in some bones now, and there would be some interesting scars, but he would be all right.

Right now the scarring was pretty ugly. If—no, when he made love to Laura, he should do it in the dark. She could be turned off by the sight of his

wounds. They didn't bother him; he was just glad he
was alive. There had been some question of survival.
He'd come to, lucid, fantastically aware. Sounds were
so clear. The colors sharp. There was no distortion.
He'd known he was alive!

Then he looked at himself. If he was still alive, and
it was no illusion, he could be saying farewell to his
life. His body was in very bad shape. His left arm at
strange angles. His stomach was a mess. The thigh...
He touched his stomach, but he had to stop walking
to lean down and hold that thigh as if reassuring himself it was still there...and thank God it was. How had
he been so fortunate?

All his life he would send blessings to the people
who helped him. The fragile-appearing woman who
had wiggled into the car, as close as she could get to
Tanner, and snaked an arm over to hold the pressure
point. She had kept him from bleeding to death before they got him out. She had talked to him calmly,
explaining what had happened, what they were doing
and how. She told him who they'd called to come help,
and she'd told him that he would live.

There was a brute of a man who was so gentle and
who wept for him. The contrasts. Why wasn't the
brute the one who was businesslike and the woman
leaking tears? Why must we go through horrendous
trials before we know how compassionate and unself-
ish people are?

All through the struggle to release him, there had
been the threat of explosion. The fire truck couldn't
get there to wash down the car for more than half an
hour. His rescuers would have waited for the experts.
They would have left him alone except for stopping the

bleeding. But they had to try to free him before the car blew up.

No one was so unmindful as to just grab him and try to yank him out. Too many people are harmed by inept good intention. It was the threat of explosion that made them try to bend the metal, to pry space so they could get him away.

Tanner learned later that the man who'd crossed the centerline going mindlessly pell-mell was killed. They were generally the ones who survived. That time the victim survived. Tanner had used up another of his nine lives.

And now Laura was there in his house.

He didn't sleep well that night. He was more restless than he'd ever been. He lay awake thinking about his restlessness, and he wondered if it was because now he knew how tentative life was. He'd learned that it was not to be wasted. He'd had that lesson underlined for him. And with Laura there, had he a chance to fill his gift of life with love?

Could she love him?

He was awake early. He got up and dressed, wearing a long-sleeved, cotton shirt and soft cotton deck trousers to hide the scars, and he remembered to carry the crutch along. He checked his messages, for he never took a straight phone call. He returned a few and erased the rest. He worked on his computer, with its involved system of codes, and he took coffee out on the kitchen deck. A strange almost melancholy mood had seized him. Could she love him? Why should she?

In that early-April dawn's stillness, with its soft taste of summer, she came to him out of the kitchen door with her hair brushed down around her shoulders. She was wearing a wraparound dress of cotton. The lime green with dark blue print made her eyes a strange slate color. She wore someone's thongs from the guest closet, and as the almost summerlike breeze molded the soft dress against her body, she had to lift her hand to brush away the strands of her silken hair from across her face. She smiled at him, making his heart hurt.

"Don't get up," she told him quickly.

"I didn't think you'd waken this early."

"I'm a morning woman. I love the early hours. Of course, then I tend to fade out early in the evening."

"I could hear you snore clear down here."

"How unkind of you to mention that." She gave him a sparkling-eyed, humorous snub that was pure sass.

"What do you eat for breakfast?"

"Everything in sight."

"A woman after my own heart." Such careless, flirting words, but he lowered his eyes quickly so she wouldn't see how vulnerable she made him. "I make the world's best waffles."

"I do bacon and eggs."

"How?"

"Any way at all."

"We'll combine."

They went inside and as they emptied the dishwasher and put away last night's dishes, Laura asked, "Who cleans this place?"

"A cleaning crew. Top to bottom once a month. They vacuum and mop and change the dust covers. There are ten of them. It's safest for us bystanders to just leave—you could find yourself mopped up or with a cover thrown over you. But don't panic, they aren't due until the first of May."

The waffles were frozen and commercial, so he had time to lean against the counter and watch her do all the rest. When all was ready, they again ate on the deck, and she laughed. "Imagine all that house and we eat outside on this old wooden deck."

"You can begin painting it tomorrow."

"You're giving me a whole day of rest!" she exclaimed.

"That's because you're non-union."

"Speaking of work, I need to report in. And I've some drawings to do. I'll need a large space. Do you have a recreation room? A game table?"

"I have a drafting table I'm not using," he offered.

"Incredible."

"I can arrange for anything your heart desires." He leaned back and crossed his arms on his broad chest as he watched her intently. "I can construct, provide or commandeer whatever you need."

"Well, with that offer I believe I could use a sampling of silks in all the colors, some swatches of sample patterns, tempera paints. Brushes, of course. And a good electric pencil sharpener. Butcher paper. You know, the kind of things all artists need." And she laughed because her request was ridiculous. "Actually, if you have a drafting table, I have what I need for these next several days. Where's your phone?"

"I'll have to show you." He stacked the plates. "I have some small modifications on the system but it's only the matter of a couple of switches. This way the phone never rings."

"You're allergic to phones?"

"To time wasters."

She could see where, having been through that wreck, he wouldn't want intrusions on what must be precious time. They dealt with the dishes, then she followed along to the study. He showed her the main phone and how to flip the whole ensemble back into being a plain, ordinary phone.

"What *is* all this? I have a message taker, but this is silly. What are all these gadgets?"

"A filter, a scrambler, a tracer and a few other little odds and ends."

She frowned and gave him a careful look. "A... scrambler?"

"Some of the information I receive is confidential."

"Secrets?"

"Well, people's financial information, or private numbers. Nothing exciting. Just personal."

"Oh." She picked up something reasonably similar to a phone and asked, "Now?"

"Sure. Those are the switches. If you use the phone, flip them off. See? Let me know if you do use the phone so I can be sure they're back on and working. Okay?"

"I just have to report in. I won't give this number."

"You can call out anytime." He didn't move but leaned against the wall with his crutch and quite blatantly listened.

She was amused by him, as she sought and punched the speaker button so he could hear both sides of the conversation. She wondered if he would allow her the same privilege? No, he couldn't. If he could, there wouldn't be the scrambler.

She punched in the number, and Jeanine—her secretary—immediately answered. "Laura? How'd it go?"

"Looks good. I got the go-ahead for mock-ups. It will be interesting. I'm staying with friends on the coast and will do some of the preliminary sketches here. I'll call every day about noon? There's no phone for any other calls. Everything okay?"

"Fine. How long will you be gone?"

"Good question. I'll let you know."

When she'd hung up and watched as Tanner adjusted all the switches, he asked, "I guess I didn't ask what you do?"

"I was an art-design major. I did portraits first because that's my love. But lately I've expanded into decoration, coordinating color and texture for specific places and moods. It's fascinating, different, a challenge, but I'm not sure it's exactly what I want to do.

"My first big job was to decorate a company's holiday house for guests and selected employees who'd pleased the boss. It's on the shore of Lake Michigan. It's big enough, but a small house compared to this one, and I was told to use my own judgment. So I fixed it up as the ideal place for a vacationing family. Sunflowers in the breakfast room, teddy bears and balloons in the smaller bedrooms, pretty flowered wallpaper in the master bedroom. It was all fresh and clean. I finished and reported to the owner.

"He came by my studio in South Bend, looking placid and bland. He waited until we were alone and

then he said, 'I believe there's been some kind of mis-
understanding. When I said the place was for weekend fun, I didn't mean for a *family* but for fun and
games. Now do you understand? For men to take
women who aren't their wives.'"

Tanner smiled. "You innocent. What did you do?"

"After an almost overwhelming episode of blushes
and stuttering, I said, 'Oh,' and eventually managed
to stammer that I'd take care of it."

"And...?"

"The teddy bears went first, then the balloons and
sunflowers. I found the whole project distasteful but
I felt committed to correct my error. I changed the
colors, put in mirrors and as a rather wicked after-
thought, lacy palms. An upright piano." She paused.
"I resisted the black woven string and tasseled door
hangings."

"Noble. Did he try to get you to initiate it with
him?"

"How could you *possibly* have known that?"

"I know you didn't and that he's still after you,
right?"

"Yes." She watched him a minute before she asked
curiously, "How could you know? Is this typical male
behavior? He has a wife and half-grown children. He's
a corporate power. Why me? His wife is a very nice
woman. She likes him. I think he likes her. Why does
he want to fool around? And why with me? I'm hardly
the type to be a mistress. At best I'd be inept. I've been
very businesslike and formal with him, I've never
flirted or teased him. I've never brushed up against
him or indicated in *any* way that I would be interested.

"And since then, I make sure what sort of place I'm supposed to decorate. I've refused two other 'fun' places. I don't want any part of something like that. And although I accept jobs from him and his referrals, I don't feel obligated to sleep with him to 'repay' him. My work is excellent. I've won awards...."

Tanner's eyelashes screened his eyes as he said mildly, "He was probably surprised to find a woman who can still blush, and that intrigued him. Plus the fact that you *didn't* try to attract him."

She scoffed. "Ridiculous. You're saying that in order to be free of him I should try to entice him and..."

"No!"

"Well you just said..."

"You're handling the situation in the most professional way possible. You're doing it exactly right. Don't be too friendly, stay courteous and business-minded when you have to talk to him."

"You're a man, why would he want to fool around?"

"I'm prejudiced." He meant prejudiced about her attractiveness and how she affected him.

"So you think whatever men do is okay?"

He shook his head. "That isn't what I said."

"You said that you're prejudiced. Do you go after every woman within your scope? Do you trail after them and hunt them down?"

"I've always been selective."

"But—"

"I can only say I admire the man's taste in women."

She smiled just a bit. "Do you find me attractive?" The words were out before she could stop them, and she was appalled!

"Unbelievably so."

"Why, how nice of you!"

"I'm not sure about 'nice.'"

"I know, you want me to help 'initiate' this house? I would suspect there have been others who've made love here."

He licked his lips slowly then intoned, "It's worth being sure. Consider all the cousins here with their parents. It's very doubtful there's ever been the privacy for any love making, only furtive, hasty sex." He shook his head sadly. "That's probably why the house sighs and creaks so restlessly. It's unfulfilled."

She laughed. She had to put her head back to laugh. "Oh you!" she gasped and put her hands to her face and the laughter bubbled from her. "You're so clever! I probably would have succumbed to him if he'd been as clever as you! You're so inventive!"

"I can be exquisitely so." He allowed a small smile.

She sobered a little and looked at him. Her own smile was still there. A soft, inviting one. But her eyes were still a bit wary.

He took her into the morning room and showed her the drawing table with its high "Bob Cratchit" stool.

"It seems unusual for you to have a drafting table. Who used it?"

"We needed something high enough to keep puzzles, community scissors, papers and so on away from small children. By the time they could stretch up to the top of it, or climb up, they would know enough to leave things alone. Our family tends to have hobbies that involve small things or sharp things or dangerous things."

"How dangerous? Poison mushrooms?"

"Guns, knives, scissors."

"Guns?" she asked in surprise.

"We've lived on this coast for a long, long time and it's isolated. Then one uncle became intrigued by the progression of weapon utility. The innovations in weaponry. Some are exquisitely ornamental. We have an extensive gun collection that is now concealed and protected very securely. They'll eventually go to a museum."

"Guns scare me."

He told her, "It's like dealing with rattlesnakes. You do it carefully."

"I can shoot one."

"I won't tempt you to try."

"My dad said we should all know how. One never knows what sort of cards life deals you."

"Logical." He nodded with his words.

"So I *can* shoot one. But I don't ever want to. I'm dreadfully afraid of them."

"There'll be no need. I'll take care of you." He moved to her carefully, carrying the crutch, and he slid an arm around her unresisting body to pull her to him. Their eyes locked, and slowly he leaned his head down and kissed her.

Being close to him wasn't any different. She felt the same old chaos. The same maelstrom of sensation. Plain, ordinary rioting of cells. Body disaster. So how could she resist? She kissed him back.

For some reason, unknown to her, he released her. She carefully re-sorted her brain cells to figure out why he'd done such a foolish thing, when he suggested they return her car to the rental branch in Myrtle Beach.

She had to blink several times in the reorientation process before she could ask, "Can you drive all right? I mean, will it hurt your leg?"

"No problem. Only my left leg gives me trouble. My right leg's fine."

"You don't mind following me in and bringing me back?"

"Not at all. I'd be happy to do it." He could hardly wait to get rid of her means of escape.

As they returned to the Moran cottage, he drove along a track close to the ocean, and she relished doing that. "I think I must have been a pirate in another life."

"A past life or a parallel one?" he inquired.

"Parallel? I hadn't considered that. I was thinking a past one."

His glance touched her hotly as she looked out over the rolling waves, with the wind streaming her hair back and molding the thin cotton to her chest. "Being a pirate could come in handy under many circumstances."

"What would you steal?" she asked. "Treasure?"

"You."

She laughed as if he was teasing.

He wasn't.

Four

Laura spent the day working in the "silence" of only natural sounds. She could hear no motors or buzzes or ringings. She didn't even hear any relentless wind chimes. The Moran place was truly isolated.

In Columbia, Laura had been given a stack of floor plans for the leisure houses. She had been one of several decorators offered the opportunity to show what could be done with color and texture to make identical layouts look individual.

She jotted down some general ideas: old-fashioned, Oriental, stark colored, contemporary. And with the great selection offered by the crayons, she began to experiment, making pencil notes on the borders, lost to her imagination.

Her stomach mentioned lunch was lacking. She surfaced from her work and lifted her nose to sniff.

Chili? She laid her pencil aside, swung around on the stool and left the table to follow the aroma into the kitchen where Tanner was stirring a pot on the stove.

He looked up at her. "I thought chili would do it. I was pretty sure it needed to be something with a tantalizing smell. My goodness, you do concentrate! Did you notice I changed you and your table to another room?"

Her expression was blank for just a brief minute before she smiled. "No you didn't." But she was sure only because she could actually recall coming from the morning room. "Toast?"

"With melted cheese and in the warmer."

"I'm famished."

"It's the sea air. I suppose, after you've been here awhile, I'll have to widen all the doors so you can waddle through."

"Ummmm." She was sampling the toast.

"Don't take my corners," he warned.

"You're a toast corner devotee?"

"Yep. We had an old cat who recognized any sound that involved the toaster and would come a-waddling for the corners. I didn't discover toast corner madness until I was twelve! I'd been psyched out by that old cat into thinking the corners were only for him!"

As Laura began to scoff, there was a call from beyond the kitchen deck. "Tanner! Come help."

Laura followed Tanner's hobble to the door and looked past his shoulder to see a tiny blonde labor up the deck stairs, her arms burdened with packages and baskets.

"It's my neighbor," Tanner explained as he opened the door. "Hi, what'd you bring me this time?"

This time? So *this* was the neighbor who baked him pie? Um-hmm. And the neighbor who probably wouldn't "share her secrets" with Laura? No wonder Tanner had laughed when he told her that. What sort of secrets had she been showing Tanner?

The Other Woman—her title was already in capital letters—looked dismissively at Laura and said, "I do hope you're not here for lunch, there's only enough for two." And she smiled sweetly at Tanner.

Possession is nine points of the law and, being in residence, Laura stepped back and held the door with a courteously welcoming smile pasted on her face. "Well, hello!" she said to the intruder. "Are you the apple pie? Or the quiche?" She'd fabricated the quiche and was pleased she thought of it.

"Quiche?" The woman's lovely face was blank. "No quiche." And, ignoring Laura with polished talent, she went on into the kitchen with pointed familiarity.

Quite remarkably, Tanner didn't ask about a nonexistent quiche. But he smiled just a little. Laura gave him a precious look that made him cough discreetly, as if with a throat tickle, before he said, "Laura, this is my neighbor, Pam Howard. My house guest, Laura Fullerton."

"House guest?" Pam then did pause to pierce Laura with a narrow-eyed look.

Her face commendably placid, Laura explained, "Old school friends."

Pam smiled. "I have just begun to notice how older women search out unmarried school acquaintances."

"Have you been successful?" Laura inquired kindly.

Apparently Tanner had another throat tickle.

Pam ignored Laura and said sweetly to Tanner, "I thought we'd go out on the beach. You do have a rug we can take along? Don't you have a clay wine cooler? I brought your favorite..."

"Moonshine? Where'd you find some?"

"...chablis." Pam looked a little miffed.

"I love chablis," Laura contributed in a friendly way. "If it's dry enough. But we have some red wine for the chili. Don't we, darling?"

That was very bold of Laura. And he *was* amused. However, although she wasn't looking at him, she was waiting for his reaction to the "darling."

He replied readily enough, "Let's ask her to join us, shall we, honey?"

Had there been just the least bit of hesitation to emphasize the "honey"? He was wicked. Of the choice in responses to asking Pam to join them, which should she select? Not "no." It would seem insecure. "If you want to" would appear as if Tanner would choose to have Pam there. So Laura smiled brilliantly as she exclaimed, "I insist!" Then she turned to Pam and begged, "Oh, do stay! It'll be such fun."

What could Pam do? They didn't go to the beach, but instead ate in the kitchen. Laura put out two glasses each for the kinds of wine and they had a smorgasbord. It should have been fun.

However, when Pam relentlessly spoke of things Laura knew nothing about, Tanner supplied *elaborate* backgrounds to each comment. He was enjoying himself, and his eyes shared that with Laura.

So when Pam tried to shut Laura out by speaking in French, Laura absentmindedly corrected her grammar as she pulled some meat from a drumstick and examined it with a critical frown.

Pam didn't stay long. She insisted Tanner help her carry her baskets home, but he was using the crutch and simply put out his hands helplessly. Laura volunteered to help, even insisted, but she was ignored. Pretending Pam was behaving, Laura waved her off from the deck. However Pam neglected to look back so didn't know to return the wave.

"My, my," Tanner said. "I would never have dreamed you could hold your own with Pam. And there I'd worried she would make mincemeat out of you."

"As a sophomore, in the sorority's schedule, I was assigned to room six weeks with Tabby. You must remember Tabby Cat? I had a six-week crash course in cattiness. She was a senior then and two years older than me. On my way down to Columbia, she spotted me in Chicago's O'Hare and I had a quickie refresher course. I also found out she's now three years younger than she was before.

"Pete was on the same flight out of O'Hare. He did call you?" she asked Tanner. "He said he was going to. Do you know that innocent is only thirty and only been out on his own for eight years in the wilds of air travel and I left him to the tender mercies of *Tabby*?" She put a hand to her forehead. "They were both going to Miami. I dread to think of him now, almost forty-eight hours later. Poor Pete."

Humor radiated from Tanner's eyes and, restraining his grin, he shook his head. "Poor Pete." But he didn't sound sincere.

* * *

Predictably Pam had left before the kitchen was tidied. As the two straightened it up, Tanner stretched over for something to add to the dishwasher. His shirt rode up and Laura saw the dreadful, healing scars on his left side. She laid her hand there and said, "You should strip down to shorts and get those outside in the sunlight and fresh air. I suppose the new skin is too tender for sunbathing?"

When she touched him, he'd frozen, braced for her horror. And his relief over her natural reaction was intense. "I could stand a little time on the lounge in the shade of the deck. Come on out with me."

"I won't chat. I'll go to sleep. I suppose it's the sea air. I slept like a dead woman last night."

"I'm glad I don't revolt you," he said softly.

"Oh, no. I was a candy striper volunteer in the surgical ward back at the age when everyone was going to be either a doctor or a veterinarian. Hospital people think of scars as successes, so I learned to look on them that way too instead of anguishing over the hurt that caused them."

He was very conscious of her as they moved out to the deck. He was a little stiff and nervous. He took off his shirt and spread it on the plastic padding of the double lounge, sat down and patted the other side in invitation.

She couldn't *not* lie down beside him. He was very conscious of the healing wounds, and she was open to his vulnerability. Laura sat down by him to stretch and yawned. Then she told him. "You ought to be in shorts."

"I will be soon." His thigh was appalling. He decided he would let her get used to the lesser scarring on his body and left arm first. Then he would expose the leg.

"This is a work of art for a surgeon." She lightly traced the curving incision that had allowed them to repair his arm. "As an artist, I can also appreciate how the doctor cut along the clearest path to do the least additional harm. When it fades, you'll appreciate it more."

He thought if she could see his injuries in that way, she could probably handle seeing his thigh.

With the same interest, she looked at his chest where the tear had been from the splintered steering wheel and the dashboard. It wasn't as artful, but the salvaging was ingenious. "Have you really looked at this?" she asked. "Obviously, it's your stomach, so you must have. See how this tear was repaired? Patched. Clever. You lucked in to a genius. Was the doctor someone you knew?"

"Pot luck. She happened to be there in the hospital."

"You have a guardian angel."

"I begin to believe it."

She leaned down and gently kissed his healing wounds. "I'm glad you survived."

"Me too."

She moved away to lie down beside him.

"Laura..." He turned onto his left, scarred side concealing it from her. "I can't believe you're here. I've dreamed it so many times, that I would turn over and find you beside me, that I can't believe it's true and you're here."

"Oh, Tanner..."

"I want you."

"It scares me a little."

"Don't be afraid of me," he urged.

"Not of you. Of me. I'm not sure whether this attraction is really 'love' or simply intense desire. I'm boggled by sensation when I'm around you. And I'm not sure I'm ready to be distracted from my own life. I've only just begun to learn independence. It's a heady feeling to run my own business, to have all the decisions and responsibility and for it to be successful. To be in control of my life. I went from father to the university to husband. I've just started to explore a business potential that's endless. It's exciting. And I'm good. I... hesitate to be distracted from it."

"Do you find me distracting?" His voice was husky and he lifted his good right arm so his fingers could move a strand of hair from her face.

"You're really smooth, Tanner. Why do I suspect you're trying to lull me into a seduction?"

"Never." She watched his lazy smile as he explained, "I'm only showing you I'm interested, and willing."

"You believe I'll seduce you?"

"I wouldn't struggle." His smile turned quite wicked. "I don't believe I've ever thanked you properly for helping clean up the kitchen." He leaned over and kissed her. When he raised his head she could see his blue eyes were vulnerable with desire and shaded by his surprising lashes. He smiled a little.

She gasped and he kissed her again. Her hands were in his thick hair and her back arched as she pressed her breasts to his chest. His hand slid into the conveniently accessible wraparound dress, and his strong fingers closed around the taut mound of her breast. She made a soft sound in her throat, and his chest rumbled in a very pleased male sound.

She recognized the volcanic urgency in that sound. His passion rumbled there ready to explode, but she wasn't yet really ready for the consequences of what would happen if she made love with Tanner. She drew back. He protested and frowned, and his hands resisted her leaving him. It would have been very easy to simply allow him to convince her to stay there with him. To lie with him on that double lounger in the soft air with the sea breeze—and they would make love. She wanted him very badly. She could have him. It was her choice.

However she rose from the lounger and, gathering her scattered wits, she managed to say quite primly, "I believe the best thing for me to do, under the circumstances, is go for a good long run on the beach. Too bad you can't, too. But the time will come when you're stronger and then you can chase me."

He'd raised one knee and propped his foot to keep it there, as he put his hands behind his head to lie there watching her. How could blue eyes look so hot? He made his voice curl through her nervous system as he inquired, "When I can run, you'll let me chase you?"

"Perhaps." She gave him a sassy look.

"It'll be an incentive to work at my recovery." He made the words a threatening promise that did strange things to her beleaguered innards.

She went up to her room in order to change into the purple shorts. Although she made a concerted search, she could find no shoes that fit well enough and that wouldn't risk blisters. She decided to run barefooted on the water-packed sand at the tide's edge.

When she left her room to go down the stairs again, Laura found Tanner leaning casually on his crutch as he waited for her at the bottom of the stairs. He was a very strong presence. She smiled a little, and his return smile was like a predator's watching his victim. His eyes were like a hunter's. He looked excessively dangerous. To a woman. She felt a thrill go through her body and curl in her stomach. She wanted him to pursue her. And...to catch her.

He said, as if it was natural, "You need to kiss me goodbye."

"I thought the kisses were just for good-night?"

"And goodbyes," he corrected the rules.

She lifted her brows a little as she tilted back her head, but she couldn't prevent the slightest little smile.

He intoned, elaborating, "Today we also kiss goodbye...and then hello."

"I hadn't realized that. When was the decision made?"

"It was there all along. So you might just as well get it over with." He moved a step toward her in order to help her.

"I suppose I might just as well." She heaved a big, enduring sigh and met him halfway. She raised her mouth and closed her eyes.

Nothing happened. She peeked and he was watching her very seriously. She opened her eyes all the way and looked up at him. She too became serious. She slid her hands up his chest and around his shoulders to the back of his head, then she met his lips and she kissed him.

It was a stunning kiss. His arms went around her body and he pulled her to him hungrily. His kiss was deep and intense, and his reaction was passionate as he reveled in the feel of her against him, the sensations she aroused in him. The thrill of her. Her hands petting the back of his head, her body so soft and feminine against his, her sweet mouth kissing him back. He finally lifted his head to gasp air and groaned before he looked down at her with a rueful smile. "Scat! Go while you can."

It was a commentary on her condition that she obeyed him. She wasn't in control of her own mind, and she accepted his direction. She almost staggered to the front door, fumbled with the latch, practically fell out onto the porch and made it to the top of the steps.

He watched with smoldering, pleased eyes as she stood on the porch and breathed deeply, in order to orient herself. She pushed her hair back several times, although the wind was already doing that for her, and she looked around as if trying to remember why she was there on the porch.

Running? her body asked. Running was the last thing it wanted to do. It wanted to go right back to Tanner and experience all those promises his kisses offered. Why had she decided to run? While she was trying to figure out why she was outside, her mind directed that she go on down the steps and across the deserted road. She automatically remembered to look for traffic before she crossed, even though there was never any traffic out there. She slipped out of the thongs, and did some warm-ups before she slowly jogged off up the beach.

Since she wasn't used to the endlessness or the sameness of deserted beaches as opposed to city blocks or tracks she went too far. So she was a long time coming back. Tanner found her tiredly returning, as he drove along the shore road searching for her. She fell into the car gratefully. This car was another Porsche to replace the wrecked one.

"You have to set a landmark," Tanner explained. He didn't scold her or mention how anxious he'd become when she was gone for so long. "That way you judge how far you'll go and remember you have to come back the same distance."

"Glad you mentioned it." She was lying back, really exhausted, sipping a can of orange juice he'd brought along for her.

They drove in silence. Laura became relaxed and contented. Tanner was still coping with his uneasiness over her long absence.

She broke the silence to tell him, "Look for the dog."

He slowed, frowning, seeing no dog. "What dog?"

"I think someone threw him out or he's lost. A black dog, like a Scottish Collie. No tags. Not frisky. I'm afraid of dogs so I didn't examine him closely. But there's no houses in sight around here. He didn't look like he was adventuring but just waiting by the road."

"We'll watch."

They were silent as they looked. The longer it took, the slower he drove, and they were all the way back to his house and he hadn't seen the dog. "I suppose he went on home?" she suggested uncertainly.

"Let's go take another look." He swung into the drive in order to turn around.

"Oh, Tanner..." Her smile melted his heart and he leaned to kiss her. As he lifted his mouth, she asked, "Is that the hello one?"

"No, that's an I'm-on-your-side one."

"It felt like a hello one."

"You've still got that one to anticipate."

"Oh, I suppose..." But she smiled and her eyes were warm.

They had to go back and forth still another time before they found the dog. He was curled up out of the wind in a slight depression so he could watch the road. In the darkness of the depression his black coat seemed only like a deeper shadow.

They had a tough time coaxing the dog into the car. He watched along the road one last time before he slowly climbed into the back seat and carefully sat down. His eyes were dulled but intelligent.

"Is it sick?" she asked in concern.

"I think he's only hungry. We'll take him on over to Henry the vet right now and have him looked at. Poor mutt."

The veterinarian's office was in an old farmhouse. There were pens for dogs and a goat. Two horses came to a fence to see who was there and there was a world of cats.

Henry squatted down and talked to the dog first. The dog was a little anxious and was looking around. They gave him water, and the dog lapped it up. Then Henry gave him a little dry food. The dog was starved.

Henry told them, "I can see no injuries. There's nothing to identify him, just the flea collar and that's

new, oddly enough. Good thing. This is supposed to
be the Year of the Flea. His coat isn't too bad, his
teeth are all there. He's a young dog. Beautiful animal. It kills my heart, people think animals can survive on their own in the country. He could be lost but
there's been no notice about such a dog running loose
around here. I'll inquire around. Thanks for bringing
him in. He'll find a home."

Tanner and Laura turned slowly away but as they
started to get into the Porsche, the dog made a sound
in his throat. Not a whimper or anything begging. Just
a questioning. They both turned back.

Quite cheerfully Henry said, "We'll give him the
shots and you can take him along." And he grinned at
the pair.

Tanner looked at Laura. "We have a dog?"

Five

They took the dog back to the Moran beach house and, with the April day bright and warm, they bathed him outside. He stood obediently for their convenience and he didn't appear to mind the water. Tanner took off his shirt, unselfconscious now about his healing body, and he first rinsed off the dog.

Laura held the hose and kept her distance while Tanner soaped the patient animal. "He's charming. I never thought I'd say that about a dog."

"Someone must have lost him. No one would throw away such a dog."

"He always turns to face the road," Laura commented.

"Yes."

"Tanner, neither of us has the time nor the place for a dog. This interlude is unfair for him. He could become attached to us and then have to go on to someone else. He's obviously loyal. He's looking for people in a car to come back for him."

To soothe her worry, he told her, "When school's out in another month or so, this place is going to be overflowing with little cousins. Dog can choose a new attachment. I'd like to keep him in the family." With old towels Tanner began to rub the dog dry then brushed his coat. The dog held still for it. "What'll we name him?"

"I'm not sure we should," Laura replied thoughtfully. "What if the next person who has him wants another name? It's asking a lot for a dog to remember changing labels."

"We could call him Dog. That way it won't be a name but it's still a label."

And just then as if responding to canine labeling, Pam came around from the front of the house. She was beautifully dressed in a dinner dress and heels, and her hair was perfectly done. She paused as she saw Laura, and asked abruptly, "You're still here?"

Laura didn't know how to reply to that. Obviously she was still there.

Tanner said, "Hello, Pam, want a dog?"

"Oh, Tanner!" she exclaimed in shock. "Ugh! Put your shirt on!" And she covered her eyes.

He looked blank for half a pause before he said, "Of course." And he slipped into the shirt to screen his healing body. "It's okay now."

"That's better." Pam then looked at Tanner. "I thought we could go into town for dinner tonight."

"I'm sorry." He smiled at her. "We have plans. Thanks for asking us."

She gave Laura a cold look that should have shriveled her, and after a mouth-working frustrating minute, she left.

They didn't say anything for a while. It had been a strange intrusion. The Tanner said, "It's interesting to see Pam under these circumstances—with you here. I'd never have dreamed she could be so rude to you. How can she be as old as she is and so unthinking about my scars?"

"I've had the advantage of working with people who've had either horrendous injuries or surgery. Both men and women have a tough time dealing with disfigurement, even if it's only temporary. Pam probably doesn't think about you being scarred, she relates it to herself, and how she'd feel if it was she who had those injuries. She really didn't mean to be nasty to you."

"How can you defend her?" He stopped brushing the dog to look at Laura, as he waited for her reply.

"Rather grudgingly. I don't like her, but she wants you. That shows she has superb taste."

"Granted."

"And in my sojourn on this planet..."

"Sojourn?" He grinned at her word.

"I'm an observer and a firm believer in reincarnation. And in this particular life, I've learned that rude people are unhappy. I can endure them for the brief time I must, but they have to live with themselves all the time. No relief. That's burden enough."

"I like you."

Laura smiled as she watched Tanner's big hard hands on the dog. "You're so gentle."

"He's been weather worn and hungry. His skin is probably a little tender. His feet are sand roughened. I have some oil Henry gave me. In a few days he'll feel well and strong again."

"I just hope some of the kids get a chance at him." She caught his eye and smiled, teasing him.

How strange that a man could be so gentle, especially one who lived such a rootless, potentially dangerous life as Tanner. He was really a very tender man. The way he'd searched for the lost dog, and cared for it now, seeing to its health and comfort proved that. "Why did you choose the particular work you do?" Laura surprised herself with the strange change of subject.

"I'm a civilized man."

She laughed. "Hunting crooks is civilized?"

"Absolutely. I'm for law and order and the rights of individuals to be treated honestly and fairly."

She waited but he added nothing more. Then she examined his words and found he'd explained civilization quite adequately. Impulsively she said, "I love you, Tanner."

He smiled but his eyes were on the dog. "I know you do."

"I've only been here two days, and I've slept upstairs out of reach. How could you think I love you?"

"Love is more than just sex," he told her complacently. "You stayed with me. You came here, and you didn't want to leave. You aren't all the way committed to me yet, but you're considering it. You're a little afraid of it. I believe you consider a commitment as similar to a sacrificial maiden being coaxed to fling herself into an active volcano.'' He turned his head to grin up at her, but he kept on gently brushing the dog.

"An active volcano?'' She considered the comparison. "That's really very close.''

"I've never known anyone who kissed in such an abandoned, committed way. You lift my hair right off my scalp. You do some other interesting things to me too.''

She scoffed, "I think you're just susceptible.''

"To you.''

"Do you feel this amazing pull between us, too? I've never felt it with anyone else. I get in the same room with you and it's almost frightening.''

"Don't be afraid of me, Laura.''

"I would bet they said that to all the sacrificial maidens.'' She frowned as she said, "If you are equated to a volcano, for Pete's sake, how do you survive?''

"Not at all well. I need my fires banked and tended.''

The most surprising wave of sensation washed over Laura. It went through every cell and nerve and tingled so that she was astonished her atoms didn't become confused and fly off in all directions. Impulsively, she asked, "Did you read that we're not solid but just clusters of atoms that are magnetically attracted?''

He chuckled. "Now whatever made you think of that?''

"*My* atoms are vibrating.''

"That's serious. I hope I'm involved when they explode.''

"It could blow up the volcano,'' she said seriously.

He glanced up and she could see the fires in the core of the inferno. "I would risk it gladly."

She watched him stand and knew he was going to come to her and take her into his arms. Vibrating, about to come unglued, she waited.

He looked at his watch. "What with you running away from home and our searching out and taking care of Dog here, it's supper time. Want to go into Myrtle Beach and have some sea food?"

Food? How could he think of food *now*? How irritating! With barely throttled sarcasm, she exclaimed, "Perfect! I can wear my own clothes for a change." She hopped up and started for the house. But she hadn't taken five steps before she stopped to turn back. "What about Dog?"

"He knows he can stay here. He can be on the front porch. I'll put his food and water and an old rag rug there. That way he can watch the road."

And she had been irritated with him! She watched with some amazement as he picked up the hose and carried it back to turn it off and wind it on the brace. He'd left his crutch on the ground! "Tanner? You're walking without the crutch!" It was a miracle!

He grinned. "You're no longer afraid of me so I can get rid of the damned thing."

"Do you mean...? You snookered me!"

"That sounds about right. I didn't want you to feel threatened. I figured if you thought I couldn't chase you or climb stairs, you'd feel more in control and safer out here all alone with me in the wilds of the South Carolina coast."

"And you claim to be civilized! You sneak!" she sputtered. "You pirate! You trickster!"

"None of the above." He was good-humored. "I'm calculating and clever. I fully intended to tell you about it because I thought of it! It was brilliant! Pete called and said you were coming down...."

"He told me he would only say a proxy was going to visit you for him."

"He lied. He told me it would be you. I had only a few hours of intense plotting to figure out how to keep you here. If you hadn't agreed to stay, I was going to become disabled."

"Disabled?"

He confessed readily enough, "I was going to wing that one. Either be sick or fall—nothing too drastic— but not able to take care of myself. That way your tender heart would have been touched..."

"Well, darn. I wish I hadn't leaped at the offer. Now I'll never know how you would have manipulated me. Just witnessing your performance would have been worth the time."

He wasn't that sure. "As I said, I'm not at all good at acting. I've never had to."

"Just snapped your fingers?"

"No, I never wanted to entrance any other woman as I want you."

"I'm a little scared."

"You unsettle me a little too."

"So." She put her hand to her chest and took a steadying breath. "So you can walk unaided."

"I can't run yet. Honest. I can't even jog yet. Stairs are still tricky, even without suitcases. But I do walk on the beach. I went almost as far as you did when I walked last night."

"But you didn't see Dog?"

"I wasn't looking for anything. I was walking and trying to calm down from that crippling good-night kiss you gave me. He probably watched me go past, tearing my hair and gnashing my teeth in frustration."

Heartlessly, she thought he was being amusing.

They drove into Myrtle Beach. It was still crowded with the seasonal invasion of Canadians and braced for the onslaught of college kids who came there on spring break. At one of the excellent restaurants on Ocean Boulevard they ate dinner and had a very pleasant evening. They spent almost three hours on good food and conversation. They remembered, they discussed, they laughed. They exchanged bites of their foods. And after the evening was out, they went back to the waiting house.

Dog was still on the porch. He got up and trotted after the Porsche as it went around the house. When the car stopped, Dog came to stand and watch them in a friendly way as they left the car. They both spoke to the dog. Tanner petted him, but Laura still kept her distance.

Leaving the dog to go back to his vigil, they went into the house. Tanner immediately went to the kitchen sink and washed his hands quite carefully. To Laura it seemed a curious thing to do. As he reached for a towel, he saw that she watched and he explained, "When I get my good-night kiss, I want to smell you, not Dog."

"After his bath he probably smells like a rose."

"Not exactly. Not bad, but still like a dog. He's a grown male." He swung his head around and smiled faintly. "And so am I."

"Don't frighten me."

"I never would."

"I'll bet you're leading up to the good-night kiss?"

"Inevitably." He seemed quite serious as he dried his hands.

The single word started her nerves shimmering. Her breathing faltered. With her hot breath pouring over her lips they would be like sandpaper when he finally got around to kissing her! She licked her lips hastily.

He kissed her just like the night before. He kissed her hands first, rather pointedly, and then he took her into his arms and hugged her so deliciously that her brain swooned. Then he really kissed her. Beautifully. He melted her bones and set her blood afire. He ruined her respiratory system entirely. After all those years, her lungs forgot how to function. It was chaos.

Then he pried her away from him and smiled sweetly as he said good-night. And again he patted her bottom in that sassy way as he started her up the stairs. How could he abandon her? She went up the stairs debating taking off her clothes as she walked back down to him. He was standing there watching her. What would he do?

He might allow her to seduce him. But then again he could very well fetch her a robe and send her back upstairs again. He wasn't predictable. Imagine his pretending to need a crutch in order to keep her from feeling threatened. It wasn't him she was worried about. It was herself!

She wanted him. She wanted to lie in his arms and have him make love to her. It would be so...nice. But he was thinking long term and she was thinking greedy. Wasn't it generally the other way around? Was she the victim of role reversal? Was this what the columnists were talking about?

She'd always been told to behave. Especially if she cared for a man. The saying was that a woman is a prude until she loves a man, then she has the morals of an alley cat; while a man will take anything offered until he loves a woman, then he's pure as the driven snow.

Perhaps that's what the trouble really was. The hang-up wasn't role reversal, but the male-female confrontation that was old as time. They loved each other and were reacting typically. Nothing was new. It was the same old thing. And she'd been as guilty as had every other generation in thinking anything was different.

So he was waiting for her commitment. He was giving her time to know him. To be sure he loved her, but how well could she love him? That was an important question. She was most assuredly attracted. God knew that. She had always been drawn to Tanner. He was so superb, so special and so attractive.

Bemused she went about the automatic routine of preparing for bed. She heard without hearing, the surf, the wind in the palms, the house shifting, the car drive by and... A car? It was probably the first she'd heard since she came here! How amazing. Civilization did exist.

She gazed at herself in the mirror, and decided she looked like a klutz. Pigtails, T-shirt and panties. Old cotton panties with loose elastic. What a dream woman.

What if he came up the stairs to say good-night again? What if he decided to coax her into taking a sample of Tanner's other talents? He'd take one look at her and forget it.

She peeled off the T-shirt and panties and took out a slip that was navy blue and made mostly of lace. She considered it as a nightgown. It would have to do. She unbraided her hair and brushed it back into silkiness. She added a little eye shadow and then just a touch of blush.

She smiled into the mirror and pursed her lips in a phantom kiss. Not too tacky. She swaggered a little as she went over, eased down and wiggled between the sheets. She was ready.

She went to sleep listening for him on the stairs.

With dawn she found herself wrapped in the sheet with her slip wound around her so uncomfortably that she was reminded why she slept in T-shirt and old panties. She lay there, irritated, thinking disgruntled thoughts at Tanner.

Why blame him? she thought. What if she wasn't interested? What if he came up the stairs to try her and she didn't want to? There they were, out here all alone, in the middle of nowhere. If he tried to rape her what could she do about it? If she hadn't wanted him, why was she staying there alone with him? The rules of convention were good practical rules that simply had to be observed.

But she *was* willing. That was what surprised her so much when she had agreed to stay there with Tanner.

The only man she'd ever slept with had been Tom. She had never cared much for Tom's lovemaking and therefore had never been tempted to try another man...until now. She was now willing. It was Tanner who was being obtuse. She would simply have to indicate that he had a free hand, so to speak. She smiled.

How does a woman go about a seduction? she thought. A good meal, low lights, sexy gown, loose shoulder strap. Right. She would seduce him. That decided so handily, she got out of bed and unwound her slip so she could remove it. Then she looked over her clothes. Obviously she'd not packed with seduction in mind.

She went into the hall and checked through the guest closet. There was a fascinating collection of odds and ends of clothing, and she found a cigar box with an assortment of costume jewelry. It was the type gathered for children to use while playing dress-up on rainy days. But nowhere in that practical closet was there anything near to what she was looking for in seductive clothing. A bikini that was a little tired looking was about the only thing that came even close, but the Atlantic in April tended to be quite cold. So, that eliminated the excuse to wear even the tired bikini. It was apparent that seduction could be a problem.

She heard a truck drive up. Last night she'd heard a car, today a truck. It was time to move on west. Civilization was intruding. Long ago, a pioneer in Indiana had moved west because someone homesteaded twelve miles from him, crowding him.

She put on the wraparound and thongs and went downstairs. Two men were delivering boxes into her morning room. Well, she hadn't needed the entire room, she told herself, but it still seemed intrusive of Tanner to put the boxes there when other rooms weren't being used.

She went into the kitchen and saw the grill on top of the stove and pancake batter ready nearby. The way she was eating, she would have to find some more wraparounds.

After setting the table she worked at making their meal. She listened to Tanner's deep voice as he spoke to the delivery men. When Tanner realized he was being seduced would his deep voice tremble and squeak? Well, she'd soon find out!

Within that creaking house on a palm-studded sea coast, she felt a little like a woman pirate. Ho ho ho and a bottle of rum. Rum! *That* was the other missing ingredient to seduction. Candy's dandy but liquor's quicker. How could she have forgotten?

Tanner came into the kitchen as the laboring sound of the delivery truck faded away, and he found Laura up on her Cratchit stool with her head in an upper cupboard. "What are you doing?" he asked her.

"I'm studying your liquor cellar for rum."

"For *breakfast*?" He seemed surprised.

She pulled her head out of the cupboard and gave him a slow, enigmatic smile. "You've never had rum in your pancake syrup?"

"I don't believe so," he replied unsurprisingly.

"Let's live a little."

"I have a surprise for you."

Her smile crept back salaciously. "Ah, and I have one for you!"

"Do I get it now or after breakfast?" He gave her the choice.

"After. Everything's ready so let's eat first." She smiled still. Once they got in bed, they might miss several meals. She thought he appeared . . . a little stimulated. Did he suspect she planned to seduce him? He seemed anxious to get through breakfast, and they ate with very little conversation. He was nice about the rum-soaked pancakes and agreed they were different. She smiled at him and made her eyelids heavy.

Tanner had studied her through breakfast, trying to figure her out. She acted a little drunk. On rum-soaked pancakes? Curious. Nevertheless, he hurried her along. He was anxious to see her reaction to the things he'd ordered.

She insisted on clearing up the kitchen. There was nothing more depressing than to return to a kitchen and find the ruins of a meal waiting to be dealt with. She quickly hurried the mess out of the way. "Was Dog fed?"

"Long ago, sleepyhead."

"He's still around?"

He nodded. "On the porch, watching."

"I thought maybe the car last night—"

"Car? You heard a car? When?"

"Yeah. When I was getting ready for bed. I think we ought to move on west, partner, it's getting crowded around these parts."

"What kind of car?" He frowned and his question was quickly asked.

"I didn't see it, I just heard it! It's a public road, you know. I thought it might be Dog's people come back for him."

"No."

He had become a little distracted from her. She went to him and put her arms around his shoulders and lifted her mouth. "Good morning."

"You train well. I am pleased." He kissed her sputtering mouth and he laughed.

"Train...!" she began indignantly.

But he only patted her bottom and said, "Come see."

He led her into the morning room and immediately began to open the boxes. He clamped the holder for the butcher paper on one end of the drafting table, and found the giant roll of paper it would take a year to use up, if she worked at it diligently. Artists use butcher paper in many ways, as a cover to prevent smears, as scratch paper, as a clean surface, as a paint tester. It is marvelously versatile.

Then he put out the brushes. Beautiful sable ones, from a brush of a single hair to a Japanese hand brush to one to paint huge ink letters on paper and on cloth. He went to the kitchen for pots and crocks and set the brushes in them on end. His generosity boggled her mind and twisted her tongue so that she could only stare with her mouth open and itch to try them all.

All those inks and paints! With such an inventory, she could start classes! Then he opened the boxes. There were swatches of material, from Damask to the finest silks, from burlaps to linen. Laura was overwhelmed. She started to laugh and cry.

"Are you pleased?"

"Oh, Tanner..." How could she tell him she was crying because if she seduced him now, he would think it was in gratitude for gifts.

"I think then, that you could kiss me for a thank-you, don't you?"

"Oh, Tanner..." And she flung herself into his arms and hugged him for a long time, which he permitted. And then she kissed him very sweetly, which he also permitted. He cooperated, and she could have snatched him bald for causing the delay of his seduction! Another night in that bed alone.

The weather continued its taste of summer for several more days. Laura and Tanner breakfasted together, then separated to their workrooms until lunch and walked along the beach in the afternoons. Dog sat on the porch or roamed along the road, but he walked along the beach with them as he watched the road.

And they kissed. Every day Tanner added more reasons for kisses. And Laura agreed readily and cooperated with an eagerness that spun his head around. He smiled to himself and thought it wouldn't be long before he had her.

In her turn, Laura also plotted. How interesting that they were each so involved in the other's seduction they couldn't pay attention and realize what was going on and work together.

Being her thrifty mother's child, and one of four daughters, Laura could sew. She chose a swatch of blues and lavenders in lovely swirls. Using an elderly machine she found in the upstairs sewing room, she made herself a dress. A dress for a seduction. It turned out very sweet. It wasn't at all sexy. Disgruntled, she put it aside. She wanted something to curl his toes.

She again went through the swatches and found a fiery red. Men like red. It was almost as clingy as parachute silk. It was horrible to work with, and she grimly finished it. It was perfect. She did look a little like a streetwalker, but at least there was no question. She didn't look unavailable. She was ready.

The red dress demanded some adornment besides the pearl buttons she wore in her ears and sudden inspiration sent her back to the guest closet where she went through the box of old jewelry. There were lots of beads, some bracelets. But mostly single, clip-on earrings.

One earring was a white rhinestone cluster with only two stones missing. It also had strings of rhinestones hanging in a bunch. It was, of course, a singleton. She found another that was also made of white rhinestones mixed with a pinky violet that went quite well with the red. It, too, hung to her shoulder. She would wear them with the dress. They looked like something a loose woman would wear.

That made her wonder a little about how the earrings had come to be in that house? It had probably been the woman whose "ghost" she'd heard on that first night. She'd had a rather knowing laugh.

So she had the perfect dress and earrings. She was ready. However, after two concentrated days of furious sewing she was tired, cross and had a headache. The weather was turning sullen and gray. She'd really pushed it by making two dresses in two days. It was no time to try for a seduction, she'd probably snap at him and ruin everything and then cry in disappointment, and he'd turn her out of the house.

With the weather muggy and still, she took her headache down to the kitchen to go through the freezer. Being on the coast, there were shrimp in plenty. There was also frozen lobster bisque, some shrimp creole and long slender loaves of bread. He should be pleased she didn't have to cook it herself. She wasn't that imaginative nor was she any kind of cook.

She thawed a large container of stew and a loaf of Vienna bread for their supper. Then she added a Mountain Top pumpkin pie. Let Pam eat her heart out.

Tanner was surprised to find supper ready. "How nice of you!"

"Do you think you're the only one who can thaw things?"

"You're my guest. I'm supposed to take care of you. You're working too hard. I shouldn't have gotten you all that stuff at once. I should have stretched it out over the summer."

"I can't stay here all summer." She was softly regretful.

"We'll see." He was dismissive to such a problem.

She explained, "All your family will be here in another month."

"They come in layers. They peak on the Fourth of July. We have a hell of a party then. It's fun. You'll have a good time, and they'll all love you." His eyes never left her.

"We do that on the Forth at home, in South Bend."

"Are you feeling okay?" He was frowning at her.

"Fine."

"Let me feel your forehead." He laid his big, warm hand on her hot, blushing face.

"I'm fine, really. Just a little tired."

"I think you have a fever. You look a little too bright-eyed and flushed. I'll get the thermometer." He began to look through cupboards.

So she had a headache. All that was wrong with her was sexual frustration. Did he mistake thwarted passion for an illness? "You could take me over to the veterinarian like you did Dog," she suggested.

"I wouldn't let Henry touch you to examine you."

"Why not?"

"I change around you," he explained brusquely. "My teeth sharpen, my arms get long, my forehead slopes back sharply, my knuckles drag on the ground."

"Really? I hadn't noticed that. Why?"

"Didn't you see how he leered at you when we took Dog over there?"

"Henry acted perfectly normal. Friendly."

"See?"

"He was supposed to be rude?"

"Only professional." Tanner shook down the thermometer and poked it in her mouth.

Around it, she said, "But you—"

"Be quiet."

She subsided. With the thermometer in her mouth she felt even more rotten. She had a cold? That would postpone the seduction of Tanner for another couple of days. She felt sour.

In broad humor, he asked, "Are you acting sick just so you can stay? How unoriginal of you. I'll allow you to stay without being sick."

"Good grief." The thermometer rattled between her teeth.

"Be quiet."

Six

She had no fever. He frowned at her bright eyes and reddened cheeks. He seemed so concerned that she explained herself to him, well enough, "I just need Vitamin C and a Tylenol. I'll be fine. It's all this sea air." She was on a roll. "My lungs and blood aren't used to the salt. As a prairie woman, of pioneer stock, I'm genetically too many generations removed from the primal salt swamp. The readjusting takes a while."

"You need an early night. I didn't mean to overwhelm you with all that junk to sort through."

"Junk! Oh, Tanner, it was like having five Christmases at once. All those gorgeous things! I must at least share in the costs. The bill will be staggering."

"They're gifts. No true courtesan offers to pay...in money." He smiled.

"Oh? Compromising gifts? How shocking."

"At times your eyes are such an innocent blue and
then there are times like these—with rum-soaked
pancakes and with my suggestion you can trade your
body for priceless gifts—and your eyes are very very
wicked. My mother never mentioned women like you.
She always told me to be kind."

"And what did your dad tell you?"

Tanner squinted his eyes for a minute, as he recalled, then he quoted, " 'Don't turn down anything
until you check it out to see if it's worth it.' Hmmmm.
Do you suppose he meant women? I always thought
he meant stocks! He was an investor. Why, I do believe he misled me."

"You idiot."

"I believe I have been." He smiled. "Shall we cure
your headache?"

Regretfully she said, "If my heartbeat went up even
one more notch, my head would explode and that'd be
a god-awful mess."

He nodded thoughtfully. "Might be a turnoff."

"Oh, Tanner, you are something else." She smiled
at him.

Outside on the road, the sound of a car went past.
Tanner simply disappeared. Vanished. She saw him
and then he was gone! There had been no sound,
nothing. She stood up, her eyes enormous, and she
looked at the floor. She peeked into the center hall and
then went into his study. Nothing.

She turned back to the hall and looked around,
getting spooked. What if there was something strange
about the house? What if there *wasn't* any family and
he was the only surviving member and the house fed
on the souls of strangers lured into . . .

And there he was in front of her!

She shrieked, and he looked very surprised. He reached for her and she backed away, saying a moaning, "Oh, no!"

He thought she'd flipped. "Laura?"

"Is it you, Tanner?"

"What did you see?"

What was there *to* see? She stared at him with huge, haunted eyes. "How'd you do that?"

"What?" he asked a little puzzled.

"Disappear like that."

He frowned, trying to understand, and told her, "I went to the front door to see what kind of car went by."

"Did you fly? There was no sound."

His face was blank, and then slowly a smile came into his eyes and his mouth quirked. "You think the house is haunted and I'm a spook." He nodded, very amused.

She agreed, "You didn't really survive the wreck. You weren't ready to depart this vale of tears."

"Ah. Am I a vampire?"

She frowned at him. "No. You do go out into the sun." That would tend to eliminate the vampire theory. "How did you vanish from the kitchen that way?"

He became serious, knowing now that she was, too. He took her arms and moved her to one side. He went to the kitchen and dashed out, past her and to the front door. He made no sound at all. She had followed him and they stood there in the soft darkness.

"I thought you couldn't run."

"I didn't. I only hurried."

It was true. "Are you real, Tanner?"

"Painfully so." He watched her.

"Did you ever read about the Englishman a hundred or so years ago who said he could run between two towns and there were bets for and against him, and a carriage of witnesses went along to see there was no cheating, and he appeared to stumble on the bare roadway and he simply vanished. They never did find him."

"You thought I was gone?"

"It scared me."

"If I left I'd take you home with me." He took hold of her upper arms, his strong hands didn't hurt her, but he held her very firmly. "Your time has come, Laura Fullerton. Face it bravely." His voice was low and husky.

"Tanner..."

He kissed her. Beautifully. Marvelously. Then he slung her over one hip to carry her awkwardly with only his good right arm, and his limp became pronounced.

"You can't do this. I'm too heavy."

"I am doing it." He was struggling along.

"This is ridiculous."

"It's romantic," he corrected. "I want our first time to be romantic."

"You're ruining my stomach."

"I'll soothe it in just a minute."

"You're not going to try for the stairs are you?" she asked in alarm.

With a bit of uncertainty he replied, "Well...if you really prefer to be on your own bed ..."

"No no no. Why are we going anywhere? What was wrong with the rug in the front room?"

"I would hate for our grandchildren to gossip about their grandmother's first time being on the floor, and their grandfather being so greedy that he couldn't sweep grandmaw up in his arms and carry her to a decent couch at the very least. A bed sounds a little too deliberate, don't you agree? Not at all impulsive but more calculated."

"Grandchildren?"

"I'm going to marry you, Scarlett honey. I can't keep waiting to catch you between husbands. One might live."

"I was divorced," she said in a record-keeping way, then she asked, "Scarlett honey? You read GWTW?"

He paused as if to consider, but he was really catching his breath. "GWTW? Ahhh, of course, *Gone With the Wind.* Why naturally I read it. All the women go bonkers over Rhett, so I had to plow through a couple of thousand pages to see what turned them all so eager. All I could find out was that he kept trying to get Scarlett into bed. Now *that's* something *I* could do!"

Quite pensive, she told him, "I've always wanted to make love with you."

"You could have mentioned it." He sounded a little annoyed.

"I didn't realize that was what it was until you kissed me in the receiving line when Tom and I were married."

"It was a little late by then."

"Yes. I've thought about you a time or two."

"Me, too."

"You ought to put me down," she suggested. "You're ruining your lungs trying to carry me along this way."

"It isn't carrying you that's ruining my lungs, it's your soft body against mine and me knowing I'm going to make love to you."

"This must be killing your arm."

"You may have gained a bit."

"I haven't either!"

He leaned an arm against the wall to rest, but he still held her over his good hip. "You have the most gorgeous hips."

"You haven't even looked at my hips. I was watching."

"I've made a concerted study of you. I know your hips in detail, if you'll pardon the expression."

"Put me down, Tanner."

"I've offended you? Most women wouldn't mind if—"

"I can't wait any longer."

"Here on the floor? My God, Scarlett. What will our grandchildren say to that? Shocking. Shocking." But he put her down. He was trembling and as he kissed her his breath was harsh.

"See? You've exhausted yourself! You won't have the energy to even—"

"Don't worry."

"I can't have you ruin yourself just to satisfy me."

He laughed with such amusement. "Laura, baby, don't you worry. I'm fine. Or almost. I will be pretty soon now. Kiss me."

But she went on fretting. "You're trembling. Your muscles are—"

"It isn't exhaustion, it's desire." His voice was gruff, but amusement laced his words.

"Really? Tom never...I didn't know. I thought...Tanner. Oh, Tanner."

"I do like wraparounds. Oh, my love." He drew in his breath as he opened her gown and surveyed her body in the soft light. Then he slid the garment off her shoulders to the floor.

"Let me help you." She reached for him.

But he moved away. "Let's go over here into the dark." He still hadn't exposed his left thigh to her eyes. Very quickly to get past it, he told her, "Don't move your right leg against my left thigh. That's the only thing. You can do anything else you want to, but just watch the left thigh."

"I love you."

"Marry me."

"We'll talk about it."

"Now, Laura, just..."

"Kiss me, Tanner."

"We..."

She kissed him lovingly and he cooperated quite nicely. She breathed, "Oh, Tanner..." Then she undid his trousers very boldly, surprising them both. She knelt to slide the soft material off his legs and it was then she saw the night-shadowed wounds in his thigh. Very softly, she ran her hand over his healing leg in an accepting caress. She filled his heart and he drew in his breath as he watched her fingers slide higher. She murmured, "You are so beautiful."

And he looked down at her, kneeling before him, and his voice was unsteady with emotion as he said, "Laura!" in a passionate whisper.

Before then, she hadn't thought how abrasive even so soft a rug might be on his wounds. She led him to his bed and lay so he could be on his good right side as they began their explorations. Their appreciation of each other.

They kissed almost as if to consume, their hands searching, their fingers stiffened with their desire. With the fire that burned in them. She made little squeaking sounds and tears slid from her eyes, her emotions ran so high. So overwhelming. He was there in her arms!

He had planned to be tender and loving, but he was swept up in her passion and they spiraled far beyond anything either of them had ever experienced. It was out of control. They could only helplessly ride it out, frantically holding on, disoriented, plunging recklessly into another world. A place of thrilling sensations that obliterated all else.

After some time, their sated bodies lay as contented victims on his bed, there in the soft darkness. They could hardly move. They carefully turned their heads to smile at each other. But it was a little while before they were able to touch and clasp their hands. It was even longer before they spoke. At first they made only sounds. Sounds of pleasure.

"I never dreamed it would be like this." His voice was a rumble.

"I thought I was hallucinating. Is this some kind of psychedelic drug that's habit forming?"

"Whatever it is, I'm sure it's habit forming. I want more."

"You jest," she protested.

"Well, I didn't mean right this minute."

"I couldn't wiggle a muscle if my life depended on it."

"Oh, yes. Want me to show you that you could?"

"Don't threaten me."

"If I could move my arm and that hand," he promised. "I would prove you could move."

"I'll wait. Don't push yourself."

"You're the other half of me."

"I sure was," she agreed easily to that.

"I mean, we're meant to be."

"You are awesome." Her voice wasn't more than a whisper. "It was a little scary."

"Another dimension."

"Ummmm."

"You're so sweet and soft. You are such a lady and such a surprise in passion. I'm stunned. I wish I had the energy to see if it was really true."

"Not right away."

With some lazy effort he leaned up on his elbow to look down at her. He smiled into her eyes and gently kissed her swollen lips. "You look like you've been very very friendly with some willing man."

"How strange." Her eyes were sleepy and heavily lidded.

"Who was the lucky guy?"

"Some handsome stranger I ran into in the center hall who appears and vanishes."

"How's the headache?" He smoothed back her hair from her forehead.

"I have no idea. I believe I'm splattered some-where in the marvelous inner space of fantastic colors. I feel so boneless and melted. What in the world did you do to me?''

''That was a restrained application of Tanner Moran's simple headache remedy. If you are a satisfied customer you owe me payment.''

''What sort of payment?'' She swiveled her head on his chest and her silken hair felt erotic to him even then when he was sated.

''I'll think of something.''

''Not right away.''

He laughed softly, lay back down beside her and held her hand curled in his. ''The sheets are damp from your sweat.''

''I never sweat.''

''It couldn't be mine, I'm never sweaty or excited, either. I'm always calm and in control.''

''Oh, yes?'' She laughed softly.

''Well, perhaps a little 'excited' got in there somewhere tonight.''

''Just a little?''

''You are fabulous.''

''So are you.''

''You are more than I.''

They debated that and then each told how much the other was loved, how gorgeous each was and how sweet. And they argued who was more passionate, and eventually they had to prove their words. And they made sweet tender love that was entirely different but no less beautiful. And they smiled as they slid into peaceful sleep.

Neither heard the car drive by, but Dog watched it pass.

*   *   *

When Laura wakened to the bird's chatter it was to find Tanner propped on one elbow watching her. He had a knee over hers and one hand moved sensuously over her pleasured stomach. He smiled at her. She laughed.

"You find it amusing to wake up in my bed? When I've told you what all you did to me, you'll find it hilarious."

With great, droll humor, she informed him, "Upstairs, in my closet, is a red dress of asininely soft silk that clings like a second skin. I made it for your seduction tonight. And in the freezer is shrimp, lobster bisque and a shrimp creole to lure you into a good humor so that I can *coax* you into submitting to my carnal desires."

"I jumped the gun."

"Somewhat," she agreed.

"I'll wipe that from my mind…" But he had to put back his head and just laugh over how impossible that would be. "Well, what I can do is, I can pretend I've wiped it from my mind and your seduction can go along as scheduled. I can hardly wait."

"Oh, no," she said airily. "The element of surprise is ruined. I'll have to just forget it."

"Hey! I insist. Surprise me tonight with a full-out, calculated seduction. I'll behave."

Spacing her words with deliberate drollness, she instructed: "The purpose of a seduction, you idiot, is to get you *not* to behave."

"I hadn't realized that."

"I think initiating men is one of the most difficult things a woman must cope with."

"I need some lessons?" He couldn't even hold his voice steady. He knew how good he was.

"In some of the finer nuances. I believe in time, and with practice, you could be quite adequate." She lifted her brows and gave him a cool glance.

Deliberately he leaned over and his kiss was cunning. He changed the kiss and introduced his tongue into play, touching her lips and teasing hers into an assault of her mouth so that her tongue then touched his tauntingly as she resisted his intrusion. His hands moved, one stroking her susceptible stomach, which caused her breasts to rise, wanting attention. He lowered his mouth to them, and she began to breathe brokenly.

His own breath changed. It scorched along on her cool skin and his tongue was scalding. His muscles hardened, and his hot hands were a little rougher as his mouth nipped along her throat and began to seduce her ear. Little sounds escaped her and her body began to writhe.

"How'm I doing?" he breathed it hotly into her ear.

"Quite well. You are, however, neglecting my... thighs."

"Sorry."

"Mmmmm."

After a time, he questioned in a clogged, foggy voice, "Anything I've forgotten?"

"Uh, you haven't, uh, seen if... the parts fit yet."

"Oh! Well." He shifted their bodies. "How about... thisssss."

"Ahhhh. Ohhhhh, yeesssss."

* * *

Some time after that, as they changed the bed linen, she gave him a verbal clearance, showing he was reacting properly to a potential seduction. She said if she could arrange the time that evening, they would have a full, dress rehearsal, just to check him out in case his passing the test had been a fluke.

He was grateful.

She continued, "Anyone can do anything once. We have to be sure performance is at level before any certificate can be issued."

"Of course."

"You might get in a couple of naps, and eat oysters, olives and..."

"Of course."

"Is that all you can say?"

"I'm still speechless. In shock. An innocent boy like me tangling with a rapacious woman of the world like you! I have to adjust."

"Good. Be brave."

"That's what all you wicked women say to us innocent young boys."

"Of course."

"That's my line." He kissed her very gently. "Thank God I don't have to go out and do something drastic like mow the yard or drive to the grocery or anything like that."

She laughed at him.

At noon, when Laura phoned her office, Jeanine said, "Mr. Perry called from Columbia, Laura. Sorry, but it seems his partner's wife wants to do the coordination. She thinks 'It'll be fun.' Sorry, honey. There is some mail, shall I send it on?''

''That'll be fine. Send it to General Delivery, Myrtle Beach, South Carolina.''

''You ought to phone your mother. She called a message in yesterday.''

''Call her for me and tell her I lost the Columbia account and I'll be in touch. Thanks, Jeanine. I'll call tomorrow. Bye.''

When Laura hung up, Tanner inquired, ''General Delivery?''

''It's easy to remember. And since you don't get mail here, I thought you had reason not to. Anyway, it's easier for the Post Office to forward it directly if there's anything.''

Tanner explained, ''One of the reasons I don't get mail here is that I never stay any place for very long. All I need is the computer and the answering equipment. When I'm through here, I just load the stuff into the car and move to another place and post that number for contacts.''

''A wanderer.''

''My job takes me around.''

She smiled. ''Live for today.''

''And tonight for my dress rehearsal.''

''I believe I'll need a nap.''

''Fortunately I have clean sheets on my bed.''

''A nap... alone. I can't deplete my resources if I face a dress rehearsal.''

''Are you tired, baby?'' He smiled and came to her to take her into his arms. ''Do I wear you out? You are just too delicious. Let's go sit on the porch and relax, then you can sleep.''

* * *

Dog sat stolidly on the porch, watching. He turned to look at Tanner and Laura, but he continued his vigil. They cleaned his bowls and freshened the water. She shook the rug and folded it comfortably. And she even leaned down with her hands on her knees to speak to the dog, who watched her gravely.

She straightened and held Tanner's hand as they looked out over their view of the road, the beach and out over the restless Atlantic. The sky was sullen, low, and the breeze humid and fitful. A cold rain was predicted coming across the land, to ruin for a time the promise of summer.

She stretched and smiled up at Tanner and he returned the smile. He led her over to sit on the padded porch swing, and he leaned her against him as he swung it gently. She curled up with her back along his body, and they were contentedly silent.

"Maybe it's a good thing Mr. Perry's plans folded," Laura said. "I haven't done anything for two days."

"I just made love to you last night. Today is the only day I've wasted for you."

"Wasted?" She laughed a lovely, throaty laugh. "For two days I was sewing dresses like mad and planning your seduction."

"That's hardly wasted time."

"I can't hold my eyes open."

He coaxed, "Let's go to bed."

"Oh, no you don't."

He chuckled a rumble in his chest that she could feel in her back. "There's no way I'm going to spoil your seduction of me tonight. Go on upstairs, hussy, and get to your plotting of my downfall." They kissed nicely, and he patted her bottom as she rose from the swing to go upstairs.

The weather forecast said there was an enormous weather system approaching the east coat, there would be rain and the spring storm promised it would become much cooler. With the promised change in weather, she sorted through the guest closet for some long-sleeved sailor blouses made of soft cotton. She also found some trousers of deck cotton with an elastic waist.

In a cavernous, linen storage closet she found another quilt. How carelessly those handmade works of art were actually used on beds when they should have been hung on walls. They were lovely things. She ran her hand over the tiny quilting stitches and appreciated the work involved in making them. She chose an intricate Double Wedding Ring design and carried it to her room. Stripping, she lay down on the bed and pulled the quilt over her, then she snuggled down. Ah, Tanner.

How could this man be so different from other men? She could remember when she was married to Tom and she had wondered "Was that all there was to living?" She'd always had the feeling of being incomplete, of expecting there was more, of missing out.

She and Tom had never had the sharing of humor that she had with Tanner. And the passion! How could it be so different with Tanner? A man was only a man. The parts only fit together. Why was their fitting so different? How could he be the one to make her so aware of him? Why him? How remarkable.

He wanted a relationship. But for how long? He spoke of grandchildren. She lay there somberly thinking of what she wanted and how honest she was in being there with Tanner at this time in his life. He was at a very vulnerable crossroad. Physically weakened, how strong was he emotionally? Could she trust his emotions as being reliable and his own decision concerning his wanting a commitment from her?

They needed to talk.

When she'd heard Pete say Tanner's name again and knew he'd been hurt, her own judgment had gone askew. It was totally foreign for her to have come to him when she had never really known him. And to stay with him so impulsively! With no hesitation at all. That could be instinct.

It could be sex. And now that she knew how miraculous making love with him could be, why this sudden questioning? Why this hesitation? Did she really want to go back into the servitude of marriage? She had only begun to taste the ramifications of independence in these past few years. She'd gone from father to college to husband. She'd never been on her own.

To have divorced Tom had been unusual behavior for her. She had been surprised she had that much courage. But she'd looked down the dull years of sameness and she couldn't stay married to Tom. He'd been offended by the divorce. He'd been bitter and he'd cleaned her out financially.

It had been worth giving up the money and property in order to be free. She'd never felt companionable with Tom. In spite of how hard she tried, they were never friends. It was as if they were cordial acquaintances. She'd never felt fulfilled with Tom. Even when she'd been satisfied, it hadn't been such fulfillment as she'd had the night before with Tanner.

Was her present conduct because she was more mature? Her child-bearing years were waning. Was old mother nature pushing?

She did love him. She cared for and about him. But did she want to risk marriage again? Better just to live with Tanner, keep control of her own life, until this bloom wore off, and he began to treat her the way the men in her experience used women.

She and Tanner had to talk. Yes.

But it wasn't talking with Tanner that made her smile as she drifted into sleep. She slept like a log. Motionless, deep and still. She awakened and smiled before she even remembered Tanner, her love. Ah, Tanner. What was she to do about Tanner?

Seven

When Laura wakened from her nap, she bathed, sprayed her naked body with a faint mist of Chanel No 5 and painted her finger and toenails a bright red. She dressed in lace briefs and that wicked wicked clingy red silk dress with its shadow panel. She put on quite a bit of eye makeup and some red lipstick. She brushed her hair so it fell loosely around her shoulders and she wore those sparkly, mismatched earrings. Since she had no suitable shoes, she went barefooted.

With the creaky stairs, her descent was heralded, and Tanner was at the bottom of the steps waiting for her. He was in a suit... and a bow tie. His unruly hair was parted unsuccessfully in the center and an effort had been made to plaster it down. What a miserable attempt he'd made to look like an innocent rube! She bubbled laughter.

There was no answering laughter. He was solemn and his eyes were glued on her. With him there to witness it, she made a slow-motion production of her descent. "My God," he breathed as he watched her, and she put back her head and laughed. He asked, "That's my dress? The one you made for me?"

"Yes."

He said, "Okay, I give up."

She frowned at him and slumped. "You're really very irritating. Show a little backbone."

"Show backbone? You want me naked? Okay." He reached up to his tie, never taking his eyes from her.

"No! I mean you ought to show a little resistance."

He amended, "I'm not easy, you know."

"I haven't even *asked* you yet!"

He explained, "That dress does it. And I think the bare feet with that outfit are the most erotic thing I've ever seen. It makes you look abandoned."

"Left by the roadside like Dog?"

"No morals." The fires in his blue eyes flamed up as he smiled. He reached for her as she came to the last step and her mouth was almost even with his.

She turned her head as she protested, "You'll smear my lipstick."

So he did. Quite thoroughly. And he made low, throaty sounds while he did that. He looked her over, as she released herself, and he watched her walk as she went to the kitchen. She allowed herself a restrained swish and flirted over her shoulder at him. He leaned against the wall and put one hand to his head to steady himself, making her laugh again.

Her laugh sounded very like that ghost laugh the first night: very knowing. As Tanner followed her into the kitchen, she asked, "Was there a woman here that first night I was here?"

"Why?"

Not "No" but "why?"

"I thought I heard a laugh."

"A nice, sexy laugh?"

She turned around and gave him a startled look. "There *is* a ghost?"

"We aren't sure who she is—or was—but that's all she does. The laugh is such that the men all smile and the women get prickly. You laughed that way last night."

"I don't recall having had any time to laugh."

"The sound's exciting to a man. You laughed that way again, just now, when you came down the stairs, and knew it wouldn't do me any good at all to resist."

She smiled a slow smile at him, amused.

"Smiles like that drive a man right up the wall." He took a deep breath. "I hope you get to eat your supper."

"This isn't supper, it's dinner." She opened the refrigerator door. The shrimp cocktails were already made up, in two iced bowls with the sauce as a side dish. "You fixed the shrimp and made the sauce!"

"I was restless." He licked his lips.

She gave him a look from under almost closed eyelashes and whispered in a huskily sexual parody, "Licking lips like that makes a woman lose her mind."

He came to her and smeared what was left of her lipstick. He couldn't be still and he fidgeted like a man who was getting ready to race in competition. He said, "You jiggle."

"It's the dress."

His chuckle was delicious, his hot eyes slid over her, and his hands had to touch her.

She stopped, as he blocked her way and kissed her, holding her to him. She looked up at him and when she could she asked, "Who is seducing whom?"

"I'm not seducing you! I'm just being friendly."

"Very. You're *supposed* to be casual, interested in business, courteous, helpful with the dishes, and completely unsuspecting. You're no challenge at all."

"Unsuspecting? I'm supposed to be unsuspecting with you in that dress? *In that dress?* You must be joshing! I'm surprised I didn't take you on the stairs. It was only my iron restraint—be serious! That kept me from—Laura!"

She handed him the tureen of shrimp creole, and he took a deep, steadying breath. She instructed, "Put it on the table on the pad."

He said, "Hmm?"

She sighed, "You're no challenge at all."

"You want challenge? Madam, and I mean no sly or slanderous innuendo with that address, if you want challenge, you get challenge." He carried the tureen into the next room and didn't reappear.

She half waited, then took the shrimp plates from the refrigerator and went into the dining room. He was sitting at his place with his hands neatly folded in front of him. He rose, held her chair and sat back down. He put his napkin on his lap and said, "The hogs have been doing fine this year. Lots of little hogs and fat, feeding momma hogs. The year is looking good."

She gave him a patient stare.

"The weeds are growing up between the rows and I'll be all week getting them chopped back."

In a studied way, she commented, "I thought bore farming was coming into being. Leaving a covering of old growth on the fields and drilling holes and putting seeds in without plowing."

"There's no place in a man's world for a smart-tongued woman who reads. Barefoot and pregnant, that's how to keep a woman."

Something flashed in her eyes.

"This is a right smart meal. How are you at lifting bales and picking cotton?"

"As good as any man."

He raised his eyebrows and smiled. "I like you feisty and challenging. How are you at cleaning wells? And the roof needs patching."

"When I said I needed challenge it was not as a laborer but as a seducer. You aren't supposed to test my muscles, you're supposed to appear unaware of the fact I'm female."

"With you in *that* dress, I'm supposed to forget you're female?" The idea seemed difficult to him.

Coolly she replied, "Yes."

"Oh. Well." He sipped his wine, as he seemed to reorient himself, then he took a bracing breath, cleared his throat and inquired, "How do you think the Cubs will do this year, old buddy?"

"I'm a Mets fan."

That appeared to rock him back on his mental heels and he asked in an argumentative way, "Now why in the world would you go with the Mets? Their pitching is the pits, they can't catch a ball with a basket and they wobble when they run. Zeros."

She put down her fork.

"Just testing!" He put up both hands from the table. "There are lip-service fans and then there are your kind who wade right in there and slug it out. I don't slug, but I might be tricked into a little wrestling?"

"One never pokes at the loyalty of a Mets fan," she informed him sternly.

"Learn something new every day. Do you drink beer?"

"I've never been able to get past the smell of it."

He nodded.

She elaborated, "I understand the taste is an acquired one."

"Umm. Like olives and raw oysters," he replied. "Do you ski?"

"I like snow skiing, but I'm not really athletic. I'm not skilled enough. Team sports have always been beyond me. I feel I'm hampering the rest, holding them back."

"I know one sport you do as a partner that is extremely skilled."

"Shhhh!" She was exasperated. "I am working up *gradually*. We aren't supposed to mention anything about it yet."

"Oh."

"What exactly do you do? Why does a car driving by here make you vanish and reappear at the door to see whose it is?"

"The way one stays whole and healthy in this world is to be aware of one's surroundings," he began. "When you said you'd heard a car and then another, I was curious. I called a contact and inquired if there were any hostiles out for scalps. They are checking on it. Since Dog doesn't react to the car, it's not someone searching for him. I asked Milo to—Milo's the area Law—I asked him to keep an eye open."

"There's danger? Someone after you?" She sat straighter feeling quite belligerent and ready to help.

He watched her, thrilled as much by her reaction as by her. Her loyalty included him, right up there with the Mets! "There's no danger. Only cause to be alert. It's probably someone visiting the area. We'll find out."

She asked cautiously, "Someone of those who, you told me, was caught and got mad at the catcher?"

"There's always that possibility."

"What exactly do you do? You said it involved white-collar crimes."

"It's very complicated. My role is less and less physical involvement, especially since the wreck. I'm just not as lively as I was. I mostly check records. I'm a skilled computer hacker. As reported in *Time* magazine's cover report on computers, and in user groups, a hacker is a proud name. A 'cracker' is someone who uses a computer for illegal purposes. They are some of the ones I search out. I watch for 'footprints' showing someone has been snooping in files or records.

"We now have the means to trace the snoopers—the crackers," he continued. "There are all kinds of reasons for people to want to see files. Like watching how someone invests and in which directions, who's selling stocks and bonds, or intruding into more personal files. And we look for unusual bank deposits or withdrawals.

"Most of what I do is part of a greater investigation. There's good reason to suspect something is wrong. I'm small potatoes. What I do is tedious and most investigators haven't the patience for it. I find it fascinating. It's a chess game of sleuthing. The criminal is clever and I have to be more so.

"I'm not the only one doing this. There's a network of us. We compare notes and make suggestions. We work to keep confidential files confidential. We try to keep ahead of the criminal element. White-collar criminals are just as wicked as the ordinary crooks. Anyone who cheats someone else has a flaw that could jeopardize our country if the price was right. There's no villain greater than that." He shifted in his chair and smiled at her. "Sorry. I get carried away."

Quite seriously she said, "I'm proud of your feelings for our country."

"I don't like cheaters. It isn't just the biggies. It's also the guy who thinks the laws are for everyone *else*, who runs stop signs, and ignores speed limits, and gets mad at the cop who catches him. Then he's surprised when his kid cheats."

"How did you get into this particular field?"

He opened out his hands as if to reveal it all. "After Nam I was at odds with the world. It was a stupid war. We had no business there. It was so unorganized. There was us against everything else, armies that weren't armies, fighting that was completely different—no lines drawn, no identifying uniforms, chaos. It was a strange experience and one to age you fast, if you survived it.

"It seemed to me the easiest thing to do, in order to solve the problems of mankind, was to reorganize the world into a more identifiable system. Separate things out better. And computers come along, the personal ones anyone could have, that lead the way to another form of almost instant communication. It was astonishing. The scope of computer communication and storage, the potential, is just boggling. It's like our brains. We still don't know how our brains really work or how to use the rest of them. And computers are like that.

"I was a pioneer hacker when the modem came along." He paused and explained, "A modem allows computer-to-computer communication via telephone. And there were other people who were fascinated. Hackers learned the ramifications possible with the modem. Learning the usage takes time. So a lot of my first contacts were kids fifteen and sixteen who had the time to explore the scope of computer communication. They're all older now. Some have drifted into other fields, but there are still a core of us who are very involved in the detection of devious intrusions."

By then they were spooning sherbet from frosted bowls. And their wine bottle had been replaced. They sat back and smiled at each other and Tanner said, "So what makes Laura tick?"

"You do."

"My God, what an opening line," he said quietly.

"I'm glad I know you."

"I return that wondrous thought."

"The wind has picked up and it's getting quite cool. Don't you think Dog should come inside?"

"Is that Laura Fullerton, disgusted dog dodger, actually inviting a canine into her castle?"

"It's just a little chilly out and he's been very weather worn."

"I'll ask if he'd like to join us."

Dog hesitated. He went out to the steps and looked down along the road, then he came back to the door and looked up at Tanner. But he didn't come inside. He'd indicated he understood the invitation, but that he must keep the vigil.

Tanner went to the storage room and found a sturdy cardboard box, one that had held some of the swatches he'd ordered for Laura. He took the box out on the porch and set it down so Dog could go inside it out of the wind and still see the road.

Laura watched Tanner do all that. His actions touched her heart.

"It's really cold," he said. "I need to go around and close a few windows. And then I'll build us a fire in the library. We can take our wine in there."

While Tanner closed windows and brought in wood, Laura filled the dishwasher. When that was done, she went into the library with a feeling of inevitability.

He'd brought in the pad from the swing, for it was beginning to spit rain, and he laid it on the floor in front of the fire. He brought a plush throw from a closet and laid it on top of the pad, then he collected pillows from around the lower floor. They now had a Sultan's nest.

He took off his jacket, pulled the bow tie loose, then undid the top several buttons of his shirt and rolled up the sleeves. He slid off his shoes and dropped down into the nest as he said, "Bring on the dancing girls." Then he poured more wine in their glasses.

"We need some music."

"I could hum," he offered.

"Some lovely, soft music. No record player?"

"You're being very picky." He got up and went outside to his car, got some tapes, stopped off in his room for a tape player and returned to the fire and Laura.

He put in a tape and set the tape player to one side. Then he sank down beside Laura and kissed her. His hair was tousled and wet and his shoulders were damp from his trip outside to his car. "Anything else? Tell me now."

"I can't think of anything that's out of reach." She grinned.

"Oh yes?"

"Oh, yes." And she kissed him.

"Ahhh. At last."

She piled up pillows and curled on her side, then she directed him so that he lay with his head on her thighs. She asked him, "Who was your first love?"

"You."

"How quick you are. A diplomat."

"I didn't know what love was until I knew you at school. You used to make my nights into the most sensual, the most frustrating madness. It was tougher than the war. Then I was only terrified, but with you I had no hope."

"Why didn't you ever ask me out?"

"You were going with Mike. And when I heard you'd broken up with him, you were already engaged to Tom. You never gave any indication that you noticed me."

"I noticed you."

"Kiss me."

She scolded, "I'm in control here. I'll let you know when there's kissing to be done."

"Now?"

"Yes."

"You drive me mad."

"I don't know exactly what you do to me, but it scares me. I'm glad you're free. You aren't involved with any woman, are you?"

"You."

"Oh, Tanner..." She curled around so that his head was on some pillows and she was across his chest as she kissed him. She raised her mouth to breathe, and he nudged it down, holding the back of her neck, controlling her. In a foggy voice she asked, "I'm not hurting you, am I?"

"You're killing me," he told her gruffly. But as she tried to lift from his chest, he held her there. "You're paralyzing me." And he showed her how.

"All of you is so tense. How different we are. I'm like mush, and you're like rock."

He smoothed his hands on the dress down her, his palms taking sensual pleasure from the feel of the silklike material on her feminine body. "You made the dress for me?"

"To attract you."

"It's like silk on satin." His hands confirmed that. "I think it's interesting you felt I wasn't paying you any attention."

"I'm glad the dress pleases you, the stuff is ghastly to sew. It slithers."

"Take off my shirt and slither on me."

"You make me sound like a snake."

"Wind around me."

She chuckled low in her throat and his eyes burned into her. His breath was a steam blast, and his hands scorched her. He commanded, "Touch me."

She smoothed his hair back from his face. "Your hair is very independent." Her fingers slowly combed through the rough silk, but he twitched with impatience. She leaned and kissed him, but he took over and turned the sweet meeting of their lips into a devouring feeding of a starving man. She pushed a space between their mouths and said, "You're rushing." By then she was on her back, and he loomed above her. He kissed her again—his way—and she laughed.

"What's funny?" he growled.

"This here 'rube' is betraying himself. You lied. You're no innocent country boy."

"Oh, I forgot I'd used that old tack," he rumbled in her ear as he did all sorts of sensational things to it with his tongue and nibbling lips and breath. "Undo my shirt."

"Do I look like a valet?"

"I'd interview you for the job."

"Let's see, I suppose we undo the buttons first? Or does it come off over your head?"

"Try the buttons," he suggested.

"They are lapped over wrong. What a silly way to button a shirt. Backward."

"I'm used to it. You're doing very well. You can have the job."

"The belt buckle's wrong too. We'll have to change that."

"I could just not wear any clothes at all." He was helpful.

"Great! But then how would I justify being your valet?"

"We could think of something for you to do."

"I don't do windows...."

He kissed her, gently rubbing his chest against her silky softness and he purred in his throat with the sensual sensation. "Oh, Laura..." His breath seemed to steam, and his hot hands were hard on her silken curves.

She'd already lost one earring and her hair was tumbled in a very careless and attractive way. Her eyes felt heavy and her lips pouted as if waiting for his. She was quite languid in her movements while he was almost feverish in his. When he manipulated her to suit himself, it felt as if she was boneless.

As she stretched, she moved slowly, and he began to tremble. He pushed the straps from her shoulders and smoothed the material from her breasts so he could look at her there in the firelight. "Ah, Laura, you are so beautiful."

"Tanner..."

They spoke in incomplete sentences, with the need to talk to each other, to hear their voices, but with nothing to say. As they moved in their dance of love, tempting completion, there were moans and gasps and turning as they followed the patterns of enticement. Their thighs rubbing, their hands seeking, their lips caressing. Their faces stroking along the other in their passion, as they made love.

Her dress and briefs were abandoned into a small fiery heap and his clothes were discarded. They lay naked in the firelight as they entwined, their need accelerating, their movements hungrier, their hands rougher, fingers tensed and pressing. She was frantic and on fire. The storm's sound rising outside the house played the counterpoint of their crescendo, heightening their emotion with the elemental sound.

Tanner orchestrated their love with great finesse and carried her on that exquisitely thrilling experience to its ultimate release, and to the spiraling aftermath with its delicious echoes of passion.

Still awed by the scope of their love making, they lay coupled, depleted. He moved to put his arms under her, bracing himself painfully on healing muscles as he held her, cherished her and hugged her to him. Then he moved from her carefully, in spite of her small sounds of protest, and he lay on his back beside her, trembling now with the residue of his expenditure of power.

With only a minute of rest, he rolled up onto his elbow to lean over her, watching her, his breath still not steadied, and he kissed her, his sweat dripping, his hand still shaking with his spent passion. "Laura..."

She smiled softly, sleepily. "You are simply fabulous."

"So are you. Beautiful."

"Let's do it again." She was boneless and droll.

"Okay. Any time next week."

"Next *week*?"

"I might be somewhat recovered by then."

Lazily she chuckled. "I never had a chance."

"True. You're mine. What chance?"

Her voice slow, she explained. "My great seduction! All that work making the dress and compiling the perfect meal, and you never gave me any chance at all!"

"You'll have the next time. You'll have full control. I won't move a muscle. I'll hum and look out the window." He kissed her very gently on her eyes and cheeks and chin. Her lips were available, and she turned her face to help him, but he ignored them and went on with her forehead and temples, her nose.

"I can use all my wiles the next time?"

"I promise."

She raised up, and he allowed that, and she pushed so that he went over to lie on his back. She smiled and her eyes danced.

He demurred, "Laura."

"Be still."

"Sweetheart, there's possibility and then probability, but there's 'not now,' too. Honey, uh, careful. Why don't you just lie back and rest a while? Uh. I'm a little tender there."

"It was only just a few minutes ago that you *put* my hand there. Why then and not now?" she inquired with a great, contrived need to know.

"How about a nice little nap?"

"Your attention span leaves something to be desired." She shook her head, then she did it again so her hair tickled his chest.

"We'll get back to the desire part in a week or maybe two. You're a tiger. I believe you're the woman they were warning us about in basic training. They said there were women like you who use up nice boys for their own pleasure. We were warned to beware."

"Kiss me."

"I might manage a handshake."

She lay back with a delicious laugh and they held hands.

He murmured, "I never dreamed I would ever be so lucky to find you again and love you. This is a dream."

"Isn't it."

"Did I satisfy you? Was it good for you?"

"Oh, Tanner. You are fantastic. I had never known what love was like. I was married for almost two years, but I never had such love. You are perfect."

And their conversation went on that way as they debated who was the greater lover. They never agreed. They lay in the firelight, still naked, touching, petting, smiling, teasing, laughing, murmuring. And they made love again some long time after that. Gentle love. Not frantic or wild but sweet tender love. And as the fire crumbled into only feeble coals they slept.

The beep wakened Tanner like a bolt of lightning. He was up and into the study in the wink of an eye. Laura felt him leave, and his urgency alarmed her. She waited, hearing a whirl and two computer sounds. Then silence.

She got up, picked up her dress and slipped it on before she went cautiously into the hall. All was dark. There was a glow in the study and she walked carefully to that door.

Tanner was naked in the subtle light, and she was aware how beautifully made he was even as she questioned, "What is it?"

He was taking several pieces from inside his computer. There was a basket and in it he'd put the tracer, the filter, the scrambler and several other parts from his computer. He didn't even look up but said tersely, "We're leaving. Grab a change of clothes and any important papers. We'll probably be very isolated. Take what you'll need. We'll leave anything else. Take only what can *not* be replaced.''

''What are you doing?''

''These are enhanced cards, expanded, I'm taking with us. Hurry!''

''Tanner...''

''I'll explain everything later. Hurry!''

Eight

It was still blowing and raining outside and quite cool. What time was it? Laura wondered. It was long after midnight. In her room Laura pulled off the seduction dress and put on a warm cotton jumpsuit from the guest closet. She looked around, mentally sorting as she discarded her possessions. She grabbed several pairs of underwear and her toothbrush to stuff them in her purse.

What did she actually need? She took the thongs, then a pair of her pumps that had low heels. She folded the two cotton sailor middies and the pair of elastic-topped trousers she'd found earlier in the guest closet and set aside to wear in the cooler weather. And she took a large bandanna to carry it all in, like a hobo's pack.

She snatched her linen raincoat, which any traveler carries in the spring and fall, and took her purse. She left her two suits and their blouses neatly hanging in the closet with her high-heeled pumps lined up underneath.

Rushing down to the morning room, she took a deep breath for courage in order to ignore the treasures she would have to leave behind. She scooped up her folder, some pencils, the crayons, and eyed the butcher paper with regret, before she caught up her sketch pad. She gave a last, quick, regretful glance around at the tumble of materials in a cascade of colors before she hurried to the study.

Tanner wasn't there. She went back toward his room, but at the kitchen she found him putting some fruit into a plastic bag. He was dressed much as she was, and he had the handled wicker basket, which held his computer parts, by him on the floor. Tense, he gave her a quick smile as he laid the fruit on top of the computer parts and reached for her folded clothes. He carelessly disordered the clothing as he put them on top of the basket. It looked like a laundry basket.

"Why are we doing this?" A very logical question.

"The cars that have been going by aren't local," he explained. "We're still not sure my wreck was an accident. We're just being careful."

"Someone could be . . . after you?"

"We're just being sure."

"Oh." Then she asked in quick concern, "What about Dog?"

"I'll call Henry in the morning and ask him to take the dog back. Dog has enough food and water. And his rug in that box will keep him warm." But when they went out to the car, Dog was there to watch them enquiringly. And when Tanner opened the car door, Dog got in.

"He knows we're leaving." Laura looked at the calm dog then to Tanner.

"Dogs are smart," he agreed. "Let's go."

"Where?"

"There are always contingency plans. We're directed to use our plan B."

"Is this really serious?" Laura was still having trouble with their exodus.

"Probably not."

"Oh. *Probably* not. That's why we're sneaking out after—" she looked at her watch "—three in the morning, going God only knows where?"

"I have to make some quick contacts on the CB. It will be in code. I can't miss any segments. So you must not talk. I'll tell you all about it later."

Apparently Tanner's contact did communicate sensible information, in the brief combinations of letters and numbers with station switches, for they hadn't gone twenty miles when Tanner pulled up, flicked his lights and a Chevy came up in back of them.

In a terse voice Tanner told her, "Wait here until I'm sure." He got out cautiously and stood by his door, and so did a man from the Chevy. Again they spoke in letters and numbers. Then Tanner leaned down and said to Laura, "It's okay. Let's go."

The whole episode was so unreal that it bordered very closely on ridiculous and Laura felt the semihysterical nudging impulse to giggle. She got out of the Porsche, into the rain, Dog followed unquestioningly, and they walked to the Chevy. The other man held her door, and Dog hopped into the back without being told.

Tanner told the man, "Take care of the Porsche."

"With pleasure," the man replied. Then he added, "Good luck."

Tanner lifted a hand, got into the Chevy, backed away from the Porsche, and they took off down the road.

Laura looked back through the rain-splattered rear window and saw the Porsche's lights sweep around as it headed back through the rain toward Myrtle Beach. She turned forward again to sit and stare out the windshield, which was relentlessly swept by the wipers, and her eyes were big and her adrenaline pretty high.

She turned her head to check on the dog, but he'd curled up on the back seat. He opened his steady eyes and watched her. She faced forward again, scrunched down in her coat and was silent.

The car hurried through the dark and rainy night, and Tanner's profile was serious but calm. He was a good man to have around. He was a good man period. He was important to her. What in the world was going on? Well, obviously it had to be some white-collar crook who bore a grudge.

If Tanner was in danger then she was, too. She looked out into the stormy night. It was strange, she didn't feel scared. Not yet. She felt…like manning the battlements. Womaning them. That was an odd reaction. She was a card-carrying coward. Why this defensive reaction for danger to Tanner? She loved him. She did understand that. But he was a whole lot better trained to deal with danger than she was. Why should she feel so strong and combative in his protection?

She thought back over their short week together, reviewing his actions with finding and caring for the dog, and his gentleness with her. She also thought of their conversations. And she knew she thought he was valuable, not only to her, but to the country as a whole.

Tanner was a doer. She was on his side. She leaned back. She was his partner in whatever came. She would see to it he survived. Then her mind was entertained with scenes of her protecting Tanner, and she had to smile it was all so silly.

This wasn't silly. For a man like Tanner to leave for parts unknown in the middle of the night was deadly serious. A little shiver went up her spine. She must obey him exactly. These people knew what they were doing. She could ruin any of their plans by being stupid. She would be very careful.

After a time there were more cryptic communications via the citizens band radio. And Tanner gave minimal responses.

Laura listened silently, asking none of the myriad questions, nor did she offer any of the avalanche of comments. Those did pile up. Why those symbols? Did they change? How did he remember them? Who thought up the codes that Tanner and the unseen voices were using? Little old ladies in apartments with geraniums in the pots and cats by the fire? How would they dispense the information? Did they mail out a weekly newsletter?

Codes too were probably done by computer. All the romance was gone from spying. Not wit against wit, but computer against computer. Of course someone had to run the computer and tell it what to do and to understand what was needed to make it do exactly that.

Computers took some of the magic from human endeavor. But that magic was replaced by opening up such computer resources! It wasn't like physics, which took the magic away by explaining everything and making it ordinary and understandable. The scope of computer potential was limitless. Just with color schemes! With a computer an artist could view sixteen hundred combinations of color in eye blinks of time.

Five lifetimes wasn't enough to experience all the wonders of living. That was one reason she believed in reincarnation. God could never be so unkind as to give us each just a taste of the wonders of living and then let it end. Laura's mind twirled on, entertaining herself, as she dozed. And before dawn they arrived... somewhere.

The weather was clearer inland. The clouds moved with the wind and there was occasional moonlight. In it, they saw the house that was small and isolated. It was tucked into a dimple of earth and surrounded by acres of trees. Even a searching eye would have a hard time finding it. They wouldn't have found it if they hadn't had exact directions. It was a hideaway.

The Chevy moved down the faint track through the trees. The house was unpainted and blended well. The garage doors were open. Tanner drove the Chevy into the gloom of that haven and turned off the motor. They sat in the silence.

Softly Laura said the obvious, "We're here."

He touched her arm. "I'm glad you're with me but I wish you weren't."

They got out of the car and stretched, and Dog also stepped down from the car and looked around before he nosed out the door and walked around with curiosity.

Tanner took the basket from the car's trunk, and as he closed the doors on squeakless hinges the back door of the house opened and a tall man stood there. He queried, "K?"

And Tanner replied in a jumble of letters and numbers. It was all strange to Laura.

"Welcome." The man was long-limbed like Tanner and he came outside in an easy slouch, his hands in his pockets. "So you brought her along." His eyes stabbed at Laura.

Laura looked at Tanner who said, "There was no way I could leave her. She's okay."

"No one is."

"As I'm okay, so is she."

"Ah," he said in response. "I'm Brodwick."

Tanner shook hands. "I've heard a thing or two about you. This is Laura Fullerton. Honey, this is Brodwick."

Brodwick gave a formal nod to Laura but he replied to Tanner, "I've heard a thing or two about you, Tanner. We have a computer set up in the living room. Use it, do as you please. There's an override for messages. You must be a genius! We have orders to take very good care of you. You're valuable, but, as I understand it, a lousy driver." Brodwick smiled ruefully as he referred to the wreck.

Responding to the easy ribbing, Tanner explained, "Well, there was a ditch with trees. Solid, big trees with awesome root systems that kept them upright."

"That would influence an evasive action. You look mobile."

"Getting there."

"Let me carry that?" They moved into the softly lighted house. "You brought the scrambler?"

"And my cards."

"Good. I'll enjoy seeing them. I heard you're innovative."

"I'd be pleased. You have any here?"

"None here." Brodwick shook his head. "We had to get you some place fast and this was closest."

"Something going?"

"We didn't chance it. Better safe than sorry, to coin a phrase. You kids hungry?" He called them kids but he wasn't much older.

Tanner asked, "Do you have anything for the dog? He was abandoned or lost and he's had a couple of days on regular chow and has probably gotten used to eating."

"When I saw the dog I understood you bringing him. He's a dandy. Is that a new flea collar?"

"Yes."

"Is he trained at all?"

"I've never been around a trained animal. He's obedient. But if he's a pro or not—" Tanner shrugged his shoulders "—I have no idea. He's loyal. It was his idea to come along."

"I'll check him out after I feed him. If he allows me to feed him on command that will tell us something. Come along and I'll show you the 'dungeon.'"

He led the way into the kitchen and through a door, down stairs to the basement. He slid aside a false wall, pushed a light switch sideways, touched a concealed button, and a section of brick moved.

They entered, Laura unbelieving of anything so bizarre, and they were shown how to close both the false wall and shut the section of brick. Flashlights were stacked on a shelf, and the tunnel went off out of sight, lighted minimally with something like Christmas wheat lights at spaced intervals. It was sufficient light. Laura simply stared.

In a perfectly normal voice, as if their circumstances were not unusual, Brodwick explained to Tanner so that Laura too could hear and understand, "If push came to shove, if someone came into the tunnel without the password, or if the place was on fire, you'd go on down the tunnel. It exits along the creek into bushes. Be very careful under those circumstances. Unless you must, don't leave the tunnel for two days. Someone would come if we didn't report in.

"We've never *yet* had to use the tunnel," he said bracingly as Tanner went through the procedure. "It's only precautionary. We don't even know if there's a problem for you. We are all Boy Scouts and take the motto Be Prepared quite seriously. It's only fair you're prepared too. Now, Laura, you work the walls in reverse."

She did, and she watched the light-switch plate slide automatically back into place. It was all unreal. After that they went back up the basement stairs.

"You two can have the second bedroom," Brodwick told them. "The bath works adequately. Food in the fridge. Make yourselves at home. I'll be out and around. Two others are assigned here. They'll be in about noon. We should know what's up shortly or if anything is happening. We're still going over the cases you've worked on, and as you know, it all takes time. But it shouldn't be long before we have a handle on this thing. We're watching your house on the coast. Relax. Enjoy." And with a half wave, he left them.

Tanner turned to Laura. "Okay?"

"This is weird."

"Granted."

"Have you ever done anything like this before?"

"No. That's why we're doing it this time. I can take care of me. I'm expendable. You're not. I won't risk anything happening to you. When they told me the car that kept going by the beach house was driven by a stranger, I would have waited it out, but with you there, I opted for running."

"Oh, Tanner." She went to him. He took her into his arms and held her almost too hard. Her fingers spread out to touch as much of him as her hands could reach. Danger to herself wasn't as important to Laura as danger to Tanner. Her hands went from his head to his shoulders, smoothing, feeling the reality of him. Nothing must happen to Tanner.

He kissed her temple and eased away from her. "You have to be hungry, let's eat."

"Somehow I'm not." She rubbed her face. "But I would like to stretch out."

"Come, let's see what's in the kitchen."

The little house was furnished with only the essentials. The furniture was as anonymous as the facade of the house. No rugs; shades but no curtains. No bedspreads, although the four twin beds were neatly made and blankets folded at the foot of each bed.

In the kitchen there was ample food, paper plates and cups, plastic spoons. It was clean and tidy. Without interest, they poked through the cupboards and refrigerator and mentioned what they found. Each was trying to coax the other to eat something.

There were doughnuts, sugared and squishy, and they each absently ate one and drank a small paper cup of milk.

After they finished, they stuffed their cups into the plastic waste sack. They went to the bedroom Brodwick had indicated they were to use and closed the door. With a very serious expression, Tanner watched Laura as he helped her undress. He lifted the sheet for her to crawl into bed, then he shook out a blanket and covered her.

He stood there watching her eyes following his movements as he slowly took off his own clothes, crowded into the small bed and into her welcoming arms. And he made love to her. He said nothing, and in the silence of that different kind of loving, she too was silent. Their loving was as strange as their circumstances. Dictated by their danger. It was no lighthearted coupling. It was another of the many echelons of love.

Her skin prickled in response. The threat of danger had stiffened her body. Her body still was tense, and now it was hungry. The tips of her fingers dug into his shoulders, and her knees and hips urged him.

Their coupling took on a kind of desperation. His taking her wasn't from body need as much as it was a declaration of possession. She was his. All of him possessed her. His mouth searched her with a deliberation as if his hot kisses branded her as his. And his hands searched her out, his fingers strong and demanding. His body was sure and powerful. And when he finally took them to a shuddering completion, Laura fiercely held him to her as he slid into a deep sleep. For she too was possessive. Tanner was hers.

The three men came separately into the house for lunch so only one was inside at a time. The other two prowled the grounds. It was an apt term for their actions. They were like civilized beasts. The way they walked, moved and the way their eyes watched. They were soft-spoken, they assessed Tanner and Laura before they saw the two "visitors" as personalities.

Besides Brodwick, there were Daniels and Reed—all long-limbed, easygoing men. Tanner was very like them. Tall, well-made. Quiet. No hearty jokes or backslapping. They were from the same breed.

It was Reed who told them, "We put two operators into your beach house. They drove the Porsche in just like home folks. They found a bug on your car. Good thing you switched cars."

Tanner's head snapped up. "They did? I thought I was careful. Was it a new bug?"

"We don't know. You did travel a ways, and they could have used one that had been used before. As to not finding it, it could have been put there at the last minute." Reed shrugged.

"A . . . bug?" Laura's eyes widened in amazement. Such things only happened in books and films.

But it was Tanner who supplied the reply. "For a tracer. It's a good thing we changed cars."

Neither man appeared alarmed. Reed looked over at Laura. "We couldn't find an agent that fast with your hair color, so she has on a wig."

"Could it be dangerous for them?" Laura asked.

"They are very, very good." Reed smiled at her, his eyes lazy. Then he said to Tanner, "Since you chose to use the crutch when Laura first arrived, he's using a cane." There was an amused, almost unnoticeable stretching out of the words.

Laura realized then that someone had to have been watching over them all along! How else would they know about her or of the fact that Tanner had used a crutch to fool her? Had they watched at the Moran house? Or was it in Myrtle Beach? When? It was spooky to realize anyone could be watched and not have a clue it was happening. It didn't make her feel protected, but a little hostile.

"That dog is really something," Reed commented. "Had him long?"

"He was either abandoned or lost," Tanner replied. "He'd apparently been on the beach for several days. He kept watching the road."

"He isn't a security dog, but he's very intelligent. We've already taught him to bark when we clear our throats. And we're teaching him hand signals. He's eager, or else bored because he's so unchallenged, and glad to be occupied. He looks back along your trail. Wish he could talk."

"I was careful," Tanner said. "Especially with Laura there."

"You have good reason. Don't fret. This is our job, and we're like Dog. We hate being idle."

* * *

Apparently Daniels was in charge, it was he who gave them permission to be outside. "Never be out of sight of the house, but only in a circle around it. There's a nice little creek and just below us a fishing hole. You can fish." He smiled. "Or if you're talented enough, you can skip stones. Wear the jump suits and the hats. No use advertising our presence here."

The jump suits were in mottled greens and browns. Camouflage. That was what really brought home to Laura the reality of what was happening. They had to hide. Someone could be hunting them ... to do them harm.

When she got back home again to South Bend, Indiana, Laura decided she was going to take judo and karate. Maybe even get marksman expertise, if she could learn to be comfortable with guns. She muddled over the facts of life, the ramifications of living in this dangerous world.

Tanner's strong hand covered hers. "You'll be all right." His voice was calm, but tension lived in his body unabated.

She wasn't the only one who saw how tightly triggered Tanner was. He never relaxed. It seemed each man, Brodwick, Daniels and Reed all sought to make things seem ordinary and to make this impossibly abnormal situation appear placid and unthreatening. Even as they checked their guns, and moved soundlessly away to watch, they talked of mundane things. "Weather's beautiful for this time of year. Different where I come from," Reed offered.

"Where'd you come from?" Laura felt invited to ask.

"Up north of here." He smiled in apology for the close-out reply.

Brodwick told them, "We're going to have a contest as to who catches the biggest fish from that hole in the creek. I want high stakes because I'll win."

"You any good as a cook?" Daniels asked Tanner. He ignored Laura as a candidate.

"I do fairly well," Laura offered.

But Daniels protested, "You're a guest! You mustn't work. We'd be embarrassed to ask a guest to pitch in."

"I believe that's a psychological trick to get me to volunteer," she guessed. He seemed very shocked and so elaborately offended that she laughed.

Whoever was off duty would lure Tanner into explaining how he'd altered his cards for his computer. To Laura, it was as if they spoke another language. The words were English, but they made no sense at all.

As the afternoon waned and evening came along, Tanner and Laura put on their camouflage jump suits and the floppy camouflage hats, and they went out into the soft light to be joined by Dog.

They walked only as far as directed. But they were outside when the helicopter was first heard. It was Daniels who jerked them under the shield of some trees.

"What . . . ?"

"Not a word." Daniels squatted with them. But the helicopter flew straight across with no side trips or circling.

An insignificant-looking band on Daniels's wrist said, "One of ours."

Daniels lifted the same wrist and replied, "X."

* * *

That night as the lovers lay in the single bed, crowded close, Laura said, "This all seems pretty strange and unreal."

Tanner held her tightly to him and didn't reply. His arms hugged her almost too tightly. And his love making was again very strongly possessive. It was as if he could never get enough of her. He didn't allow her night clothes. "I'll keep you warm." And his hands on her were feverish, greedy.

He drove her mad with desire. She tried to smother the sounds of passion that escaped her, and she was embarrassed by the rustle of bed clothes and the furtive movements of the bed. She was on fire, and his mouth scalded her. She shivered with the heat of him and almost fought for him to take her. He delayed as if he needed her frantic.

His hands were so hot, rubbing down her body, and his heat burned her as she was pressed against him. His desire for her raged in him, but he was silent as he made this strange kind of love to her. His hands shaking. His breath rasping, laboring as he worked at her, undistracted, intense, shivering with his need.

It wasn't "making love" but something else entirely. Were they using their coupling to prove they lived? That they were whole and together? It was as strange as the rest of the adventure. As puzzling.

Not really understanding, Laura did as he wanted, wanting him, wanting to fulfill whatever it was he needed from her. With skill he prolonged the exquisite agony in keeping her on edge for an endless time before finally taking her to completion, exhausting himself and her. And at last they slept.

Nine

The next morning, Daniels told them, "There's nothing going on at the coast. Zero. No cars. Not even a stray jogger."

"False alarm." Tanner said it as if he was casual.

"We'll make sure."

"I appreciate the fact you take this seriously."

"There was the bug on your car. When it was put there or for what specific purpose, we don't know, but it was there... and we left it in place for now, out of curiosity. They've been driving the Porsche around looking for a tail. It gives them something to do."

The days passed. Nothing happened. Laura reported in to her office, she worked on current projects. They gave her more paper and pencils. They already had a pencil sharpener.

Laura volunteered to fix supper one night. She made a meat loaf using some of the boggling supply of hamburger. And she made a pie using pudding mix for the filling. They were nice about the meal, but they went back to fried hamburgers with ice cream for dessert.

She did endless sketches of Tanner as he worked on the computer or talked with the other men. She sketched them, too, but they secretly, regretfully burned her drawings. They could allow no pictures. She did drawings of the dog and gradually became friends with him. He was learning more commands and was very clever. They all enjoyed his company.

Accompanied by Dog, the guests walked often through the picture postcard setting. They went through the piney woods with its young underbrush and the cushioning carpet of needles. In the spots the sun found, there were tiny flowers, and in the deep shade there were toadstools and mushrooms. It could have been idyllic, but Tanner never really relaxed.

The pond was lovely. There were trees that reached out their limbs overhead, and the new leaves cast shadows on the surface of the greeny gray pond. They fished and watched the dimpling of the pond as the watery residents chose surface bugs instead of the tempting, baited hooks.

They were never far from a shelter under which they could duck on command. The three guardians never relaxed their vigilance.

When some mushroom hunters went through a corner of the woods, Tanner and Laura were sent to the tunnel for a tense time. The mushroom hunters didn't come near the house, apparently didn't know it was there or that they were avidly watched. After a time the intruders went off.

Of course their car's license number was traced. The car belonged to a high school physics teacher whose wife worked as a check-out clerk at a grocery. Their companions were another teacher and his friend. They had no connection with anyone Tanner had ever known or investigated. It was a false alarm.

There were other false alarms. A plane flying low and circling turned out to be hunting a stray horse. A car that cruised and parked in the woods was an amorous couple who ducked a suspicious husband.

But it was an all-day Boy Scout camp-out that gave them the fidgets. Boys tend to roam and are so intensely curious. And they tell about things, like a tunnel that emerges in bushes by a creek. But even that threat to their solitude passed harmlessly.

Tanner was busy, using the now exquisitely enhanced computer to help research his past cases for some clue to explain their present circumstances, living in a hideaway under protection. So he worked hard. Tanner could work wherever there was a computer.

Then there was Laura who had a business that she was neglecting. She needed to complete her projects, search for other prospects and reschedule postponed appointments. Something had to be decided.

As April drew to a close, there were decisions that would have to be made. The decoy couple in the Moran house on the coast would soon be inundated with Morans, who quite understandably would be intensely curious as to why a strange couple was living there. They would have to leave. There was Tanner's Porsche. Should it be left where it was? Sold? Stored?

Daniels said, "We could move you to an apartment in St. Louis. We could change your identity, go the whole course. Or you could stay here forever, but that might be a drag. We three are darling, but you might occasionally like to see other faces, buy your own supplies, that kind of fun thing. Talk about it."

In their room Laura said to Tanner, "I'll do whatever you decide."

And he replied, "I love you. Never forget that I do. But we need to split. You need to be free of me. We have no idea who's doing this or what's going on, or even if anything is! Laura, I can't stand to have you in any danger. I have decided to give you up."

He sat on the side of their bed but he wouldn't look at her. She reached out to him, but in a strangely harsh voice he said, "For God's sake, don't touch me."

She was stunned. "Tanner..."

"Don't say anything. It must be this way. If anything happened to you, Laura, I don't know what I'd do."

"We could go away. We could find a place to live. You are enough for me."

"If anyone is really looking for me, they'll find me. Wherever we were, I could never quit worrying about you. I can't live that way."

"There is risk to everything we do in our lives, Tanner. In any decision. I could live with risk. I will."

"No." He shook his head. "Don't you realize what that would do to me? I can't see you in jeopardy." With a groan he turned and took her into his arms and made that desperate love with her. As if there would never be another time.

When they lay spent, she said very low and seriously. "But to live without you would be another kind of death. I can't handle that."

"Oh, Laura..." And a ragged, choked breath escaped his iron control.

Laura could guess some of what haunted Tanner. But could she solve it? Carefully she acted as ordinarily as the situation could allow. She thought of things that were amusing, their guardians helped with that, and she talked to Tanner as if their circumstances weren't so strange.

Her efforts were wasted. Despite his facade of languor, his muscles were never uncoiled. He was constantly ready for danger. He was exhausting himself.

To live as they were was so unreal. There in that lovely April weather, with wild flowers growing in charming clumps, with the weather smiling down, or raining down, in the ideal setting of a cabin in the woods and discreetly kind caretakers. It was very strange to live as hostage to an unknown.

Their nemesis finally appeared one beautiful day. They'd been fishing and were going back to the house with their catch, when a man holding a gun stepped from behind a tree like an apparition. He was simply there. So quietly, so amazingly still. They couldn't believe their eyes. But Dog growled.

That drew Laura's eyes to the dog. He had never growled. Why now? And she looked again at the life-threatening stranger who confronted them.

"Just me," Tanner's voice was a soft command. He almost smiled in a terrifyingly wolfish way. Here was his adversary, and he was known to Tanner. "Leave her out of it." Tanner appeared to drift from Laura's side without actually moving. And Dog moved the other way, silent now.

The man said, "Yeah."

"You're Rockwell. Does your uncle know you're here? Tell me that."

"I'm here on my own. I'm going to take you out. I've been in prison all this time because of you."

"You don't learn easily, do you? You went to jail because you manipulated those securities. I only caught you at it." Tanner had moved farther from Laura.

Rockwell's voice was a dog's snarl. "If it hadn't been for you, I'd have made it. No one else had a clue."

"How did you find me?" Tanner's voice was almost conversational.

"I hired some private investigators, just like anyone else." He turned his head and looked then at Laura, and his eyes narrowed.

In that split second, Tanner moved. He was a blur of camouflage against the wind-tossed background. At the same moment, snarling viciously, Dog attacked.

Dog's attack was probably what caused Rockwell's first shot to miss. As Tanner hit the man, knocking him over, there was another shot, which plowed along the ground. And after that, there was a wild, dog-growling, man-grunting melee as two of the guardians ran up from opposite directions.

Daniels ordered the dog aside and pulled Tanner from Rockwell. Tanner's avid eyes immediately sought Laura, who was standing there in wide-eyed shock. He went to her and grasped her arms to shake her just a little to be sure she was alive. She said, "Oh, Tanner!" in shuddering disbelief. He put his arms around her and hugged her too tightly as he groaned with his relief... or was it a growl of triumph?

For the moment no one paid any attention to the body still on the ground. Rockwell didn't get up. His neck was broken.

The two guards carried Tanner and Laura to the house and ordered them to the basement tunnel until they knew the extent of the invasion. Then the two men took Dog and disappeared immediately into the woods to search the area... and to find Brodwick.

One of the two men found Brodwick still out cold from a thrown rock. He'd known someone was around, he'd already alerted the other two, but he'd turned wrong. The others were already converging on their guests when the shot was fired. When a sweep of the area revealed no one else, Tanner and Laura took Brodwick to the local hospital in the Chevy station wagon. He had a concussion and would be kept there for several days.

Meanwhile at the hideaway, Daniels and Reed examined Rockwell's car and found a tracking device.

That made the men look at each other. That's when they looked at Dog's flea collar. The bug was there.

On the way back from the hospital, Laura had the opportunity to ask, "Who was he?"

"George Rockwell," Tanner replied. "His uncle is a crook, and George Rockwell helped him. The uncle paid an impressive fine, but he didn't go to jail. Rockwell did."

Back at the cabin, the couple was shown Dog's collar and the bug. They'd all asked if the collar was new, but not if Tanner had bought it. They had to speculate quite a bit. Dog was attached to whoever it was who deliberately dropped him by the Moran beach house. It had not been Rockwell. The dog didn't know him. So someone else had been involved.

"How would they have known we would take Dog in?" Laura asked.

Daniels replied, "It was the only house around. When Dog got hungry enough, he'd have come to you. You would have fed him. Whoever dropped him there was hired by Rockwell to locate you and keep an eye on you until he could get there."

"Why would he think to bug the car? What made them think we might leave?"

"They were taking no chances. Under normal circumstances, the watchers would just keep track of you, but these guys who found you were pros and they were covering every possibility. With the change of cars, that tracking bug was lost, but there was still the chance you had Dog with you and the flea collar was still on him.

"Tracking is limited in range," he went on. "With you gone, they had to get within a reasonable distance to pick up the signal. So Rockwell had to cruise in a widening circle from Myrtle Beach in order to try to find the signal. And he found you. It was incredible that he did. That's what took him so long. If we had taken you farther, we might have thwarted him...for a while. He'd have found you eventually."

It was Laura who said, "The crook who hates not his crime, but the one who catches him." And the others agreed.

There was no charge brought against Tanner. There was no question it was self-defense. They were free to leave their haven.

It was rather strange to part from their three companions. A closeness had developed among them as happens when people share something unique. They had depended on each other, and by living in close quarters under such conditions they had come to know each other unusually well.

At the hospital Brodwick had said, "Don't say we'll be in touch, or send Christmas cards or anything. You can't prolong this kind of relationship. You two are good kids. Good luck to you."

Then as Laura and Tanner collected their various possessions, Daniels said the same thing. "We're glad the time is over for you, but forget it and get on with your lives. If you should ever need us again, we'll be there."

It was very strange.

But, of course, it wasn't over. It was only beginning. How does a woman convince a man that he is

more important to her than her life? She and Tanner
had changed roles. Now it was she who was committed and he was not. So how does a woman bring a man
to commit himself? To know there is danger in just
living?

She tried. "There are people who get killed by
buses," she argued. "Tornadoes, lightning, stairs and
unloaded guns. And there are a great number of people who never experience any danger at all and who
finally die in bed, bored to death."

She talked all the way back as Tanner drove the
borrowed car to the rendezvous with their stand-ins
from the beach house and picked up the Porsche.

Laura was hardly distracted by the meeting. She
thought the woman looked rather like her, but they'd
missed matching Tanner altogether. No wonder
Rockwell had ignored the decoys. As they drove off,
Laura mentioned that to Tanner who had nothing to
say.

They arrived at the beach house and it seemed years
since they'd been there. It was dear and familiar, and
she walked around and smiled at everything. Tanner
was uncommunicative, busy as he replaced all the
parts inside his computer and added the accoutre-
ments to the phone. Dog wandered around seeing if
anything had invaded his territory while he was gone,
and he no longer watched the road.

"Tanner."

"Umm?"

"Will you marry me?"

"No."

"My mother will be shocked with me living in sin. I do hate to disappoint her. And then there's the influence on my younger sisters, and I have young female cousins that might also be influenced by such conduct. I've always been a role model for them, so you can see that you're probably wrecking another whole generation of young Fullertons, and then there's the Nance side of the family and those kids. They're still a little young but kids are underestimated and they are like walls, they have ears. And on the other side of the family—"

"I'm not going to live with you either. We'll separate and go our own ways. I can't handle another time like this."

"And I have nothing to say about it?" she challenged. "What about what I can handle? What if I demand that you not drive another car because you could get in the way of another idiot? How about if I say you can never drive another car?"

"You know what I mean."

"I'll take your keys away and get your driver's license revoked."

He glanced at her, and when his eyes rested on her a spark appeared in their depths. "How?"

She watched him stubbornly. "I'll find a way."

"Laura, you must understand."

"I can't. I only know you don't love me enough to take any chances. I am willing to take whatever risks are required. Rockwell was a fluke. He could have been anything dangerous. He might have been a blue racer, or a falling meteorite, or some fool's 'arrow shot into the air.' If you don't love me enough to marry me

and take your chances, then you don't love me at all.
You've had some pretty free sex lately, and you were
very clever about it. I was under the mistaken impression that I meant something to you. I told you I'm not
a bed hopper. The next man along the way will have a
tough time breaking through the—"

"What next man?" he asked quietly.

"A brave one who will love me enough and be willing to take a chance on me."

"And I'm not brave enough?"

"Yes, you are. There's no going back. You love me.
You need to realize how much. I need you. I want to
share my life with yours. I love you very much."

"Oh, Laura, don't tempt me to risk you. I'd never
be sure you were safe." He took her in his arms and
held her tightly.

"I know, darling. This has all been very unusual."
She moved away from him slightly and began to take
off her clothes quite slowly. All's fair in love and war.
This was both. She said kindly, "You need some normal time to balance out this past week. I can't guarantee you wouldn't have a dull life with me, but I'd try
to keep you from being too bored." Quite seriously she
discarded her panties and came to him, stark naked,
standing against him and putting her arms around his
shoulders and her hands into his hair holding his head
sweetly.

"Laura, I do love you." He, too, was serious and
his words were gentle.

She smiled, her eyes moist, and her fingers were
moving in his hair. "I know you do."

"We have to separate."

"I think we should contribute our share to the horde of progeny who are privileged to visit this gorgeous old wreck of a house. Whose feet are causing the stairs to wear next to the banister, and whose hands are—"

"The stair treads are worn?"

"Quite noticeably... and whose laughter will be absorbed—"

"You're only making this harder."

"And whose fingers—"

"How many children?" It wasn't a question of curiosity, it was one of anguish.

"If I recall you're an only child. Only children tend to go overboard and have a veritable *horde* of children." She paused to consider then went on, "I would be willing to consider between four and six. I could tell you more after I see how difficult the first two are."

"Difficult?"

"I find you quite difficult to contend with. You are opinionated, obtuse and stubborn; and that's something for me to think about before I give you any terms."

"Explain this 'next man to come along.' You mentioned one a while ago and you haven't replied to my question." He frowned at her. "Do you have someone in mind?"

"Why is it when I take my clothes off and stand against you this way, I have your attention, but if I'm over there and dressed you don't want to marry me?"

His deep voice was emphatic. "If there was no danger to you, and you were encased in iron and I could never touch you, I'd want to be with you."

"That's a start."

"But, my love, if I kept you with me, you might be in danger. I cannot."

Her eyes studied him. He hadn't said, "can't" but "I cannot." The "cannot" was more serious. It was something insurmountable, which he'd studied and which he could not do. "Tanner, I love you more than my life."

"And I you. More than mine. I must let you go free. If I bind you to me, I put you at risk."

She leaned her forehead against his chest in despair, then she lifted her face to his and said, "Well, what will be, will be. Make love with me one last time."

His lips parted as he took in a sharp breath. "You're ... leaving?"

"Yes. There's no purpose in staying."

"I ... don't think I can let you go."

"What do you mean, you can't let me go? Make up your mind! I can't hang around waiting for crumbs."

"Is there another man?"

"No!" She was becoming impatient with him. "How could I have carried on with you this way if there was another man? Don't be ridiculous!"

His hands slid down the silk of her naked back and his fingers ran along her spine's dip at her waist. "Laura... It would be madness. I cannot. I must not. I can't risk you." His eyes were no longer filled with despair. They were focused on her in suffering.

"How boring."

"What?"

"You've said that forty times and I'm tired of hearing it!" She pushed away and began to pick up her

clothes. She was deliberately slow, as she shook them
out, and she turned with some knowledge of how she
must look to him.

"Laura."

"It occurs to me that the only thing you want of me
is sex. You could hardly wait to tumble into bed after
not seeing me in years. And I was so easy! It's rather
annoying to admit that..." She frowned, her temper
rising.

"Now..."

"So now the fun's over, and reality rears its head.
All of a sudden I am 'at risk' and you dare not 'expose' me to danger. You're the danger, you rake! I
came here—" She was a little hostile by then.

"You've got it all wrong."

"Do you want to marry me? Yes or no."

"Laura."

"A simple yes or no."

"No!" He was getting irritated with her. With some
strained patience he began, "You have to understand..."

"I do. And I won't hound you, or beg or pester you.
Goodbye. It's been fun." With her beautifully curved
naked back to him, she began to dress.

Now it was he whose intentions turned around. He
asked silkily, "How do you intend leaving? You have
no car and I won't drive you."

"I'll call a cab." Over her shoulder she gave him a
quick, enduring stare.

"The phone has been deactivated."

"Dog and I will hitchhike."

"No traffic."

"Then we'll walk."

Then he realized what she'd said, "*You* are taking Dog?"

"Yes. You can't have him. You might *jeopardize* him! Put him in harm's way." She glared.

"Laura..."

"Goodbye, Tanner."

Pulling her middie blouse down over her head, she stormed toward the front door in a temper. She arrived just as a knock sounded. Very irritated, Laura jerked the door open with one hand, just as she pulled her blouse down over her body with her other hand. Henry, the vet, was somewhat startled.

Her face was red and angry, and she snapped, "Henry, would you take me into Myrtle Beach to the airport? I need to go there and Tanner refuses to drive me."

Henry cautiously looked over at Tanner who was about as placid as a storm looming on the horizon. So Henry said tentatively, "Well..."

"I'll pay for your trouble." She was furious with Tanner by then and edging into being hateful to poor Henry.

"No, no, no. Uh. Tanner?"

She tattled to Henry. "He disabled the phone too."

"I gotta be going." Henry tried backing out of the situation. "Listen to Tanner. He'll figure things out."

"Henry—" she was killingly calm "—if you don't take me into Myrtle Beach, I'll have to hitchhike."

Any veterinarian has a soft heart. Everyone *knows* a veterinarian is a pushover for anything in distress. Henry said, "Tanner, I'm going to do it. If you can't solve whatever it is, right now, I'm going to take her into town.''

Tanner didn't say anything. His stormy eyes never left Laura, but he didn't interfere.

She went up the stairs to her room. Her "double" had left the room spotless and put fresh sheets on the bed. Laura pulled her clothes off and fought her tears. She dressed in one of her two suits, with panty hose and heels. She took her other things from their hangers, scooped up her shoes and threw her clothes into her bag, then she gathered the closet clothes she had worn and put them in a heap. She hesitated when she saw the red dress. It would only remind her of Tanner. She'd just leave it there, and she added it to the pile of clothes to be washed.

It was Henry who met her on the stairs and took her bag and carried it out to the car. She went back to her room for the bundle of clothes she'd worn and carried it down, through the kitchen, to the laundry room to put it into the washer, add soap and start the load washing.

"You haven't had lunch."

She looked up at Tanner but only very briefly. If she really looked at him she would cry. "I'm not hungry."

"Don't leave this way."

"How then? What would you suggest? A hot-air balloon?"

"Don't be angry with me."

"I'm not. It's just that I've never been able to endure deliberate idiots."

"Laura, you're killing me." His voice cracked.

Her heart was about to break in two. "The closet clothes will be washed; sorry not to get them dried and folded."

"Laura..."

She went on out into the big center hall, where Henry stood waiting. She looked toward the morning room, holding its supply of perfect equipment, where she could have been content to work for the rest of her life, but she couldn't bear to go in for a final look around.

She had her own case of supplies, the things she'd left home with, plus the sketches she'd done at the beach cottage, and those she'd done of Tanner at the hideaway. She had no excuse not to leave. But she stood there.

Henry cautioned Laura with gentleness, "You must not take Dog. He's gotten used to you two. To throw him into a carrier and drag him off in a plane would be cruel..."

Tanner came from the kitchen as Laura said, "I know." She looked at Dog who was alert and curious. The human emotions were running high. He couldn't figure it out at all. In her guest voice, Laura said, "Thank you, Tanner, for an interesting and... different two weeks. It's been unusual."

Ignoring an appalled Henry who didn't know what on earth to do to help these creatures, Tanner said to Laura, "Kiss me goodbye."

She couldn't see him through her tears. "I can't." There was no concealing how her voice wavered. She'd come apart if she kissed him. He probably knew that.

Very gently, Henry said, "Come along." Carrying her bag, he held the screen door for her, and she went out onto the porch.

Tanner asked her, "Do you have enough money?"

She didn't look back, she was trying to see the steps as she went down them. She mumbled a strangled, "Yes."

But then Dog went down the steps and tagged along to Henry's car. He didn't go close to it, but stopped to watch as the car door was opened and it was apparent she was going to get into that car. He made an inquiring sound in his throat that wasn't a whine or a bark.

Laura exchanged a long look with Dog and then she bent down and hugged him. He held still for it. She then got quickly into the car. Henry went around and got in to his side, started it and they backed from the drive, turned and went off down the road, leaving Tanner and the dog watching after them.

She cried all the way to the airport, and Henry didn't say a word. He found it was a lot easier to deal with animals than with people. You could pet an animal and talk to it and not have to pick and choose words or understand anything but its physical pain. People were another whole mess.

Piedmont Airline had a plane that left in the middle of the afternoon, flying to Dayton and then going on to South Bend. Laura told Henry goodbye and asked him not to stay because she wasn't good company. He agreed absentmindedly. He stood around for a while and, about the third time she told him thank you and goodbye, he shook his head and said, "You didn't seem to be such a quitter." Then he left her sitting there with her mouth open in huffy indignation.

He went back to Tanner. Along with Dog he sat around with the silent Tanner. Finally he said, "If you truly love someone, then you fight for her."

Ten

Having arrived at the airport far too early for the Piedmont flight, Laura had more than sufficient time to think about Henry's accusation. A quitter? She had never in her entire life been labeled a quitter. Was she? Had she given up too soon?

Was it Ann Landers who said, "In order to judge a relationship with anyone, you have to decide whether you are better off with or without that person"?

Tanner's face came strongly into Laura's mind and she had the leisure to contemplate all his expressions. His thoughtfulness, his humor, his appreciation of her. His eyes dancing in amused interest, the flames of his passion burning there.

Laura sat in the airport, thinking about Tanner. If he didn't want her, why had he asked her to stay with him? Why had he trapped her heart forever? Her love, her own desire. Actually he'd claimed her all those years ago with that first kiss, there at Indiana University by the Jordan River. She would have gone with him that day, lived with him and been his love, but he'd walked on off as if her presence hadn't really registered with him.

Tanner did desire her. She hadn't needed to make that red dress for his seduction, and she smiled as she remembered Tanner's hilarious responses to her requirements for his conduct. He was so marvelously humorous. And she remembered how he'd loved her. How he'd not been able to keep his hands from her, his face flushed with his desire, his eyes hot, his smile so wickedly delighted with her. How could he have done all that if he didn't want her?

Was she better off without him? No. She'd always yearned for Tanner Moran. Tanner hadn't lured her into his volcanic lair. She'd gone there wanting him. How could she leave him? Not without a better try. All her pioneer ancestors would be embarrassed by her meekly leaving without at least a more concerted effort. She wanted to be with him. She found her mind was repeating his name endlessly. She had never forgotten him. She never would.

Laura opened her sketchbook and looked at the drawings she had made of Tanner at the beach house. They were all she had of him. And she contrasted the lazy, humorous Tanner she'd drawn at the beach house to the tense Tanner at the hideaway.

As willing as she was to flaunt any danger, when it was balanced against being with Tanner, could she put him through the worry of danger to her? Not to consider his concern would be selfish of her. She worried over that with as much fairness as she could. She decided—equally as fairly—that if they were ever to be together, as fate intended they should be, then it would have to be by his choice. It was something he would have to work out for himself, however. It wouldn't be unfair of her to be around while he decided, but only to remind him she existed.

She had no problem throwing fate into the middle of her fair-unfair argument. Any fool's subconscious knows when to nudge the balance. With fate allowed into the argument, her sense of having been misused strengthened, and a healing irritation began to grow in her. She felt he'd underestimated her. She was a strong, mature woman. She could handle whatever came her way. Anyone can live a completely risk-free life in bed—alone, naturally. Of course the house might catch on fire and the decision would have to be made to leave the bed. No one lived without some risk.

How could she go back now, after she'd flung out of his house that way? How could she act, under such circumstances, so that she didn't look foolish? She *could* go back to the Moran cottage and say, "Oh, hi. I was just passing by..." Or she could be honest and tell him, "I'm here for as long as you'll let me stay. Until you ask me to leave again." That's what she'd do.

She had taken so long, in her remembering and deciding, that it was almost flight time when she returned her ticket, retrieved her luggage and snared a cab.

As the cab drove north from Myrtle Beach, a Porsche went by then, going south on the lonely road.

Was it Tanner? After the brief glimpse, she didn't look again. How could she chase him in a cab? Was he, too, leaving the Moran cottage? What if she got out there and he was gone? He could have put all his computer parts in a basket, gathered his things and left. What would she do out there if he'd gone? No phone, no transportation. She'd have to break into the house. What was she doing going recklessly back to Tanner?

Dog was sitting on the porch and he smiled at her when she emerged from the cab. But Tanner could have left Dog there, with a call to Henry to pick the animal up. Tanner had suggested doing that when they'd gone to the hideout. She said to the cab driver, "Would you wait just a minute?" He turned off his motor.

The front door wasn't locked. She went inside to Tanner's study, and on the desk the computer and all its parts were still there. Tanner was coming back. She went out, paid the driver, took her luggage and watched the cab drive away. Her last link with sanity.

She straightened up bracingly, breathed deeply and marched up onto the porch, her heels sounding on the wooden steps. She vividly recalled the first time she walked up those steps to that porch with Pete's bouquet in her hand as an excuse to see Tanner again. She went inside, and everything was so dearly familiar. Some qualms caused her to shiver. Was she right in doing this?

She put her suitcase down in the center hall and slowly walked in a circle with her hands comfortingly holding her face, then she took another deep breath and went up to her room. There she efficiently unpacked.

She went down to take the load of clothes from the washer, to put them into the dryer so that she would have something to wear. But the clothes were out on the kitchen table and neatly folded. She thought of Tanner's hands folding the clothes she'd worn, and she wondered what his thoughts had been.

As she carried the clothes up to her room, she considered what she should wear. Not the red dress. Sex wasn't all there was to a relationship. She should be dressed in a fairly normal way. Like a reasonable, mature woman. The party girl/sexpot wasn't companion material. In her room, she put the cleaned clothes in various drawers, and the red dress was nowhere to be found. It was such wispy, asinine material it was either stuck in the drain of the washer or had disintegrated in the dryer. Lousy material but...very effective. There is a time and place for red dresses. This, however, was not a red dress time. Then why was she becoming irritated in not finding it?

She put on the dark blue and light green wraparound and the thongs. She let her hair free and brushed it and she looked at herself in the mirror. Then she very, very carefully put on makeup, rejected using some of the mismatched earrings in the cigar box of costume jewelry, and went downstairs to the kitchen to sort through the freezer. She made her choice, shunning an apple pie that looked as if Pam had made

it, and paced slowly around. Out on the front porch
she spoke to Dog, then decided it wouldn't look right
for her to be waiting on the front porch for Tanner to
come back. She was going to be aloof, logical and patiently mature. Pretty soon now.

It *had* been Tanner's Porsche that had passed the
cab, and he'd noted the cab, oddly that far north of
town, and the shadow in the back seat had been...
feminine? But flight time was looming and he had to
catch Laura before she left. He couldn't risk following a cab with a shadow of a woman in the back seat.
What if it hadn't been Laura?

So he did go to the airport, and he did find she'd
canceled at the last minute, and he did drive back to
the cottage rather pressingly. He saw no difference in
the house to tell him if she was there. He drove into the
garage and, feeling stretched by his emotions, he went
up the back steps to the deck and flung open the screen
to enter the kitchen.

She was there. He stood, looking at her. She gave
him a cool glance and went on with her preparations
for dinner. He moved to her with an anguished,
"Laura..." and she stepped neatly aside. She didn't
say anything.

She'd had all those neat things to say, so coolly and
maturely, but she found she was very annoyed he was
actually safely back... and there. She didn't really intend her lack of warm response as punishment for her
own tears, but she was rather surprisingly angry with
him.

And since he was meltingly loving to find her there, her coolness puzzled him. He stood there, watching her with tender eyes. With a needless busyness, she walked around him, with pointed impatience that indicated he was in her way. He said in a throaty purr, "You came back."

One is not always in control of one's tongue. Quite coldly she replied, "I believe I missed the name?"

He looked surprised, then he said warningly, "Laura..."

"Well, if you know mine, I should indeed know yours, give me a hint." She was very prickly.

He was, too. "A hint? You asked me to marry you not too long ago."

"Oh," she said dismissively. "One of those." She turned away very efficiently and continued her preparations.

He was at a loss. He had no idea why she should be angry with him. But she *was* there. He stood in the middle of the room, watching her, trying to find a way to talk to her; and she finally told him "Move."

He went over by the door to the dining room and stood there, and he leaned against the jamb, as finally he just relaxed and watched her. She was really mad at him. Why? She moved so beautifully. Her color was a little heightened. Her body was just inside that handy wraparound. What would it take to placate her?

In silence they sat down to eat, and she had no real idea what she'd served, or if it was edible food, or even how it tasted. She was well aware that she could not continue this ridiculous behavior, and her color was high because she had embarrassed herself by being so silly. Mature and in command was the only way to behave. She was girding up to speak when he said softly, "I'm here, Laura, look at me."

She blurted, "I'm not speaking to you."

"Why?" It was a reasonable question.

"Because I'm mad that you would discard me so readily. You didn't give me any say in anything."

"Honey—"

"For me to leave was only pandering to your idiosyncrasies."

He straightened up and inquired, "My...idiosyncrasies? Being concerned for your safety is hardly in the category of idiosyncrasy, Laura, you—"

"I'm not through. I believe we should have some time as just friends." She watched him laugh, then said sternly, "Just because I'm furious with you that's no call for you to laugh. I may not be speaking to you, but I believe I need to explain why I'm here."

"I don't care *why* you're here, so long as you are."

She ignored that and continued, "We've had a week of sex and a week of danger. That isn't anything like most people have, and our emotions are very unreliable. I believe we need some time to have an ordinary, friendship relationship. No sex. Just a courteous time with ordinary conversation. Learning about each other." Her words weren't as smooth or reasonable as she wanted them to be. He distracted her from what she was saying. He did that by giving her his entire attention, which was well enough, but his eyes were so amused that the flames were obvious. He wasn't accepting her premise. He was indulging her. How like a man with a woman.

She told him primly, "I'm in love with you. No, sit still. I want you to listen to me. I'm not sure if I'm truly in love or if I'm mesmerized by the idea of you. I've always been unreasonable in my reaction to you. I really came here to exorcise you from my dreams. Tanner, if you don't sit still and listen to me I'm going to leave here. I'm much too susceptible to you. We could go right to bed and I would never know if I stayed here because I really love you or if I just wanted you."

He smiled and leaned back in his chair. "There isn't any question at all, Laura. It's like that with both of us."

"I'm from pioneer stock. The women in my family coped with men who had to see what was over the next hill, who settled in dangerous places, where there were unwelcoming Indians, cholera, saddle tramps, isolation and hard work. I'm no ninny. I can cope. I need to know if what I feel for you is true."

"Oh, my love."

"Don't get mushy. This is serious. Pretty soon all your nieces and nephews will be here, and you'll have to think of something to explain me. They'll know I have no honorable business here. They'll point at you and scrape the opposite forefinger along the pointing one in a shaming sign. I'd be ashamed."

"Don't you trust me?"

"The government might, but I'm not sure I should. While I do love you, right now I don't much like you. I can't understand why you made me leave."

"But you came back to me." He smiled that Tanner Moran smile of his.

She looked away from him before she could reply soberly, "You never took me sailing."

That confused him and he inquired, "Sailing?"

"When I first came here, you asked me if I sailed and when I said I was a prairie woman, you said I needed to try sailing. You could do that while we're being friends. Can you behave for a week and be friends?"

"How about friendly friends?"

"It won't work, Tanner. We need time to know each other."

"I know all that needs knowing about you. Haven't you learned anything about me?"

"I know you're more complicated than I thought. There are depths to you I hadn't known about. I saw you move like a shadow, so fast, and you attacked that man. I hadn't realized that you could do something like that."

"At all costs, I had to protect you."

"He didn't want me; he was after you."

"I was surprised he didn't shoot from ambush. It's ambush that scares the hell out of me. I was almost sick with worry that you would be hurt."

"In Fort Wayne, Indiana, the Children's Zoo has an alligator in the moat around the monkey island." Tanner looked a little blank, so she explained, "The alligator was put there to add stress so the monkeys don't get bored. Life without some stress is too dull. So to be healthy, you need some problems. I'm glad you got Rockwell."

"I believe the killing was an accident. When I saw Rockwell come from behind that tree with a gun, I thought only to stop him. I'm not completely sure that Dog's simultaneous attack threw me off that much. I'm not sure I didn't mean to kill him. That's a tough question for a civilized man to have to live with. Rockwell did have other problems. We're finding out more about him. He wasn't balanced or he'd never have come after me. Any criminal who blames the catcher isn't working with a full deck. He had a gun. I knew how to handle that. But I hadn't expected Dog to feel such loyalty so soon. I hadn't realized Dog meant to help."

"I was no help at all."

"I'm only grateful you didn't try. You did exactly right. You did nothing to attract his attention to you, and I could keep it on me."

"I was terrified."

"We are, too, when we're in danger, but we've been taught to use the adrenaline to help ourselves. It's the same channeling of emotion used by fighters before a big bout, or by actors who have stage fright. We'd be stupid to say we're not afraid. We simply use the fear productively in our own protection. In all this there was only one loose end. We needed to know who had found me and why they'd helped Rockwell. It was they who'd dropped Dog and bugged his collar and the Porsche.

"We found the finders are professional investigators. They're ordinary businessmen. They're very good at their job. They're busy and had no trouble believing finding me was quite routine, search and find. They'll be more careful after this. Do a little more thorough checking on their client." He looked at her very seriously. "Laura, I can never let you go free again."

"I never wanted to be free of you. You're the one who was dead set against my staying with you. Why have you changed your mind?"

"I almost missed getting you off that plane, had you been on it, because I really put the pressure on the organization to finish the scan. To find if there could possibly be another, potential Rockwell. There is no one. Life from here on out should be quite routine and very dull. You have to save me. That's why I went after you. But you were here." It was important to him that she'd returned on her own.

"Save you?" She frowned at him. "Save you from what?"

"Boredom. A loveless life. Loneliness. Be the alligator in my moat. I love you with all my heart and soul. Marry me, Laura."

"Your... alligator?" She stared. Then she whispered, "I'll think about it." And her eyes were enormous.

"You know you have nothing to be afraid of with me."

"No?" She moved a little, lifting her chin, again in touch with her situation. Rather saucily, she asked, "How many times have you pulled this caper? Seducing and then relinquishing a woman for *her own* safety? You're really a scoundrel."

His smile was slow and very dangerous. "I? I was here all alone, unable to walk well, and you came along and seduced me."

"That isn't true. You could too walk! You sneak! You deliberately fooled me with that crutch."

He went on smiling that smug, naughty smile. "If I recall correctly, it was you who made a red dress to catch my fancy."

"You did too seduce me. You lugged me across the floor over your hip and displaced my whole rib cage. I had to have my whole chassis realigned."

"Really?" He rose from his chair at the table. "Let me see."

She stood up and backed toward the center hall. "You're to keep your distance," she warned, holding one hand out to warn off his advance.

It is a rash woman who pushes a man too far. She had. His long swift stride closed the space between them. His arms went around her, enclosing her closely, so close her breasts were squashed against his hard chest and her arms flew out. Then he kissed her.

Her head felt as if it floated off. Of course it couldn't actually, he was holding it with one big hand so she couldn't move from his kiss, but it still felt that way. Her whole body seemed unorganized, swamped with sensation and a little out of control. It was as if she ought to hold on to something in order not to become too disoriented. He was handy, being there so close to her, so she held on to him.

She should resist. This was to be friendship week. No hanky-panky. He was pulling this same thing again. He was going to seduce her. She should resist.

She wasn't a pushover. He was kissing her unfairly with the Tanner Talent that drove women wild. He was doing that to her. She should... His mouth was marvelous. How could he be so gentle and so masterful and so sensual at the same time?

Her body relaxed, aware how lovely it was to be against Tanner. To have his hard arms around her and to feel him close, to hear his unsteady breath, the sounds in his throat, to feel his heart thundering....

His hands moved along, on, over and cupped. So strong, so nice, so... She really ought to...what should she "ought" to do? Kiss back? That had to be the feeling urgently trying to communicate to her. That she should do...what? She couldn't figure anything else she wanted to do, so she kissed him back quite willingly.

Her fingers worked their way through his hair in slow, sensuous combings. Her body squirmed a bit and trembled with desire, and her breath gasped. Her knees bent and pushed her hips against his, and he made pleasured sounds.

She really...what? She really was glad he was there. When he lifted his mouth from hers, or actually he only slid it from hers to kiss along her cheek in greedy nibblings, she was surprised as she said in a gasp, "Where is my red dress?"

He laughed; a low, deliciously wicked chuckle that rumbled in his chest. "Don't forget, it's mine. You made it for me."

"That's silly! What would you do with it? It's mine!"

"I *would* let you wear it for me."

She hadn't meant that, not now, maybe next week. She said, "I couldn't find it. If it went into the guest closet, it could well shock someone." She lay back in his arms, her fingers still at the back of his head and she looked up at him. Her heart turned over and she couldn't remember what they'd been talking about, he was so dear. She loved him so much. She might have lost him. But he was there, holding her.

"It's in my inside jacket pocket. But it's mine."

The dress, he was talking about the dress. "It wouldn't fit in there. Let me see."

"Only if you intend to put it on."

"No." Her lips said the word very slowly and her lashes drooped by themselves.

He said with soft urgency, "I have to make love to you."

She shook her head so minimally that it could be ignored. He released her and moved back a step as her hands trailed off his shoulders as if they'd been abandoned. She frowned as her lips parted to take in a breath to protest his leaving her, but she forgot to voice her protest because he just stood there and looked at her.

His eyes looked down at her hotly, and then he smiled that Tanner way, as he reached into the pocket and pulled out a thin streak of red, just as a magician might do, and the streak floated out and became a limp garment. She'd worn *that*? How shocking!

He looked at her as he shrugged out of his jacket and began to unbutton his shirt.

"Oh, no you don't," she cautioned.

He pulled off the shirt and tossed aside shoes and socks. Then, in front of her captive eyes, he unbuckled his trousers and slid them off his hips and kicked them aside. He watched her as he discarded his briefs and stood there before her.

It wasn't only because she was an artist that her eyes consumed him. He was so marvelously male. The streaks of healing scars only enhanced his pirate image. He could make a *fortune* for *Playgirl*. She'd break his neck if he did. She had to paint him. What was she thinking?

He came to her, and she didn't turn away, or run, or even take a backward step. She opened her arms to him. He undid and opened the wraparound dress. She didn't say one word of protest. He peeled the shoulders down her arms, and she moved them to help him. He took her panties off, as easily, and they joined the growing pile of discarded clothing. His eyelashes moved down over his eyes as he looked at her, then his relishing hands began.

"Tanner..."

"Well, how about that? You do remember my name!" He picked up the red dress and pulled the flimsy, wicked thing down over her head, then he tousled her sun-streaked hair into a careless, wanton mass. With narrowed, smiling, passion-flamed eyes, he said, "There you are." And he began to touch her through the fragile silk. He groaned and held her to him. "Put your hands on me."

"Oh, Tanner, what are you doing to me?"

"I'm going to make love to you for the rest of our lives. You need to marry me so the nieces and nephews won't be shocked."

"Marry you?" She acted as if that was the first time marriage had been mentioned.

His eyes were deadly serious as he looked down at her. "Yes."

"Oh, Tanner..." He really made her a little unsettled. "This is our friendship week." That was an odd thing to say when she was plastered there against his naked body.

"I like being friendly with you."

"Well..." she began. She looked up at him, and he was so confident.

He acted as if that had been the reply he wanted to hear as he said, "Me too. I do have to know how many kids we're going to have, so I can build a house that's big enough." Then he kissed her in such a lovely way, hugging her tightly in that red silken dress. His eyes were brimming with amusement and the flaming coals of his passion. He lifted her and carried her to his bed, only limping somewhat. He laid her on his bed and followed her quite easily.

The bed was soft and sensuously welcoming, enfolding them. By degrees he removed the red silk that covered her so seductively, so invitingly. And he made love to her.

Laura helped. She made it easy for him, in that first of their friendship week. Helping was a little embarrassing under her blatant disregard of her rules, and she blushed a little. She turned for him as he relished her and her breath became a little ragged. Soon she squeaked and wiggled and moaned as she twitched, and the fires of desire flamed high and hot in both of them. She felt abandoned and quite reckless.

He nibbled and kissed and suckled as their skins filmed from their labors causing them to slither as they rubbed together, enjoying the differences of their bodies. Their mouths were eager and demanding, their hearts racing with their thrills as they loved each other. She cried out with her need and he took her with care, then they rode the glory trail with exquisite movement, delaying, hesitating, writhing and finally flying off into ecstasy.

As she lay dormant, he trembled still, his kisses softened, his hands gentled. He moved minutely, no longer desperate. He sighed and his words were sweet. "I love you. You're my own. My dream. My love."

And she heard herself: "You're here. You're *here*! You're real. Oh, Tanner. I love you, too. Marry me."

"How soon?"

"Soon. Very soon."

He stayed with her as he kissed her, propped on his elbows, his fingers playing with her hair as he talked to her, petting her, and eventually he again made love to her. She laughed then, and wiggled and teased. And so did he, but he had his way with her, and then—like their bodies—their lives came together just as fate had intended all along.

* * * * *